Richard Henry Savage

In the Old Chateau

A story of Russian Poland. A novel.

Richard Henry Savage

In the Old Chateau
A story of Russian Poland. A novel.

ISBN/EAN: 9783337298678

Printed in Europe, USA, Canada, Australia, Japan

Cover: Foto ©Andreas Hilbeck / pixelio.de

More available books at **www.hansebooks.com**

A STORY OF RUSSIAN POLAND

A NOVEL

BY

R. H. SAVAGE

AUTHOR OF "MY OFFICIAL WIFE," ETC.

COPYRIGHT

LONDON

GEORGE ROUTLEDGE AND SONS, Limited

BROADWAY, LUDGATE HILL

MANCHESTER AND NEW YORK

1895

CONTENTS.

BOOK I.

THE GATHERING STORM.

BOOK II.

REAPING THE WHIRLWIND.

BOOK III.

EXPIATION.

IN THE OLD CHATEAU.

A STORY OF RUSSIAN POLAND.

BOOK I.

THE GATHERING STORM.

CHAPTER I.

IN THE CHATEAU ROYAL AT WARSAW.

"If I could only crush them, . . . the traitor dogs!" and the noble Count de Berg clenched his fist, with vain imprecations of rage as he spoke. His eye roved in discontent over the sleeping city of Warsaw. With his head bowed, and his hands clasped behind him, he slowly paced the grand terrace of the Chateau Royal. The breeze of night stirred the leaves of the trees fringing the superb terraces sweeping down to the Vistula. There was no sound, as the Governor-General communed with his anxious heart, save the distant sentinels turning wearily on their posts. "I would be happier, if I were a simple sergeant!" bitterly mused De Berg. "A medal, a pension, a few days of vodki happiness, and the coarse joys of barrack frolics, with the rough fidelity of peasant love, these things are the lot of the contented common herd! And I, ruler of the Kingdom of Poland, with an empire's whole resources to aid me, am baffled here by a few beggarly malcontents. I have tried in vain to break their lines.

"Will my failure cost me these gew-gaws, or, perhaps, doom me to Siberia? Who knows!" His restless, nervous fingers thrilled with a mad desire to tear off the stars and jewelled orders glittering on his breast.

"I will never live to be the butt of every court fool,—every would-be dictator. And a false step now may cost me all that thirty years of service has won." He sighed heavily as he gazed into the few windows still lit up, where his merry official staff were yet pledging the Czar. The eight hundred feet of the grand façade was deserted, save by the guards, and a single aide-de-camp, who followed the perplexed Governor at a respectful distance while waiting his slightest signal.

Count de Berg paused, and noted the glitter of the stars in the dark gliding waters of the swift river. The leaves of early autumn rustled down beside him as he sought a lower terrace, and threw himself down on a marble seat.

Great Warsaw lay couchant like a sleeping lion around him. The hail of a distant sentinel alone broke the oppressive silence, as the noble turned and gazed at the grand old pile where first the Dukes of Mazovie once held royal state.

" Accursed palace prison!" he bitterly cried. " Your halls are only dens of traitors, your very air is poisoned with foul intrigues, and heavy with the breathings of revolt! Kings have been driven broken-hearted from your throne hall, heroes betrayed within your spy-haunted walls, the state basely sold, and humanity itself abased! What will my fate be here? Will I suddenly meet my successor—some upstart of the hour, or receive an order which will carry its banishment for life. For in this game of brute-force against sly Polish intrigue, I may have frittered away an Emperor's confidence! I have lost, even with my crowded camps, my corrupting gold, my secret powers.

"To say, at last, that I cannot trace out the secret plots of these fomenting disorders, means my utter ruin.

"At any moment my downfall may be announced, and my punishment begin! If I could only read the stars—what waits for me in the future—when they swing up pitiless from the eastern skies. The Czar demands but one thing, success. He exacts an absolute obedience, and at the gage of my very life, perhaps! I must find a way to win in this blind game of counter-conspiracy, of foul intrigue. I claim no second-sight of genius, and yet, great Napoleon was as blind, when he walked these paths, as blind as moody Wallenstein at Eger, or the misanthrope Charles V. on the battlements of the Escorial! For the stars swing on in silence while man drifts along to wreck, to ruin, ever blindly struggling against the awful decrees of Fate. My last report was harshly received by the Czar as unsátisfactory. The utmost rigor, the most searching probing of society the lavish bribes thrown away, all have failed me!—And, here under my feet, in this foul nest of Warsaw, the glowing coals of treason's fires are being fanned into some mysterious uprising! Now at any instant, I may hear——" He turned his head, as below him, a single officer, dashing along at a mad gallop, rode up toward the great sally-port of the garrisoned old palace of the Jagellons.

Behind the reckless rider, a squad of Cossacks clattered along on their fleet steeds,—with tall lances gleaming pale-blue in the crystalline starlight.

"A courier!" wearily sighed the Governor-General, as he left the seat where Sobieski had vainly battled with his cares, —where Augustus of Saxony had sadly thought of his fair Aurore, far away: and the minion Poniatowski had dreamed of the mighty Semiramis, whose wayward love had led him, by the path of shame, to Poland's ill-fated throne!

Wearied of his gloomy presages, the man whose iron hand ruled couchant Poland, in the name of Alexander II., retraced his steps to enter his secret cabinet. Tired of the fulsome formalities of a banquet given to the higher officers of the reinforced garrison, the ruler of conquered Poland had quietly escaped for the quiet of the midnight hour on the terrace.

"I can trust no one," he muttered: "I only dare to think when alone out here; my letters, my reports, my secret measures all seem to be open to these plotting mongrels. It is only a gilded siege, this palace life here, for in the three hundred thousand who swarm here, racial division and villany foil me at every turn. A hundred thousand vile Jews, a hundred and fifty thousand Poles, all mad with their treason villany, and the Czar's few friends are only the soldiery and the lazy pampered officials. And of these last, how many, seduced by Polish glitter and womanish arts, may not have betrayed their trust.

The Count de Berg started back, as an aide, hastily approaching, saluted, and in a low tone reported: "A special imperial courier, with dispatches for instant delivery."

"More useless orders, more commands, impossible to fulfill!" sighed the Governor-General, as he alertly strode toward his own special retreat. "There is but one thing left! To wipe out every trace of the Polish autonomy, to extend the regular imperial system of Russia to the very western frontier and to build a new fortress around Warsaw— with its guns pointing inwards!" The Count did not smile at his involuntary witticism, as he passed from the great eastern wing, out of the haunted chambers of the shadowy Polish kings, on through the silent Senate Hall, and deserted Chamber of Deputies, through the huge Throne Room, to the great western wing, with its nucleus of an army. His two aides strode swiftly on, and noted the fierce Mongolian-eyed Cossacks, standing with drawn sabres, at every portal!

An involuntary shivering made the noble's teeth chatter as he walked through the violated shrines of an enslaved nation.

"Do I go to my disgrace?" he mournfully thought. "If it were not for Xenia and Serge, I would welcome the farthest post, the meanest place the Czar's anger may assign!" He gazed from a window, looking out on the Place Zamkowy. It had seemed to him that the pictured Polish kings glared down and cursed him as he passed, and new legions of rebels started out from the huge battle-scenes on the walls, showing how Poland's flower had once carried their lance-headed banners in victory into the very heart of Russia.

On the heavy black clouds now gathering over doomed Warsaw, the reflection of twenty thousand lights threw a faint, angry glow. "I would like to fire this nest of rebels with my own hand!" he snarled. "Fire and sword for the Pole! Peace! The peace of the grave!"

His stern soldierly face lit up as he strode into the hall where his generals received daily his secret orders to tighten the links of the galling chain of repression.

"Admit him!" was his brief command, as an adjutant, springing to his feet, whispered to the man whose signature could bring the proudest head in Poland to the halter.

The anteroom door opened, and a swarthy Circassian Captain of the Guard escorted a single officer to the Count's side. Through the open door a score of the wild mountaineers, dirk, pistol and sabre in hand, cast eyes of mingled curiosity and fierceness on the Petersburg dandy as he passed. Their astrachan turbans, gleaming silver cartridge-cases, and national garb lent a farouche air to the men whose fidelity as body-guard still proves the value of a Mussulman's oath! Even the stains of travel, the weariness of a forty-verst night gallop could not hide the singular beauty and graceful elegance of the man who, saluting as a soldier, bowed in deepest respect, as he handed a sealed dispatch to Count de Berg. "From His Highness the Grand Duke!" The last words were lost to the waiting aide-de-camps, who started involuntarily.

The Governor-General's eyes flashed, as, tearing open the envelope bearing the seal of the Czar's private secretary, he eagerly scanned its contents. Signing to the waiting soldier to be seated at his side, De Berg drew a long breath, as he heard the whispered answer to his single query: "In an hour, Your Excellency, I am to report at the head of the Pont d'Alexandre, on the Praga side of the river." Without a word, the Count de Berg turned to his adjutant, who stood, note-book in hand.

"Colonel," the Governor said, with practised decision, "double the guards at the Chateau. Send out twelve companies of the Guards instantly to line the Pont d'Alexandre. Four sotnias of Cossacks also to patrol Praga. Two more to accompany this officer. My guard, my horse at once, at the main guard-post. Send General Alexandroff and the Palace Intendant to me, in my cabinet. Silence, and not a moment's delay! Let the Circassians on duty guard this officer over the Pont d'Alexandre."

"A soldier, every inch of him!" decided the imperial courier, as he sprang into his saddle at the sally-port. Around him, forty dark riders started out of the gloom, grim children of the night, and with no sound of voice or bugle, the palace grounds, the Place Zamkowy, the terraced garden, the river banks and the Place de la Vieille Ville soon swarmed with two thousand armed men. Not a human being was allowed to enter or leave the Palace after Count de Berg sprang into the saddle, and with an anxiously beating heart dashed over the bridge, whose every recess now held a score of riflemen. For it was in the year eighteen and sixty. Murder, assassination and dark deeds of night made the streets of Warsaw a path perilous.

Not one of the mute soldiery, grimly clutching their loaded guns, knew whose form was hidden by the shrouding cloak—whose face was buried under the great nodding white plumes of the Field-Marshal's chapeau, as Count de Berg, Governor-

General of a captive kingdom, the ruler of enslaved Poland, sprang from his horse, and respectfully kissed the hand thrust out from an Imperial britzka. Without a word, he rose from his bended knee, and entered the carriage which dashed along over the guarded bridge.

Through lanes of gleaming steel, the mud-spattered vehicle rolled into the court-yard of the Chateau Royal. The kingly postern gate was opened, and the gleaming lights of fifty liveried footmen only revealed the form of a powerful man of middle age, as the Count de Berg with profound deference led the way to the state apartments of the Polish Kings! Every nook of the tapestried chambers had been searched, and the glare of wax chandeliers showed the faintest tracery on every richly decorated wall—but not the four armed Circassians, standing behind a canopy—in the corner of every room!

When Warsaw awoke to its varied games of a cunning greed or traitorous intrigue, its daily round of dance and lust and laughter, its mingled schemes of Russ and Pole and Jew— the great yellow imperial banner, with its huge black double-headed eagle, told the half million of slaves that a Romanoff had slept in the palace, the way to which was watered with Poland's best blood—shed in vain!

And, late toward the dawn, the Count de Berg had turned his keen eyes in anxiety toward the man whose searching queries racked his very heart. For in a little jewel-casket room, where fair queens had once burned with love's avowals and blushed in passion's thrill, the chosen brother of the mighty Czar secretly debated the fate of Poland with the Governor.

Even lovely Countess Xenia, waiting, pale-faced, for her lord's return, dared not whisper the dangerous question of the identity of the midnight visitor. Too well she knew, in her splendid misery of isolation, that all doors opened at a touch of him who came in Alexander's name! That, though now loaded with an Emperor's honors, her gallant husband's tenure of place might be forfeited by one imprudent word, a single awkward disclosure. For even in the safe retreat of the marriage-chamber, the noble pair were watched by officer, functionary, spy, servant, and the gliding servants of the Third Section! The fall which might doom De Berg himself to an exile of years, would close the gilded doors of the Court to its shining social star, the Countess, and send the dashing young Guardsman, her son, to the devoted martyrdom of the war raging in the defiles of the Caucasus.

The Governor-General trembled at the suspicions of his doubted trust and faith which had led a Grand Duke seven hundred miles in a mad incognito race, galloping unceasing, to pounce suddenly upon him at night and perhaps demand a final account of the stewardship of Poland! For while the yellow and black flag would float over the crumbling walls of the great palace, the fateful dispatch gave up to the Grand Duke the absolute authority of mighty Alexander II.

There was no shade of either friendship or distrust upon the face of the imperial visitor, as he commanded the Governor-General to observe the strictest silence. "I shall see no one but yourself and such persons as I may send for," briefly answered the Grand Duke, as the Governor ventured a question of ceremony. They were alone, and the feast already served waited in the private royal salon, while Count de Berg vainly tried to read his fate in the impassive face of the Grand Duke. A few sharp questions showed that the visitor possessed the fullest secret details of his own latest reports.

"Your last report was unsatisfactory, my dear Count," said the Grand Duke, throwing the document on the table. "The Imperial will demands of you, further action—grave, earnest, sweeping, relentless! I am charged by His Imperial Majesty to say to you that he reposes every confidence in your zeal, your activity, your courage and firmness. But I have been charged with the gravest mission of my life! As a last resort, before a wholesale 'repression,' I am directed to confer with you, and to see if we jointly cannot reach the heart of the hidden mystery. You are in a growing ferment here, and I am authorized to tell you alone that West Russia is aflame! Kowno, Vitebsk, Wilna, Grodno, Minsk, Volhynia, Podolia and Moghilev are now only nests of rebels! The crisis is very near. An outbreak may occur any day."

The Count de Berg lifted his eyes in astonishment, as the Grand Duke's voice sounded solemnly in his ears. "And I did not even suspect this!" he stammered. "I have tried to do my duty!"

The anguish on the Governor-General's face touched the stern Grand Duke. "My friend, we have all been deceived by the apparent quiet. Dismiss your personal fears! The Emperor trusts you more than ever! The proof—you alone will know of my mission. It is the personal order of my august brother. The plan of action will tie you in even closer relations to the Imperial family. The Czar sends you this!" And the noble's heart leaped up in pride, as the Grand Duke fixed on his breast, while he dropped on one knee, the star of the one order whose attainment had been the Count's life ambition. "We ask no greater fidelity; we claim only your continued activity and absolute silence! For, a slip of your tongue now might balk the designs of Holy Russia!"

Spreading out a little sketch-map on the table, the visitor sharply said: "Fix your mind on this: The line from Konigsberg to Odessa is the shortest transverse diameter of Europe. You see here the Kingdom of Poland thrown out, like a bastion, far beyond it. Its possession gives us the entry into Prussia and Austria! Dropping all the juggling of the three partitions of Poland, the Russian power must spend its last drop of blood, its last million of treasure to hold this natural fort! We are not ready for a great war yet. The Russian hand moves slowly, but its grasp is of iron!

"Forty years from now, a network of railroads, a series of great works, a planting of military depots, will make the Kingdom of Poland one citadel, against which all Europe could hurl itself in vain. Forced to watch Constantinople and guard the mouth of the Danube, our first enemy is Austria. We count on another power to soon break down Austria,—the rising giant of the north,—Prussia! When these jealous western nations have humbled each other, we will be fresh, and our work will be soon finished. We can then tear to tatters the work of the Congress of Vienna, sneer at the Paris convention, and, before the twentieth century dawns, throw ourselves on any one European enemy and easily crush it. Our motto is the Prussian one, ' Drill, educate, watch, and, at our very strongest, fight our weakest enemy!' In twenty years Poland, girdled with military railways and bristling with forts, can be easily held by our reserves, while we freely fight Turkey, England, or menace Prussia, in force!

"'To do all this, we must rub out the last vestige of Polish coherence. Napoleon was right! Passionate, fickle, fierce, and foolish, the Poles are doomed. You see now, my dear Count, that we must hold Poland, even if the heavens fall! The fate of Christendom was once decided on this same short line, when Sobieski crushed the Turkish hosts in 1683. The domination of Europe will again be debated on the plains of Prussia or Austria. France is tottering to its fall, with the corruption of wealth. England, day by day, shrinks behind its trading flag, and its money-getters rule the land of the Queen of the Sea! The red revolution we fear now is behind your lines. The eight interior Polish provinces are ripe for arising! Any émeute there would cut you off, and you might be left as a Varus among modern barbarians. We could easily replace our butchered armies. But we must not lose Poland! It is the key of Russia's western lines. If we ever fight en masse, we will fight in the enemy's country. They shall feel the Russian heel from the very first gun!"

"And your new plans?" The Count was mystified.

The Grand Duke thoughtfully regarded him. "When all your well-meant zeal gave the Emperor no definite information, the tension in your territory, the personal activity of the nobles and dangerous classes led us to look elsewhere. Our keenest spies, our ablest agents, were soon scattered through West Russia. It is natural with one-third of your population, Jews who hate us, that the same proportion of Israelites in the other eight provinces, would aid the plotting Poles. These Jews look to see their ancient privileges restored by the Poles, as far as the Dnieper. The Polish nobles, from our old lines to your western extremity, fear the coming abolition of serfdom. There never was a land where the gap between noble and serf was as wide as in the old realm of Poland! And there the Jews, as middle-men, reaped the golden harvest they so eagerly crave. So, noble, Jew, and Polish peasant have at last united. They are ripe for a rising behind you now! But, when our secret spies had dogged these midnight assemblies, these veiled conspirators, in all their movements in the Provinces I name, the Emperor decided to crush them forever!"

A cruel gleam flamed in the Grand Duke's eyes, as his voice rang out pitilessly.

"Your leading dangerous nobles have been mysteriously lurking over in these Russian regions. So you were baffled! But we will let them go on blindly. We will trap them! The Emperor will not try to avert this rising. He only waits to bring it on. You are strong enough here, and two corps d'armée, under Michel Mouravieff are ready to sweep in over the Dnieper, and smite the very last offender." In a whisper, the Grand Duke closed. "Then, the unification of your charge with Russia will be vigorously carried out at once."

"But the Poles ?" timidly said Count de Berg.

"Let there be no longer a Polish nation !" growled the Grand Duke. "Catholic, foreign refugee, mongrel Jew, Polish hound, all this scum shall be swept away ! But first, we will let the great nobles run into our trap. When it is sprung, they will fall into our hands. Punishment, exile, confiscation will follow. The scum will revolt! We will force it on. And every domain to the frontier shall soon have a loyal Russian noble as its head. Now," said the Grand Duke, "follow my orders exactly. Let the whole troops under your control be at once reviewed and inspected. Begin with the Warsaw garrison to-morrow. It will divert these dogs! Report to me at orderly hour to-morrow with a list of every Polish noble under your government who holds an estate. I have the same for our eight western provinces. Send instant orders to the maréchals de noblesse of every sub-government to report to you forthwith." The Emperor's brother paused, and smiled at the embarrassment of the Governor-General, who was standing, all attention, before him. "My dear Count, recognize no one in your relations with me, save the young officer I sent you. Alexis Dournof is Major of the Cuirassiers of the Guard, and he is charged with springing the net upon the Polish nobles. He bears them no good-will, for his father fell under Baron Meyendorf at the deadly grapple of Grochow, when the cavalry died to a man to save Diebitch. Dournof is the only human being, save the Czar himself, who knows of our design to lure these nobles deeper into our hands. "

"And why ?" murmured De Berg.

" Because, getting them all implicated in one questionable affair, they will soon be scattered forever, and their domains be peopled with loyal Russians. Here ' we piece out the lion's hide with the fox's skin !' You know the old proverb,

Count, 'One Greek can outwit any ten Europeans; one Jew, ten Greeks; and one Russian, ten Jews.' The Polish proprietors have hidden safely behind our privileges, and their plots have been sheltered by their ardent, passionate women, aided by the Jews, and our policy has even been tampered with by the foreigner. They shall have their lesson soon. Now, silence as to my identity! I will leave here secretly at night. Only the Countess and your son may be presented. I shall soon need her help."

The Governor-General raised his eyes in astonishment. " My wife ! "

" Precisely," calmly answered the Grand Duke, as he dismissed the Count for the night. " You will give a grand ball here, under Dournof's direction, and I will give one, on my return, at Wilna. I propose that we shall find out the weak points of the whole Polish and Lithuanian nobles."

" But the troubles ! " suggested the Governor-General.

" I shall fight behind flowers ! " smiled the Grand Duke. " With gold and flattery, I will win my way to the weakest elements of Polish womanhood. While the army waits for the word, some social dalliance may help us on our way ! "

Profoundly bowing, the Count de Berg receded from the presence of the man who, striding to a window, gazed out into the night. Count de Berg shuddered as he saw the heavy-set Muscovite raise his clenched hand in a gesture of ominous wrath. Standing in his long gray coat, edged with priceless sable, one gleaming white cross on his breast, a soldier booted and spurred, his gauntlets and stiff cap in his left hand; the bullet head, the gray eyes, the bristling mustache and bronzed hardened features of the rough, resolute, imperial magnate indicated the trained force, the resistless energy, and the ferocious activity of the Romanoffs.

There was a pitiless smile on the thin cruel lips, under which the strong white teeth flashed, for the Grand Duke held in his heart alone the secret of the doom of a nation !

And all night, to the resounding tread of the sentinels, the Count de Berg, who had cheered his timid wife to her rest, pondered upon the meshes of an intrigue which, spreading out before him, veiled the waiting scaffold and the prison-cell's horrors behind the glamour of the ball-room. "There will be no more Polish nation!" he mechanically repeated, and before his eyes rose up the stony face of Mouravief the terrible, the Silent General, whose finger-tip pointed only to the felon's grave. For Michél Mouravief was the haunting curse of Poland, and his blood-hounds bayed even now in the distance! And so the dreaming night mantled sleeping Warsaw, with its thousand lights glittering on the blood-stained banks of the Vistula. .

"Good!" cried the Grand Duke, as in the morning light, he scanned, at his ease, the list of the Polish nobles handed him by the Count. "One hour to the society of your charming wife, and then,—to work."

The roll of drums and scream of fifes broke out upon the morning air, and the sunlight glittered upon the waving pennons, flashing bayonets and gorgeous uniforms of the Czar's soldiery pouring out to the Champ de Manœuvres at Mokotow. The rumbling of heavy cannon deepened the cadence of the strong tread of the solid regiments moving along in ominous silence. Crowds of grinning, inert Jews thronged the avenues, and the thin-lipped Poles with dark eyes, flashing in hatred, turned away into the side streets, and left the great avenues to the rabble, the strangers and a mob of idle, half-frenzied students. No martial music resounded in the air. It was a demonstration of irresistible brute-force, the hoarse commands of the officers breaking the gloomy silence, like the ravens croaking over an unreaped battle-field!

While Countess Xenia de Berg personally inspected the room where the visitor would sit in the place of departed kings, and a dainty repast was spread, the Grand Duke, led by Count de Berg, threaded in curiosity the vast tangle of the Chateau Royal's interior. A solid line of troops enclosed the Chateau Royal in a mighty square, now reaching from the Quartier Juif to the Place de Saxe, and from the Arsenal to the River. On through the great lonely ball-room, haunted by the bright-eyed Polish patricians, whose slender feet twinkled no more in the gaiduk, or cracovienne, the two plotters against the haughty rebel nobles, passed through galleries lined with statues of the great who have vainly died for Poland, that unhappy land, the battlefield of the Swede, the Russ, the German, the Austrian, and the fierce swarming Frenchmen of the man of Austerlitz. Empty niches, yawning gaps in the superb collections of centuries drew the Grand Duke's eyes. "All sent to Petersburg, Your Highness, in 1831," the Count replied to an inquiring glance.

"I shall advise the dismantling of the whole!" grimly answered the Grand Duke, "and a new citadel planted here on the ruins of the rat-hole of Polish thieves!" When from the tower, the secret emissary turned his eyes upon the superb panorama, he slowly said, with a proud glance, "Russian it must be forever! It is a royal scene!"

The Grand Duke's glass swept the scene with the skill of a strategist. From Praga, with its bloody fields of Bialolenka, Grochow and Wawer, past Wilanow, with its memories of princely Lubomirski, and Potocki. On past Morysin, Natolin and Powaski, the Grand Duke scanned the princely palaces, the splendid parks, and the charming chateaux of the ruined magnates of the White Eagle. The Emperor's brother smiled when he recognized the Praga suburb which from its bloody triumph of the Black Eagle, made Suwarrow a field-marshal, and enabled Catherine to point her diamond wit over forty thousand dead and wounded!

Sixty palaces, thirty superb churches, lay below him, and to the west stretched out the plain of Wola. It was there the equestrian order of Poland were wont to meet to elect their king. There, they proudly boasted that their lances would uphold the very heavens in their fall!

The Grand Duke closed his glass at last. He had recognized the famous "redoubt of the dead," and the scene of Paskiewitch's terrible death-struggle at Wola. He cast a glance of scorn at the crowds of the meaner sort, far below him, clustering like flies. "I would like to turn my brave Cossacks loose upon that rabble now!" he said with a deep disgust! "Let us go down, Count. I think I see our future plan. The citadel wants more outworks, heavier guns, and a chain of forts around the tower. This, with a good military hedge there," he pointed to Praga, "will help us to hold those wolves at bay. And he smiled in cunning glee.

The Count de Berg was pale with the varied excitements of the night. He seemed to hear again on the breeze sweeping over the forty battlefields in sight, Kosciusko's last despairing cry: "Finis Poloniae."

And the Grand Duke's charming courtesies to the beautiful Countess Xenia at the tête-à-tête breakfast, soon proved to the Governor-General how easily the tiger could sheathe its claws.

It was only when the doors of the Royal Cabinet closed that the Grand Duke's eye resumed its cold official stare. In half-an-hour, the Count de Berg, and Major Alexis Dournof were engaged busily tracing in official cipher, the secret directions of the White Czar. For even a brother of the blood was only trusted to keep them in memory.

Two hours later, the Grand Duke dismissed the Governor-General. "You can go and officially show yourself at the review. Bid all your commanding officers to an official dinner to-night. I may need some of them. And verify the presence or absence of every noble whom I have marked on this list. Let the maréchals de noblesse all await your orders as they arrive. It is my purpose to assemble the Polish and Lithuanian nobles before the official balls."

When the door closed, the Grand Duke's manner at once changed. His voice was almost caressing, as he motioned Major Dournof to a seat near him. "Now, Alexis Fédorovitch, my departure will leave you free to act. Your temporary duty near the Count de Berg will be an excuse to find your old friends. The clubs, the staff, and regimental messes, the halls of society, even the lingering foreign adventurers, all these must be gleaned of every bit of gossip and news of use to us. I shall leave you a half company of my own Circassians as messengers. Write nothing save to me, and in the private cipher. You are not the man I take you for, if you cannot in a week penetrate the surface of the veiled social intrigues of luxurious Warsaw. In the train of Countess Xenia, your credentials will be of the highest. I will speak to the Count guardedly. But it is to you, to you, tried friend, that I must look to find through the easy license of private life, the one man we need for our purpose. Remember: Flattery! Gold! The social arts! Every man of them whom we can lure to these two great feasts will be shadowed on his homeward way. I have wagered with the Emperor that in one month I will know all their meeting-places, also their system of outwitting De Berg! Now, if we can chance upon one of these assemblies, we can snare all the birds!"

"But the evidence, the incriminating papers, the proofs needed to justify severity!" suggested the Major.

"Bah! The Government will supply that! If these fellows dare to meet over our border, the whole swarm will be at once severely dealt with! This first sudden action will separate their leaders, break up their plans, and afford us a public reason for the legal reorganization of Poland! Remember, Major, your Colonelcy depends on my winning my wager! You will see one great branch of these wild border aristocrats here, at the Warsaw ball; the others, naturally, will flock to Wilna. I will delay that fête two weeks, so that they may have time to venture over into West Russia, in holiday guise.

"But the man whom we need is a Polish noble of rank, whose social needs for money are great. Some desperate fellow, in other words, a man who will be easily worked on. Find him; the Government will guarantee his future, in luxury, and secret protection, for life,—abroad!"

Major Dournof stood with bowed head, in silence, for the Grand Duke had closed his orders. There was a blush on the soldier's cheek.

"I would sooner win my rank in the field, your Highness," he confusedly muttered.

"Ah! Never fear!" laughed the Grand Duke. "These fellows will fight like rats when stirred up. You will soon see fighting enough for even your impetuous nature. If our railroads were now finished, it would be an easy matter, but to chase these fanatic devils through the gloomy forests of the Land of Shadows, is disheartening work. Mouravief is right. 'Level the forests, hang the rebels!' That, our faithful troops will do. But, Dournof, we must forever break up and scatter this rich rebel nobility! Then the sword can do its work on the masses. Go, now, you shall be pushed to the front, where honors are to be bought with blood, but first, first finish this secret quest, for the sake of the Emperor, for Russia. Go, now, and prepare to pay your respects to the loveliest of allies,—the Countess Xenia!"

Seated alone, gazing out on the proud city, beleaguered from within by its stern conquerors, the Grand Duke's brow grew black. "Cursed rebellious horde! I counted thirty of their own churches, and only five of the Holy Greek Faith! There lies a deeper quarrel here than mere race hatred. Jew and Catholic band together against the orthodox faith! I wonder if Rome nourishes in secret their border feud of creed. It seems that they will cling with desperation to their dogmas. Every barren, marsh-bordered field, has its Polish cross, and the sly priests call this land of fens the 'jardin du Sainte Vièrge.' Silence first, the silence of defeat, and then, the Russian plowshare: Let Poland be obliterated!"

CHAPTER II.

THE GOVERNOR-GENERAL'S BALL.

THE Imperial ensign fluttered slowly down at sunset of the day on which Count de Berg's mysterious visitor left Warsaw at midnight. The city of Warsaw was convulsed with an anti-climax to the review with its ominous display. For a thousand eager gossips had failed to discover in any increased activity at the Chateau Royal the effect of the Czar's long arm. There were no military displays or unusual movements. A dozen of the keenest Polish spies, from a disguised noble acting as a kitchen servitor in the palace, up to the reigning beauty of Warsaw's rebel loveliness, were all strangely disconcerted. A calm of lulling softness settled over the captive kingdom, and the fact that some Russian imperial fête, or the passing of a princely off-shoot of the blood had caused the display of the family banner of the Romanoffs was generally admitted. Even in the clubs, veiled boudoirs and the students' secret meetings, the unusually suave politeness of the garrison and higher officials created the hopes of a modus vivendi of millennial kindness. But the grave-faced maréchals de noblesse presided over continued meetings of their gathered patricians in which a concensus of opinion on the great question of serfdom was asked for. For the Russians, serfs themselves for long years to the Mongol invader, had, after pushing beyond their safety-line into Poland, been enslaved by the union of Lithuania and Poland. The old battle of Piast against Slav had its currents and counter-currents. The Muscovites, victors in the Kingdom of Poland since the dark days of thirty-one, now desired, while secretly strangling the Polish nobility, to release the mingled serfs of both nationalities.

The aspect of graver things drew the Polish mind for a time, from their wild dreams of seeing the White Eagle soar above the Black once more!

Hopeful men of mediocre influence began to dream that the last convulsive struggle of the Pole against the swarming Russian might be averted. That at least one generation of Poles might escape that grim reaping-hook, the Russian sword. For all knew well that Poland's choicest blood had drenched the tattered guidons which moulder now as clustered trophies in Vienna's halls, in the Prussian Zeug Musée, or in that crypt of buried nation's spoils, the Kazan cathedral at St. Petersburg. There in the Kazan church, behind the hundred splendid columns, in the dim interior where every art and the treasures of Crœsus add to the splendor of the silver shrine, the myriad flags of Poland, furled forever, are offered up to the meek and lowly Saviour, the apostle of love! Three revolutions brought these grim trophies, the hacked lance-heads, the fluttering ribboned silk, shot-torn and marred, to gleam where, in face of the church, the bayonet-pricked Poles driven out on the awful journey to Siberia muttered their last prayer for Poland, as they passed in chains. These last brave tokens of self-immolation were wrenched from the hands of the slaughtered cadets of Warsaw, as the " Redoubt of the Dead," and " Io Polskie," tells its mute tale of fidelity to death, still shining on the rebels' treasured flags. For, where the captured keys of a dozen great cities of Europe are held up by French bâtons de maréchal, and the standards of Napoleon, of Prussia, of Turkey, and of the brave Swede, are displayed, these Polish trophies are eyed with a ferocious glee. Men have crept in there in the guise of ragged beggars, on their knees, to kiss

these lame staves and murmur a prayer, which is a memory
"Io Polskie."

There were cautious denizens of Warsaw who suspected a
fine strong hand behind this new comedy of peace, but none
dared to dream that an Imperial Grand Duke moved the
puppet play!

It was even so!   The Czar's brother had smiled in a quiet
satisfaction, as he pressed the hand of the Governor-General.
A secret departure for Berlin, at midnight, had astounded
De Berg.

" I think that our two weeks have not been entirely thrown
away!" laughed the Grand Duke. "You and Dournof
have now my final orders.   Follow them explicitly.   The
sly nobles are swarming in here.   Our own West Russian
Polish aristocrats are all moving towards Grodno and Wilna
on the summons of my representative.   Do not spare your
magnificence.   I wish our friends to always remember—the
Governor-General's ball!"   With a last whispered word of
secret import, the great magnate disappeared in the night,
his fierce Circassians swarming closely around the princely
equipage.

Count de Berg passed through the royal postern with a
sigh.   Though new honors crowded upon him, the pale
aristocratic face of the old soldier was flushed with shame
as he thought of the work before him.   For he knew all the
dark snares now ready to entrap their wily adversaries,
under the guise of new concessions, relaxed severity, and a
public programme, which in lying protocols would emblazon
the crowning mercies of Russian rule with diplomatic art.

" It must be done!" he mused.   "It is hard, and yet, of
all the world's glittering charlatans, the Pole is the most
specious and unreliable.   Celts of the East, Gauls of the
modern idea, their myriad changes of dissimulating elegance exact the finest Russian duplicity, in self-defence!"

In the anxious days before Dournof returned to report that

the Grand Duke had safely slipped back into Russia, and had appeared in royal state at Wilna, the Count and Countess de Berg were deeply engrossed in their preparations for the magnificent ball. "After all, Xenia," said De Berg, with doubtful self-consolation, " we only open a royal puppet show on behalf of the Czar. The future acts of the drama will be played on other scenes than our official theatre here. All court life is but dissimulation at the best. We are not morally responsible."

And yet, they shuddered to admit that with smiling faces they would greet the train of haughty nobles, from whose ranks would be selected the shining victims of the first pitiless Russian vengeance ! " Note their faces well, all these unruly fellows, we may need you to certify to the identity of some who may drift into our net over there ! " said the Grand Duke, as he pointed to the far Lithuanian border.

From every one of the thousand windows of the old chateau, the blaze of lights told at last to the outer world of the Czar's celebration of the conclusion of the Convention of Nobles.

It was a night of royal pageantry, when the unwilling flower of Poland's beauty and bravery passed in a brilliant review before timid Countess Xenia, shivering with womanly dread, as she stood on the lowest step of the throne, her husband at her side. In a great city which was princely when the wild boars roved over the sedges of the Neva, which already boasted its jewelled shrines of the Virgin when the pagan Tartar yet ruled at Moscow, no such splendor had been witnessed since magnificent Charles Radziwill in 1786 opened to the world the Namienistkowski palace in a matchless fête remembered for a hundred years !

" This rivals the work of Aladdin's lamp," mused Major Dournof, as he aided the glittering staff officers in the presentation of the guests. Music's dying strains beat passionately upon the perfumed air. The sheen of jewels, the gleam of snowy bosoms, the sparkling of eyes brighter than star or golden order lit up the fairy scene. Defiant, elegant, haughty yet courteous to the Czar's representatives, the dark Polish patricians swept along in the pride of unrivalled beauty and vivacity. The intoxicating excitement of the witching hours, the magnetic tension of the hundreds of beautiful buoyant natures, lifted up the pageant to a dream of every delight. Here, on every hand, the cool. Russian officers, with scarcely veiled entreaty, wooed the Polish beauties for that forgiveness which loveliness always extends to valor! A gratified feeling of growing sincerity moved the versatile men of the fated race to a lofty truce of elegant demeanor.

"It is a pity that these fine fellows are Poles!" mused Count de Berg with dreaming regret, as he gravely returned the salutations of his semi-rebel subjects. Splendid in address, elegant and supple in figure, graceful in step and with unequalled skill in dress, the tall nobles, thin-lipped, with eagle glances, murmured their salutations to friends parted for years by the gloom of that occupation, which had closed the salons of the nobility. For the greatest princes of Poland were long forced to avoid each other or merely communicate in secret. And the ruined heirs of magnificent Arkadia, superb Skiernuvice, of royal Pulawy—the nobles who held state at Morysin, Natolin, Piotkrow, Jasnagora—the lords of the proud old land of Boléslas the Brave, were now houseless! The Potocki, Krasinski, Zamoyski, and a hundred other palaces were in stranger hands. Bold Russian officers from the vast camps of Powaski, with their bright-eyed Russian friends, now chased the deer in the beautiful parks of Chateau Lasienski, of the Belvedere, of Bielany. The lords of the soil were houseless fugitives!

It was a strange assembly, for the Radwills, the Batthoris the Czarytorskis, the Lubomirskis, the Poniatowskis, Paskiewitchs, Zborowskis, Lasienskis, Potockis, Zarnoyskis,

Branickis, Walewskis and other children of kings were making merry though held at bay by a conquering soldiery in their own land!—Their absent brothers were either in foreign or in alien lands! Their mournful colony in far-away Paris plotted and daily knocked at the doors of the third Napoleon, the arbiter of Europe, for a recognition as a body of the local noblesse! Gay Paris was the world's queen.

Beautiful women descended from him who hurled back the Mongols at Lowicz, when the Russ was still a slave,—had only their beauty,—their blood, and a few jewels which escaped the spoiler's hands. Their dowries and lands swelled the Czar's treasury.

It was a touching scene when the proud children of conquered Poland saw their fairest women, with passionately appealing glances gazing on the past glories of Poland still shining pictured on the walls of the palace of the Russian Viceroy. And it was before the despoiled throne of Poland itself, that they bowed to the impassive Count de Berg.

In all his semi-royal state, the Governor-General envied the poorest Polish noble before his eyes, for he was playing a hidden part which seemed to the soldier's eyes,—pitiful, cruel and mean! And yet, the Czar would be obeyed. Cæsar's stern orders.

De Berg would sooner have seen his brave Russians shrink in defeat on a lost battle-field, as did their fathers before Étienne Bathori in 1577, than to stand, and feel that the jaws of fate were closing in upon these helpless doomed children of fortune. It was, after all, but one more turn of the screw crushing the very memories of fair Poland out of existence.

Major Dournof, too, was busied with other duties than mere beauty-worship. His secret mission weighed heavily on his mind. He could not forget it, for a dozen of the most dashing Warsaw officers had been told off by Count de Berg, to initiate the handsome major of cuirassiers into all the gilded coteries of Warsaw. In the two weeks of his special duty at the Chateau Royal, Dournof had already learned every current and counter-current of the social war of dissimulation between Pole and Russ. Proud and haughty as the local nobles were, there were yet common meeting-grounds. Though the sacred blue blood of the land mourned in private, and kept an invisible barrier before its highest salons, there were debatable grounds where the chevaliers of the two races met in a seeming friendship. Distinctive Polish and Russian clubs were jealously raised to a haughty exclusiveness, but there were also many club-houses open to the polite foes. In public resorts, a quiet but guarded aversion classified the meeting votaries of fashion by their sympathies. The gay young officers clustered around Major Dournof had now done their very utmost to expand his acquaintance. Feasted in every nook of the great chateau where a thousand officials dwelt, he knew also the resorts of the mad gamesters of society, and those shadowy parlors where fair spiders were ever spinning webs to ensnare the too vivacious Russian lover.

"Now, Alexis Féderovitch," laughed young Boris Milutin of the guards, "they call me the 'mad wolf,'" and the young officer of twenty showed his alleged fangs in a gay smile, "but you set the pace a little fast, even for me! I think I can safely leave you to walk alone, in Warsaw. Or else, some other man of the mess must take up the running."

Major Dournof smiled quietly. "I shall not be here very long, so you need not fear that I will rob you of your dangerous fair friends." The only son of the patrician General Vassili Milutin, the handsome Russ had already won a Parisian renown for plunging.

On this festal night, young Milutin little knew that the Major had called him to his side only as a walking directory of fashion. Dournof, in his cabinet at the chateau had all the secret reports of the Governor-General daily spread before

him. Spy, mouchard, feminine agent, and every paid in-
triguant of the Czar knew by a mysterious warning that Dournof was their master for the hour. After frequenting café,
theatre, opera, the jockey clubs, and all the thousand
booths of the Polish Vanity Fair, the cuirassier officer
glanced kindly back on this night at many a passing fair
face of recent acquaintance. The men were nearly all
known to him, as the artful Grand Duke had thrown his confidential agent designedly forward in the conferences of the
gathered proprietors so deftly arranged. With his cipher
lists of reference, Major Dournof could easily follow the
merest introduction to a complete knowledge of the surroundings of every suspected Pole. And so, here, in the great
parade of the conquered, at the grand ball where none
dared to openly refuse an Emperor's bidding, sent through
his Governor-General, Dournof was yet searching for some
fitting victim of the Grand Duke's wiles. "If you will excuse me now, Major, I will go over to our wing, and try a
little game of baccarat. Some of these fellows play desperately, and our improvised Yacht Club branch here is open to
them.

Major Dournof was carelessly nodding assent, when he
suddenly grasped Milutin's arm. "Stay a moment! Who
is this?"

"Heavens, what a handsome woman! Ah! I do not
know her,—but I do her escort."

"He is the very one I want, not the lady," eagerly whispered Dournof, as Milutin returned an incredulous smile!
For the Major of Cuirassiers was as stately a soldierly son
of Mars as his renowned regiment ever boasted. Tall, well-
knit, with a bronzed cheek, his fair hair, cool, steady eye,
and stern, resolute face were a marked contrast to the rosy
cheeks and dark boyish beauty of the pet subaltern beside
him. The queenliest one of the beauty-show might have
favored the man whose cuirassier uniform gave full effect

to his splendid personality. It was with a secret joy Dournof heard Milutin's answer, as the youth exchanged a warm
recognition with the passing cavalier. "One of the really
best of these fellows I ever met. I always used to tell him
in Paris I would have him baptized as a Russ! A prince of
good fellows is Count Étienne.—But, here he is himself!"
And, as the boy spoke, Major Dournof riveted his eyes
upon the singularly fascinating looking man of thirty who
grasped both Milutin's hands. "I have just left my wife
with the General. I see that he is looking even better than
in Paris."

"Ah, Count, allow me!" cried Milutin. "My friend
Major Dournof,—Count Etienne Wizocki," and the secret
wish of the cuirassier was easily gratified. For the shifting,
eager restlessness of the Polish noble's eyes had caught the
Major's instant attention. It was a face dowered with every
manly beauty, and bore the stamp of the race of pleasure in
every line. "You did not tell me you were a married man,
while we were in Paris!" maliciously whispered the guardsman.

"Ah!" carelessly said the noble. "Cecile is devoted to
her little girl, and she prefers the pure air and grand old
woods of Nimovitch! By the way, my dear Milutin, I can
give you the very finest hunting in Volhynia, and I should be
glad also to have your friend Major Dournof as my guest!
"Come to Nimovitch."

"You are now on your way homeward?" queried Dournof,
with a strange, growing interest.

Count Wizocki bowed. "I was abroad all last winter,
and my place in Volhynia needs my occasional care. At any
rate, I must take Cecile back to her beloved lakes and forests."

The Major started! Fate seemed to have brought to him
a possible instrument. Volhynia lay just over the line in
Western Russia, and was one of the Grand Duke's suspected
provinces.

" Come along with me and have a little roulette or baccarat,
Étienne. They play high enough here, even for you."

Another gleam of light shone in Dournof's mind. The
noble was an absentee, and a gamester. Perhaps he might
be the very tool needed! For Alexis Dournof thought with
a blush that, as a rule, the Polish nobles clung to their unhappy
land, even in its sorrows, while the serf-owning modern Russians of rank eagerly abandoned their Siberian wilds, their
Ural fastnesses, their limitless steppes, and lonely domains,
to hurl their gold foolishly away in the capitals of western
Europe.

While agent and intendant robbed, plundered, and ground
down the serf, the Russian noble gained, at a frightful cost,
all the vices of the politer lands.

" I'll join you for half-an-hour only, if you wait here,"
cried Count Wizocki, his eyes lighting up with a born gambler's fire. " I must take Cecíle to our, old friend whom we
wish to meet here. This is a full parade of all you have left
us !" said the Count, smiling faintly at Dournof.

" Is he dissipated?" calmly asked the Major, while
Wizocki sped away to gain a respite from his evidently careless guidance of his beautiful wife.

" They say in Paris that he pours acres down his throat,
and throws forests away at the gaming-table. But, I am
astonished to know that he is married. For I must say that
while I am a pretty giddy youngster, Wizocki is by no means
averse to Gallic charms !" The youth concluded with some
chivalric charity: " I suppose the fair Countess wanders
alone under the arching trees of Nimovitch. She does not
look like a woman who would go astray ! And, yet, neglect
and loneliness may, some day, do its work ! Hello ! what's
this?" added Milutin, as Wizocki approached with his own
father the General. Boris frowned impatiently.

" I suppose he has told my father of the partie de baccarat ! Now, I cannot with any respect for the service, go and

play at the same table with my own father, a commanding General," and the youth's eyes then wandered strangely, to the other side of the great ball-rooms, where Cecile Wizocka's fair face shone out as a bright particular star.

"I'll make him introduce me!" was a lightning thought of mad Boris Milutin, who was a very squire of dames. And, while General Milutin conferred a few moments with Major Dournof, the youthful soldier on his presentation bowed deeply before the lady of Nimovitch.

"Do you know this Count Wizocki intimately, may I ask, General?" said Dournof, his eyes following the graceful civilian.

"Fairly well! His social renown makes him a feature in the gay circles of Paris," replied the General. "He is throwing away the remains of a splendid fortune, I am told. I have followed his career with some alarm. For he married a sweet Polish princess, the sister of a woman whom I once admired as our only loyal Polish lady of rank! I never met her till to-night. She seems to me to be unhappy."

A sudden impulse guided Major Dournof to say, in a low tone, as the Count returned. "I would like to call on you, to-morrow, about ten; I wish to speak to you about him." And the Major whispered a word in the General's ear which caused him to start and significantly bow assent, as Wizocki gaily joined them.

"Let us go over now, General," he eagerly cried, "I have only gained a single half-an-hour's furlough." As they bowed and threaded the sparkling stream of pleasure-seekers, Major Dournof bowed his head in conviction.

"Just the very man, if he could be only trapped!" and then, to the Russian's mind came up the old proverbs of the gambler's fatal passion.

"If he could only be encouraged to play, to involve himself, while he could be watched and worked on! Thank God, my share of this mean work is done when I name him as open to apparent approach ! The Grand Duke must give the future trapping over to other hands. "I wonder if I dare speak freely to General Milutin." After an hour's deep thought, while carelessly eyeing the changing shapes of the spirited dancers, Dournof had decided upon his course. Before him, in the coquettish mazurka and polonaise, under the crystal and silver chandeliers, the dancers swayed to and fro ! But the beautiful Countess Wizocka was still sitting listening to Boris Milutin's murmured conversation, as the gallant youth bent to her fascinations, though her eyes wearily sought the door through which General Milutin and the Count had vanished.

It was an hour already, and Major Dournof himself chafed for the return of the two friends. "I will send a courier at once to the Grand Duke, and have him place this whole thing in the General's hands. The Pole would not distrust Milutin," and then, the Major's head was bowed in shame. For there, facing him sat the young wife who awaited the return of her reckless lord ! "By heavens ! It is too bad ! " thought Dournof, and he raised his head in eager inquiry, as General Milutin and the Count at last returned. They were exchanging sober whispers, and a thrill startled Dournof as the Count anxiously said, " You will give me my revenge at Nimovitch, next month. Remember, you are of the hunting party ! "

The victor General bowed, in some confusion, as Dournof quietly interjected. "Do you make a long stay in Warsaw, Count ? "

"Only a week ! " lightly said Wizocki. "I am going to rally some of my own old friends here for a grand hunt next month. My forests are overrun with beasts. They have not been shot over for several years. The General has posi- tively accepted ! Will you join him and be my guest ? "

The Pole's voice rang out, frank and manly, and Dournof thanked God that his path led him no nearer to the now imperilled domain of Nimovitch. "One Russian guest at a time is enough, my dear Count!" laughed Dournof. Besides, I must soon report at Wilna, for winter duty!"

"Then, I shall surely claim you now, for next year," cordially cried Wizocki, as he observed a mute distress signal from his waiting wife's fan. He moved over to the corner where Boris still sat.

"By the way, General, was fortune on your side?" remarked Dournof, with some effort.

"I won a fair sum,—four thousand crowns,—mostly, I am sorry to say, from Wizocki. But, he is headlong! nothing will stop him! If I do go to his fine old chateau, where he bids me, I shall stop on fair terms of honor—double or quits, —I do not want to win his money!"

But, General Vassili Milutin was himself in the hands of Fate, and it is human to change one's mind!

"What's the matter with you, Dournof? You look strangely pale! Are you ill? Come along with me and have a glass of wine!" and Alexis Dournof thrilled with a sudden chill, as, at the grand portal, they gravely bowed to Count Wizocki bearing away the pale-faced beauty of the evening.

Drifting, drifting! It seems they are doomed to be ever brought nearer! Can he be the fated man? Is it an omen? and, long after he had laid his handsome head on a soldier's pillow, that night, Alexis Dournof was haunted by the reproachful glance of the fair stranger's eyes. "I pray Heaven that she did not think I have lured her wild husband on to play high!" was the last reverie of the man who was perhaps fated to be the instrument of his country's shame.

General Vassili Milutin wrapped his sable pelisse around him, and threw himself in his carriage in deep thought. On his long drive back to the Powalski camp, he evolved a certain indignation at the long-drawn-out tête-à-tête of his reckless son with the lovely Polish patrician who would not dance. "That young cub is growing troublesome! I think a tour of outpost duty will do him good!"—and so it was not altogether for "the good of the service," that Boris Milutin was next day suddenly sent on a tour of detailed inspection which lasted three months! Leaning back in his carriage, clasping a richly-jewelled sword, an Emperor's gift, Vassili Milutin was the personification of a successful Muscovite general. Rapid promotion and daring deeds had carried him up quickly to the high rank he held, before reaching fifty, and the only son of his early marriage was almost a brother in appearance. Milutin's broad breast bore a golden line of jewelled orders and sparkling crosses. Vigorous and graceful he possessed all the graces of the courts, and the arts of the camp. His sweeping soldierly mustache hid a sternly-cut chin, and only the round, deeply-set eyes, which could soften or glare at will, proved the cruel craft of the Tartar blood, lurking under all the polish of the Czar's court.

He was thinking of the beauty and fresh graces of the fair Polish woman, who, a wife at eighteen, now had walked alone the park of Nimovitch, with her baby girl for two long years, and waited in vain for her prodigal husband's return from Paris.

Vassili Milutin had never remarried after the sudden death of the girl-bride who had brought to him an enormous fortune and also given him as a sole heir, the son whose present headlong social career was only a picture of his father's mad youth. Time had not yet cooled the Tartar noble's passions, nor chilled the hot blood now leaping to his wild heart. He was of a pitiless race,—a man who had seen his brave squadrons go down headlong in the mad charge of battle without a single sigh of regret, and yet he now tried to lie to himself! "I must see her again! Certainly! For her husband has asked me to this great hunt in Volhynia."

It was only after he had watched the sparkling white stars from his open window, for a half hour, that he remembered the lateness of the vigil. The great Russian permanent camp lay sleeping silently around him, and he at last vacantly remembered his appointment with Major Dournof. Even as he slept, he thought again, with some strangely awakened eagerness of pursuit, " I shall see her again—at Nimovitch ! "

The lights were darkened in the great ball-room, and the wearied sentinels alone watched the windows of the great palace, now all dropping one by one into the blackness of night. When Alexis Dournof had finished his letter to the Grand Duke there were already at the chateau gate, four Circassians waiting to take the private report to the distant master, now eager for Dournof's important news.

."I cannot plot this crime out in all its mean details ! "— thought the officer, as he pondered upon the last words of his dispatch, at once a suggestion and a report. " If His Highness really cares to trap the game,—then, Count Wizocki is the very man ! " It was easy to see in the Polish noble's face that his gambling debt to the General was carried homeward as a leaden weight on a heavy heart !

The flying Circassians were fifty miles away on the road to Wilna with Dournof's cipher letter, before Warsaw awoke to the lingering memory of the night's wonderfeast. It was not a dream ; it had been a display of all that wealth and power could throw around the old historic scene of many great fêtes, whose garlands were long faded. There had been no such dazzling reunion in recent days to speak of the growing nearness of the opposing social lines. Even the satisfied Count de Berg, communing with the graceful consort who was glad to see the trying ordeal over, never fancied to himself that there had been no real reason but Russian duplicity for the tempting allurement. It had all seemed so real, the bounding pulses of life had beat so proudly under the glare of the thousand wax-lights, to the impassioned, tender, witching national music !

General Vassili Milutin, however, galloped gaily up at ten

o'clock, to meet his appointment at his headquarters, with the anxious Dournof. "I have been out trying some new horses, Major!" he merrily cried, as he sprang lightly from the saddle. He did not inform the cuirassier that his swift ride had led him back to the heart of the city where he had already left cards upon the Count Wizocki. It was thoughtful in the soldier to so quickly yield to the demands of local etiquette, and his eager mind seemed to be relieved by the slight formality. "I shall see her again at Nim-ovitch!" he repeated, for the most definite plans of his future did not now lead beyond the acceptance of the hunting invi-tation. It now seemed to him to be almost a duty to his social code not to decline.

Over the morning breakfast, en militaire, between very careful directions to his chéf, and a few hurried reports from his busy aides, General Vassili Milutin graphically sketched the history of the illustrious line from whence the lovely Countess Cecile sprang, and told the story of her ro-mantic marriage to Etienne Wizocki! "There was abso-lutely no fitness in the match, my dear Major," mused the General, as he leisurely sipped his hock and soda. "But the man himself you have seen! He is of fairly good rank, and is now the Maréchal de Noblesse of Volhynia. Undecided in politics, and an absentee, he has grown lately very unpopular by neglecting the hospitalities due to his rank as chief of the nobility.

"I have asked some men here who know him well, and they tell me that his whole career has been one of uninterrupted foreign extravagance! For a short time at first, his pride at winning the loveliest heiress in all Poland, caused him to remain in Volhynia and discharge his duties. But soon the force of old habits returned to draw him back to Paris, Baden and Monte Carlo. As for his proud and stately bride, wedded at eighteen, she is but twenty-two years of age now. Her vast estates have nearly all vanished under his wild lavishness.　His own beautiful Nimovitch is sure to follow, in time, her lost patrimony, for, with a true Pole's pride of race, he has kept his own land to the last.　The term of his four years as Maréchal de Noblesse has now nearly expired, and these hunting invitations, I suppose, are meant to pledge future votes and gain over family influence among his old friends.　For the angry Volhynian proprietors have all banded together to defeat him."

"What do they say against him?" slowly demanded Major Dournof, as he registered in his mind every word.

"They allege that he is but half-hearted in Polish patriotism, and, besides this, his wife's proud relatives resent his ruin of her estates."

While Dournof, with burning brows, made a semblance of enjoying the noble General's early hospitality, he muttered;

"It is the decree of Fate, he is the very man!　But, I will leave it to the Grand Duke!　Can there be already a plot behind this?　Is he even now a revolutionist?　Perhaps; for when all patrimonial property is lost, the ruined conservative usually becomes a blatant radical!　It is true that the poor and desperate have nothing left to risk in any local agitation."　With a concealed impatience, Dournof ran through the slowly dragging luxury of Vassili Milutin's exquisite menu, for this Russ à la mode, was both epicure and General; and yet, while he could dally at Vèry's, or the Trois Frères, for hours over a raffiné déjeûner to please some finical Parisienne, Vassili Milutin's very sweetest meal had been black bread and water from the trenches stained with blood, as he rested after driving the thrice victorious English out of the Redan, at Sebastopol.

"I must leave you, General," finally said with deep regret, the Cuirassier, as he profoundly thanked the host.

"And will you not come and try the woods of Nimovitch for a ten-pronged elk, or a monster bear!"

The General's eyes were dreaming in pleasure.

" Ah, my dear General, your own career is made !   I have my laurels yet to win, and a grave tour of duty waits for me. I cannot accept."

" A gallant fellow," mused Milutin as Dournof rode away. "He will surely make his mark !" The General was pleased with Dournof's neat compliment. " My career will be made,—when I meet her at Nimovitch !" He sighed.·— For, crafty Milutin had now decided to indulge Count Wizocki freely in his revenge at baccarat !   " Lucky at cards, unlucky at love ! " he laughed, " We will see !" In an hour, Alexis Dournof, impatiently listening to young Milutin's babble of the ball, indited a cipher dispatch which astounded General Milutin, a week later, with sudden orders to report to the Grand Duke at Wilna.   He grumbled, " But I *must* go to Nimovitch for the hunt ! "

CHAPTER III.

AT THE CHATEAU DE NIMOVITCH.

IT was a month later than the epoch of the still, outvaunted grand ball, when, with a pale and thoughtful face, Countess Cecile Wizocka walked under the doric-columned south portico of her Volhynian home. The lake, dreaming at her feet, was leaden-colored, and chilly gusts scattered the leaves of October now lightly rustling down in the great encircling park. A faded autumn sun was sinking towards its rest in the long line of evergreen forest to the west. The lady of the manor shivered slightly, and as her light foot touched the threshold, passed the two liveried servants awaiting her return with her head bowed, and crushing a brief note in her slender hand. Her soul was strangely shaken.

For, a Cossack dashing up at full speed, had astounded the lodge-keeper by vaulting his pony over the high masonry wall, hedge-hidden, which marked the northern line of the Chateau grounds. The great red waxen seal, a mailed hand grasping a sword, was unfamiliar, and yet a sudden pallor made the roses on Cecile Wizocka's face whiten to ashes. It was a brief announcement in courteous etiquette, of the speedy arrival of General Vassili Milutin. "The debt of honor is not yet paid! It is shameful," she murmured, and a strange feeling of dread entered the disturbed mind of the proud Countess, when she met the General on the threshold of her home. "He is the only man living who can charge my poor foolish Étienne with dishonor. It must not be!" For, in the temporary absence of the Count, the spirited aristocrate knew that before the two men could meet as equals of their lofty caste, at her board, that yet unpaid four thousand crowns should be in the Russian General's hands. Like many other consorts, the gentle Countess shared her husband's misfortunes loyally, even though others, strangers, divided his hours of mad enjoyment. But, the perfect demeanor of Vassili Milutin disarmed even the self-conscious Countess. Though he had fifty times muttered, unconsciously, "I shall meet her at Nimovitch," in his mad onward ride from Wilna, and the two hundred versts seemed to have been two thousand, Vassili Milutin was only the beau sabreur, par excellence, as he bent over the trembling hand of the beautiful hostess, kissing it lightly with his courtly grace. The Russian patrician was a philosopher in love, though a tyrant at heart, and a reckless fiend in the field! He well knew "that all things come to him who waits!"

So, the only distinct thought he bore over the threshold of stately Nimovitch, was his purpose not to prevent Étienne Wizocki from wooing the fickle "painted ladies" on the cards! He had never given a second thought to the I. O. U. which the crestfallen Count had pressed upon him. "You can pay it whenever you will, my dear Count! See, it is better so!" He tore the little flimsy paper to tatters, and simply said, "Send the sum through your Intendant to my bankers, De Roque, at Wilna at any time. It will then, be simply a business matter."

With that perverse mingling of qualities which always proves the unequal grain of humanity, Wizocki had not lied to his wife when she gently reproached him for his late return at the ball. "Luck was against me, Cecile! I lost, and I cannot see the way to pay as I should." For, the twenty-four hours rule of debts of honor, tied up in anguish the soul of a man whose gentlemanly code had survived the wreck of all his principles! He, who had scattered his loyal wife's

fortune in crazy rioting abroad, and showered dearly bought
jewels on "strange goddesses," yet loved, trusted and feared
his beautiful young wife. In her stately loneliness, she
directed all the affairs of their joint estates, managed twenty
villages of serfs, and found a silent joy in guarding the little
girl of two years whose eyes hardly knew a father's face. The
minds of all three were fixed upon the gambling debt when
the General rode into the park at Nimovitch! For the
Count had secretly convoked several rich Jew traders to en-
deavour to borrow at once the needed sum. As he rode away,
from the Chateau on this errand, he bore the choicest of his
wife's jewels as a security. The fair woman waiting his return
was only another sacrifice on the altar of "barren honor!"
To what hellish deeds of rakish wickedness has not the
cowardly egoism of manhood for centuries given the thin
mantle of "Honor!" Bowing low, two servants with silver
candelabra, with astonished eyes, conducted the Russian
foeman Vassili Milutin to the guest chambers of state. For,
though twenty nobles were already assembled in the east wing
of the chateau, awaiting the sound of the hunting-horn, the
Czar's representative was the chief guest in rank and precedence. The stars peeped out in the evening sky, as, far away,
riding afar with his wild escort, young Boris Milutin grumbled,
"He is at Nimovitch now." Major Alexis Dournof, bending over crafty new secret plans and reports at Wilna, tossed
aside a curt note from the General. "Thank God! That
is off my hands, and I now have duty which will not stain a
soldier's sword." For, closeted for days with the Grand
Duke, the wily General had carried away alone in his bosom
the final plans, for the enthralling of the nobility of Poland
and old Lithuania. "It is just as well that no one man, however loyal, should know the whole scheme," mused the
Grand Duke, as he watched Milutin ride away from the
Wilna palace. "It is well, Vassili Michailovitch is brave
and cunning. However he brings the game on, we will

be ready to detain and incriminate all these Poles. But
the birds must not be frightened. They must trap themselves !"

The same cool, cruel thought agitated General Milutin's
mind, as he gazed at his noble entertainers, across their own
board. For he would fain tame this shy, polish falcon, and
the eyes of the timid dove met his, in a long searching glance
which made his bosom thrill. The Count had returned in
time to sit at the head of his board, in the halls of his chivalric forefathers. It was fortunate that a number of his noble
comrades of the chase were present, for the rising gayety of
the dinner chased away the slight embarrassment of the
single hostile Russian at the board. The versatile Polish
nobles soon entered into the acquaintance of the powerful
General with an apparent bonhomie. While the Czar's
agents grimly watched the land of the old Polish power from
the Vistula to the far west, the Poles themselves, in the safe
secrecy of their clannish veiled conspiracy, waited with
unslaked revengeful thoughts, to entrap, disarm, delude and
betray any sudden movement of the Black Eagle. Over the
great land of the Piasts and the Jagellons, a feeling of haunting unrest had slowly crept, as haunting as the fogs hanging
over the undulating plains, the great lonely marshes, the
silent forests and rolling savannahs of the bosky wooded
plateau of Poland! Every chance of a future conflict had
been carefully studied on both sides. The intending rebels
were well aware that the great cities, Warsaw, Wilna,
Grodno, Kowno, Minsk, Vitebsk, Moghilev and Jitomir formed
a ring of hard-held fortified camps, which even dauntless
Polish bravery could never break. But, the whole wild land
was a natural cover for partisan warfare. From the bare
open Russian plains on the east, to their dreary Prussian
bare frontier stretches, and the foothills of the Austrian
Carpathians, the copses, forests, woods, marshes, fells, lakes
and tangles of gloomy Poland offered myriad safe nests

for the rebels. Every peasant knew the almost pathless woods. They were even yet unmapped.

And, as Vassili Milutin's jewelled orders and golden stars glittered when he raised his glass to drink the official toast, "The Czar," the bright-eyed nobles near him longed for the moment when such dashing generals as he would head their great trains of heavy Russian troops into the sombre woods. For, then the Polish Eagle could stoop to an easy prey! They smiled and dissembled! At this hour of joyous social reunion, the easy-going nobles plied General Milutin with their infinite graces of society.

For, beside insurrection, and the fathoming of Russian wiles, each rebel eagerly burned to know the official plans which proposed to free three hundred thousand serfs, throw them on their own resources, and give to them great unpaid gifts of the now useless lands of the Polish grandees! It was clear to all that the Russian government contemplated easing the yoke of the loyal Russian serf at home. But, this step in Poland would suddenly deprive all the conspiring nobles of the unpaid labor which tilled their fields, tended their herds, and turned the virgin forests into ready money. So, while with artful grace the General met and parried all the searching politeness of the witty and vivacious Poles, the Count himself was free to exchange a glance of sorrowful defeat with his proud and silent wife.

He had not obtained the full sum desired, but one-half of the amount was already his, and the remainder was promised in a few days. While the Jewish traders sent out secret messengers to gather in the gold, by Judaic accommodation, Count Étienne suddenly found a royal road to victory. "If I can only play to good fortune, why not try the luck again to-night."

He had, in an unacknowledged cowardice, lingered in his dressing-rooms, so as only to meet his agitated wife in the grand salon, when the silver gong had sounded, and the

old butler—a family heirloom—had announced that the
" Countess was served." With delicate dainty grace, Cecile
Wizocka presided alone, unembarrassed by the score of men,
all stealing eager glances at her pale loveliness. It is the
fortune of the noblewomen of Russia to be obliged to often
dispense social attentions alone, in the great Empire, where
the nobles' palaces stud the lonely wastes at great distances,
and the traveller of gentle caste must be entertained. There
are no hostelries or inns. The great gulf between noble and
peasant has never been filled in either Poland or Russia. A
middle class is almost without existence, the furtive intelligence of the hovering Jews supplying all the duties of an in-
telligent bourgeoisie. It was, therefore, unsupported, that
Countess Cecile stood at the head of the table, radiant in its
crystal and gleaming with rich ancestral plate, as each guest
in order approached and kissed her hand as the dinner
closed. She swept away through a line of gallant cavaliers,
attended to the door of the salon by the courtly General,
whose cool glance had never once wavered, as his eye roved
over her exquisite charms. Something of the self-protective
element of motherhood stirred the lovely woman's bosom,
for she was met at the door of the salon by the dainty child
Marguerite, proudly conducted by her nurses.

Clinging to that slight form, in an appeal for the sympathy of her sex, the lady of the manor sought her boudoir.
Her life was a sad and strange one ! On an estate twenty
by sixty miles in extent, with two thousand serfs scattered
in six villages, there was not a single woman near to whom
she could extend her hand, and the nearest patrician, either
Russ or Pole, who could sit in her presence, was sixty miles
away ! Etiquette forbade a free personal acquaintance with
the one or two women attendants who were of her household. The studied politeness extended in Slavic lands to
tutors and governesses excludes them from ever crossing
the line of inferiority. And, in the scattered manor houses

of Poland and Russia, the rarest womanhood withers alone in a solitude unbroken by the beating of a kindred heart! It was natural that the wine-drinking nobles soon crowded around the Count and the General, and, while the "silver-necked" flagons were foaming, the idea of a game at baccarat was joyously hailed by all. The General followed Count Étienne slowly, as he led the way to the east wing. At this particular moment he cared little who played, or for what stake, for a gloomy settled purpose crept into the heart of the man who had noticed that Count Étienne winced as he passed the rooms where his wife was now safely hidden from their gay wassail shouts! Neither hawk nor victim knew that Cecile Wizocka was on her knees before a jewelled shrine on her marble "prie-dieu," praying that black and bitter ruin might not cross the threshold of the old chateau! How many ashen-faced women, hiding an anguished love in a sorrowing heart, have vainly begged the Great Disposer for the sparing of the last sad, crushing, chastening stroke! Rake, roué, spendthrift, mad votary of the bowl, and the crazed devotee of Fortune might pause if these sanctuaries of sorrow were violated, and the breaking wifely heart be held up to awe the wicked. But there is no limit, no human bound to the infinite capacity of all womanhood for Love and its Crown of Sorrows!

The train of men high in the vigor of the lust of life wound on to the great guest wing, through a corridor lined with the old servants of the house. Doubled doors, duplicated behind them, left the main chateau to be the theatre of Cecile Wizocka's sobbing entreaties. In the far west wing the countless dependents carried on the patriarchal organization of a baronial home, wherein no modern luxury was omitted! For a second point of Étienne Wizocki's morbid egoism was the stately profusion of the daily life which brought Paris into the heart of Poland!

In later years the pillaged homes of the ruined Polish

nobles have furnished the curious of Europe and America with a wealth of costly treasure trove. And to-day, bare walls and grinning broken windows attest the touch of Time and the finger of Fate. Seated with her child nestling in her arms, still robed in her dainty dinner-dress of rich clinging white silk, with ropes of shimmering pearls encircling her fair neck, the bringers of tears, Countess Cecile, born a princess, was only a broken-hearted woman at twenty-two! The pangs which rent her bosom had not marred her dark exquisite beauty. A noble, wistful face, with earnest, tender eyes, glancing honestly under brows crowned with the rich flowing tresses of youth, she was the perfection of the startling beauty of the land of sorrows. Her still girlish form was slowly ripening toward the richness of young wifehood, and her exquisite girlish grace still lingered with her. Though now pent up in a lonely home, Cecile Wizocka, born a princess, had once thrilled the onlookers, a moving dream of delight, a vision of beauty and grace, when she had shown to the rapturously applauding nobles her impassioned grace in the mazurka. The delicacy of the distinguished Polish beauty gave to her face a patrician cachét, and the slender hands clasped around her lisping child were the fitting adjuncts to the arched Cinderella foot.

Nowhere in the garden of the once haughty and victorious nation ever moved a more heart-loyal child of Poland's defiant, undying spirit. In the slowly-crystallizing grasp of her silently-borne sorrow, Countess Cecile clung yet to that wild love of Poland which came with the very milk of infancy to her days of prattling childhood. The very sun seemed to smile brighter, leaping up over the exquisite eastern valley of Nimovitch, than even in storied Italy. For, when she had been led on from land to land abroad, her spirited and tender heart turned always fondly back to Poland! Her daydream was to see it free; her glory to know that it had been once so in very truth.

And so, while her desperate husband gambled, under his own roof-tree, with the artful enemy of his race, the young Countess murmured, " If I have no home left, if our fortune is ruined, still my heart will break—at home, in Poland." And she had ever resolutely refused to go abroad, and mutely watched the daily swing of the pendulum of ruin. " Étienne, my place is at home—here, in Poland ! " she had replied with the sad courage of womanly martyrdom.

In Warsaw, whose colleges and seminaries are famous, even in the silence of a nation's fall, in her own princely home, the fair girl had been carefully fitted to grace the Court she left when Étienne Wizocki bent his pleading eyes on her in a matchless wooing. Of all the graceful lovers of the world, the Polish Lochinvar is absolutely irresistible. It seems that a mad grace, a spirit of untold poetic frenzy sweeps these cavaliers into an exaltation almost beyond the human. Étienne Wizocki believed in his heart of hearts that he truly loved the brilliant bride—and it was a truth, for a time. His rapture was unmeasured when he first led Cecile under the great chestnuts shading the Lovers' Walk, by the lake at Nimovitch, and, pointing to the storied old chateau, whispered, " Here, darling, you will make a heaven for me on earth ! " Alas ! It was not two years until the deathlike lethargy of a lonely noble's life and the chains of vicious former habits led him back to the ever open halls of pleasure on the Seine. The draught of Circe Paris was too strong, too sweet to refuse ! It brought back his headlong days when, as a rich absentee, he was the star of the youngest, maddest Paris ! And the dull shame which smote him at first softened to regret, and then finally dwindled to indifference. His wife's singular, distant nobility of soul made her suffer in a proud silence, and the husband's letters which, in the first weeks, had been passionate protestations of his unfaded love, cooled down at last to mere drafts upon his intriguing Intendant. He, a hireling, was filling his purse by every chicanery before the final downfall of the historic house, for the Count always came empty-handed back from Paris. The Intendant was himself a Pole, and fitted the grim Russian proverb that "every Pole is a traitor at heart!"

There was a dreaming silence by the lake, the light wind faintly rustling the leaves, and the guest wing of the chateau only gleamed with lights, when the noble circle sat down before the fatal green table. Hawk-eyed devotees of chance, it was now "every man for himself," and the courteously studied code of the gambling club lifted up the reckless Poles to the levels of Chesterfields. It is singularly inappropriate that the greatest ceremonial of the Church, the most gorgeous pageant of the palace, can never match the calm, refined, inexhaustible etiquette of a game of cards in the realm of strict "high life." It would seem as if "trifles light as air" took on here the magnitude of mountains. It was in view of the refinements of this exacting code that General Milutin gravely observed, when they drew to see who should bank the game, "Gentlemen, I play only for one hour." And in a low tone he whispered, in excuse, to Count Étienne, "Madame la Comtesse has kindly offered to drive me over the grounds to-morrow." Count Wizocki passed over, in his eagerness to read the mysteries of the innocent-looking cards as they lay spread out, backs up, in the first "parade," this innocent stratagem of his loving wife.

She would fain have made the dangerous ordeal as short as possible, and, in her defenceless womanhood, these simple home arts of cutting off Milutin from her husband's society came to her. For, she, a nobleman's daughter, knew that Count Etienne had not the right to face the impassive noble Russian, now the banker at baccarat, until the score of honor had been paid in full!

She only feared General Milutin, for well the Countess knew that the glittering Polish nobles of her husband's circle were all travelling abreast with him on the same road to ruin.

Careless and irregular in the handling of ready monies, they tacitly spared each other in high play, for, by some lingering bit of national pride, they wished yet to keep up at least a show of state in the equestrian order of human nobility. The high rank, station, and great wealth of General Milutin made his name a household word in every aristocratic circle of western Europe, and, with the instinctive aversion of the Pole for the Russian, she desired to guard her husband, and but one last resort appeared to be within her use—a final personal appeal to the haughty Russian not to gamble against Count Wizocki. Even as she laid her tired and aching head to rest, knowing that the night-hours were now crawling on, in a silence which was haunted by fears of the worst, the young Countess would fain respect her husband's personal free-will. For after all, he was a nobleman, a gentleman, and a Pole at heart! "Only at the very last," she murmured, as she kissed her sleeping child. It needed not the clang of the door with which Count Étienne entered his dressing-room, long hours later, in the sickly gray of dawn, to awake Cecile Wizocka. Through the darkened room she had stolen in the vigil of this sad night, to await his return. An ominous feeling of the coming absolute ruin slowly gathered in her sad heart.

The fatal story of that eventful night never reached Cecile Wizocka, for the affrighted guests had drawn out of the game two hours before Etienne Wizocki finally threw down his cards, and dropped his head upon his breast. "I have enough," he hoarsely murmured, glancing at Vassili Milutin, who slowly rose and bowed gravely to the gentlemen who stood aghast at the mad duel of cards to the death, which had followed the ceasing of the general game of baccarat. It was not cool, steady, remorseless Milutin, who demanded dice! It was not the Russian with the Grand Duke's plans revolving in his unshaken mind! It was the haggard-eyed Polish Count, who demanded his absolute right to play double or quits ! With one grave appealing glance to the listening circle of honor, Vassili Milutin said calmly, " You insist, as a right !—I beg you !" but the flush of desperation was on Wizocki's face, as he sternly eyed the Russian General. " Am I not qualified," he cried. The blood leaped to the Muscovite's bronzed cheeks, and he bowed, simply saying, " The word of a gentleman qualifies him in life and death !" There was a sinister ring in the accents of the soldier at bay. It was not the gambler who spoke, it was not reflected by a growing desire to linger near Cecile Wizocka's passive beauty, it was the triumphant secret agent of Russia, who suddenly felt his heart glow in triumph. "Now! He is mine !" and Milutin knew in his heart that however the fateful dice might fall, one lucky turn would at last sweep the whole immense stake back to him. For, impregnable in his vast riches, secure in the Grand Duke's secret orders, Vassili Milutin was lord of the " stronger battalions," and the tide of fortune was with him.

In the courtly grace, with which even the cruellest duelist may pass the face of his mortal enemy lying prone and dead at his feet, the victorious Russian bowed and passed out to his own apartments without a word. The Polish nobles filed off sadly to their own rooms without daring to speak, as the ruined Count staggered away through the lonely corridor. His hand was clenched upon his bounding heart !

The bright and sparkling morning flashed out in beauty over the Volhynian forests, and the sunlight glittered on the lake where the swans glided, bringing the bird carolling to the bough, and the beast to the field. There was no outward sign of the ruin which had been wrought at Nimovitch, for the uneasy visiting nobles galloped early afield. The Russian General trifled alone over his dainty breakfast service, awaiting the summons to ride with the beautiful Countess Wizocka. As the unhappy woman arrayed herself for the ride, she was yet without definite news of the night's battle. But she divined all, as the gray-haired old house butler, handed her a note brought back by her husband's groom. Its words were few.

"Pardon me for not waking you! I have gone to Rowno to see Prince Lubomirski, on a grave matter which will not wait."

And well Cecile Wizocka knew that the bolt had fallen at last; for Rowno was eighty long miles away, and she would be left on this dreary day alone, to sit, in mocking state, among strangers in the grand ceremonial of the formal dinner.

She would not admit that the coward dared not face her, for the morning had brought its bitterness of death to him.

"Poor Étienne!" she softly whispered, as the note fell at her feet. For her hands trembled as she went forth, in a dazed day-dream to meet the enemy of her race. The Countess from earliest girlhood had known the fierce light of the excited society of the dashing Polish nobles. No other race lived so headlong! and yet, as she bowed, in a stately greeting to General Milutin, the frightened faces of the servants told her that some unusual occurrence had been the source of a general shock. Servants, the world over, are never deceived! They inertly fatten in the prosperity of a house, and instinctively scent its downfall. But there was no outward yielding in the manner of the beautiful patrician. Vassili Milutin was as graceful as a Cæsar Borgia in the calm courtesy of his address. He knew how to wait!

Together they slowly walked through the great rooms of the chateau. Its general plan was that of a central hall, with the wings joined by galleries. Its entire front of three hundred feet was of solid masonry, and the white walls of the main chateau towered twice the height of the wings. From the beautiful plateau on which its great park enclosed noble lawns and stately groves of trees, the eye swept away to the forest line sweeping mile on mile. Facing the south, built on an easterly and westerly line, each front bore up a severely grand portico of lofty and massive Doric columns. Within, every treasure of a family for hundreds of years patricians, adorned the old chateau—whose three greatest halls, salon, reception, and dining-hall—made an unrivalled vaulted apartment, when joined, stretching in stately splendor a hundred feet by fifty.

Below the south front, the lake with its exquisitely wooded island, opened a view of the smiling green valley stretching out twenty miles to the east. From the quaint dormer-windows of the great chateau, the nearest serf village, lying on an avenue to the east, was traversed by the main Moscow highway. Herds of horses, vast droves of cattle and sheep, dotted the fragrant flowery plains, while, from the six scattered villages of the Wizocki manor at morn, the peasants drove afield their own swarms of domestic animals. Slightly-rolling hills swept out to the west, where a vast rich upland for miles ·was dotted with the teams of the laboring plowmen.

As General Milutin slowly made the circuit of the beautiful manor-house, he noted with a grim smile the old Catholic chapel of the ardent Polish Romanist believers, with its graveyard studded with memorial crucifixes of enormous size. These bore a representation of the " thirty pieces of silver," gleaming under the terribly realistic life-size images of the Saviour. Polish inscriptions carefully distinguished the generations of the Catholic dead in the lonely wooded graveyard on one side of the highway, while at a gun-shot distant, the four sub-domes and lofty great central tower of the Greek Orthodox church, glittered in gaudy blue and gold, above the dark enclosure of the dead of the Greek-Russian faith. A grim opposition.

" Even in death, it seems we are divided !" remarked Vassili Milutin. as his beautiful monitress easily read his thoughts.

"Nothing can ever bridge the gulf between Pole and Russ, not even Death !" sadly murmured Cecile Wizocka, who had vainly tried to pierce the perfect mask of Milutin's polished manners ! Even in great disaster,—in times of shock and change,—the last impregnable tower of human refuge, is the perfectly equable manners of that refined society which absolutely ignores all human feelings—" good form ! "

"I wonder if awakening Love could not work a miracle ! " secretly mused Milutin, his delicate hand gleaming with the sapphires and turquoises of the superstitious Muscovite as it lay resting on his jewelled sword hilt.

With a sigh, the silent lady signed for the magnificent equipage, which, with its four black pure-blood steeds harnessed abreast, awaited her signal.

There are natures so refined and keenly clairvoyant that the clear soul needs not even the mechanism of the eyes. Countess Cecile, seated by the side of the proud noble, felt even in his courteously-veiled politeness, the coming menace to heart, hearth and home. And yet, simply conscious of her own upright inner nature, she nursed in her pure heart a last prayer to a merciful God to keep her wayward husband out of this crafty Russian's power.

"There is something in the very essence of his presence, here beside me now, which bodes a terrible disaster,—disaster to us all," she thought in a sudden affright. They swept away in silence. The round of the parks and lawns showed to the polite visitor all the adjuncts of the chateau. Its massive ice-houses, wine-cellars, granaries, the manége, and stables, with huge store-houses, were reviewed, and in stations around the lake, the two silently inspected the varied adjuncts of the gardener's art.

"It is a superb estate," said Milutin at last with enthusiasm, as the Russian gazed at the rich livery of the driver and footmen, the exquisite appointments of the equipage.

Their eyes met, and, defenceless before the frank gaze of a spirited woman, Milutin's eye dropped. The story of the night's huge risks was unwittingly revealed in the reddening blush of the passionate noble's cheek.

He tried to feel as they dashed along through the two villages where a thousand serfs in each were appanages of the old fief, that he had no lingering feeling of remorse. "It is only, after all, like riding down a regiment of the enemy," he reflected, in a vain attempt at self-excuse. And yet, he knew at heart, as he muttered, "Some one must always perish in the shock in this wild border world," that his half-formed secret purpose was deepening hourly. That, in the involvement of weak and desperate Étienne Wizocki in his future schemes of dread import, he would also lay his snares so as to control the destinies of the peerless woman shuddering at his side!

Her very refined, stately self-protective attitude charmed and thrilled him. Passing without a glance, the rows of log huts, where double-cabin, stable for kine, and sheepfold were uniform hovels marring the little village plots of the serf, he raised his costly turban in reverence as they dashed past the great stone-cross in Nimovitch village, marking the spot where the great Empress Catherine had first set her foot, on her voyage of inspection of Suwarrow's bloody conquest. A tottering Polish Catholic shrine leaned over it, hung with the votive garments of those who had prayed for health and help to the Saviour sculptured here in an awful realism of torture. Far over the fields, gleaming mournfully in glaring white, the Polish memorial crosses towering thirty feet high, were mute emblems of a silent defiance to that Russia, whose peculiar Greek cross shone only on the five domes of the official village church. Below them in the valley, a swift dashing river, winding through exquisite groves, turned the five mills of the manor. These reposed with their huge double water-wheels, floating on joined barges, so as to allow the passage of the vast rafts of timber drifting down, to be marketed abroad. The forests were moving on to Paris—Count Étienne's reckless work !

Milutin eyed the Countess warily, as he asked himself, " How long will it take all these superb forests to disappear in the champagne-stained coulisses of the Grand Opera, or slip away over the gaming-table." With a sense of a certain latent humanity in his heart, he hoped that the enormous sum he had won of the mad Count would not send him forth absolutely homeless. He had not wished, even in his own dark schemes, to push the victory too far, but his hot blood rose at the implied sneers of the irritable and luckless Wizocki. When, after a two hours' drive over the beautiful plains, down through the forest arches, now golden with the turning leaves of autumn, the General sprang out and gallantly aided the Countess, his invincible bonhomie had almost disarmed her gravest fears. For almost any miracle is possible under the encouragement of that strange, burning, resistless passion which men call Love ! Now sighing as soft as a summer wind, now invoking the sweetest minor chords of the human heart, now swelling into passion's mad cyclones, the love-fever is as incapable of measurement or analysis as the lambent flare of the lightning stroke. Through the world, witching the young, maddening the old, filling soft white bosoms with maddest joys, driving the flinty heart of manhood to despair. levelling the great, raising the humble, Love goes driving along on its resistless course, sweeping on as madly as the Indian typhoon. To the exquisite realization of the first moment when the lover feels the pride of the one victory of life, no other human joy can compare. For, heads which have worn the crown, or shone under the laurel, hands which have wielded the truncheon of command or the sceptre of Empire are bowed and busied in the ceaseless labors of the worship of Love !

Vanishing as the breath upon the glass, outliving in the

memory of man, the Pyramids,—Love, unsubstantial and fraught with its mingled sighs and tears,—rules the world unchallenged when all other feelings have died in the callous breast.

The desert jackals may howl yet over the crumbled ruins of the all but eternal Pyramid, but the human heart will never tire of thrilling to the tale of how a mad Antony threw the world away for a witching but worthless Cleopatra! It is the old, old fashion, and will so go on while there is a heart to break, or a bosom to burn with the flame which never dies. For the fiery invisible spirit of Love lingers in all things, when the corporeal has passed away. It seems that each quivering heart's passion goes on tingling to the stars forever. Eternal and all bending,—it has brought the saint to the block, and raised the defiant sinner to heaven. The first mighty throb of the master-passion sweeps away all law, and bursts beyond human restraint. The coolest philosopher, the meekest prelate, the keenest sophist, has never yet found the golden key to the mysteries of the un-found, unknown Law of Love. For manhood and woman-hood have worn away with lingering footsteps the flinty blocks covering Abelard and Heloise,—and no one yet has dared to say where the right ends, the wrong begins in the wayward course of that mad Ariel of the human heart,—in-comprehensible, uncontrollable Love. Across icy seas, be-hind prison bars, it mocks at time and distance—and has drawn up the vile and humbled the mighty. Oh! Mortal, proud in self-control, towering in the citadel of intellect, mock not once, ever so lightly, at the winsome demon, Love, lest he drag you down in all your foolish pride!

There was no fibre in the rugged heart of the sybarite soldier Milutin, which thrilled to the weak notes of senti-mentality, but he only knew, as the splendid steeds swept them on, in the golden haze of that autumn day, that he too had been touched at last with the magic wand! For, in the

Russian's heart there was to this day of days, but one real feeling, " Fidelity to the Czar! Loyalty to his military oath!" Beyond the sworn determination of his brave spirit to render all up, at the glance of the one august commander, to hurl even his life away, without regret, Vassili Milutin's only mental possession hitherto was the unbroken code of the man of honor. And this, with an easy self-adjustment, did not restrain him from swearing, in his inmost heart, as he watched, furtively, the graceful form swaying at his side, " She shall be mine—no matter whither the pathway leads me on!"

CHAPTER IV.

IN THE VOLHYNIAN FOREST.

DURING the absence of their dangerous enemy, the Polish nobles, by twos and threes quietly left the chateau, riding afield on various pretexts, until they all met in the deserted park of an old chateau, a few versts east of Count Wizocki's seat. A superb sweep of the great Nimovitch valley left here a magnificent bend. There the crumbling ruins still showed the blackened interior, where the torch had ended the deadly work of the Russian sword in thirty-one. Strolling through the still lovely woods, as witching as the glades of Fontainbleau, furtively watching around, they hastily exchanged views as to Count Wizocki's probable future. Men from proud old Vitebsk, haughty nobles of Polotsk, whose chivalry was splendid in the ninth century, long before Rourik the Norman came at the bidding of the savage Muscovites to rule over Russia, the Patricians of Wilna and Grodno, were all aghast at the coming ruin of their absent host. With the bridles of their steeds thrown over their arms, the anxious Poles brooded over this inopportune gambling mania of the Count.

"This ends forever his career as Maréchal de Noblesse," said one moody baron, who had yet an estate to lose. "His duties were always neglected, but now he cannot even keep up the state of our social honor. I shall vote against him!"

"You are right, Balthori," cried an ardent conspirator, "At this time, when stirring-events may occur," and as he spoke they all exchanged significant glances, "to call for every one of us, he could have watched this gay Commanding General, and have hoodwinked him, while we met safely here in Volhynia."

"True," cried a third rebel, "I always stay by a friend in his sorrows, but this man is surely mad! He has crucified poor Countess Cecile. She will be soon homeless, and if any rising occurred, God knows where her feet will stray!"

"But what is to be done?" grimly said a sullen scarred veteran, whose face bore a Russian sabre slash. There was a gloomy silence until one flashing-eyed rebel, cried, "Let us agree right here upon one candidate, and at least keep one man at whose manor we have a legal right to meet without fear of arrest. This new project as to the serfs demands our one social leader to be a true son of Volhynia. Étienne Wizocki is a fool! A dancing eye, a foaming glass, the glimpse of the green cloth would lure him away from the very altar of our salvation. A man who cannot trust himself, cannot be trusted! And, in these dangerous times, God knows where his madness may lead him!"

"He may join those cravens, the poor lick-spittles who sneak into Russian favor, or else drift abroad with the men who have gone down in foreign mire!" a harsh voice cried. "Let us name our man now, and may God curse the craven hound who is false to Poland!"

A ringing shout of "Amen," woke the dim forest arches. When the meeting broke up, Étienne Wizocki was already a dethroned chief.

"We must loyally remain, and finish our secret duty," said the first speaker. "We are not safe unless we carry out this hunting festival to its end. This clear-eyed Russian visitor would suspect! If we were tied up at home now, even by temporary arrest, our friends, the poor humble herd who die on Russian bayonets, would be left powerless."

"For the world's long story of unripe revolt tells how unfit all revolutionists and reformers are to command others, and to govern themselves. On us, the old nobles, hangs to-day the fate of Poland! No! Wizocki must learn only of his retirement when we meet at Jitomir to elect a marshal for the next four years. His term has only three months, now, for his successor could act if—if——" the gallant noble hesitated.

"If what!" cried a dozen voices.

"If he should take to flight, or fall a victim to Russian seductions!" sorrowfully concluded the speaker.

"I will stake my life on the honour of a Polish noble, in his own home. He could not betray us!" a brave young cavalier generously cried.

"Our very lives are all staked on his honour!" growled in answer the old veteran. "And, God help us! I myself have lived to see a Pole sell his brothers' blood."

There was no contesting voice, for Poland's sorrow is also Poland's shame! The dark story of Hungary bleeding under the Austrian rods, the secret archives of the three bloody revolts of failure, wring every breast with the knowledge that, while Christ's disciples carry down His Message of Love and Truth, that Judas also left his poisoned seed to curse the world, until the heavens shall roll away as a scroll.

How many hands have clasped in friendship the traitor's palm! How often fond lovers have kissed the daughter of Judas, in love's last impressioned greeting, when the lips, trembling under the heart's-blood thrill, have betrayed already to the waiting doom!

The arts of patience are the golden talisman of the hunter, the lover, the man of high and dangerous emprise! It was not a new rôle which Vassili Milutin played, as during the day he courteously conferred upon the general future of the border kingdom with the anxious Poles. He knew so well how to charm!

The long hours wore away, but Countess Cecile's dainty form did not grace the branching shades of the Lovers' Walk.

Secluded until the hour of the evening assembly in her lonely rooms, she went out in heart with her absent lord. Prince Lubomirski—the heir of a lofty line—the descendant of a great chief who had ruled Poland, and beautified Warsaw, was still of enormous private wealth. Would he now aid Étienne in his hour of need ; or would beautiful Nimovitch, pass at last from the line of the Wizocki's ? The splendid domain, the home of a hospitable and princely race was renowned for the brooding calm, the haunting rest, and the splendid gifts of Nature's kindly alchemy gathered there. It was famed for its richness, its superb forests, its peculiar "nirvana" bringing ozone, wafted from its dim woods. The old home was still very dear to Cecile Wizocka ! Though sorrow had found her out in this beautiful lonely valley, still her woman heart thrilled to the memories of the days when, still a lover, Count Étienne, ardent and impassioned, had clasped her to his breast, under the whispering trees whose leaves rustled down a gentle benison. And, though her wayward husband had been lost to her, for absence and estrangement had at last killed the love once so brightly burning in her breast, she clung to Nimovitch, for here she had found her child—that beloved fairy whose dainty fingers had unlocked the golden cell of fortitude and self-devotion in her breast. For, alas, Love with averted eyes and extinguished torch had closed the chamber in her heart wherein the but once awakened love of a life had died away in cold embers. Count Étienne had thrown away the key in far-away Paris ! For love, outraged, is its own avenger. Foot of panther, eye of lynx, ear of fox are not lighter, quicker, keener, than the consciousness of a woman's love betrayed ! The fatal knowledge may creep to its work slowly,—or it may come with lightning flash. It may be the heartbreak of years,—or even the story of a clumsy accident, but, when that thrill of wounded womanly pride has once wrung a fond woman's heart, let him who wrought the woe, beware !

There are no dangers to appal, no binding ties to restrain the one who whispers in her bitter sorrow,—" Never,—never any more ! " It is the blasting stroke of annihilation ! For, so fond, so true, so loyal to the one love of a life, are Eve's sorrow-burdened daughters, that the scar upon the heart quivers under the disloyal stroke of that discovery, until it beats in vain agony no more ! . . .

With a quick decision, Countess Cecile, calling to her aid the most trusted of the elder nobles, sent forth to rally around her some of the neighboring ladies who were nearest in creed and station.—" If Count Etienne is delayed, I will give you a ball ! " she smiled, with a last faint attempt at coquettish hospitality. For, even divided by creed and hatred, hospitality is Arabian in the land of the Pole and the Russian ! No welcome a whit warmer ever greeted a guest than the light shining from the open doors of these Eastern Slavic dwellers ! It shines out in the hearts of these different warring races, to both of whom hospitality is a law, beyond the faintest suggestion of possible weariness !

And so the stately lady prepared to play her defensive part in the peculiar dignity of a border châtelaine, until Count Etienne should return. As she robed herself with unusual care, she murmured to her mirror, " He shall never see me quiver under the lash of fortune ! " It was of the virile and scheming Muscovite, she spoke. Though the graceful tact and perfect bearing of the sleeplessly polite stranger had masked his inmost feelings,—as a wife, Cecile already feared him for her husband's sake,—as a mother, she hated him as the possible enemy of her impoverished child, and,—not as a woman,—she distrusted him by that peculiar thrill of self-defensive femininity which baffles often the keenest pursuer. " I must act a hard part," she murmured, as she prepared to do battle on her own hearth-stone, for all that fate had left to her, for all she still held dear, and for the man who had carelessly thrown away the golden key which her ennobling love had placed in his eager hands. When the splendor of the proud beauty they awaited, touched every heart among the assembled guests in the grand salon, Vassili Milutin's eyes gleamed. He drew a hard breath. "She acts the part just a little too well!" he mused, as he turned his eyes away to the exquisite lake view,—to hide the cruel flame which leaped into their steel-blue depths. And as he bowed, in gravest respect, there was that upon his face which would disarm all cavil! For every great passion has its seal and, whether foolish, criminal, or blindly hopeless,—the love of a tyrant nature had set its seal upon the bounding heart of cold Vassili Milutin. He was already a slave in very thought to the woman he would betray!

"An empress of nature's own crowning—a queen by the rare gifts of God," he mused, as the passing evening hours still told him of newer charms, of varied graces, of hitherto hidden arts, and the unsuspected wealth of feeling loosened by her high-souled nature, now battling in the open!

Cecile Wizocka was of that finer clay which genius moulds with its divinest touches! From girlhood, impassioned and versatile, possessing a singular emotional range, with all her heightened gifts, none could withstand her crystalline voice pleading in the songs of her native land, or voicing the poetry clinging to its glorious past!

Count Étienne, under a gloomy mental cloud, rode slowly homeward through the vast extent of his domain on the next evening. As he threaded the sunset woods on the Rowno road he marked, with hidden sobs and heavy sighs, every familiar reach, of the grand old forests! He was returning in dejection and despair! Forced to own at last, the extent of his heavy involvements, even gallant Lubomirski was constrained to answer with a sigh:

"Do not wring my heart with asking the impossible! I cannot, for even your sake! Make your best terms with this Russian, or else Nimovitch must go!"

His servant riding stolidly behind, marvelled at the Count's manner, for it was a heavy heart which his bosom carried past the remembered haunts of happy boyhood hours. He gazed at the forest aisles of whispering pines, the grand oaks out-spreading their sturdy arms, the silver shining birches, the golden-tinted maples, and the huge green chestnut trees where the grouse now drummed in peace. Clumps of waving stately elms marked the openings of the superb prairies, and all that Nature's artist hand could lend of glowing touch, lit up the land which he rode through to face, powerless and empty handed, his remorseless creditor! "I will kill my-self," he muttered, as the white walls of Nimovitch shone at last bowered in the grand park's gracefully bending trees. A pang smote him to the heart. "And, Cecile!" He had never dared to face with manly avowal of his errors, the woman whose sweetly shining eyes carried a mute reproach, as she clasped their child to her breast, when his britska waited, for that unreturning path to Paris. Rolling on his load of secret shame and hidden self-reproach before him, the Count had always sheltered himself behind the knowledge of his own treason to her very life.

Loving, young, trusting, and ardent, a woman who had made a throne in her heart upon which he sat, love-crowned, he had left her, raised up by her rank to daily solitude, to burn out her young love alone before its deserted shrine. The spring sunshine wooed her heart for the lover who was not, the summer glories found her "but yet a woman," even if patrician, chafing deserted under the whispering arches of the Lovers' Walk. Beautiful in womanhood's young morn-ing, though her lips were sealed, though her heart was locked, she suffered in a burning passionate unrest, as the golden sun swung over her lonely forest isolation only a jailer's lamp!

For never yet was nature equally strong at all points, and the fairest castles yield, at times, to sudden assault upon

the unguarded wall! Day by day, Cecile Wizocka's heart
had called for him in vain! Devoid of lover, husband,
friend, counsellor, companion, though her lip trembled not,—
her love had slowly hardened in neglect, into the cold ada-
mant of a mother's fortitude. But when, at last, the knowledge came, one day, by the public clamor of an awkward
foreign episode of Etienne's deliberate and unnecessary
treason. Cecile Wizocka sealed her lips and walked, broken-
hearted, with trembling steps, to her own chosen shelter.
There, after hours of an agony which can but once sweep
over a woman's soul, she drew from her blue-veined hand
the golden wedding-ring which had bound their souls together. Bitter tears fell upon the little packet which she
locked away in an old casket of her own! It bore the inscription, " For my child." And even Étienne Wizocki, in
far Paris, the gilded theatre of a world's vainest feats of vice,
might have quivered in repentant shame, if he could have
seen the beautiful face of his wife when her lips, kissed last
by him, the very last time, in unfading love, whispered,
" Never any more!" It was no relief, no respite, from the
life-sentence of her outraged heart that he did not hear this
sad decree! A woman's vengeance, when it falls, tells all
its story of the hidden past in one blinding flash!

To this estranged wife, whose plotted path of duty divided
them now with the invisible line of honor, the Count wearily
returned. He had never marked the change, but still love
was dead, slain on its own holy altar, by the man whom she
had invested with all her heart craved in nature's nobility.
When, this night, Étienne Wizocki rode slowly into the park,
he was heavy-hearted and sore! His outlying foresters
had already told him of the departure of some of the of-
fended guests ; he also feared to face the Russian creditor,
and he knew that his election was doomed! Even the tur-
baned Polish peasants, wrapped in gray rags, with sandals
of bark, and tattered leggings, eyed their master in surprise,

as they pulled off their head-gear, and a dull surprise crept under their shock-headed skulls. With a sullen face he answered each humble salute, as the serfs clattered by in their little box wagons, dragged by uncouth diminutive steers, or half-savage ponies.

" Those peasant's breasts are happier than mine, to-night," he muttered. As the master of Nimovoitch reined his steed up to the grand entrance, he saw a gentle, wistful face glancing from the windows where once Love sent out his kindling golden shafts. Though many ladies were flitting through the grounds, with their ardent cavaliers lingering in fond attentions, the Count feared to face the silent woman whom he had wronged, betrayed and ruined. "My God! what can I do? She must not know!" he groaned, as he threw himself heavily from the saddle, and in his sad heart he vowed to make any terms with General Milutin which would save his pride from the last awful task of a gambler's utter self-humiliation. Confession seemed almost impossible.

Fool! He did not know that the woman, burning for months with unsatisfied love, with neglected affection, would have gone out happy to a cold world's buffets, at his side, if he had not cruelly slain the lamb of love! Gentle, wistful, tender and true, Cecile Wizocka had not openly repined at seeing her fortune melt under his touch, for she still loved him! A daughter of an ardent princely line, she could pardon a Polish noble's wayward acts. But, even in his torment of these bitter moments it would have chilled his heart had he known how the outraged wife had lifted her head in secret scorn when the shame had been cast upon their vanished married love.

" I belong henceforth to myself, in this world!" she resolutely said, and yet, up to this bitter moment, Étienne Wizocki had never missed the thrill of truth in those caresses which drew the line between earth and heaven. The light had faded slowly in her glance. The angel at his side had vanished, alas! never to return. And yet, a parting sigh of the spirit of love had never reached his ears.

When he entered his wife's boudoir, the Count eyed her steadily. "Have you anything to tell me?" she sadly said, with her hands clasped on her exquisite bosom, and the flash of light which entered his darkened soul at last, told the ruined gambler that it was too late to plead before the beautiful form once glowing and clasped in his adoring arms.

"Nothing! nothing yet!" he abjectly said, as he hastened away to his dressing-room.

That night, the guests learned with surprise of the delay of the grand hunt for a week, and then, with an artful show of hospitality, the Count threw the labor of amusement upon his consort. Days slowly followed in which, by stealthy plans of the hour, the Maréchal de Noblesse often rode scores of versts afield with the Russian General. His Polish guests looked for him in vain!

To the relief of Cecile Wizocka, the sound of nightly revelry was stilled in the west wing, and, though she heard no word of cheer, her husband's face seemed to be strangely lightened!

The preparations for the chase were now eagerly urged on. Hounds, and beaters, guides and foresters were streaming in, and the impatient nobles waited for the echoing horns. For these secret political conferences were over, and General Milutin, after an absence of three days at Sarny, a neighbouring manor village, where he had gone to meet some passing Russian dignitaries, also returned to the chateau, in time to welcome home Count Étienne on his return from a second long voyage to Rowno.

"Étienne must have come to some satisfactory terms," said one of the anxious Poles. "He seems much happier. . I am glad of it. For, at this dangerous time, we must watch every passing moment."

"Have you heard from our friends in Paris, yet?" eagerly whispered his listener.

"Yes, the hour of action draws momentarily near. I wish to see all our friends soon in their appointed places for secret duty. This cursed Russian who kills with soldierly grace, is far too near for safety." The wary speaker was suspicious, for every heart in the Polish rebel circle now bore the dangerous tidings of specific plans of revolt.

"Come out into the park, Stanislas," said the rebel, gravely, "and I will give you some news which we dare not put on paper."

And, in sight of General Milutin, bending in chivalry before the beautiful Countess among her flowers, the Pole told him all the story of their hopes. It was the old story. The eager, restless Poles in Paris, coquetting with the spiritual ministers of the Empress Eugenie, hoped to lead the inscrutable Louis Napoleon into an active support of the revolutionists on the Prussian frontier. "He clings yet to two of the great Napoleon's guiding principles, the control of the mouth of the Rhine, and the establishment of a Polish kingdom, to check Austria and Prussia, and offset Russia in the far east. England and France will menace the Czar with their fleets, for France now holds the balance of power in Europe. The time is ripe. Let us but once light the flame of revolt in West Russia, in the Polish fragment still bearing the name, we will be aided with ready gold, arms, diplomatic pressure and the fleets. Christian England will surely listen to the cry of suffering Poland. Louis Napoleon is our friend. All that we here have to do now, is to concert the·day of a general rising. Our secret messengers at Paris wait only for the last appeals of the Empress to gain the great French Emperor's plighted word. Even now, our brave nobles, trained in his foreign legions to arms, are stealing quietly homewards. They will bring us the secret help. If we wait till winter, the Russians, lulled to sleep, will not gather their great armies till spring. All aflame with holy zeal, if we nobles lead our peasants into the forests which we only know, we can decimate the heavy-witted Russians as Schamyl did for thirty long years. Now is the hour!"

"Is this the last word?" gloomily said Stanislas, as the speaker paused, fearful lest his very looks might betray him to the sly Russian general, who eyed them curiously from afar. The tiger scented blood.

"Yes, yes, we are ready now!" the enthusiast cried.

Stanislas dropped his head sadly on his breast. Then, we are doomed; we will either fill Russian prisons, or Polish graves. I choose the silent grave. England hears unmoved the howl of weaker sufferers, she gives Bibles and Mansion House advice, and then possesses herself calmly of all fragmentary colonies, or ruined communities open to her patent hypocrisy.

"Louis Napoleon is the one notable liar of Europe. He only seeks to distract Austria and Prussia, and thus check Russia. We will be the bloody sacrifice, our peasants will perish like flies, our nobles will be swept away. Russia is irresistible, and the last vestige of our old autonomy will be swept forever into the Russian general dominions. Our own estates will go to the minions of the Romanoffs, to the triumphant butchers. Think of the Stuarts, and their feeble foreign aid. Look at all the abortive Carlist efforts. No land ever won its independence from the outside. Let us finish this hunt, then, each to his post, to die for dear Poland. But," he almost sobbed, "to die in vain."

They slowly wandered back to join the mingled valor and beauty on the terrace.

It was fortunate that Count Étienne Wizocki was busied with the details of the great drive of a week which was to sweep the domain of Nimovitch from east to west. It afforded him a relief from the ordeal of facing his estranged wife, now busied with the duties of hospitality to the few ladies who had answered her hasty summons. For the late October, though the woods were royal in gold and russet, was chill, and the rustling leaves told now of the dying year.— The deposed Maréchal de Noblesse was spared the pain of the growing aversion of his guests, he only saw their eagerness to reach their own neglected domains.

General Vassili Milutin with impartial courtesy exhibited all the winning charms of his tiger-like nature in repose to the fair aristocrates, who listened to his words, although they faltered from a Russian tongue. For with cool premeditation, he narrowly watched the Countess, as the fierce flame, so lately kindled, was wildly raging in his breast. Day by day in cool stratagem he selected some one of the graceful enemy, and smiled in his heart, to think how easily he, a Russian, could bring a quiver to the gentle bosoms of his fair foes. His vanity deceived him.

They listened, smiled, and bent to his varied arts, yet, for all his knowledge gained in bower and hall, in court and camp, the Russian General had not learned that all the arts of a Machiavelli are feeble beside the infinite ways of womanhood!

The thousand moods, the hidden wiles, the secret arts, the cunning femininity swathed in clinging laces and rustling silken robes, all these give repression, expression and impression to the tide of wayward passion sweeping over the level of the woman heart.

Secret and still in the bosom's depths, the woman nature lies hidden like an Alpine lake, though from every icy gorge, gusts of tornado force may lash it to fury, the sunlight breaking through the clouds finds its regained level, trembling in the silence of its sapphire depths, to the fall of the drifted forest leaves.

Trifles will turn a woman's love, awake her heart, and exalt her soul where even a tyrant's mandate would find her resolute to the death in denial. Ever quivering, and unpoised, the needle of her wavering affections may swing at any moment in wildest sweep to an unseen attraction veiled to all human eyes. But the witty, wily Polish beauties who played with Milutin the Russian, were all secretly admiring him as a man. Still, he was a type of their country's foes, and for all this, even their white bosoms had pillowed in feigned self-surrender, the enamored Muscovites who had rashly sold themselves often to death,—for a desperate rebel woman's smile.

The plan of the Nimovitch hunt included three days. On the first a forest drive was projected at which the ladies could see the animals fall before the unerring aim of the border nobles. The second was a great valley battue of the superb grouse and game birds haunting the fragrant copses, and the third,—for which the cavaliers would leave the chateau at the previous midnight, was a circling of the gloomy trackless forests of the eastern river, sweeping west-wardly to join the Pripet in its hide-and-seek course to the Dneiper and the Black Sea. The dangerous chase in these black wooded depths was forbidden to the ladies, by the fatigue, the midnight hours, and the fierceness of the formid-able animals lurking there.

The day of the forest drive dawned clear, crisp, and sunny. Long before the streakings of the rosy dawn, a line of knightly cavaliers filed away from the great portal of the Cha-teau. A half dozen troikas and wagonettes were tenanted by the spirited Polish beauties who, buried in furs, thus hid their rosy faces from the crisp gusts of the cool dawn. Led in state by the Intendant of the domain, and the chief forester, the cavalcade swept along the north park walls, and passed, in the gray of the dawn, the two rival churches, with their embattled dead resting under the tall waving trees of the Russian and Polish graveyards. For, though the domain of Nimovitch boasted its two thousand serfs in the three vil-lages, these two silent villages of the dead were tenanted by greater numbers, gaining yearly with sad certainty of proportion.

Nodding in the dawn, on their horses, the fretting Polish nobles were now eager to finish the unwelcome dissipations of this long-delayed chase, and they greatly feared the Russian General's keen eyes, for, though the Intendant, and chapel priest, and the forester, with the house servants, were loyal and even fanatic Poles, the Staroste, the chief of the gendarmes, the chief of the post station, and many of the newer underlings of the chateau were Russians. And here around them every Russian servant or minor official was a possible spy.

"It looks like riding down into our death," gloomily said young Count Stanislas to his enthusiastic orator friend of the previous day. He pointed as he spoke to the forest of tall Polish crucifixes, leaning in broken disorder over the graves of their forgotten dead.

"Russian work,—half of them," growled the veteran as they emerged on the beautiful prairie sweeping in a splendid expanse around Nimovitch from the north to the west, and south. His eye rested malignantly on Vassili Milutin's soldierly form, riding with incomparable grace, at the side of Countess Cecile's own troika. For all the best horsemen of the world can learn from the Russ, who is still the heir of the arts of the vanished Scythian !

The sun broke out in a gleam of golden glory as they galloped over the frosty prairie. A pearly haze hid the dark evergreen forest of pines and elms which they were moving toward, and from its deep silent bosom spurs of heavy oaks, their scorched twisted leaves burned to a bitter red, with clumps of graceful golden maples, were thrown out as outposts into the smiling valley, where the faintly visible green shoots of the winter wheat even now struggled up, under the straggling, waving, stubble stalks. Down in the romantic wooded waterways, the thousand shades of Autumn's pensive gilding lit up the silent dells below them, Cranes and geese clanged overhead slowly flying northward, while the Polish wood-eagle hovered above, towering saucily in the morning air.   But, Vassili Milutin noted a vast flight of black, repellant-looking gray-winged ravens ominously croaking over the fields in their low flight. They crossed the line of the restless Polish nobles, and the Russian smiled "Already!" as he drew his rein nearer to the carriage of beautiful Cecile.

Though attended at the chateau by no staff-officers, a grizzled Russian sergeant and four men ministered to their master's chargers, and, long before dawn, by the flaring lights of the small salon, while the hunters took a hasty morning refection, Vassili Milutin, in his own rooms of state, had read, with a fierce secret joy, the few lines of a hurried despatch brought in by his body-servant.

"Ivan, tell me who brought this news here?" said the General, as he leisurely donned his huntsman's coat.

"One of Major Dournof's command gave it to the sergeant, who was at the appointed place, Your Excellency."

"Good," sternly said General Milutin, and as he picked up his furred turban, he muttered: "Then, Dournof is at hand ready with his troops. I wonder if two sotnias of cavalry are enough. There are over fifty of these would-be rebels here. Va banc," he grumbled as he lit a cigarette! "The few who may by chance get a few miles away, can easily be run down later, for Dournof will surely picket all the roads."

And, while the fearful nobles plunged into the forest in search of big game, the Russian secret agent grimly smiled, "They are only bringing themselves to bay!" In his leathern jerkin, lined with fleece wool, garnished with a belt with a revolver on a snap-clasp chain, and bearing a heavy knife attached by its sliding knotted cord, in his top boots, and sheathed in his chamois gauntlets, the handsome

General was the beau-ideal of a chasseur as he gave his orders to his gun-bearers trotting by his side.

Milutin had attached himself quietly to the Countess. None other dared to dispute with him the coveted place of honor at her side, and the pale-faced Count Etienne, as host-head of the hunt and Maréchal de Noblesse, was riding far away in the van. When Vassili Milutin had at the outset with courtly deference raised his cap and begged Madame la Comtesse to allow him to offer her the view of the chase from his shooting post, under his experienced guidance, the lady's brooding eyes trembled slightly, but she bowed her head in a quiet assent. The sly patience of the Russian would-be lover had not for a moment disarmed her. While he was tranquil in these last days, and his easy politeness was offered in turn to the fair guests, a sinking in her heart and an ominous fluttering of her nerves told her of his deliberately formed purpose to be near her and alone through the long day. "It is but one more ordeal—the last!"—she murmured, for the second and third days would be engrossed by the fair spectators in preparation for the ball at the chateau which would end the chase, and for this the guests were bidden even from distant Warsaw.

The strange attitude of her husband had greatly alarmed her! No lines of care streaked his forehead, however, and his demeanor was even light and cheerful. But no clear rapprochement had brought them nearer to each other. Studiously attentive to his guests, and gravely cordial to the General, Étienne Wizocki always avoided his wife's questioning eyes. He even looked down confusedly when she directly questioned:

"Did Prince Lubomirski aid you?"

"Not yet—but—he will—later," hastily replied Count Etienne, as he quickly hurried away on some small detail of hospitality. His eye had scarcely noted his little child, in

these days of estrangement.   Cecile was sorely troubled at
heart.   Well she knew the gallant and kindly soul of princely
Lubomirski, but her husband's changed manner and his
strange avoidance of her presence told her of the unsettled
raging conflicts of his mind.   Countess Cecile had never
stooped to watch him in his amours after his one flagrant
baseness.   He had shivered the crystal vase on the altar
with one blow.   She had never looked to discover any future
treasons.   For her betrayed lonely womanhood had in its
outraged pride closed forever against all things but the
sharing of his woes !

He had profaned to her the very sacred name of love, for
in her heart of hearts she had given herself to him with a
feeling as sacred, in its wifely purity, as the devotees bending before the Host under the chime of the silver gongs in
the great cathedral where they had been wed.

And, so he had violated the very shrine of love !   Betrayed
her for another—for others, and coldly turned away from her
warmly-beating heart, her open arms, her glowing bosom !

An eternity of regret would not suffice to have built up in
that fair woman's breast the love she had once cherished for
her husband, for she had brought a high soul, a noble heart
and an entrancing womanhood to the man who kneeled beside
her at the marriage altar.

At the edge of the forest a hundred beaters, led by the
sub-foresters, awaited them in the faintly crimsoning daybreak.   It was a silent and even depressing scene.   The
songless forest was lying dark and impenetrable before them.
As they drove into dark wood roads to reach the line of the
hunters' stations in the dim forest depths, the beaters, in
squads of ten, and their directors, moved slowly away.   Men
and boys clad in coarse blanket frocks, armed with batons, or
old fowling-pieces, plunged into the copses to await the gun-
shot signal that they were to move forward with an uncouth
clamor and to drive the hiding game on the guns.   Count

Étienne had not spoken once to his pale-faced wife. As the cortège halted at a line two miles within the outer forest, the Polish noble rode up in search of his chief guest, the General. The rays of the rising sun now lit up the sandy under. growth, with its tangle of pines, elms and hoary oaks. Already at a distance the faint hallo of the line of noisy beaters was heard afar, and the different nobles moved away, with each a fair companion, to their allotted stations on the line of undulating ground, whence, a hundred yards apart, on one knee, with breathless attention they waited the coming of the forest monarchs. Deer, boar, wolves, and other game of note were the chief tenants of the lonely woods where the drifted leaves now lay thick below their feet.

" I have reserved the very best station for you, General ! " hurriedly said Count Wizocki, as he bowed with a tender grace to his wife. He was the very picture of a cavalier in his graceful, manly bloom, and his dark expressive face lit up as he aided Cecile to leave her troika. Robed in a national hunting-costume of dark green, lightly edged with fur, her steadfast face was shining out as pale as marble under the toque of priceless dark Khamschatka sable. Her eyes sought her husband's face in a strange surprise as she noted a quick glance of intelligence wafted from the Czar's general to the Maréchal de Noblesse. " What was this strange entente cordiale " Her heart froze; but the daughter of the Jagellons drew up with stately pride as she followed the master of the hunt to the distant wooded dell, near the best runway on the line of retreat of the animals. She had at last parted with Count Étienne with a few hurried whispered words in answer to his strangely clumsy attempts at a last morning greeting. Count Étienne sprang to his horse and then galloped down the road like the sweep of a storm-driven wave. She was now alone with her enemy !

As Cecile lost from view her husband's graceful form, she stole a fleeting glance at Vassili Milutin, now striding lightly along at her side, with a step which had been trained from the Alps and the Caucasus to far Irkutsk, in every art of the woodsman. A controlled smile of quiet contentment lingered on the soldier's face. "What dark secret can bind these two foes together?" thought Cecile, with a sudden new alarm. For the secret understanding had betrayed itself! Vague fears of some humiliating concessions made by her husband made her mutter, with outraged Polish pride, "I will save his honor! My husband shall take no boon at the hand of his country's enemy!" Her princely kinsman might, perhaps, aid her, though the head of her house, now stricken in years, had left his land forever, his frail body torn with the wounds gained in the mad death-struggles of Thirty-One. He was proscribed. "My last acre, my every crown, shall go to free Étienne! And then we can go away together and face the world anew—for the sake of—Marguerite!" The unhappy beauty sighed as she was passively led to her station between two sturdy oaks, in front of which the eagle-eyed Vassili Milutin took his post. His heavy rifle was ready, his extra cartridges prepared, and, crouching on one knee, he waited the coming of the frightened animals. Distant hallos and the nearing shouts of the gathered peasant horde were faintly borne to their ears. The line of a hundred men was sweeping down through the dense copses a mile away. The Countess, with suddenly awakened uneasiness, would fain have been far away. True, the etiquette of the hunt made it her bounden duty to accept the escort of the ranking guest. And the Czar's high officer outshone in precedence all the ruined princes of Poland! It was her own husband's duty as Maréchal de Noblesse to supervise the whole line.

And yet she gazed now on the kneeling soldier with a vague and growing distrust! The silent woods dreaming around them, the leaves murmuring to the moving breeze of morning, the fragrant odors of withered flower and drifted leaf, all

wooed her in vain, to a repose of soul—as the morning sunlight glittered brightly on the dewy grass! The nervous
strain of the exciting days and the present suspense weighed
heavily upon her. With clasped hands, she regarded the
magnificent figure of her country's foe as he crouched, ready
for the coming forest kings. A second loaded gun lay ready
at his side, and he had also placed his heavy army revolver
within easy reach on a crumbled log. Never once during
his stay, had the Russian magnate raised his eyes in passion
to her—but, as she turned her face from a quick glance to
the south, when a dropping shot, far down the line of hunters,
rang out on the still air, she saw Vassili Milutin now furtively
regarding her with a glowing look which shook her very
soul. She started! It was too late! They were far away
from the others. Buried in the wild Volhynian forest, the
nearest hunters were hidden, far out of sight, lest the wary
game should be turned back! Even the flutter of a single
kerchief or the crackle of a careless footstep might rob the
sportsman of his coveted honors. And, with the strange
intuition of womanhood, she stepped lightly forward and
picked up the General's heavy revolver. He turned to her
with gravely-questioning eyes, as her light foot crackled the
golden leaves beneath her springy tread. " Something might
happen ! " he hoarsely whispered, as he saw her firm white
hand close on the pistol-butt.

"I am a soldier's daughter !" she whispered, and then,
she hid her sudden alarm behind the mask of pride. Had
she known that her husband had learned by one guilty glance
of the secret stationing of Dournof's fierce cavalry, there would
have been nobler blood staining the brown heath on that
brilliant morn than ever welled from buck or wolf ! Cecile
could have been a Judith ! But she only feared baseness !
Her husband had seemingly accepted the gift of Nimovitch,
at the hands of his patrician creditor ! And, now, with the
coarseness of the cruelty of man in the woman-chase,—this

haughty stranger dared to lift his eyes familiarly to hers! Her very heart was frozen in the solitude of the lonely forest reaches, with her splendid enemy at her feet !

Leaning slightly forward, seated on a jutting boulder, her thoughts wandered far away to her girlish days, when she had dreamed of her unknown lover-husband to be,—the star of men, the very pride of Poland ! And now that dream had faded into the cold gray truth of her uselessly-fettered woman-hood ! The days when she had wandered with Étienne Wizocki, through the romantic bowers of Villanow returned to her mind, as a child of the great Potockis, and Lazienskis, an heiress of the blood of the Radziwills and Zamoyskis, she had walked at her ardent lover's side, through the silent paths of old vanished family glory ! And she had loved him so! even more than Poland ! Before the sacred statue of the Holy Virgin, in front of her own old palace of the Kaza-nowskis, she had bade him vow, before she took his hand, to be ever true to Poland, for her sake ; and in the white moon-light they had together lingered on the marble terrace of the Lazienski chateau, where King John Sobieski, still in heroic bronze, still waves on the children of the Land of Sorrows to vanished victories!

"Be a man ! Be what he was !—and, be mine ! " the ardent girl had whispered, as her lover poured forth his fond oaths of eternal fidelity. The girl's proud heart was thrilled with the songs and poesy of Poland. Its old legends were her family histories, and her gallant princely ancestors had fought at Sobieski's side before Vienna ! They had watched the haughty Turks, as prisoners raising up the storied walls of Villanow, and divided, with their great chief, the thanks of an affrighted Christendom !

It was in the leafy alleys of Marymont, where the haunt-ing footstep of Queen Marie—Sobieski's bride—still seemed to linger in the silent flower-strewn paths, that lovely Cecile bowed her head in maidenly blushes, as she placed her slender hand in her lover's. The fond girl would fain have invoked the blessing of the vanished Queen upon the love-tryst of her gentle descendant! The dream of the past was sweet!

It came suddenly to an end, as the silence was broken by sharp shots to right and left. She woke to realize that she never found the fairy realm she dreamed of! That land where men were true and loyal, where women fair were white in soul, and where Love's witching song resounded in a key-note of solemn and eternal truth!

For now, her heart told her she had found all her dreams to be but the roseate mirage of her own splendid youth! One by one, her fresh hopes had failed, and the shattered altar of her pure heart was tenanted no longer by the god whom she had herself set up! "False, false even to me," Cecile wailed in her warring soul, as she was stirred by a renewed vague distrust of the Russian who had seemed to be a wolf stealing out of these passing days upon her unguarded womanhood! But now, he was like a crouching tiger! For the one glance of implied suggestion bade her man all the walls of her heart's citadel.

"Am I to fall into this man's power!" she murmured in affright. "No! For the wide world is open to the Polish exile, and Étienne has at least kept one half of his oath to me! True to Poland,—if not my heart's true king!"

The moment was agonizing in suspense. She dared not look into the gleaming eyes of the man whose heart was madly beating in restrained passion before her, but she gazed steadily down the aisles of the forest, now resounding with loud cries. "After to-day," she silently pledged her soul, "he shall never see me alone again!" For she knew that this hunt would be the very last opportunity of a tête-à-tête. The peopled passing hours of the gay ball would be given up to general hospitality, and she could then seclude herself! The crisis was past!

"Why did I not plead my sudden illness? I can now, at least, soon retreat to my faithful cousin's at Warsaw." The woman's tender heart quivered with a danger signal strangely ringing in her wildly-throbbing pulses.

With a quick cry she started up, as a loud crashing shot rang out in her very ears! She was transfixed with astonishment as a huge bear dashed from the nearest cover directly upon Vassili Milutin, who fired pointblank into the great beast's shaggy breast! Wounded deeply once, the raging animal had turned in his rage along the line of hunters, whose guns were now ringing out in a death fusillade! Vassili Milutin sprang lightly to his feet, with the second gun caught up like lightning, and covered the animal, now so near that his hot breath almost touched the cheek of the surprised hunter. Quicker than thought, the Countess, her soul transfigured by the sudden peril, glanced, in a woman's utter helplessness, at the resolute Russian, who, throwing his hunting-cap in the bear's face, with a wild shout, pulled the trigger as he marked the curling hair directly over the mad beast's heart, now rearing in all his towering height to grasp his gallant human foe, for two heavy balls had already torn and lanced the brute to the quick, maddening him into the utmost desperation in his frantic rage. A hoarse yell rose as Vassili threw away his useless gun. It had missed fire! Before he could spring to her side and grasp the heavy army revolver from Cecile's trembling hands, the bear turned fiercely upon the helpless woman, who, even in the excitement of the moment, saw her Russian foe, brave, resolute, and fearless of himself, throw himself deliberately between her and the cruel beast. His left arm, shielded in its thick leather sleeve, was thrust into the great bear's face, as Milutin madly plunged his heavy Toledo hunting-knife again and again up to the very hilt in the fierce animal's shaggy breast! There was the quick mingling of an involuntary shriek of pain and a dying growl, as the great animal dragged Milutin down with him in his heavy fall. It was over!

When her frantic screams drew the nearest hunters to the spot, Cecile Wizocka was kneeling by the side of the man whose love had come at last to blight her pure life! His pale face was lifeless, his left arm lay helpless and bleeding at his side. It was half stanched with Cecile's blood-stained scarf. But his head rested now on her heaving breast!

Beside them there, the dying beast was groaning out, in churned foam, his very latest breath.

The first comer never knew from the calm of her resolute pale face, that when she sprang to his side, as he made a last feeble effort to rise, with her whole soul aflame in her glowing cheeks, in admiration of his desperate bravery, she had cried, unconsciously:

"You saved my life!" And, as the excruciating pains of his crushed arm and gashed side, sapped his failing vigor, the bleeding Russian noble feebly kissed her trembling hand!

"Give it to me, Cecile, to the last sigh," he whispered, as, kneeling by his side, her eyes gazing into his, her lips almost touched the pallid face of her country's foe!

She could not tell from whence came that mad impulse, her very nature melting in a warm glow, her eyes kindled with the strange light of nature's highest exaltation, but she had pressed burning kisses upon the pallid lips of the man who was her mortal enemy.

For, since the world began, womanhood's last restraining art is useless before such a display of peerless physical courage.

CHAPTER V.

JUDAS.

In five minutes after the Count Étienne had galloped up, a dozen peasants carried the senseless General Vassili Milutin, to the nearest opening near the road. The line of fire had now ceased its ringing work, and around the heaps of slaughtered game, the dull-eyed peasant boors wondered over the aspect of each ferocious boar, gallant stag, grim bear, and gray wolf, snarling even in death, as they lay stiffening with glazing eyes. A dozen Polish wagons, with their deep wedge-shaped boxes, were clattering all along the mile of the hunter's position, and the astounded beaters nodded in admiration of Milutin's prowess.

For the neglected woods, though swarming with game, had never sent forth as monstrous an object as the gaunt old she-bear whose claws were now stained with the Russian General's blood. On a hastily-made hurdle, its body was dragged in triumph, to the road.

When the bearers glanced inquiringly at the Count, to know where the wounded General should be placed, the lady of Nimovitch, in a strange low voice, said, speaking as if in a dream, " Bring him here !" and, as the nobles, riding up, all crowded around the carriage in which the General's head lay back, in ashen pallor, on the bundled furs, with a general surprise they saw that, unconsciously clasped in her hand, Cecile still held the knife with which Milutin had slain the giant bear !

Its heavy blade was crusted now with the blood of both

man and bear, and as Count Étienne gently strove to take it from her grasp, she turned a glance upon him which told him for the first time that he had lost his wife's heart.

"I will keep it!" she said, with cold contempt. For in her heart of hearts, she was now persuaded that her recreant husband would willingly have had her aid him in suing basely for the mercy of the creditor at cards.

Dragging on slowly homeward, the cortége moved back to the chateau, and long before the wounded man had arrived, the nearest village doctor of the serfs was waiting at the portal of Nimovitch. The excited guests, though wonderfully successful in the chase, were all drawn in gloomy groups, hovering in the salon, as the wounded General was carried to his state apartment. The strong brandy forced into his mouth had revived him, and sustained him, but only until the motion of the carriage angered his swelling wounds. For, under the rough bandaging his lacerated left side was already knitting in the first flames of a fever. The left arm, crunched and lacerated, was almost stripped, and the simple village doctor shook his head as the soldier was divested of his outer garb. The pain of the examination revived the Russian. He glared around, as if recovering from the shock of some wild cavalry mêlée in which he had gone down stunned and bleeding.

But, a faint wintry smile crept at last over his face, and his stern eyes softened, as he marked the Countess Cecile standing at the foot of his bed. He called feebly, "My sergeant, at once," and in a few moments, the grizzled old veteran stood by his master's bed. Vassili Milutin drank the brandy held out by the excited doctor, and then, husbanding his strength, whispered to Cecile, who now obeyed every summons of his eyes, "Write for me, only a few lines!"

While the beautiful enemy of Russia sought the materials, in a low voice, with eyes flashing in all the stern pride of command, Milutin gasped out a few directions to the old sergeant. Those around marvelled at the strange tongue! They did not know the Circassian language, learned by hardy Milutin, in the heyday of his youth, when, after chasing Schamyl's bold warriors all the day, he had often lingered in the yellow moonlight to whisper to the dark beauties who loved the boldest of the brave Russian riders.

Brief were the words of command, briefer yet the sergeant's quick replies, and still a look of satisfaction shone on Milutin's face, as his weary head sank back on the pillow. When he next opened his eyes, the pale Countess was gazing down at him, with a glance which sent an electric thrill bounding through his whole nature.

"I am ready," she said, and her slender fingers moved swiftly over the paper. A brief note to Count de Berg, at Warsaw, to instantly send his best army-surgeon was the whole burden of the fair amanuensis.

The fever was already mounting to Milutin's head, his raw wounds now began to inflame, and the stiffness of his lacerated side to affect his whole circulation.

"Hand it to me," he murmured, with a look which made Cecile Wizocka quiver in her inmost heart. With faltering fingers he feebly grasped the pen and traced a few scrawled characters, under her own lines. Turning his head to the sergeant, he threw his whole soul into one word, as he cried eagerly in Circassian, "Go!"

Before the man had sprung from the doorway, the General's head lay low, in a senseless stupor. Cecile Wizocka, seated in the nearest chair with averted head, waited until the surgeon had closed his first labors. The arm, though torn and bruised, was not broken, and the feather jacket alone, with its wool lining, had prevented the beast's claws from reaching Milutin's heart.

"He will have a high fever, but a week will show him a different man," said the surgeon, bowing low to the lady of the manor.

Without a word, Cecile Wizocka walked out of the room, and it was only in an hour, when the sufferer had sunk into a slumber, that she returned to gaze upon his silent sleeping face. She was strangely calm, but the look upon her face might well have waked the late repentance of the man who had left her alone, to dream out her young womanhood in the unbroken solitude of a Volhynian forest. For nature avenges itself, with a remorseless justice, in this world, and always chooses the most direct path ; even though it leads in the strangest direction !

One hour of real breathing life, in any human soul lit up with the fires of repressed feeling, will sweep away, under the sway of Fate, more codes than all the crawling moralists of the world ever patched together, in their pious zeal !

The Countess suddenly laid her hand lightly upon the sleeping man's brow. She sprang back, with a sudden fear as his fevered lips moved, and, shivering at her act of rash indiscretion, she passed like a gliding vision, swiftly to her room. But, she had left her heart behind her !

Even as she forced herself to go out, and cheer the other guests, who were now debating the future of the interrupted hunt, two mounted Circassians were madly urging their horses away along the Sarny road !

Their real destination was Major Dournof's secret camp. Another courier was already far away, riding as the crow flies toward Warsaw. The evening stars had not swept down to the west, before the Man of Iron, Michél Mouravieff, at Wilna, had read the secret dispatches telegraphed by Alexis Dournof from the nearest military post—forty miles from Nimovitch. He smiled the devil smile of Cain !

One by one the noble hunters passed silently through the room where the General lay, to reassure themselves before they separated for the night. At Count Étienne's earnest solicitations, the two remaining days of the hunt would be carried through as originally planned.

For, there was a secret reason which gave a pleading energy to Count Étienne's entreaties. As the châtelaine leaned over the wounded man, before the doors were closed to all, Vassili Milutin suddenly opened his eyes. His right hand feebly grasped her slender, unresisting fingers. There was the light of fever burning in his wandering eyes. "I shall meet her at Nimovitch!" he whispered, "and the work,—yes, the work shall go on! I must rise!" His voice grew stronger. But he sank back in pain, muttering, "Yes! Dournof! Dournof,—at once! Ride! Ride! For your life!" and again his eyes closed.

Countess Cecile passed out into the silence of her boudoir Love had closed its doors often there upon the happy dreams of the two married lovers, dreaming heart to heart! But those days had fled forever. There was only a dim light softly shining, and the room was silent. The woman's brooding face grew strangely pale, as she saw sitting by her table her estranged husband with an anxious face. "What do you wish, Étienne?" she said calmly, as she seated herself facing him. Between them, cast down in her hurry, lay the heavy knife with which Vassili Milutin had killed the grim old bear!

"Tell me how it all happened?" he said, with his eyes vainly searching to read the story of his wife's now strangely indifferent mood. In the by-gone days, her question "What do you wish," would have been an impossibility! But, he himself had built up the wall between them. His cold neglect and his long absences doomed her to the inanition of the unmarked round of a solitary life. His foul treason to the sacred oath of Love, all these, had changed her. She was at heart another woman! The glad-eyed girl who clung to him with love's freshest, fondest embraces had vanished forever. He did not dare to own that he had coldly slain her love. But, in some half-hearted way, it reached his dulled nature that he now missed something in the woman whom he had led to these Volhynian shades!

It might have dawned upon him that her love was lying cold and dead! Though her voice raised up no accusation, her heart was murmuring, "Never, never any more!" And on this fatal night there mutely passed from the beautiful wife to her lord, facing her in his dejection, the knowledge that the light which once burned for him alone, had gone out forever, in the windows of her soul. Darkened now, as she gazed at him, would the red fires glow within them ever again?

In an unconstrained manner, she related all the incidents of the hunt. It was easy for Count Étienne, an accomplished hunter, to see that the second gun, missing fire, had nearly cost the daring Russian his life. Beyond that, he could not follow the scene, even in his thoughts. "It is wonderful that he was not killed outright. The bear was very old, and but for her teeth being almost worn out, his arm would have been munched into fragments! The sharp claws would soon have finished him. He behaved with the greatest gallantry!" concluded the Count. He dared not clasp his wife to his breast, and cover her lips with kisses! He dared not strain her to his bosom in the delightful joy of her safety. For, there was a hidden reason, and he could not reason. He dropped his eyes when his watchful wife murmured, "Very gallantly!" in an echoing refrain of his few awkward words, and then, suddenly rising, she grasped the knife lying between them. With an unfaltering step she swiftly passed into an inner room and placed it before the cabinet, wherein she had with bitter tears entombed her golden wedding-ring.

Before he had raised his head, she was standing again beside him. Her hand rested lightly on his shoulder as she said, "Étienne, what brought this man here? Why does he linger? Have you any secrets with him? You know your re-election as Maréchal comes on soon. You should not openly caress your country's foe."

"There is nothing at all beyond the hunting invitation," her husband said sullenly, "and his wound will now tie him down here, I suppose, for some time." The natural excuse seemed to cover all to the cowardly guardian of an untold secret !

" Have you in any way released yourself from his claims of honor ?" said his wife, as she firmly gazed into his unsteady eyes.

" That is being arranged," he stammered. " It will come out all right," he muttered. But he did not face her glances !

" You are deceiving me," she said coldly, and rising she passed into her inner room without another word. For an hour after all the other lights were extinguished in the chateau, Étienne Wizocki paced the floor of his cabinet alone. The great house was still, and the moonlight streamed down on the sleeping lake and the softly murmuring forest. Above him on the walls the escutcheons of his noble line met his eye as he nervously glanced at the captured arms hanging in trophies on the wall. A sudden idea smote upon his brain. Before him on his table lay a superb pair of Lefacheux duelling pistols. He had once owed his life to their directness when an Austrian count had vainly tried to win from him the vicarious smiles of Delphine, the last Parisian lionne. Taking out one of the loaded weapons he pressed it to his temple ! The chill of the cold steel recalled his wandering mind. Already in his fancy he saw the finger of scorn, unwavering, unpitying, sternly pointing at the yet unstained crest of the Wizockis. But his weak nerves gave way ! Throwing down the pistol he drained a glass of fiery cordial. " No one can ever know ! I can trust to Milutin's honor !" His knees smote together as there flashed over his mind the consciousness that never again would he dare to gaze frankly in the clear eyes of the woman who had once drawn him down to her bosom's rest with all the fervor of the dead love now grown strangely dear.

" She must be protected," he murmured, " and no one will ever know over there in Paris." There is also Italy, and——" He abruptly threw himself upon his couch. The strong liquor had deadened his mental agony for a time, and the secret of his shame slept within his breast a little time longer.

Judas slumbered !

When the evening brought back the guests, now all re-assured as to the Russian's rapid recovery, the great hall rang with the excitements of the glorious chase. Beyond an intense soreness and the certainty of a disabled arm being an uncomfortable reminder for some weeks, the dis-tinguished visitor was practically unscathed by the rough handling of the struggle. Silence and a copious blood-letting had abated his fever. The frame of the soldier was most vigorous; his vitality, distinctive of his singular nature, was also a wonderful agent in meeting the shock. By his side now, a Russian army-surgeon, who had also brought with him several grave-faced attendants, took entire charge of the disabled man.

Cecile Wizocka, going on her way with an unruffled brow, had relapsed into the cold outward calm which her solitary life had brought to her. It was with a heavy sigh she parted with the noble ladies who returned to their homes on the third day of the hunt.

They fled gladly, for the projected ball had been aban-doned.

The Count Wizocki, a strange restlessness on his face, had ridden out alone to meet the returning hunters, in the evening shadows, for at last the stars shone down on the distant eastern forests whence, all day, the pent up elk and wolves had vainly tried to break the armed lines of the hun-ters. Riding out slowly, with only his own groom, Étienne

Wizocki parted with his wife, as she stood at the portico of the great hall, her last duties of womanly hospitality achieved. He bade her a formal adieu, with all the courtesy of his graceful nation, and, when she was left alone, Cecile stood, stormy at heart, watching him gallop down the avenue toward the great valley of the East. The lonely rider turned, seeing her lingering there, and, from a distance waved his hand, as his superb charger bounded on.

With the premonition of a coming disaster, the Countess re-entered her stately home. There was no sound of the olden laughter of the merry past. There was neither music nor the glancing of love-lit eyes. A brooding stillness seemed to haunt the splendid lonely halls. Cecile knew well that at daybreak the chafing nobles would gloomily separate, perhaps forever!

For, high in the councils of the secret cult of their rebellion, the Countess had recognized the Paris-bred scion of a great Polish house, in a new visitor who had been ushered by the old steward to the easy friendship of the east wing during the last morning. "The time draws on ! at any day, the storm may break ! And, Étienne !" she murmured. Though she feared for the final result, self-devoted and loyal to the traditions of her blood, she was willing to face ruin, and even the loss of her home, for the cause. She paused in the great salon, standing alone before her own portrait, from whence the loveliness of her bridal days gleamed out upon the witching canvas. Resolutely nerving herself, she placed herself before a mirror, and then glanced again at the face of the girl whom Love had crowned with the roses of that happy time. "I am another woman, now," she sadly sighed, as she paced the deserted hall alone. The beautiful woman gazed out on the glittering lake; the woods where love had led her willing feet, the far smiling valley, stretching out, the natural fortresses of her martial race. "The foot of the stranger may soon pass over the threshold; I may soon wander as a houseless fugitive. My child may be despoiled. But, if Étienne is true to Poland now, in the field, he may yet find a way to win back what seems buried forever now—my vanished love, my burdened heart!" She turned and then passed into the room where her sleeping child smiled in its peaceful nest. "Here, I will find my future life, here, at this child's side!" and, as she sat watching the sleeping girl, the face of its father came back to her, as first he bent with delight to kiss the little heiress of the Wizockis. A kindly touch of nature melted her debating heart, as she gazed upon the child who still linked her fate to the man on whom she smiled no more! "I must provide for Marguerite's safety, should this rising occur!" and, in her troubled mind, she bethought her of a far distant castle on the Galician frontier, where one of her own loyal blood still ruled over the remains of a great Polish estate. "There will be a sure safety there for the dear child," she thought, "while its father is riding under the proud banner of an awakened Poland!" Glad to see still open one avenue fitted to her husband in regaining the standing of his once proud station, in the country side, she tried to put down and forget all the venial wrongs of his later years.

Sitting there by her sleeping child, musing over the patriot husband, who was even now exchanging the last secret words with his fellow-sympathizers in the cause without a name, she could not hear Vassili Milutin, under her own roof-tree, whisper hoarsely to one of the Russian attendants, who had been gliding around the chateau for two days, "Are the papers all distributed? Is everything ready?" When the man's eager eyes answered the dangerous question, Milutin dropped his weary head. "Gather here, all of you, the very moment that they come!"

In the superb moonlight, the long line of cavaliers came riding wearily back to Nimovitch. The thirty versts of the journey, the midnight vigils and the chasing the wounded elk through swamp and morass had worn them out. But the great purpose of their meeting was achieved! On the long ride back, secure in the silence of the autumn footpaths, and the lonely roads, they formed up, two and two, and successively interchanged their last heart views and warmest pledges! Brave and devoted, with everything to lose, their very heads at stake, it was a touching hour! Not as of old, with banner and sparkling lances, did the flower of Poland ride along on the very highways whence they had once chased the Russian in defeat.

No armor glittered, no martial music rang. Only the sighing of the night-winds marked their onward midnight march! Passwords were exchanged, the last secret pledges made, and the rendezvous for all the nearest levies of the peasantry planned out. It was their very last chance to confer before they entered on that road which led on to perhaps death, and the dishonor of prison life followed defeat, or to the black scaffold of shame!

Many a stout heart quivered as they thought of wife and child, of the far, misty future, and of the tighter grasp of the stern power which held Poland now before her open frontiers as a buckler against any European storm.

It is only the trifles of life which draw out to an interminable length! Few and solemn were the words which were exchanged, as the great rebel nobles vowed their personal devotion to the death! Each had the liberty, perhaps the life of the other in his hand, and they relapsed into a gloomy silence, as the cavalcade neared the old ruined chateau on the high-road above Nimovitch.

It was a singular omen of bad fortune that there, under the gloom of the deserted park, a single horseman waited for their coming. The night-owls hooted in a dismal refrain as they flew afar, frightened out from the lonely trees by the Polish chivalry.

Count Stanislas riding in the van, drew a heavy pistol

from his breast, with instinctive fear of surprise or treachery. There was no hostile hail, but a cloud passed over the moon, and then the young Pole saw his host, Count Étienne, waiting there on his charger, and peering forth from under the shade of the gloomy trees. It suddenly flashed over the young man's mind that Count Wizocki did not know the last of the final arrangements made on this homeward march.

The next day, the returning peasants and beaters would bear the slain elk, bear and wolves back to the chateau, whence the trophies of the chase would be sent to each huntsman. This would offer a chance for undisturbed communication in the future, without exciting the argus-eyed Russians.

Recognizing at once the courtesy which brought the noble host out to meet them, riding on side by side, Count Stanislas whispered to him the very last secrets of the finally matured conspiracy.

" You were not with us, Wizocki," he warmly said, as they rode up together to the park gates of the chateau, " but you need to give no pledge. You are our leader. Our Maréchal de Noblesse. We count on you."

Étienne Wizocki dismounted without an answering word. but his face was ghastly pale, as, hat in hand, he saluted each returning guest, standing under the flood of bright light pouring out of the opened doors of the old hall. Its hospitality had never yet been violated, and over its great arch the arms of the princely Wizockis bore their proud motto, " Loyal en tout!"

In the east wing, a royal table was spread out for the tired hunters, and the silence of the main hall was broken by the wassail shouts of the men who, under pretence of the rejoicing of the time-honored chase, were drinking, unmindful of the future, the gallant old toast, " Io Polskie!"

" You are not yourself to-night, Étienne," whispered a friend of his university days, as the conclave broke up at last.

He feared that the enormous gambling losses were still hanging over his host's head with a dark monition of coming ruin. The friend's greeting was never answered, for, with a faint smile, Count Étienne bowed to all his assembled guests and then passed out, preceded by his old steward, bending under his silver chains. He strode across the deserted corridors, and went through the silent great halls to his own rooms, immediately adjoining those of the wounded Russian general. There a faint gleam of light still showed that the watchers were yet lingering near the Czar's high representative. But, all was silent as the grave!

Count Étienne Wizocki double-locked his doors, and then, carefully placing a brace of revolvers on his table, threw himself, still dressed, upon his furred couch. Before him, on the great carven mantel, a superb silver clock with two knightly figures holding up the crown of Poland, marked the approach of the hour of one. Only a few minutes lingered until its faint muffled chime would start the silver maces in the cavalier's hands in a mimic signal!

Count Wizocki rose with a last fearful glance at his double-sashed windows, and then stealthily approached a closed door leading to the state apartment. Though apparently barred with a portion of a great cabinet of arms, it easily swung back at his touch. This concealed mechanism was a relic of the days when both dark intrigue and light loves were secret practices of the gay lords of Nimovitch. Many a fluttering heart had waited in tender anticipation to see that solid barrier give way. And often had the old silver clock, in its thrilling crystalline chimes, told off the hour of love's fond tryst!

But, only a man racked as Judas was, when he said, "It is the hour," gazed upon the figure of the recumbent General and softly whispered, "It is time!"

Only a gleam of two resolute blue-gray eyes, a half start of the man buried in the downy robes of a sick bed, and, as the door closed again, a single wave of his one free hand, told Count Wizocki that his fearful secret summons would be obeyed. For as the breathless man threw his head down upon his folded arms on the table, and burst into tears, a dark silent figure, one of the grave-faced attendants of the wounded Muscovite General, leaped noiselessly out from his low window on the velvet turf and disappeared in the darkness. For the moon had gone behind a cloud, and the brightness of her glances silvered no more the unhappy land of Poland!

Crouching in haunting remorse and fear, Etienne Wizocki lingered long after the clock had struck one, and then suddenly started as the trampling of many chargers' hoofs resounded on the still night air. The distant shriek of a woman was followed by the loud wail of a frightened child.

In an instant, the sound of oaths, yells, and a few straggling shots rose on the night air, for the chateau was ringing to the crash of broken windows and the strong blows which forced the four main doors of the old hall at once. It was but another moment before the feet of the frightened servants, hurrying in flight, were adding to the growing din. A dozen dark forms burst in the low French windows of Count Étienne's own room. Though he snatched a pistol and quickly fired shot after shot, when the smoke cleared away, he was pinned down to the floor by a knot of troopers in the uniform of the Circassians of the Russian Guard. Over him stood Major Alexis Dournof with drawn sabre, a captor, who sternly said, "Close the doors and let no one enter!" Turning to a young officer he said, "Find the General's room and tell him that I report for orders. Ask him what I shall do with this prisoner!" There had been a dozen ringing shots heard in the direction of the guest wing, and soon the babel of a new melée added to the grim horrors of the hour.

The young officer soon sprang back with a torch in his

hand. " I am to take charge here! The General calls for you !" and the youth held a pistol at Count Wizocki's head as Dournof, still with his naked sabre in his hand, went out into the great hall to learn the will of his wounded chief and to gather up the fruits of the night surprise. For all was still. The Poles were captives !

The Chateau de Nimovitch was now in the hands of two strong sotnias of Circassians armed to the teeth! And, among these ferocious mountaineers, there were those who, replacing a cartridge or wiping a sword now reeking with Polish blood, showed their white teeth in a ferocious joy over the bloody work.

" Take charge of the Count ! Let him speak to no one ! Bind him and guard him in his own room ! An officer to be placed in charge of the Countess' rooms ! No interruption there ! All her servants are to have free access ! Let no one leave the chateau ! Are your lines drawn around the house ? "

These were General Milutin's eager orders.

Dournof bowed. His strong frame was rent with a soldier's anguish. And yet, he must obey! It was brutal work. The General sank back exhausted as he finished. " Secure every Polish prisoner ! Hold them all in the west wing ! Pinion them and place a soldier over each ! Shoot the first man who tries to escape ! Make report to me at dawn of all the details ! My men here will search the hall ! Give them every aid they need !"

The sickly gray dawn slowly coming on showed the wrecked glories of the Countess' lovely gardens, and in the park the savage ponies of the Circassians were now nipping the tender grass. Broken sash and doors forced off their hinges told of the rough surprise. A picket guard on the high-road stopped every chance passer-by, and even by the dreaming lake, the sabre of a Circassian glittered in the morning sun.

The frightened servants were all busily engaged in arranging the wrecked chateau for the comfort of the victors, and no sound was heard in the great halls. Not even the sobs of beautiful Countess Wizocka, now lying with her cooing girl clasped to her bosom, for she was moaning "My husband! My husband!" And not even the assurances of her frightened women that Étienne Wizocki was alive, though a guarded prisoner in his own rooms, stilled the wail.

And, deeper than the fears for her own, the blood curdling in her heart, told her that all the chiefs of the Polish nobility were now in the power of the grim Russian commander. "Had any one escaped? Who was slain?" These questions tore her agitated heart, and it was four long days, before she knew that but one daring noble had sprung through the fusillade of the soldier's carbines to the sedgy lake! Its chilled waters had warmed his heart in freedom, and hid him from the eager pursuers. That, another fortunate one had found an old boyhood haunt in the crypt of the gray Polish chapel, and, given a mantle by the faithful priest of his own blood, had followed down a ravine to where, on the edges of the fringing forest, he dismounted the first passing peasant, at the point of a pistol, and fled on to bear the news to the waiting network of Polish peasant spies. Alas! Cecile Wizocka did not know that while she mourned the loss of her dearest hopes, a young officer was respectfully bowed, over the stiffening forms of four men, all proud in manly beauty when the day had unfolded the golden curtains of the East, on the morning of the fatal elk-drive—her own slaughtered guests!

Scarcely a man, young Count Stanislas lay there, dead, with a pistol-ball in his brain, for it was his own hand which took a life dear to Poland. Summoned to surrender by a score of voices, pent up in a solid angle of the guest wing, he chose the freedom of death to a Russian prison's gloom!

Cecile Wizocka dared not breathe, as she thought of the

haughty General now lying disabled under her roof. "Had he a part in this carefully-planned descent?" No! It was impossible to foresee that he would be wounded struggling in the embrace of the ferocious bear. Had some Polish traitor sold himself for Russian gold? Falling on her knees before the ebony and ivory crucifix, which had last rested in her dead mother's hand, the Lady of Nimovitch begged the God of vengeance to shower His curses on the man who had —a second Judas—sold the Polish name to shame again, and made leaderless the chafing rebels now all ready to rise!

The few orders given to Major Dournof by General Vassili Milutin, were brief and imperative, as he listened to that officer's final report at dawn. "Send all the prisoners, each guarded by two men, to meet the troops from Sarny. Let your ranking Captain take half your force for this. He is to bring back a written receipt for each man. And you can retain the command here till I am able to leave this room. Have you had all the men begin searching?"

Major Dournof bowed.

"Your four police agents are at work now, each with two soldiers." Vassili Milutin smiled a grim smile.

"Then, all you have to do is to order your own convoy down from Sarny, and make ready for the Odessa journey. You know your duty. Stay. Send one of your lieutenants who saw this whole affair as a despatch-bearer to General Mouravieff at Wilna. He may need him as government evidence. Mouravieff will dispose of all these cases. My duty is done when you leave here with your convoy for Odessa." The General dropped his eyes gloomily.

And yet, as Dournof saluted and walked silently away, the clock ticking on the General's mantle seemed to chant, "Mouravieff will dispose! Mouravieff will dispose."

The forests, decked with dangling corpses, the graveyards where the dead, despatched by summary court, soon crowded each other, took up in the fatal flow of these later days that grim refrain, " Mouravieff will dispose." And the man without mercy, was soon at his grim work ! For Poland's shame was Poland's doom !

It was sunset at Nimovitch once more ! There was no sound heard beyond the regular tread of the sentinels pacing on the north and south porticos, when Major Dournof stood again by the couch of Vassili Milutin. " The Countess desires to see you, General," he simply said, and then bowed his head to hide a soldier's blush of shame. For gallant Alexis Dournof was doomed to win his rank on a grander field, in a nobler cause, under the blue-and-white cross, than the rifling of a country-house, under the secret orders of a merciless master, who hid behind the blood-stained uniforms of the Circassians.

"Tell Madame la Comtesse that I regret that I cannot wait upon her until ten o'clock to-morrow, in the salon. At that hour, I am at her service." And, as the Major walked gloomily away, disgusted with his strange command, Vassili Milutin heaved a long, heavy sigh of relief. There were thousands of mobilized troops ready to fill the Czar's behests now. There were near them dozens of eager officers thrown out with light columns, ready to check any Polish uprising in Volhynia, and the local reinforcement from the town of Sarny had already arrived. A jolly mess of gay Russian officers now occupied the vacated guest-chambers of the east wing, and the only reminder of the armed descent, was the still scarred front of the chateau, and the fresh blood of young Count Stanislas spattered over the walls of the room, where he had died alone in boyish desperation, rather than feel the vulgar grasp of a Russian jailer.

The chilly October winds wailed sadly now in the forest, and huge fires crackled on the lonely hearths of the chateau, when, in his uniform of state, with his wounded arm bandaged, and still borne in a sling made of the Countess' silken scarf, Vassili Milutin awaited the now discrowned queen of the Paradise around him. His heart was beating softly as he whispered to himself once more, "I shall see her again at Nimovitch." Steeled to his cruel work, borne up by his masterful passion, he was prepared to face an outraged princess, but he suddenly quivered to his heart's very core, as the great doors slowly swung open, and, followed by two waiting-women, the Countess, robed in deepest black, approached him in silence. The wistful sorrows of her beautiful eyes melted his stern heart, her lofty glance cut him to the depths of his quivering breast. For, what man can bear unmoved the lash of the scorn of the woman he loves! Proof against all of cold fortune's frowns, indifferent to the decrees of fate, brave against a callous and hostile world, the man whose heart springs up, in quick answer to a beloved woman's coming footsteps, whose very soul hangs on her slightest glance, cannot find the courage to withstand the torture of the scorn of the one woman whom he worships!

He bowed in a grave silence as the lady approached. "I would see my husband," she said, and her defiant voice rang out as clear as a silver bell.

"Major Dournof's private orders from General Mouravieff makes it absolutely impossible, Madame. I am not in command here," said the General, his eyes on the floor. Swept away by the passion leaping through his veins in every wild heart-throb, Vassili Milutin's tenderness shone all too clearly in his blazing eyes. He would fain spare her whitest bosom every pang. "And as yet, she did not know?"

Stepping lightly to his side, she said, with an accent which thrilled him, with an infinite pain, "Is this a soldier's honor? You have betrayed my husband! You have violated his home!"

A storm of emotion made Milutin shiver like a leaf in the wild storm. The icy winds wailed on without, and the bosom of the lonely lake was lashed into a mad unrest! He gently took her slender hand in his, and led her to where their eyes rested on the forest branches waving before them. He would speak to her alone. In a recess by a crystal window, he pointed in silence to a seat. She sank down, and, this time, his steady eyes did not quail before her own. His voice was gravely solemn as he said, "You told me once that you were a soldier's daughter; you must prove it now! You have said to me, a soldier, what would cost a human life were those rash words another's?"

She had trembled strangely when he took her hand. His clasp was that which broke the charm of her resentment. It was not the enemy of her fated race who spoke. It was the brave man who had saved her life, whose head had lain for one happy moment upon her breast, in what she deemed his death-agony!

"Cecile! I would spare you, but our lives must flow together now. The man who betrayed Poland, the man who sold his guests, his boyhood friends to prison and to shame, the man who should cower under your glance," he paused, for she had started up, and her hands were now clasped upon her heaving breast,—"Speak! My God, only speak!" she gasped. "Is Étienne Wizocki—your husband?" he solemnly concluded.

With one last effort of her failing strength, she cast his clasping hands away.

"You lie," she screamed, and it was only a pale senseless beauty which glanced up in his arms, from her proud face, as she lay silent in a deathly swoon. Burning, in his crazed passion, mad with the love of her very footprints, and filled with a tenderness new to his cold heart, yet, Vassili Milutin never pressed a kiss upon her paled hands,—he only murmured with bated breath: "She shall be mine, mine forever, and I swear I will make her happy!" There, kneeling by her side, as the frightened women crowded round them, he waited breathlessly to see her eyes open again, on a world of sorrow, misery and shame.

After a time which seemed interminable to the love-thrilled Russian, smitten sadly at heart to see her suffer, the Lady of Nimovitch slowly opened her eyes. She feebly sought to read the eyes of the foe of her house. But, Vassili Milutin was standing far away in a distant window recess, his stately head buried in his hands.

Steeled to a thousand scenes of woe and carnage, yet he could not brook the agony which was imprinted on the noble Polish wife's face, as her wild cry rang out in answer to the crowning infamy of his bold accusation!

"Tell him to come here!" she whispered to her one companion of rank above the peasant caste. The General slowly crossed the hall with a bowed head.

Vassili Milutin stood before her, now mutely regarding her flaming eyes. For, she gazed as if she would tear the truth out of his very soul—"Étienne, my husband! False to Poland! The blood of the slain upon his head," she cried. It was impossible. She clasped her hands over her aching heart as she leaned forward. "The proofs! ah, the proofs! You have them, or else you are an infamous coward! You— our guest," she trembled in rage.

"I must speak with you alone," he hoarsely whispered, for his self control had fled. His brows were burning under her hostile glances. "My duty—to the Emperor," he muttered. ·

"Leave us," signed Cecile to her two women, as she glanced across the great hall at the distant corridor, where an armed sentinel walked now before her husband's closed door.

"If he could only face his accuser—if he could but meet this Russian, and die in defence of his honor." Her haughty bosom rose and fell.

"What do you wish me to do, Cecile," said Vassili Milutin, softly. "Do you wish your own husband to confess his treason before ME? Before YOU? I must now tell you that my orders from the higher authority which he negotiated with are to send him away under a safe escort, to Odessa, with all his effects and baggage, and also such members of his family and private servants as he may choose to take. Then, to see that he leaves the limits of the Russian territory in safety, with the gold which pays for—his complaisance ! "

" It is a foul accusation," cried Cecile, "incapable of proof."

" Ah ! " softly sneered Milutin. He was cut to the quick. " The Greek priest, the staroste, the chief of gen-darmes, will be all important witnesses against the others, in whose baggage this whole treasurable correspondence has been found. Their evidence alone would hang Count Wizocki before Mouravieff's court. It is to save his own wretched life that I am ordered to send him out of Russia, with passports, under an assumed name. I dare not inter-fere with him, or even to question him now. For—he has richly earned the golden price of his dishonor ! These lower officials for months have aided him to entrap these poor hot-headed Poles. They will not be so very hardly dealt with," Milutin paused and said slowly, " but they will never rebel again.

" What do you mean ? " Cecile murmured, her tortured heart freezing.

" Some will be imprisoned. Some others deported to Asia, and Siberia, and, I hope, none executed. Their estates, however, will be all forfeited when they are found duly guilty. But none will be executed unless a general bloody rising occurs ! "

Cecile's pallor was only a treachery of her weakened mental state. " Cecile," gently said Milutin, " let me take you far away out of these scenes, far away to a land of sunshine. I shall have a six months leave. This foolish rising will be abortive. I may save your own life." A second time, he took her unresisting hand and kissed it.

"You would use the hours of his imprisonment basely," she cried, as she threw his hands off in scorn.

"Listen!" solemnly replied Milutin. "I know that you yourself are not innocent of this mad patriotism. You have a plundered woman's born right to rebel! I might even send you to the underground corridors of the Neva polygon! But you know, in your heart, you cannot fear me." His voice was almost tender, and the beautiful eyes were downcast, as Cecile dared not accuse him in this. For, he had taken no liberty, not a lover's plea had escaped his trembling lips. If she knew of his passion, by a woman's intuition, he had spared her insult so far, he would spare her forever. But, her husband, a traitor!"

"It is impossible. There is some foul plot," she defiantly urged, a conviction slowly creeping upon her of Milutin's mysterious power.

"Alas! The Jewish money-lenders have all been frightened into a cowardly confession. At the Jewish bath-house, alone, down by the river, we have found enough proofs to hang your foolish husband. They, the paid go-betweens, have all whimpered and also betrayed. For we will now hold this rebel land forever. Shall I make YOU convince YOURSELF from his own lips. You can see him now, for you will go abroad with him. His contract is for life, to live in ease, in comfort. And the Russian Crown always keeps its word."

Cecile Wizocka sprang to her feet. "And Nimovitch——"

"Is mine!" simply said the General. "Major Dournof has the full price of the estate, in chests of gold imperials, near here, under the escort of his cavalry. It is even now stored in the masonry cellar of the store-house yonder, and, that with a liberal secret pension, and a shadowy rank for his protection, your husband will enjoy, for life——"

"I will never look upon his face, if this is true," she cried.

"I dare you to prove my husband's dishonor." She was an avenging Diana now, clear eyed and pitiless!

"I accept your défi, madame," he coldly said, bowing deeply, and, when I have proved this, YOU shall ask him to tell his story to YOURSELF, free from the presence of even a guard. Is that honest?" She bowed her head. The rising storm howled without in greater violence and the casements rattled anew. "Quick, the certainty! Either you or I lie. I will have the truth," she gasped, with a raised finger.

The General motioned to a sentinel. "My compliments to Major Dournof."

In a few moments the handsome cuirassier stood regarding them in silence.

"Dournof," said the General, "hand this lady your official orders." With a shaking hand, the officer extended a packet, and, bowing silently, left the room.

"Sit down, Cecile," kindly urged the Russian. "And when you are done I will send you at once to your husband. I would have spared you. I violate for you my sworn duty. But, the woman I love must not deem me a lying craven, a cur, a traitor to her hospitality!" Their eyes met, and she gave him a glance which stirred his shaken soul. "And, you dare to speak to me, thus." He bowed and walked away. Her eyes were glued upon the fatal orders. Countess Cecile, with a breaking heart, learned in unmistakable fact, that Major Alexis Dournof was charged to safely escort the Count Wizocki and his belongings, to Odessa, also to obey the orders of General Milutin, and to return official receipts for the gold in his care, the sum of which staggered her! She rose, and, walking to where Milutin lingered, said in a strained hushed voice, "And, his gambling debt?"

"I forgave that," simply answered the General. "For he is a Russian official now, and under the Czar's protection. I dare not injure him!"

"This dishonor, this last lie, never," the Countess answered. "Take me to him!"

He bowed, and softly said, "Before you speak to the Count, please hand him these," and he drew from his breast, duplicate Russian Imperial passports. They were already viséed for foreign travel, and he placed them in her hands without a word.

"A mere trick, again a trick," she cried. "See the name, General Michael Waldberg and family." She smiled in derision.

"Precisely," calmly answered the General. "That will be your husband's future designation and rank in our un-attached foreign service."

With blazing eyes, the Lady of Nimovitch triumphantly turned upon him. "Now! I am ready. Every lie shall be squarely met. Every cunning trap exposed. And Étienne Wizocki would sooner rot with his doomed friends in your jails than to stoop in the gulf of shame." She was magnificent!

"Pray ask him, then, these questions for yourself. You may also take the documents. You had better soon decide if you will accompany him, for the Odessa convoy starts to-morrow. He will take his child. He has already signified that to me in writing."

To his dying day, the look which the despoiled mother flashed upon him haunted the Russian. She was a Niobe as she turned and walked slowly to her own room. She came forth in a moment, for she had only strayed to where Milutin's knife lay, still bare and blood-crusted, before the cabinet where she had thrown it !

General Milutin walked in silence beside her to the door of her husband's prison-room. He said, quietly, "Let this lady see the prisoner entirely alone. Release him fully; only, watch the doors and windows from without." He paused, and, cap in hand, held the door open himself, when the young officer had retired.

"I will wait for you here," he said, as she passed over the threshold, and then, wolf-like in his tread, he walked the floor, with springy strides, as his cold, steady eye was sternly fixed on the closed door. He never moved a single muscle of his impassive face, for Fate was now fighting—as once before—on his side!

Beside a man, who cowered, with his head buried in his arms, Cecile Wizocka stood, the papers clutched in her left hand, but her right held something which glittered, as she touched him lightly on the shoulder. He shuddered not ; did not raise his head. A horrible sudden fear possessed the soul of the woman, who had staked all her life—her whole womanly worth—on his manly honour.

"Étienne !" she said slowly, with each word falling like a clod upon a coffin, "we part to-morrow—forever—if these papers tell the shameful truth ! I have come here," and her tender voice quivered in a wife's appeal, "to ask you by the memories of the night which made you mine, if a Wizocki can betray ?" She laid the damning proofs beside him on the table. Her heart beat on in silence. He remained motionless, and he had not dared to look into her eyes. "Look up !" she cried in despair, "let me see in your eyes, your honest denial." "Oh, God, Étienne !" her voice sank almost to a sob, as she fell on her knees beside him, "tell me that you do not go forth willingly, to take the Judas gold, the price of an eternal dishonor. I will never set foot forth, beside you in this quest. And,—my child ! A traitor's child ! "

There was still a horrible silence. Her heart stilled its beating, as she sprang up and threw the knife she had con-cealed, on the table. "For you and me both, if you are honest ! Let us die here together, now, and your love will thrill in my last sigh !" The mass of bones and sinews before her moved, in a mingled nervous dread and fear of her possible self-destruction. "In a foreign land," he muttered, "safe with our child!" and then he turned his face toward her, for the first time since the deadly carbines had rung out on the midnight air!

It needed not a single word to tell her of the fatal downfall of a human soul! "Go!" she whispered, in a voice which filled him with new and unknown terrors, "and may the curse of God send to you a death alone—the death of a dog!" She grasped the papers, and then, her firm right hand closed upon the knife with which Vassili Milutin slew the great beast of prey!

The door clanged loudly as she threw it open. In the vast salon, there was no human being, save keen-eyed Vassili Milutin, who stood with his arms folded, as she strode swiftly near him, with the gleaming knife in her hand. "Is this true?" she cast the papers down at his feet. "On your mother's grave!" Her eyes carried an appeal which touched even the heart of stone. He dropped upon his knees before her, and his arms fell. "Strike me to the heart! It is the truth! You know I do not lie!" She cast the knife away! It fell with a ringing sound, which sounded hollow in the vast silent hall. At the far window, gazing out into the swelling storm, she mused alone, while General Milutin picked the blade up and thrust it in his bosom. When she turned there was a light on her face which had never shone there before. Swift as the stride of a leopard, she neared him. Grasping his two wrists in her slender hands, she searched his eyes with a last long glance of unutterable appeal. "Then, I AM NOT SOLD WITH POLAND!" He sprang toward her, and as her head fell unconscious on his breast, her whispered sigh was as faint as the last breath of a dying child. "Only take me away! Far from here—forever!"

The grim recorder who sits at the gate where Proserpine went down into gloom, smiled as he made the record of one lost soul more!

It was a week later when the new Intendant, with a strong

body of Russian servants, took possession of the vast estate of Nimovitch for its new master. There was no debate, for already "General Michael Waldberg" was far on his way to the convenient port of Odessa. His trip was safe, for, avoiding the city of Kiev, the easy passage down the Dnieper, on a government steamboat, would at once prevent all gossip and baffle the vengeance of Polish spies. An armed officer sat in the luxurious travelling carriage of the new "General Waldberg," whose little child shrank away in fear, in the farthest corner of the great Imperial, from the moody father on whose brow the Judas mark was already plowed with the blushes of shame. For even now, far away, the gallant hunters, his betrayed guests, in chains, were beginning the expiation of their rash conspiracy. Long years later, in a foreign land, a square of linen, only a fragment of a coarse prison garment, bore, in letters written in human blood, pricked in with a sharpened nail, the names and fate of those who lived to see far Khamschatka, the gloomy vale of the Amur, the steppes of Turkestan, or who died on the convict march. But, none of the gay hunters ever saw the Volhynian meadows smile again !

Major Dournof galloped alone back from Kiev to join his squadrons and pick up the revolutionary Poles, now being chased over the border of the eight vast provinces now under Mouravieff's sway, by Count de Berg's soldier sleuth-hounds in the government of Poland proper. He rode on past the lonely Chateau of Nimovitch. Only the new task-masters and the feasting servants lingered there now. Around the wide domain the expelled house servants of the vanished Count Wizocki timidly wandered, as yet afraid to take up the residence freely offered by the new Russian master. For, Count Étienne Wizocki had disappeared forever from the ken of his familiars, and never again did his black charger bear him through the park gates, to greet the sweet face once smiling at the window of the now closed apartments of the Lost Lady of Nimovitch !

"You will be kind to my poor people, Vassili. Do not let them suffer for me." A veiled and muffled woman spoke sadly as she passed out of the corridor of the guest wing of Nimovitch, to the shores of the lake. At her side, his heart filled with a tenderness which was of a new birth, a love which was not even dreamed of in the days when he whispered in fevered visions, "I shall see her at Nimovitch," Vassili Milutin halted and clasped her to his heart. "On my soldier's honor, by our love, Cecile, I swear they shall feel your gentle hand guarding them forever!"

"Leave me for a moment. Is the carriage ready?" the grateful woman whispered.

He bowed in silence, for an agony beyond the compass of human speech, shone upon her transfigured face. It was a cold, starlit night, and the long voyage to the Austrian frontier was beginning. General Milutin wished to bear her far away, where the nature which God had made a treasure-house of every gift, could revive under the passionate tenderness of a man who had found his other soul at last! His simple obedience had touched her heart. He went on in advance, without a word, to where the great carriage waited ready, with its gleaming yellow lights. On the threshold, where the nobles of her girlhood's friendship had died—torn by the Circassian's rifles—she knelt down and kissed a dark stain still lingering there. "It is Polish blood!" she softly whispered, and, she never raised her eyes, as she fled out into the wide-spread welcome darkness of the night, which veiled her adieu to the fated house which was her home no more.

The shimmering lake and the bending chestnut shade, where she had lingered once, in another love, were hidden in the dark shadows of that night, which lay heavy on her guilty soul!

"Cecile! my life, my love, my soul is yours—till death!" was the welcoming whisper which she heard, as the wild horses sprang out into the black night!

BOOK II.

REAPING THE WHIRLWIND.

CHAPTER VI.

A LOST LOVE.

A SOFT wooing breeze was fluttering over the lazily lapping waves breaking on the shores of a little bay where Sorrento nestles among the purple crags of the Campanian mountains. It was a bright April day, and the sun, slowly sloping to the west, burned on the tranquil blue Mediterranean, a path of golden glory toward the far Pillars of Hercules.

Vassili Milutin paused upon a jutting crag, as his eye roved vainly over the silvery sands of the shore. Turning his head impatiently toward the spot where the white walls of a little villa shone out among the graceful olives, the Russian General muttered, "They told me that she was here!" All in vain before him, Capri hovered, a blue faintly-gleaming vision, a fairy argosy floating on sapphire waters. Far Ischia, storied Amalfi, gallantly perched upon its boldly carven cliffs, and grand Vesuvius hanging high over the buried Roman cities below, thrilled him not with their romantic beauty. He sought only the form of the beloved woman, who had now grown so strangely dear. He was a new man at heart. A fresher life burned upon his bronzed cheek, a glad light glittered in his steel-blue eyes. For the happy months which had thrown their glamour around him, had sped all too swiftly—alas! Over the banquet of his life hung the Damocles' sword—of a parting whose shadows were already clinging to his troubled brow. His master, the Czar, had called him back to a trust which placed almost the honors of a royal crown upon his brow! But there were thoughts thronging upon him in this hour which melted his stern heart. As he sought her wandering form among the graceful ilex and the quivering cypress, he felt how sharp the bitter pangs of the coming parting, a parting for long months, when even a half day's absence in these golden days had wrung his heart.

"My God! I cannot live without her!" he murmured, as he strode on, with renewed eagerness, looking for Cecile, in her lonely walk. The wisdom of a great government now sent him far away, to where, in Asia, the wheel of Russian conquest was crushing out, one by one, the little princes of the "Heart of the World!" But one short month remained of his leave. The parting hours crept on, and he counted every moment!

The lovely woman who had shuddered as she passed forever over the threshold of Nimovitch, had chained him to her side by the subtle charms of a love drawn out by his eager, superb manhood, now pledged to her slightest wish. Alas! The love of the present could not tear from her heart the little motherless child which the Draconian Russian law, had enabled her recreant husband to drag away from her side! Even the tenderness of chivalric Vassili Milutin could not efface the sorrowful knowledge that a long desperate, partisan struggle in Poland, had ended in a final death-blow to all the rebel's hopes.

"Order reigned at last in Warsaw." The mad students had fallen in the square, mowed down by the flashing rifles of the brutal soldiery, and the fearful remorseless vengeance of Michél Mouravieff, a human tiger, smote alike the innocent and guilty. The prisons were filled with suspects, the crowded common graves with the victims of drum-head court-martial, and the fields of a dozen scenes of conflict were yet covered with the unburied bodies of the slain Polish rebels. Wolf and raven fattened upon the stripped corses of the poor peasants, who, devoid of skilled leaders, hid under the cover of the gloomy forests and attacked the lumbering Russian columns, like a charge of the starving forest wolves. Alas! Stumbling along blindly in these dim tangles, cutting out new roads, forcing stronghold after stronghold, the steady discipline of the Russian troops finally prevailed against the desperate rebels, half crazed in their frenzy of revolt. The entrapped nobles, the destined leaders of the ill-timed movement, were now scattered, far and wide; for the detention of every one related to those arrested at Nimovitch had followed the outbreak of two months later.

The secret agents who had been sent as nurses to the wounded General, with artful skill had placed documents and papers of a compromising character in the scattered luggage of the few leaders who were really secretly doomed from the first. Those prisoners of Nimovitch who were not convicted, now lingered under the doom of a possible sweeping exile, and a certain confiscation of their rich lands.

And, Vassili Milutin, the Czar's agent, knew that the Russian machinery of a compact autocracy was being now quickly extended to sweep in the last wrecks of the decayed fabric of the old Polish Kingdom. The ill-timed revolt had swept out of their natural rank and station, the ill-starred children of the men who rode with heroic Sobieski at Vienna. And so the Russian government was now free to fill every public place, to redistribute the escheated estates, and, in the suppression of the Conseil d'Administration, to assimilate old Poland, forever, in law and government, to the rest of mighty Russia.

The final details might linger for years, but already the ashes were cold upon the altar of a dead Poland, for the last hope of the patriots was shattered, and the lingering fires of rebellion had perished in even the stoutest heart.

"Does she know? Is she brooding over all this butchery? Is it her past life, her child?" he thought. For, thrilled in heart by every fleeting shade upon her brow, Vassili Milutin had seen her pale cheeks grow thinner, even under the wooing myrtles of Sorrento. There was a speechless appeal to his utmost manhood in the wistful glance of her dark eyes. And, often, furtively watching her in silence, as she would gaze out, hands clasped, upon the gorgeous sea-panorama of the gates of the old Roman world, he feared to wake her from these silent dreams, even by the words of burning tenderness which came thronging to his lips!

In their hurried voyage to Vienna, and over the wild Brenner pass to Naples, no one had recognized them, and the little villa on the Sorrento cliffs was an old retreat purchased by the General's princely father, on his final retirement from the field. There were no prying eyes in this fool's Paradise.

As Milutin gazed along the silvery beach, he saw at last the woman he now loved with a new heart-life, slowly pacing down from a sheltered nook, where the waves had been singing at her feet. He sprang forward to meet her, and as she raised her splendid eyes to his eager face, his heart failed him. "I dare not tell her now!" he murmured, as he kissed her slender hand.

There was upon her face again that brooding look, as of some voice calling her away. He feared to question her as he drew her to a bower where the sweep of the beautiful bay showed them the dainty fisher-boats skimming out to sea, with the wild dash of the falcon. His heart told him the parting hour must come at last! That bitter, bitter hour of parting which wrings every human heart. And, yet, finding her so wreathed each day, in newer graces, in a passionate womanliness never before awakened, he fain would still fold around her every protection of the wealth and the power which his august master reflected upon him. Alas! Even heaped-up gold cannot lighten the stricken heart. Ropes of pearls and sparkling gems bring no light to eyes looking always for one remembered face veiled by cruel distance, but bright in fond memory. Countess Cecile, with a mute self-abnegation, had moved calmly among the delightful scenes of his newer daily life, the fruit of his ever-anxious love, and even mutely accepted the nameless station which she filled. And with her past sealed, her country blotted forever from the face of the earth, the helpless woman without a future, dared not look forward to the inevitable breaking of the golden chain which bound the man who had saved her life, to her slightest wish, in these days quickly fleeting.

In gentle converse, Milutin tried to approach the subject of her thoughts on this evening. The sun dipped lower at their feet, and all the stilled waves shimmered in burnished gold. There was no art in her demeanor, it was only the helpless abandon of a woman whose young life had been marred. Rustling silks and rarest lace could not keep out the cruel, chilling thoughts which lingered around her, as she saw her whitening face in the mirror which had once shown to her only a loveliness lit up with life and hope.

At last, Vassili Milutin broke down the thin wall which had been builded up between them by her womanly reticence. Despatch-bearers and secret agents had sought him out, in these last weeks, and, from Count de Berg at Warsaw, momentous telegrams in cipher, trebly guarded, gave him all the details which proved his master's coming call to a new field of action. From his dashing son, still attached to the staff of the Governor-General, many letters told of another great projected Russian advance in Asia, and, moreover, every weekly Brindisi steamer brought to the General reports from a man of history who was slyly weaving the dark web of Russian intrigue at Constantinople. He might receive a summons at any day. And then it would be too late! Milutin well knew that the woman whose love had so richly crowned his life would never cross the Polish or Russian frontier again. For, if the sad past alone would not warn her back with shadowy, spectral finger, she was now without a legal name. Vassili Milutin could not bear to think of her as the object of scorn, helpless in the penumbra of uncertain womanhood. He shuddered to leave her alone, still almost in the door of young womanhood, with her brave bright life blighted forever, at twenty-two. He had striven in some way to find a prudent means of protecting her name. It was, alas! impossible. For, already, at Constantinople, and in Cairo, the newly-fledged General Michael Waldberg, with an easy self-surrender, was enjoying the security of his new birth with an infamously gained fortune. The traitor shuddered when he thought of bleeding Poland, but it was so easy to forget; and, his innocent child was now safely lodged in a distant convent, for her education, in the south of France. "She must never know!" he muttered, shame-faced. It had been a prudent movement of the new General Michael Waldberg not to approach his beloved Paris as yet, for there the last remnant of the despoiled Polish nobility had gathered in a dejected and mourning circle. Little had they to give to each other now. Their interchange of gloomy thoughts was their wealth of sorrow alone.

And so, Michael Waldberg, having lightly buried his awful past, sought the Lotus land of the Levant. There, the Russian consuls and agents were all forced to publicly respect his official passports, and yet, too well he knew that once only in every legation, he would be socially received as a forced recognition of his secret services. But beyond that, he dared not further intrude. And, still life was so easy in Egypt, for on the verandah of his home upon the Shoubrah road he hid his shame in the easy luxury of those balmy Cairene winter days.

But, the victorious lover bore an aching heart in his self-accusing breast. Gazing at Cecile, sitting by his side, on this April evening, the man who knew he must go soon to a distant viceroyalty in the far east, writhed in his devoted heart, at his helplessness. He dared not offer Cecile the obscure ignominy of a woman camp-follower's ignoble place. For lifted up by his rank to a shining isolation, he could not hope to safely conceal her beauty and graces. And, the prying Russian officer soon knows all. "If she is left alone in Europe, her recreant husband may harass her in some cowardly way, and even work some secret villainy of revenge." Milutin groaned, "My God, I cannot shield her! I cannot take her with me. There is but one thing left. I can make such provision for my poor darling that her lonely sorrow will be a splendid one."

In the long nights, when he walked the salon, where the opened windows showed the silver flood of the Bay of Amalfic, below, heaving far below in molten glory, he had vainly studied how to win his way to make her openly his honored wife! For the noble second nature of the man was all awakened. Love had smitten the flinty rock of his nature. And, he would fain have her forever, to be his very own. But, bitter unavailing tears welled from his eyes when the stern fact faced him, that the permission of the Emperor to marry could never be his. Étienne Wizocki, now legally inscribed as a Russian citizen, had the absolute right to prevent a divorce. The Emperor alone could sunder the legal bond. And, the permission to marry could not be asked while Cecile walked in the shadow of shame—and until Death had removed General Michael Waldberg.

"If she were only some unknown stranger—even a waif, from any land. I could then make her legally mine," he groaned in his agony. But, Countess Xenia de Berg had already written him that Warsaw was ringing with the strange disappearance of the star of all the beauties of the Sorrowful Land. "Of course, I know, officially, that Étienne Wizocki has disappeared! The highest authorities only will admit that he still lives." So the graceful Russian wrote, "I have forced my husband to tell me that somewhere that shame-cursed man wanders in the Levant. But, alas! General, those who knew in her youth, this most unfortunate lady—born to a princely rank and a vast inheritance—will not be so easily quieted! They know that you were at the chateau, when these secret arrests took place, and you will be asked to socially explain her disappearance." He was on the rack! Again, over Milutin's warring soul came the memory of his rightful son Boris—the legal heir to all the dignities and honors of the family. It would be a sacrifice to all the bright hopes of that gallant soldier's career in camp and court to vainly beg the Emperor to grant what might not be asked. Boris, too, might have been his fortunate rival, and, would the son forgive? So, sadly gazing at the silken rustling curtains of the alcoved chamber of the loving and betrayed woman whom fate had thrown so strangely on his hands, Vasilli Milutin, in the rage of his helplessness, would fain have driven the sharp knife with which he slew the bear, deep into his own unhappy heart. "I will win her yet!" he swore. There was her pride. Her unviolated native honor. Could he offer a mere provision of money to her, however princely in sum, to support a secret life of guilty comfort? With the generous heart of a chivalric lover, he feared to cross the threshold of that passive reserve which had not yet been violated!

But, on this brooding evening, his softened heart was touched to the quick. He leaned to her, and murmured, "Cecile, I must speak to you. I must speak of that which is dear to us both, of our happy present, and of your own future, both so dear to me." For the delicate reference of Countess Xenia to the noisy gossip of Warsaw, was her warning womanly reminder of the terrible power of the myriad tongues whose poisoned venom would follow Milutin to the gates of the Winter Palace. He must be ready at any moment, and yet, how could he wrap the sheltering mantle of his love around her. Where could he guard her against the sorrows boiling up from within, the sneers and insults waiting her without? He had so far feared to approach this one grave matter which lay ever next his heart, and now he gazed, in tenderness at her, as she slowly turned her beloved head. She rose and pointed with a slender, wasted white hand to a bark lying far below them, in the blue gulf, with all its sails set, backward drifting toward the fanged reefs of the dangerous shore. The helpless vessel was already within the gripping line of the rocky headlands! He found her insensibly changed, for the fires of remorse had burned in her accusing soul since the day she walked in shadow at his side. "My God! How thin and pale she has grown!" he gasped.

"Vassili," she said, in a low sad voice. "Do you see that drifting ship? It may make its way out upon unknown seas. It may be carried by a current to perish on the nearest rock! It may go out in storm to reach the distant port, and then, be wrecked in sunny seas at the very harbor bar!

"Let me drift, my Vassili. Let me drive on alone! You have been so kind to me, Vassili," and her heart swelled in gratitude to the man who had tamed his own fierce nature to make these shaded days even brighter by a nobler love than had ever entered his heart. Words were useless between them. For too well she knew that he could not linger forever at her side. And in her own gentle way she would have him know that she knew a parting hour would soon come upon them! With the utter self-abandonment of despair she said, as she raised her eyes to his, "I will go

on my way alone! And, all you must do is to forget me!"
For, to her the whole world was now but a vaulted prison.
It was the mere inanition of her hopeless sorrow which kept
her from slaying herself.

One night when he was called away, she had pressed the
point of the heavy hunting-knife to the sorrowing bosom
which knew the joy of love no more. At the very moment
of her spasm of desperation, the thought of her motherless
child, far away, she knew not where—an innocent child who
had clung to her in all the wild outcry of that last terrible
night—stayed her rash hand. And it was only with a
mother's famishing love that she whispered, "Not yet—
not yet, till I have seen my child, my own, once again!
Then, I will forget—yes, forget forever!"

Vassili Milutin sprang forward and clasped the woman he
loved in his strong arms as her mournful words fell on his
ear like a death-sentence. "May God crush me in His
wrath at my happiest hour if I do not cling to you in life
and death!"

She gently released herself. He had never dared to
intrude even for a moment upon that perfect self-owner-
ship which should be the property of even the humblest
woman. She laid her light hand tenderly upon his heated
brow. "I believe that you love me, Vassili! May
God help you! For, I fear that if I lingered your love might
conquer!" And, lightly as the fawn springing away from
the leopard on the path, she passed him, and he stood alone!
The salt tears blinded him, and he did not see her passing
form. But he raised his despairing eyes. She was already
far away. While he watched her stealing past, far above
him among the silvery green olive trees, he was suddenly
startled by a servant hastening to his side. It was a man
who had followed his desperate path for years, and a loyal
subject of the Czar. A secret agent long trusted!

"Colonel Dournof has arrived with despatches. He prays

to see Your Excellency at once!" And then even a deeper
shadow settled upon Vassili Milutin's soul as he briefly
answered, " I come!" For his heart and hand was vowed
to the Czar's service. The loyal Russian General dared not
linger even to brood a single moment now on the means of
shielding from a world's sneers the dear and defenceless
woman now grown to be the idol of his heart.

" I will find the way, and she must be ever near me," he
muttered, as he strode up to where Dournof stood awaiting
him upon the portico of the villa. No stranger had ever
crossed its love-guarded threshold since Cecile Wizocka found
there an unviolated shelter in the bosom of those purpled
cliffs.

" Are we absolutely alone? This is a secret mission," cried
the anxious soldier, whose eyes rested anxiously on Vassili
Milutin, who tore open the despatches with a shaking hand.
" I am to attend you at once to Brindisi! You have but two
hours to prepare! And if you leave with me now, at
noon to-morrow you will be safely on the Constantinople
steamer."

The General bowed his head in mute assent as he hastily
ordered his own body-servant to attend to Colonel Dournof's
instant entertainment. " I will be ready. But this sudden
summons," he murmured, and his heart failed him as he
glanced at Cecile's window.

" I know it, Your Excellency," said the newly-made Colonel.
"I was bidden also at the very last moment by Count de
Berg to say that your visit to Constantinople must be kept
strictly incognito. When you are fully in accord with * * *"
he nodded, " and, shall receive a Petersburg despatch con-
firming all your joint plans, you can then return here, and,
coming on homewards, reach Warsaw as if returning from
Paris. You will be ordered from your present command to
another after you have returned to St. Petersburg, so as to
place you near your real future destination. It will take all

that time to secretly assemble and move the troops you will need. And you are chosen to take command at Astrakhan; the troops will all be moved down the Volga, instead of being gathered in the Crimea. In this way, the movement is covered."

A gleam of momentary relief lit up Vassili Milutin's hopeless eyes. "I will meet you in an hour at my hotel in the village," said Alexis. "I will prepare all the necessaries for our voyage if you will only send your body-servant at once down to me." And, the General knew from Colonel Dournof's instinctive delicacy that he would not break too harshly the spell which bound the Russian Antony to the heart of the gentle Polish Cleopatra.

Vassili Milutin stood alone, stunned by this sudden call. He was gazing around on the splendid scenes where, in the bright years before the world was old, the fair Roman beauties had looked love into the eyes of emperors. "I must tell her at least," he softly muttered, as he took a single step forward, and then the consciousness sadly stole over him of his absolute helplessness to leave her now in that safety which his love would build up as a fortress around her. He passed on into the villa and moved slowly through the vacant rooms until he found her, still gazing out on the distant bark, which had struggled seaward, and was now but a white wind-blown cloud of canvas, far out upon the darkening seas. She read the bitter tidings instantly in his face. "Do not speak! Let me simply look on your dear face," he pleaded, as their sad eyes met. "I will be with you again, my own darling, before another month rolls around," and then, taking her frail form to him in a mighty grasp, he drew her to his breast, in a last transport of speechless love!

Far down the cliffs, as he dashed away to join the waiting messenger of the Czar on that fatal night, Vassili Milutin fondly watched the light still shining for him in her window,

But, its rays also followed that unknown bark driving out to the lonely sea !

Two weeks later General Vassili Milutin sat alone, gloomily gazing out of a window of his rooms in the Russian Embassy at Constantinople. His great secret work was achieved, for the dozen of hardy young Russian officers who had already overrun the region to be operated in had exhausted every possible query of the new Governor-General of a yet unconquered realm, leaving in twos and threes from Odessa. Their official reporting for duty at the Legation attracted no attention, and now every avenue of secret information had been probed, every possible movement of the wily Levantine spies had been counterwatched. The mighty intellect of the wily servant of the Czar, who was his ambassador on the Bosphorus, had furnished to General Milutin all that matchless craft and a youth spent among the Orientals could impart. It was not the cares of a new Asiatic suzerainty; it was not the wild fury of savage tribes now crowding up to the frontiers to meet the invaders in battle which weighed upon General Vassili Milutin's leaden heart.

In the agony of the sudden separation, he had failed to give to Countess Cecile a private address at the Embassy, under which her loving words could safely reach him. It was too late when the Italian steamer swept into the lovely archipelago of the Ægean, that this thought came to him. For, his telegrams to her were not answered, and though veiled in the most cautious words he knew not where they had miscarried, for no word had reached him in reply ! His stormy bosom was rent with unceasing agony. He had broad lands in Russia, mines in the Ural, great forests in Poland, and a vast princely domain in Eastern Siberia. He would have even given his stately home on the English quai to have this mad fever of unrest in his ardent soul stilled. One word— only one word—he craved. In the watches of the night he vainly sought the oblivion of sleep. His mind was dreaming ever of her! In all the splendor of the Governor-General's ball, in the days when, with bated breath, he whispered, "I shall meet her at Nimovitch," he had only craved with passion. But now, lord of the deserted domain, haunted with all its later horrors, he would have gladly yielded it up to know her walking again with unstained brow under the spreading arms of the sheltering chestnuts by the lake. He loved her now in truth! The failure to receive her answers was an omen of dark import. For he felt that he owed her every reparation, a permanent protection, and every provision for the lonely days to come. It was with a new fear for his hidden charge that he heard the ambassador who had reported the departure of the mysterious "General Michael Waldberg" from Cairo. "We always know everything that goes on there," the great envoy said carelessly. "I thought that it might interest you." There was no sign on the inscrutable face of the diplomatist, but the soldier knew that this veiled warning was well meant. "If I live to ever see her dear face again, I will make such provision as shall wrap her in the protecting mantle of my eternal love!"

And, even on the eve of his departure from Brindisi, he had chafed all night in his sorrow. Secretly arriving on the Golden Horn from the Mediterranean, he had only met the men whose lips were sealed by the military oath, and the secret agents of the Ambassador. But, though he was in mufti, the several ladies of the Ambassador's household were all known to him.

At the last "diner intime," while he only waited for a private message to go back, boarding the departing steamer in the launch of the Embassy at night, the General revolved a dozen new plans, each at last proving fallible. "If I dared trust him," he thought, as he watched the roving, glittering black eyes of the great statesman. "He might find a way! And, he is all-powerful with the Czar!" To him, then, in a moment came also, the thought of his loyal friend, Colonel Dournof. "He is gallant, loyal, true! He might watch over her in my absence. Until,—until," his abstracted reverie was rudely broken, as Princess Anchikoff, the very epitome of womanly daring, fixing her glittering black eyes on the moody Commander, said bluntly,

"Tell me, General, did Colonel Dournof really gain the greatest victory of his life in far-away Volhynia?"

Milutin was bewildered, as he murmured, "I fail to understand you, Madame."

With a keen glance of taunting malice, she slowly said : "I am told that he bore away in triumph the Flower of Warsaw. My letters tell me that this great beauty—the missing Countess—was seen lately at Vienna, and, I am also told that Dournof himself has just returned from an Italian trip! Where have the birds nested?"

The crystal glass shivered in Milutin's hand, and his voice trembled, with the wildest rage, as he rose. "There are sorrows too deep for insult, Madame! That poor woman fled, a heart-broken pauper! I know nothing more of your heartless babble!" And, with a cold bow, he strode out of the salon. There was an astounded silence!

No one saw him again until his boat waited at the quai, and his brow was black as night when he bowed a formal adieu to the gay circle he was leaving. But through the Dardanelles, counting every leap of the swift vessel racing onward, the haughty patrician bore his burden of restless sorrows. "My poor Cecile," he madly swore, "she shall never quail before the cruel world's mocking sneers!" For, in his mad resentment at the covert insult, he would brave a Czar's just anger. He would have married her, even against her will.

"What if I married her now, and then begged later of the Czar the forgiveness due to thirty years of faithful service, as boy and man!"

And, his torn heart grew madly impatient as he waited for the moment when he should see her dear and gentle face again. Her eyes were shining on him from afar, wistful—wonderful. He forgot that the traitor Count Étienne Wizocki still existed, in the person of "General Michael Waldberg," that fictitious creation of a most unholy bargain. A man, whose subtlety and finesse, as a higher class mouchard, were even now being recognized at St. Petersburg. Dissimulation and natural intrigue were the very gifts of the versatile man, who, still under forty, could be yet trained to richly earn the bread of his secret pension guaranteed for life.

"I had once thought," smiled the chief of the Foreign Office, "that it would be a happy inspiration if some untoward accident would suddenly cut off this person." His face grew serious. The removal even of a secret service spy was not a difficult matter. "But he has really shown a value all his own. He is a graceful, educated Judas. We will let him live and earn his bread! For abroad, he dare not talk even in his cups, for, lighter than the panther's foot, is the creeping tread of the avengers of blood betrayed!"

Vassili Milutin, toiling up the winding roads of the Sorrento cliff, had now abandoned his mad idea of negotiating through Dournof, with the disguised Polish traitor, for a divorce to be obtained only on the husband's own application. Under his new legal rights, in the Russian law, he alone could effect the sundering of the bonds which still legally tied the Lost Lady of Nimovitch to the man who had snared his brethren to their cruel doom, and then sold himself to vile shame. "No! It is impossible!" Milutin cried, as the white walls of his villa shone out. "Cecile is far too proud, too noble to use a freedom gained by any base treaty with this cowardly cur! If he would only act for himself alone." His heart beat for a moment in hope. "Alas!" he cried. "This dog of a traitor has money enough now. I cannot hope to buy him, For the faith of the Government is secretly pledged forever to him. No! I will buy an Italian estate here, a home worthy of my darling, one whose revenues will openly provide her a fitting establishment. And then, sending her one faithful intendant, Cecile shall at least be as now, under my roof, until—until I can give her my name forever!"

And, happier at heart, he sprang lightly from the carriage, as he murmured, "If I could only give her my name before I go!" For he knew too well, alas! that she must be for the world, nameless, until some strange turn of fortune's wheel would bring her freedom. His eyes were blazing with the tender light which lingered in them, as when of old he whispered softly to himself, "I shall see her at Nimovitch!" His heart bounded in anticipation. But his keen eye saw no movement of the persiennes. There was no glad face beaming from the windows where all the beauty that womanhood knows was centred to his loving eyes in the dark-eyed nameless lady. His well-trained servants, grave and solemn, gathered in a group, watched him in affright, as, with a stony look upon his face, he sprang quickly through the open door. His foot rang out loudly on the waxen floors as he hastily strode on to her rooms. A sudden fear smote him, and, before he laid his hand upon the door, he called in all the willing tenderness of his loving passion, "Cecile! Cecile!" But his fond words were only thrown back in a hollow echo, and their strange accents died away in unanswered silence. For his own voice seemed to him like the cry of some strange, despairing one. There was no loving face to greet him!

And, alone in the room where she had been wont to meet him, with the wistful shining eyes, which in their liquid depths had never shown the storms of sorrow beneath her soul's forced calm,—he saw lying upon her table, a sealed letter, and beside it a vase of freshly-blooming forget-me-nots, the lover's flowers, the blossoms of Nimovitch!

Nimovitch ! Its meadows sparkling with her favorite flower. The hours of mingled joy and pain of this one heart-history of life. It all came back in a wild rush of sudden heartbreak. For, in all the wanderings of life's storm-shaded pathways, but one woman had ever unloosened the fountains of his nature. The Russian General groaned in the agony of a lonely despair.

Vassili Milutin turned. His body-servant stood at a distance, mutely regarding his unhappy master. Companion of battle fray, and dangerous quest, faithful to the death, the man still trembled at the look on his master's face, as he beckoned his servitor with a shaking finger.

"Find out, AT ONCE—tell me all ! ON YOUR LIFE !" And the patrician bowed his head on his hands, and bitter salt tears flooded eyes long unused to unmanly weakness. The letter lay there before him. He dared not touch it. A scarf of black lace was left carelessly thrown across a chair near him. It was a silent token, and its unspoken message cut him to the very heart. Before the return of his frightened valet, with a last yearning hope failing each instant, Milutin wandered through her rooms. There was not another sign of her graceful presence. But the things of beauty which he had gathered around her still spoke in a silent eloquence of the witching woman who was gone— "forever !" His heart knelled "forever !"

Vassili Milutin, wild-eyed, had picked up the scarf, as his servant entered. It was the same—the very one—which she had bound around his crushed arm, when he lay at her feet, bleeding in the mad battle for her life. There was nothing left for the servant to tell. In the deserted lover's ears there was ringing the message of her voice, borne from afar by the mystic spirit of love. It seemed to say, "Never—never again !"

The man hesitated, as Vassili Milutin nerved himself to know the worst. "Your Excellency," he faltered, "the Countess bade them place these flowers here for you, fresh every morning. It is twelve days that her orders have been fulfilled!" It was the silent message of the loved and lost!

His master gazed with flaming eyes. The man dared to say no more. There was that look on the Russian's face which comes to those, going silent and devoted, to their death. "Leave me!" he simply said, as his head fell on his breast.

Not once did the thought goad him that any other had lured her away. No! Loyal to his love, the strong soldier only murmured in his agony: "My poor darling. It is useless. She will surely kill one of us—perhaps both!"

He rose and locked the door, and then threw himself down in the very chair where her last hours of suffering had been passed, as he sat, pleading with her for that one last undiscovered seal of love which the chosen one of all the earth hides from the darling of her heart.

Though the soldier did not know all the half-hidden mysteries of her Psyche nature—the viewless charm which defies Time and Tyrant—it seemed as if her very soul was yet intermingled with his own. For in her accustomed place the invisible essence of her womanhood seemed to be breathed in his heart of hearts. And yet, Cecile had fled! Whither?

The scarf was crushed between his strong hands, as if he would tear the secret of her flight from its darkly hiding folds. Too well he knew the fatal import of its presence there. The fond woman, fleeing from the man she loved, with all the tender yearning of a womanhood whose dearest heart-throbs had mingled in love's ecstasy with his own, would not be forgotten at last.

He knew, too, the sweet message of the flowers she had always loved, and, heart-sick, he broke the seal of the letter which was to tell him of the bitter truth.

He knew that it was his final decree of fate, for Cecile, in her very soul and spirit, was the child of truth and honor.

He kissed the seal—the first word traced by her shaking hand,—as if his burning lips could call her back again. The lonely silence deepened around him, till he could almost hear his heart throbbing, as he read her tender words of parting :

"MY VASSILI:

"The flowers will tell you what I dared not. For, after I learned how you had grown to love me, I knew that I must go away now, lest I should not always have the strength. Do not seek to follow the path of the poor nameless one. I shall know of you, wherever you are. Trust to me in silence and absence, as you have always when we were face to face. It is the only way. There is no love of man which can ever enter this heart. When I say these true words, you can read in them, that you gave to our unhappy love, a sweetness which hid its bitterness even to the very end. We were enemies by birth, race, creed, and by that dark crime which swept away the Polish nobles trapped at Nimovitch. And, yet, my own darling, this, the last time, and I tell you that love's crowning miracle came to us, in that I could cross the gulf of each dark barrier between us, and be so happy in your arms. I ask you, in your loyal love,—for I know you would not have me hopeless in my exile of life,—to forgive me, to remember that I shall follow you out of my shadowed silence, even as you would have me do. You know my old race; you have proved my true heart. There is no way that you can lift me up to your side, before the eyes of the world. Fate is against us. One thing do I ask again, Vassili. My poor people at Nimovitch! Protected by your generous bounty, they will learn to love and honor you.

"I have taken with me only the knife—and, darling, you will find the scarf where I have often leaned my head, and here I have given to you my last greeting. Read it in the flowers you once loved to bring me. You will have another token at Warsaw, the very last! And now, my own, I close the record of my lonely heart, in a love which will burn until my last hour! It is better so. Forgive the pain I brought you. I bear the saddest heart, for I lose you—and, I owe it to my own heart to tell you that in life and death—I love you!"

The soldier never saw the name " Cecile," faintly traced below in her faltering hand, for a mist was driving across his eyes which blinded them in a fall of the bitterest tears. The world was shrouded in black to him now!

No man dared to break the stern silence of the lover's sorrow, and the long night had passed before the devotion of a life led his body-servant to his side. For days the Russian walked alone through the groves where her light foot had set its seal of love. His hungry eyes were resting moodily upon the places where he had so often met her, bright in her graceful tenderness. He was now outwardly calm. Seated on the rocks by the sea-shore he communed with himself. He knew that it was useless to follow. He was too fondly loyal to dare to dream that another had claimed her as his own. Colonel Dournof's faith was invincible to all suspicion, and even the recreant husband would not dare to entrap her. For, well might any man fear the merciless vengeance of Vassili Milutin, whose desperate courage would have lashed itself to madness to have known her in another's arms. His faith was fixed, for it was the self-poised calm of her high soul which conquered him.

"She would not live the daily lie while her warm heart and the bounding pulses of youth drew her to my side ; the daughter of kings could not live to fall in the mire under the world's trampling feet." On the second night, he went out of his lonely home, over the portal which she had crossed in her flight without another word of question. His face was strangely calm, for he had said a last solemn adieu to everything her dear presence had hallowed. Not even her pictured face was left to bless him. His heart smote him sadly. "At Nimovitch !" he thought, with one quick, fond heart-throb. He knew not that his dismayed servants had gazed there one winter morn, in blank astonishment, upon the empty frame in the grand salon, whence Countess Cecile Wizocka's glowing picture had been roughly cut by a hasty hand. Some Polish retainer's work, faithful even in adversity !

Alone, in his gloom, he began his journey to Warsaw. "Thanks be to God !" he murmured, "I can now thrust myself without one last regret before the Turcoman's bullets. Perhaps, some one ball will be kind as it whistles down the wind, billeted by the fates. And, he of the charmed life rode on with a crushed heart over the lonely plains of Pæstum, where, in the pale moonlight, broken arch and proud pillars still towered as a mocking monument of imperial ruined Rome. Far out on the throbbing sea he gazed! The gulf from whence the bark had struggled to pass beyond the encircling breakers lay there calm and silent under the white stars sweeping by, but the bark had vanished out on the unknown seas! He was doubly alone as he missed that one glittering sail. In sorrow he bowed his head, and swore in his inmost heart that a sacred life-quest should yet bring her dear face back to him. In mingled pride and tenderness he murmured, as if her vanished shade could hear him, "Cecile! Cecile! my darling; I would have gladly claimed you as my wife before the proudest king on earth!" And he went on into the increasing loneliness of the days which gnawed him into despair. And the lost love gave no sign.

It was at Warsaw that his heart at last found words. For, in the pent-up fever of his soul he must finally speak or die! When every vain and secret search had failed him, on the eve of his departure to the palace on the Neva to go forth to command the Czar's Asian host in battle, he sought the womanly counsel of his one friend, Countess Xenia.

In her own heart Xenia de Berg had divined a mystic link between the brooding General's new sorrows and the vanished Countess' sad story. Even the shattered fragments of the decimated nobility cast flashing eyes in questioning glances at the great patrician as he rode down the streets of the old capital with an impressive face. The burden of his hopeless sorrow was heavy on his darkened soul, and he had spared not himself. Ah! conscience, conscience! When Countess Xenia had listened to his manly story, she gazed up at him with eyes filled with a noble woman's noblest tears.

"I am glad that you have told me all, General," she timidly said. "I know that your name is beyond all the aspersions of her unreasoning Polish friends."

"I would have risked my very life to make her my wife," he cried, bounding to his feet.

They stood in the beautiful cabinet where a fair queen of Poland had once lingered in happy hours. The old Chateau Royal never heard a truer oath!

"Be my friend!" he pleaded. "I go to the field—to far Asia. But, by the God who made me, by my mother's grave," he bowed, and a sob escaped his lips, "I will make her my honored wife if God ever gives her to me again! Her love, my poor darling, has broken both her heart and mine! Find her for me—only find her!" he pleaded. "Promise me now, that if you, who linger here, shall ever see her face again, you will, on your honor as a woman, as a mother, send a messenger to me! Yes, even to Khamschatka!" he cried, as he kissed Xenia de Berg's hand in a last adieu.

And the Viceroy's gentle wife, smitten with his suffering, with a feeling of pity which kindled her generous heart, leaned forward and kissed him on his brow. Her eyes pledged him her faith.

Vassili Milutin strode out of the portal of the Chateau Royal with this one last flickering hope glowing in his heart. The Countess Xenia, as a habitué of all the world's palaces, was called by her high station to tread every highway of Vanity Fair of the continent. She must go out with her gallant husband, always on the Czar's bidding. She always heard the slightest word of the local Polish secrets caught up by the swarming Russian agents. "I will find her for you! I will bring her to your breast again," she whispered. "And—she is worthy to be a Russian—to be your wife!"

Milutin never knew if it was man or maid, that dark form which, grasping his hand as he leaned out of his carriage in the darkness, pressed into its sudden grasp a little packet! So quickly did the stranger vanish behind a recessed pillar of the old palace, that the carriage was rolling down to the Praga bridge before the startled noble could bring himself to calm reflection. Halting at the guard-house, at the far end of the long bridge, the General, hastily dismounting, opened the packet. The night-wind wailed over the misty Vistula in a requiem of the thousands slain at Praga. They wailed, too, in a requiem of Milutin's buried hopes! But, when he was alone in the commanding officer's room, he dropped his head in his hands in a burst of happy agony. " She loves me yet! Ah, God!" For the picture of his vanished love shone out upon him in all its wistful tenderness. Its shaded sorrow, proved that it had been recently painted for him. A little spray of forget-me-nots and a slip of folded paper which told him she yet loved was there. It read, "God be with you at Warsaw, my Vassili." And it was long years later, on the distant shores of the Sea of Aral, a lonely conqueror, before he knew again of her lingering here below.

CHAPTER VII.

THE OLD HOUSE AT LOSCHWITZ.

"I AM sure that they are Russians, Uncle Boris! and I will never cease till I find all the story out. I know that I shall win my wager. I may as well give you the number of my gloves now." It was the very merriest of voices which roused Lieutenant-Colonel Boris Milutin from a reverie as he sat on the slopes of a terraced garden at Loschwitz.

"I will double the penalty, Ladybird," he said, while a fond smile softened his stern face. "I would rather lose than win. It is all very possible. All this Elbe country is filled up with our border Russians now. I do not know why, but our own people do not go to Italy as formerly. Even my father has given it up."

"Has he really sold that beautiful villa at Sorrento, Boris?" questioned little Countess Vera de Berg. "I am so disappointed." For a shade crossed the wounded officer's face as he bowed assent. He gazed away from the laughing girl who was now eagerly examining a quaint old stone house below them. It lay buried in huge trees within a triangular walled enclosure.

Fifteen years of hard service had changed the laughing boy-officer, who was the pet of his regiment at Warsaw, into a man known from the court to the Caspian as one of Russia's most daring cavalry officers. Seamed with scars, his face wearing that worn look which partisan warfare always gives, he looked down the terraced walks to see if his hostess, Countess Xenia, was visible.

"I will ask her this very day. Perhaps she knows." And then, laughing, Vera, with mutine lips, told of General Milutin's offer to place his Sorrento Villa at the disposal of Countess Xenia for the winter.

"I do so long for Italy!" the child of snows murmured. "And all is so different at home now since——" She paused abruptly as the graceful form of her mother, who was robed in deepest black, neared them.

The fifteen years since General Vassili Milutin had gone forth to the Aral steppes had brought many changes to the glittering circle of Warsaw's garrison. Summoned to act as his great father's confidential staff officer, Boris Milutin did not see the final assimilation of Poland in 1867 to the autonomy of the Russian Empire. The long grass was waving in the silent Polish forests over the tumuli marking the butchered dead of the abortive rising of 1863. Crouching under the daily severer administration of the Russian officials, the last hopes of the patriots had departed. Poland was "tranquillized," and the great estates of the once haughty nobles were all in Russian hands. Lithuania and old Poland were now cut up with strategic railways, and the aged Czar could now easily hurl all his vast army on the foreign invader, behind the still gloomy forests, or crush with the heavy corps of occupation the maddest Polish revolt. Others beside the slaughtered Polish rebels, too, slept that long sleep which knows no waking!

The Count de Berg's stars and orders, now carved on the marble effigy over his tomb, were his only reward, save the undying hatred of the ruined Poles for his memory and the tenderness of the grateful Empress of Russia for his widow, who was still winning and beautiful. The Czarina loved the sweet daughter who, at sixteen, was now the pet companion of wounded Boris Milutin.

Hardship, fatigue, and the poisoned waters of the plains of Turkestan had undermined the young soldier's superb health. At thirty-five, Boris Milutin was distinguished even beyond the hopes raised by his birth and natural advantages. Desperately wounded in a slashing sabre fight with the wild Turcomans, he had been given a long leave of absence, and had now sought at Dresden the society of the widow of his dead chief, the famed Count de Berg.

Cut off in his long Asian service from the society of his equals, young Milutin had never married. But now his immense fortune in futuro, his splendid rank, and the personal favor of the Emperor made him a marked parti at St. Petersburg. He was the very highest type of the gallant profession which his valor adorned, as he slowly rose, and, leaning heavily on his crutches, raised his cap gallantly as Countess Xenia joined them. He turned his eyes on the pretty girl at his side, now eagerly tapping her foot in impatience.

"Ladybird, continue your peeping over your neighbor's wall," he said lightly, as he begged the favor of the escort of the elder lady. "I will send you two dozen pairs of gloves at once, instead of one, if you will only allow me to confer a few moments with your mother."

"You laugh, but I know they are Russians! I heard the young lady singing to-day in the garden. I think that I should really know my own mother's tongue. And, my dear uncle, you are not gallant! For she is beautiful enough even to tempt a Lieutenant-Colonel of the Guards to one stolen peep at the very handsomest girl in Desdin."

The young Colonel walked away in deep thought, along the sunlit terrace, and tried to frame the approach to a father's confidence in delicate words. "I have long wished to speak to you," he began, as the Countess gazed earnestly at him, "on a subject very near my heart. Your little one brought it all back to me by her reference to the sudden sale of Villa Sorrento. Am I right, Countess, in saying that you alone know my father's heart? In all these long years by the Aral Sea, you are the only woman whose hand has ever traced him a single line. Tell me, Xenia, what is the mystery of his strange life?"

The gentle Countess saw how earnest was the young soldier's emotion. "You know, Boris, that those old stormy days in Poland, drew my husband and your father very closely together. Tell me what is it that you wish to know? If I can lift any shadows, I will do so. But, there are some private matters which your father has confided to me alone. Even to my death—or until he passes away—I cannot break the sacred seal of his friendship. But, my dear Boris, you shall not suffer a moment, if I can ease your mind." Her eyes rested in sisterly fondness on the handsome invalid.

"Sit down here," answered the wounded soldier, and a very manly look of tenderness rewarded the graceful lady as the brave man was helped to a comfortable rest, where below them the glittering Elbe ran, a blue rushing current, down toward the gray Baltic.

"You know that I left you at the time of the memorable Great Ball, before the insurrection," the officer began, taking her slender hand in his. "I was then only a mad wild boy, and life seemed to be a mere hurdle-race—a simple cross-country gallop. Since then, if I have not cut my way to wisdom with my sword, I have at least gained some experience. My father's high command has naturally made him a lonely man. There was no one but your dead husband and General Dournof, who has now the old Aral command, who has ever peeped into Vassili Milutin's proud heart. He is not merely a changed man. He is another man, since he went out to Asia! I have talked with trusty Dournof about this. He knows nothing, and he is as anxious as I am, for Russia has few men like Vassili Milutin. It cannot be any official disappointment, for the gracious Emperor has showered upon him all that forty years of distinguished service have earned. Our fortune, too, is vast—

it is secure—and, I have tried to do him some little honor. No, no compliments ! " said Boris, as the enthusiastic woman touched with her rose-tipped finger the great white cross gleaming on his breast—bought with hero blood !

It was won in that simple devotion which makes the soldier's calling after all the epitome of human self-abnegation. "For valor !" The simple title is one which even kings cannot confer at will ! The blood-bought title of the brave soldier to his honest renown. And, women, the very children of silent Fortitude, whose lives, after all, are but helpless expressions of their best : given, alas ! often without any return, love to honour him who gives of his best under the stern military oath. Its obligations are only matched by the life-enlistment of wifehood, the never-ending campaign against cares and hovering ills of motherhood, the woman-fight against Fate !

" I know that my haughty father loves me," continued Boris, with a slight flush upon his cheek, "and that is why I would draw him out from himself—would call him back. I had some long letters from him yesterday. I have been covered with recent marks of his kindness, and he has held nothing back, save any military mention, in his despatches. When he gave me my first independent command, he said briefly, ' Show yourself to be my son. I shall know. And, the Czar is just ! ' His silent embraces when I came back from that field, told all the story of his veiled pride, his hidden tenderness. He is a strange nature.

" I have watched him narrowly for years, and yet, his lips have made no sign. When General Dournof relieved him of his command last year, Dournof called me into his own room at Tashkend, and then said, ' Boris, you know how I love you. You grew up as a boy in the service with me. There is no man in the army I would rather trust as my chief of staff. Your father says rightly that you have long earned this place, but that he could not give it to you. Now, even at the risk of losing you, I wish you to try and lift your father from the strange gloom which is slowly eating out his heart.' Absent a great deal, I had noticed no change, but Dournof said, 'He has never been the same Vassili Milutin since he came back from that visit to Constantinople. Take him with you over to Europe for a year of brightness and change. I will give you a long leave. Your father will have a princely welcome at all the courts, and you alone can win him out of his despondency. For Vassili Milutin at sixty, is still a man of a marvellous mental and physical vitality. But his soul is dead within him! There has something vital gone out of his heart forever. Find that other missing soul. If you wish to bring the last argument to bear, I can tell you now that Countess de Berg alone can sway him even in a hair's-breadth. I know nothing of his future plans.' "

Boris Milutin paused, and then narrowly eyed the graceful Countess as she bent her head in some strange confusion. Did she know anything?

"Did you then plead with your father, Boris?" she said in a low voice.

"I did, and with what result!" echoed the invalid. "The General heard me with a kindly patience, and, gently laying his hand on my shoulder, said, 'I will decide to-night, my son.' Poor old Elia—his servant of a life-time—came to me at dawn, with tears in his eyes, and told me that the burning light and the ceaseless tread of my father's step told of an all-night battle with himself. 'It is some charm, some woman witch!' the simple old country Russian murmured, crossing himself. 'For, he always wears her picture on his neck, night and day!'"

The Countess turned and gazed earnestly into the young Colonel's eyes. Her lips trembled as if she would speak. But, she dropped her eyes.

"I never knew my father's heart. I know nothing more

now," gloomily continued Boris. "All I do know is that, next day, when General Dournof ordered me to accompany my father, with his personal staff, after the last grand review of his favorite division, I was astounded when the first words he uttered, as I reported to him, were, 'I am going back to Orenburg to spend the rest of my days!' Boris sighed. He continued, "And, there he is to-day! In that old castle, sheltered by the last broken peaks of the Ural Mountains, his awful solitary life is slowly dragged along. I remained but one week with him. There is no grander place in the north than his place of refuge, but he lives only in the shadows of the past.

"When he called me to him, as the horses pawed at the door to take me back to my waiting Turcoman foes, he said, 'I have given you my Polish estate of Nimovitch. It is a beautiful domain. I wish you always to keep it. Promise me that you will never sell it. I only ask that the intendant always carries out my wishes, which he has set down in writing.' And then, he pledged me that neither I nor Dournof should take any private measures to have him summoned to the Czar's court. 'It is all over, my boy,' he said, with a hopeless look which haunts me yet. Now, to-day, I learn that he has even sold Villa Sorrento, but the money has been lodged for me at my bankers. 'If you go to Italy, on your year's absence, buy any other place you like, and I will do all you wish to have it kept up, should you go back to Asia. I hate the very name of Sorrento!' he growled."

And, as the Colonel finished his story, he said, "I can now do no more. General Dournof has exhausted his pleading, and I now ask you to aid me to trace the source of this dark spring of sorrow. What is there that cannot be mended with Time?"

Milutin, spurred on by a soldier's ambition, had so far turned his face away from women's eyes. His ears heard not that sweet undertone chant of Love which thrills still trembling through a lonely world. And no fair woman yet had chained him in the golden links which bind. But, as she listened, Countess Xenia said softly, " How can I help you ? "

" Dournof said that I was to appeal to you. It drives me mad to think of my lonely father, hidden away up there in the clefts of the Ural. What shock of sudden sorrow has driven him into the magnificent solitude of that lonely castle. True, he still goes out to the chase, but his day is done. I appeal to you, but, if you cannot aid me, I shall then speak to the Grand Duke. He has ridden often shoulder to shoulder, in the charge with my father. And I shall ask him to break in upon this unreasoning sorrow. I will not have my father eaten up by a heart-canker. The cure shall be found. It must be found ! Help me to discover it."

"Tell me, Boris," the Countess said, leaning earnestly forward, " have you ever seen anything to alter your father's usual poised calm ? " She eyed the young colonel with deep interest.

" Nothing, nothing !" the soldier said, as he leaned his pale brow in thought upon his crutch. " Only this strange aversion to lovely Nimovitch ! For the intendant there writes me that my father has never visited it once, since he gave his detailed orders for its care and maintenance. That was about the time of the sad Polish insurrection. Why he should not even look at the costly improvements and extensions, I cannot say. For, he has provided the most liberal employment for all the surrounding peasantry. Even the old house-servants of the first regime are living there yet. Now, he gives this place to me—he bids me never to sell it,—and yet, he himself would never set foot upon it. It is strange. Can there be some sad old story ? "

" Were you not with him there at the time of the outbreak ? " said the lady, with a gentle craft. Boris shook his head. " I was away on a four months' reconnoissance, under secret orders, inspecting all our posts in Poland. We, my Cossacks and I, were really thrown out to tempt the first mad attacks of the angry Poles. It is not the only time that I have been used as a mere pawn, in the bloody game of war. I never saw my father after, until I joined him a year later, at Alexandrowno on the Aral Sea. Tell me, did he buy this place, or was it allotted to him by the Crown? Have you ever been there? What has become of the family who last owned it?" Boris was moodily musing.

"Your father bought it from a noble who left Poland,—never to return. I know nothing of his fate," the lady answered.

And Boris Milutin, following his roving thoughts, never noticed that fair Xenia de Berg had passed over in fear and trembling, one crucial question.

"Thank God! He does not know, the past!" the Countess reflected, and strove to hide her tell-tale blushes.

The old servants at Nimovitch still remembered the graceful stranger lady who had tried in vain to learn from them if Cecile Wizocka's foot had ever wandered back to the dreaming lake of Nimovitch. But, the empty picture-frame still hung on the wall of the great salon, whence her portrait had been cut, and, even Vassili Milutin had learned of this strange happening first from the Countess, after her incognito visit to the deserted chateau.

Polish aversion still sealed the lips of all the old pensioners at the lonely chateau, and even the winds, wailing in the woods of Nimovitch, seemed to always whisper, "No more —never again!" There was no sign in all these years of the sweet woman who, as a girl-wife, had seen the crystal waters of the lake reflect back her glowing face in those days of brief happiness, and had later murmured her sorrows to the faithful trees of the Lovers' Walk. The charm had fled forever! Vassili Milutin, in far Asia, had groaned in sorrow, as the letters of Countess Xenia told him of her failure, and never a single whisper in Warsaw, brought back the sad story of the Lost Beauty.

"She is hiding somewhere from me! Her pride, her white-souled honor, protesting against the false position of a nameless woman, has crucified her in her loneliness. She still lives! But, my God, where?" The man holding his clasped hands on high, in the vain agony of a midnight sorrow, thought of these silent rows of convent cells, the dim cold churches, where, behind the old screens, dividing this world of sorrows from the world of shadows, the white-faced nuns knelt. He dreamed of all the lonely retreats where woman hides her crushed and bruised heart from man! "She has gone out of my life!" he groaned. And yet love's torture came again, six months later, when he had in his helplessness only begged Countess Xenia in answer to still wait and watch. He was called back to his long struggle against time and distance. For, it seemed as if her foot-fall lightly echoed in his heart again. An officer of high rank coming to Asia direct from St. Petersburg handed to him a sealed packet from the war office. It only contained a little enclosure without any external mark. There were tears in the great General's eyes as he gazed upon a little parchment strip bearing a few words which thrilled his sorrowing heart to its last hidden cell. "If it is hard to suffer, Vassili, remember that you do not suffer alone! I love you now, more than when I went away. I am still the Cecile of old. God be with you always!"

And, the parchment was tied through a little ring he had given her—a love-token—at Sorrento. It was a cluster of sapphires fashioned in a golden forget-me-not. The sickening suspense of the last years had broken down the stern soldier, when he learned that the pseudo "General Michael Waldberg" still lived in his easy retirement in some place on the continent; then the General knew why it was still useless to pursue further the woman who would not face the shame of a life of ignominy. "She knows of his existence, the traitor cur, and can it be only for her child's sake that she hides?" One ray of hope still lit up his sorrowful heart, "Cecile is far lifted above all lying and deceit. Love's miracle may yet be worked in the strange purposes of Fate!" And he bided his time, for her golden token showed to him that he was still held to her heart by the dear and unforgotten memories of the days when she had learned, against her own warring will, to love him.

"There is a hidden mystery in all this," insisted the wounded Colonel. "He was always very fond of the Sorrento place, too, and it had long been in the family. He sold it abruptly, and I myself always reverenced it, for my mother had dwelt there once. I am sure that some sad event which happened on his leave of absence, has given him an aversion to these two localities. Yet the one, he sells to mere strangers in the open market, and the other, I am bound in honor to always keep. To all my prayers, he has answered that he will never leave Orenburg unless the Czar should absolutely need his sword again. ' I am not too old to die yet, sword in hand,' he wrote, ' but, Boris, you are in the full sunshine of youth and life. Let me sit here among my mountain-shadows, in peace.' Perhaps if you, Countess, were to write to General Dournof, and then we all would work together, this mystery could be cleared up. I do not want my father's succession. He had always placed a very handsome revenue at my disposal, with no cavil. But to see him, driven like a mountain-eagle to that lonely eyrie, poisons my whole daily life, and embitters even these dear days of rest with you."

" I will think it all over," kindly replied the fair Russian widow. In all the later days of Boris Milutin's tedious recovery, Countess Xenia narrowly watched the brilliant young officer. "Thank God he knows nothing; but I am sure that General Dournof must have fathomed this sacred sorrow."

And it was true that Dournof's only answer in later days was, "Find that lost woman ! She is even now only at her zenith of beauty. Such a nature cannot always hide itself. Bring them once more together, and you will work Love's miracle."

The lively little Countess Vera was doomed to unwillingly give up her unsuccessful researches into the antecedents of their neighbors, for any further progress was stopped by the reserve of the attendants and the guarded prudence of even the tradesmen. On the hills of Loschwitz, in the great bend of the Elbe near Dresden, villa after villa, chateau and modest retreat, newer flaring palace of the money king, and stately old mansions of storied history, shelter the tired worldlings who have sought a final peace and cozy retirement there. Nerve-broken Americans, sturdy, comfort-loving Teutons, cosmopolitan English, and representatives from the whole polite world, climb the shady roads and pleasant inclines in their carriages for long years, and merely bend a curious eye on each other in passing. Egoism à la mode.

"It is a real mystery, at any rate," the laughing girl still insisted, as she teased her adopted "uncle," in the later days of his growing convalescence. "Our gardener exchanges the floral compliments of his innocent trade with theirs. A beautiful lonely girl, an invalid father, who shuns all society, and they do say that the old gray house is a very dream of luxury. But the strangest thing is, that these two live entirely alone. And, the father alone comes and goes occasionally, but always at night. Five years ago this rich stranger bought this dear old place, and has since lived alone there. A few men, foreigners, mostly, one by one, come and go occasionally. When, two years ago, the hidden beauty came home, the new attendants brought were all strangers, and this unbroken reserve thus gave rise to every strange fancy."

It was with a lingering curiosity that Boris Milutin turned his eyes on the quaint old structure. Builded long before the thunders of Napoleon's cannon shook the valley of Dresden, the mansion was a quaint old four-storied hall, with a stable foundation of solid granite. Its gray masonry walls rose high under a huge over-shadowing pyramidal roof. Its sameness was broken by the quaint old dormer windows of southern Germany. Placed so that one façade formed the side of a level street lane, the triangular inclosed garden swept downward, with a steep road on each side, leading toward the linden-shaded main avenue, skirting the river. A high stone wall with capping columns, crowned with sculptured antique vases, hid the fantastic grottoes, and summer gardens. Here, the long trellised archway of grape-vines, and the plashing of a flowing crystal fountain, lulled the wounded soldier to rest, on the long summer afternoons. Green window-shades jealously shut out the light, and the climbing vines threw tendrils of graceful tracery over the mossy walls. It was an ideal home for the wearied scholar, the world-worn wayfarer, but to ardent Boris Milutin, it seemed as if the graceful girl whose form flitted lightly among the trees, must find the shade of the old orchards wearying, and tire of the silence of the grassy terraces, broken only by the noisy grasshopper, or the chime of the distant bells of Dresden.

In the long autumn afternoons, Boris Milutin began to feel the blood of health stirring in his heart. The wine of life, which had been poured out under the Turcoman sabre, was now bounding gaily in his strengthened pulses. In the frank friendship with the delicate Countess Xenia, he found a needed repose of mind, and the rest of a soldier between war's alarm. Bright-eyed, laughing Vera was soon his delighted cicerone, as they drove over the hills daily, in search of varying scenes of smiling contentment. It was pleasant on the banks of the Elbe, where the mountain breezes, sweeping down, told their stories of far crested heights, crowned with singing forests.

There was no thought of any love between Boris and the bright girl at his side. Knitted to her mother by a common devotion to the grand old soldier, his father, now lingering alone in his lofty eyrie at Orenburg, the young man had easily glided into that delightful brotherhood of the heart, which awakens every man's best and noblest inspirations.

So, it was not love that he whispered to the budding Countess, in their long daily pilgrimages, for his scarcely healed wounds yet prevented his walking far afield. He told the fair-browed girl stories of strange past mischances on the burning deserts of Turkestan ; of ruined cities, buried far beyond the Caspian, where the tottering gates of the palaces of the old Emirs still bore aloft their gilded inscriptions to Allah.

For, fierce Genghis Khan, sweeping down into the unpro·tected heart of Asia, had brought with him the fighting Mongol hordes, to rule over the diamond oases of the once vast realm of romantic Turkestan. The pagan horsemen soon learned to bow to Mahomet's Allah, and to smite in his name with the edge of the fanatic sword, even as the great Norse warriors sought to heighten their battle frenzy by invoking the blessing of the mild-eyed Nazarene ! The great Latin race later, with upraised cross, carried a hungry sword over the plains of bleeding Europe, and decimated the fair unspoiled new world with a fearful profanation of Constantine's old motto, " In hoc signo vinces." Boris, with a soldier's frankness, painted all the wild camp-life—the romantic chivalry of the warring Moslem tribes—and these scenes, unrolling like a varied panorama, sketched by a master-hand, thrilled the heart of the young girl, as she clung to his side and whispered : " If I were only a man, I would be a soldier, too ! "

Countess Xenia, always narrowly watching the young

colonel's face, waited warily lest some chance discovery might yet lift the veil shrouding the unfathomed mystery of the Lady of Nimovitch.

But only a son's love agitated Boris Milutin's heart. He had always lingered in respect without his father's threshold, until summoned to the brief confidences of his proud heart. The fierce passion-play of Vassili Milutin's life, and his devotion to the service of the " White Czar," had lifted him high above all petty intrigue, and the banal adventures of the salon. Stern, silent, and great, in a soul which had never been softened by long years of womanly tenderness, Vassili Milutin looked back with an intense devotion to the memory of the gentle Russian wife of his youth, who had died, leaving to him her infant son, as her only reminder, as that of one who had smiled, lingered for a few brightening moments, and then, passed out, alone, to the great unknown of the Sea of Death, with gently smiling eyes.

The distance born of military discipline, the marked respect due to the Russian patriarchal family life, had held his son at the friendly arm's-length of a distant love really fondly cherished for the great commander, the Czar's splendid general.

It was to Countess Xenia de Berg alone that Vassili Milutin had in any manner, ever unfolded the treasured secrets of his rugged heart. It seemed to the stern-eyed noble, hidden in his far rocky gorges of the Ural, that the loved and lost was always brought nearer to him in this commune with one who had seen her, in her matchless loveliness, as the star of that great social pageant, which showed her first to his eyes. Unconsciously, Vassili Milutin had discovered that all women strangely love a faithful lover, and the gentle widowed Countess in her letters, which were now the only light of the self-exiled man's heart, often strove to speak to him for the one who was still hidden from his sight. " How he has loved her ! How tenderly ! How truly ! " and the Countess prayed in her inmost soul that Love's miracle might yet be invoked to calm that proud and faithful heart, beating alone in a sad unrest. She knew well that the tenderest loves of this strange, strange world are seldom gratified with the smiles of fickle fortune ! That the steadiest stars of mighty Love shine down often from afar. Sweeping on around the beloved one unceasing in their swing, they only glitter through those gray distances which ever separate the two loving souls, beating as one, across the gulf of the Impossible !

She knew well the golden seam of manly devotion entwined in the fibres of the passion which drew him still to the lost one. For, it was a sadly proven truth, that the Lady of Nimovitch, in her wild protest against the baseness of the life she would have to lead as the wife of the dishonored pensioner of treason, had escaped a slavery of shame only by pressing the crown of thorns of a guilty love upon her saddened brow. Her noble nature could not live this lower life, and, of the two parted lovers, in all these years of oblivion, Countess Xenia knew that the loving woman had suffered the most !

For, the capacity of woman, Love's handmaiden, is infinite when she, herself, bears the misery ! It is only in inflicting it on others, that the gentle bosom softens and relents, yielding up a regretted sacrifice upon the altar of her lover's suffering.

" She has truly loved him always. And, she would have him true to her still, even in these hours of pain." The gentle Countess bowed her head, in a fond wish that the clouds might yet be lifted, and the parted ones be brought face to face once more. The token of the sapphire ring had told her of the womanly love still vibrating at the touch of memory, somewhere in the far unknown lonely paths. General Dournof's hope-tinted letters filled the Countess with a renewed zeal, to find the banished lady. He wrote with a loving zeal. His heart had one frail spar to cling to on the dark sea of Fate.

" I have, on a pretext of some of the Czar's affairs, sent one of my favorite staff of officers to linger for a week in General Milutin's hospitable hall. I am more than ever anxious now. He must be lifted out of himself, and some great happening alone will do it. It is useless for me to act alone. My gallant brother of the sword shrinks daily deeper into the solitude of his princely sorrow. If you and his only son cannot rouse him, then I am powerless. If you would only discover the faintest new clue to the lost one, then, I know that he would search to the very ends of the earth, until he would find her. For, my friend, I am sure that he still dreams of the hope that she could be his wife. He would ex-piate the days of guilty passion ! Sweet as enjoyment is, to a man like Vassili Milutin, atonement has also its golden seal of perfect happiness ! This failing, I can tell you, in our con-fidence of the past years, that our strained relations with our old foes, the Turkish power, are surely swinging us into the shock of a bloody war. Boris will be sure to nobly win his generalship in that struggle, I know ; but, I am rejoiced to think that his father is still splendidly vigorous, and his scarcely-silvered hair shines over a brow fresh and manly yet. The Emperor would at once call him into the council of the very highest commands. No man knows the Danube and the Principalities better than Vassili Milutin, and his laurels gained in Asia Minor, are all unwithered still. To be brought back into the fiery glow of great events would surely chase away these crowding dreams of a lost love, a vanished past, ever lingering in his lonely heart. You may look at any time for a rupture between Russia and Turkey. Nicolas Ignatief at Constantinople is busied like a tiger at play. His brain-work is ceaseless and untiring, and the marvellous game of the intricate Eastern Question is being played once more, upon the banks of the Bosphorus.

Countess Xenia and Colonel Milutin were returning one evening from a fête at Dresden on the Emperor's birthday, when a carriage slowly followed them up the beautiful linden avenues of Loschwitz. The Colonel chancing to turn, said lightly, "There is Vera's living mystery: our pretty neighbor of the Gray House." The soldier had grown to find an idle occupation in watching the very window at which a distant face sometimes showed its smiles to the lovely world dreaming around. Below him in the dim and fragrant paths of the picturesque old garden he could often see her robes flutter-ing through the long rose arbor where she walked, followed by an attendant Ulmer dog, of splendid proportions and characteristic fidelity. Her voice, raised in lonely song, was borne up to him by the frolic winds, and the officer grew at last to wonder if her chanted words were loving or longing! He divided the childish interest of sprightly Vera, now tri-umphant in the forfeited gloves, so happily yielded up. He grew to a strange distant devotion to the beautiful girl who haunted the sylvan shades over his neighbor's wall. And, though never seen face to face, Boris Milutin had yet brought back romance enough from the vales of Tashkend to swear that she was beautiful. He had often marked at night and in the early morn, the rattle of wheels as the master of the Gray House came and went on occasional journeys. A glimpse of a stately man slowly walking at the girl's side was the only proof to Boris Milutin that a master of the Gray House existed in the flesh.

"What can he have to hide? What schemes of portent, what dark heart-history lurks beyond the mossy copings of the embattled walls of this lonely mansion?" Milutin had hitherto lightly passed it over, for the thousand and one filaments of intrigue are interlaced in every European capital.

"He will probably be known to the world only by the conspicuous failure of his plans," moralized Milutin, who had early learned that harvests are gathered only in the open sunlight, and not in the dark obscurity of midnight shadows! With his mind attuned to a daily musing over his father's brooding state, the young Colonel dropped at last the enigma of the life of the recluse of the Gray House from his mind. It was to the woman, whose unseen face he had painted as beautiful as a veiled Fatima, as fair as ever had looked out under the palms and orange groves of Bagdad, that the young soldier's romantic soul sued at a distance.

The shade of a passing carriage caused Boris Milutin to look out hastily, as for the first time his eyes rested on the face of the young girl who had chased sleep away so often from the eyelids of laughing Vera. He turned gently as his eyes fell with the polite self-restraint of a man, preux chevalier in all his ways. "Heavens! She is beautiful!" he softly murmured, and then he turned his eyes in a gay triumph upon the Countess, sitting silently at his side. And, by the telegraphy of awakened memory, before he addressed Countess Xenia, his soul was borne back to old days.

"I have seen that face before—that very face—that same beautiful woman!"

He spoke gaily. "Vera was right. She is a Russian!" and his voice changed to a sudden note of alarm as he cried, "Are you ill? What has happened?"

The lady shivered slightly, and only answered, as she drew her rich furs closer round her: "I am very chilly. Bid him drive on faster. It is nothing. It will pass over." And they swept quickly up to their beautiful villa, while Boris Milutin's eyes turned from the agitated hostess to the retreating carriage which dashed in through the opened gates of the Gray House.

Vera de Berg sprang forth to meet them with a happy smile, and was startled at her mother's ashen face. "What can have happened?" It was only behind the sheltering doors of her own boudoir that Xenia de Berg, sinking into the nearest chair, murmured :

" There can be no mistake here. And it was one face in a thousand. I must watch her, and watch Boris ! For, here I have found the missing clue. This beautiful child !"

All the long evening, secure in her own rooms from any self-betrayal, Countess Xenia listened to little Vera's sweet carols as she archly sang the passionate songs of Russia to her gallant guest. Boris Milutin, his eyes straying away from the fair singer, uneasily turned over in his mind all the passing beauty-show of his eventful youngest days. He smiled even in his earnestness. " Is it some one that I have dreamed of in another world ? The world of sleep, of rosy dreams ! Is it some embodied verification of some lost love romance whose pictured words have left a living memory thrilling in my heart ? " And so, he strove to recall every line and loving tint upon the sweet face radiant in the sweet flush of early womanly beauty which had flashed but one look at him from those deep, dark eyes. " I must—I shall see her again ! " he muttered. For the " mystic chords of memory " were now thrilling tenderly in his heart. All the days of his gay boyhood, when, a page at the Winter Palace, he first learned to watch the light of women's eyes, all the gilded scenes of the glittering apprenticeship of the Guards, came back, and yet, in the unrolling of all the pictured loveliness still lingering in his heart, he could not find the vanished shadow-face again. He bent his head in a reverie. " If I have dreamed of this fair woman in my strange life, by field and camp, she is no longer a sweet dream, for I shall look upon her witching face again. I cannot lose her ! " It was, indeed, true that the instant touch of the arch magician had waked the silent music in his heart which would echo on forever in increasing sweetness and with gathered power. For, the voice of a sudden love had broken the dreaming silence of his heart. Some hidden spirit in his soul whispered to him, " She is thine ! She is thine ! She waits for thee ! "

There was a hidden purpose in all his movements in the days which followed this accidental meeting on the Loschwitz highway. Countess Xenia, bending daily over her letters, was still the prey of every possible conjecture which could call up the outcome of the now forgotten tragedy of Nimovitch. Her mind was absolutely fixed upon the unravelling of the web which fate had woven around Vassili Milutin's unhappy lost love.

" It would be only a wretched cruelty to give him a sign now," she finally decided, but, every gentle womanly art she had learned in the wide experience of an almost queenly social life, was exerted to break the seal of the brooding mystery of the Gray House. The Russian officials at Dresden knew nothing of any family of rank, such as were the inmates of the Gray House on the Loschwitz hills. All the daily affairs of the luxuriously maintained mansion were transacted by reliable male attendants, and the days wore slowly on, in disappointment. Only one little gleam of light shone through the darkness hiding the long quest of years. General Dournof had written, " There was a child there. I know not positively, but I think that it was a girl." And the Countess clung with a new hope to this faint confirmation of the value of the clue. And yet the kingdom of Saxony was filled with the refugees of the Polish Land of Sorrow. This type of face—patrician and tender—was distinctive of the loveliness of the higher-born daughters of Piast and Jagellon. " I must not dare even to hope," murmured Countess Xenia. And so, she hid her busy quest in Dresden—her one innocent secret, from the unsuspecting Boris and gay Vera whose overflowing girlhood happiness now filled every sunny day. But, the Countess needed not to blind the eyes of Colonel Boris Milutin.

There were glances bent upon the terrace when the wounded noble lingered which were armed with some magic power, for Boris often smiled, and Boris often sighed, as he walked each day, nearer to the garden-wall!

CHAPTER VIII.

COUNTESS XENIA DE BERG had made no advances, a month later, in the following of the shadowy clue which had aroused her heart to the utmost efforts of friendship. The threads of her old Warsaw friendships had been run over in vain. Letters after letters returning to her, bore the same unvarying responses. Nothing had ever been heard of the fate of the Polish beauty of the sad rebellion year. A last expedient suggested itself. Years had elapsed since the incognito visit which had been fruitless of results at Nimovitch. "Perhaps, now, if Boris went there, his naturally awakened curiosity might loosen the tongues of some of the old dependents. They may be willing themselves to try and follow the fates of the gracious lady who once ruled them so kindly in the old days." Count de Berg's old steward, the master of ceremonies of his house for twenty-five years, was a thoroughly trustworthy retainer. "If I could only induce Boris to visit Nimovitch, his new domain, I could send Ivan Ivanoff with him. A little money and a great deal of vodki, might unlock the seal of the passing years. And, my old Russian major-domo, a very Richelieu of the Lower Hall, could soon probe the minds of the dull Russian servants who now wait there for the master who comes not." The Countess was doomed to a new disappointment, for Colonel Boris Milutin was at last able to travel. He was in fact ready to follow up his original plan of going to glittering Paris, where the very highest honors awaited him at the Russian Imperial Embassy.   But, though a new light shone in his eyes, and his feeble step was fast changing to its old elastic stride, he lingered on at Dresden ! His crutches had long been laid aside, and his tall form was seen at dewy morning, on all the beautiful footpaths of Loschwitz.   With Vera at his side, he sought out the very last attractions of the river banks, and the galleries and museums of Dresden were also his frequent resort.   The Countess saw no tell-tale flush upon the young man's face, as he pleasantly said, " Some fairy of the Elbe has certainly bewitched me.   Are there Nixies and Loreleie still lingering here, as well as under the star reflecting waters of the Rhine.   This place has grown strangely dear to me."   He laughingly put away the suggestion of a flying visit to his treasure trove, Nimovitch.   " It is time enough to go there when I am an old worn-out General.   But, a Turcoman's sword may cut off the line of promotion."   He relapsed into a lover's artful silence.   Two things were hidden behind his ready answer.   Though a very Russian of the Russians, he still remembered the dark closing days of the insurrection of 1863, with a true soldier's shame.   It was the work of the unstained sword he bore, to meet the wild Poles, pouring out of the tangles of their forests, and to fight, to the bitter death upon the barricaded roads, toilfully hewed by the Russian columns in those gloomy shades, in that partisan war. But, the upturned faces of the scattered dead lying there still haunted him.   The struggle had ended in untold barbarities which shocked his gallant soul.   Manhood had lost its last generous impulses on both sides l   The wounded and helpless Russians had been burned in their hospital wagons. Their sick officers had been poisoned in the villages that lay there, stricken with the burning marsh fevers.   And Polish prisoners had been pinioned by the Russians and half buried in the earth, for the wolf and the raven to batten on.

He had seen the wild marauders charging out, bearing the

awful signal of the black flag! It was a war to the death! The Muscovites, roused to the sternest reprisals, had filled the forests with swaying bodies dangling from the nearest oak-limbs! The Polish crosses and memorial crucifixes were used freely for the soldier's bivouac fires, the chateaux and houses rifled and devastated, while the maddened camp-followers of Mouravieff's fierce host plundered the peasants, Russian, Jew, and Pole alike. On the roads, half-starved peasant fugitives were found whose arms had been loosely flayed, in imitation of the Polish flowing sleeves of their rebel countrymen.

In the burning villages, abandoned to the vodki-crazed Russian soldiery, only helpless womanhood was left to suffer under the lusts of the victors, for Milutin had seen the last men, not hidden under the bloody sword, driven away in chained lines, to face General Michel Mouravieff's reeking death-shambles, or dragged, heart-broken, far away to Siberia.

Not a spark of gallantry had characterized the warfare of either side! The Russian soldiers were crazed by the gloomy horrors of the forests which they floundered in, and mutual treachery, stratagem, and dissimulation marked the absence of any laws of civilized war.

A circle of Russian officers, cut off in a distant country city, had been deluded to a ball, on the very evening of the carefully-planned uprising, and, on the next day, the fair women who had clasped them in the dance, drove over their dead bodies lying in the village streets, without a sigh, as these excited women fled to the shelter of the insurgent camps. Guilty Judiths. "No, I do not wish ever to go back to the scenes of that awful struggle!" mused Boris. Even the money which would be his, ground out of the cowering peasants by the alien intendant who now ruled at Nimovitch, was unwelcome to him. It seemed to be blood-money!

"What is money to me? I have money enough!" he gloomily thought, as he sought in vain the reason of his absent father laying upon him the strange injunction never to sell this unknown domain of Nimovitch! Vassili Milutin was silent as to his real reason. He would not breathe it to the gentle woman who had hidden herself in her inmost chamber of the Chateau Royal at Warsaw, when the heavy platoon volleys told of the slaughter of the desperate students in the market-place. "De Berg was in command there. He had to do his bounden duty! I would not call back that awful past to her." But, the real reason of his delay, was the strange attraction which the lovely woman hidden in the Gray House now exerted on his awakened soul. Boris was a strange compound of the man of the world, and the superstitious Russ. He had learned all the fatalism of the Orient among the wild dwellers by the far Jaxartes. And, keenly watching his hostess and the spirited little Countess, he hid within a soldier's proud heart the strangely-awakened passion which was called to life by the sweet face which swept past him on that autumn day. It is over and again true that mighty Love is the unchallenged lord of time and place! A strange new growth filled Boris Milutin's heart. He lingered near the unknown, on the hills of Loschwitz, hoping that the stars of fate would shine some day kindly on his nightly dream of hearing her voice, and drinking of the unawakened love which filled that young girl's slumbering heart.

Neither at the theatre or the opera, had he ever seen her, and his glass swept the rows of boxes nightly, without result. The daily mystery of her secluded life grew in the youthful Colonel's heart. And, after all his secret efforts had been proved fruitless, he began to think of going on farther toward the Atlantic, or of rejoining his loved comrades in the command fighting on the Aral Sea.

A gala night at the Dresden Theatre found Boris Milutin —for the very last time—searching in the great audience to see the face of the woman who occupied his thoughts. It was near the time of his departure, for the young man had at last given up all hope. "I will go back to Petersburg. I will try in one last attempt to rouse my father from his lonely life; then, from Orenberg, I can go down the Ural River and rejoin my command." General Dournof had sent to him confidential enclosures to be delivered at once, by the son, in the hopes that the old patrician would return to a world which once charmed him.

The advent of a great new actress had aroused on this night, all the local interest in a magnificent presentation of Schiller's Marie Stuart. Borne on the wings of fame, from Austria and Italy, from France and even England, the renown of the great artist had preceded her. Colonel Milutin, from the nearest proscenium box, was leisurely scanning face after face, as the magnificent theatre slowly filled to overflowing. Beautiful Countess Xenia had left for once, her usual retirement, and dozens of levelled glasses attested the interest excited by the Russian aristocrate and her rose-like child.

Boris dropped his glasses at last with a sigh. It was his only chance to verify the promise of the passing face, the distant glimpses of the hours when he had strayed near the garden wall to gaze on the fair girl straying under her rose vines. He had not noted the rise of the curtain, and it was only when he heard the clear crystalline resonance of a matchless voice, that he turned and closely regarded the new idol of the public. Across the wide stage he could only see a woman ripely beautiful in form and face, and whose magic voice breathing the lines of genius swayed all hearts as she grandly moved in the pathetic helplessness of Scotland's ill-starred queen. The house was breathless in its riveted interest, and with heads bent forward and heaving breasts, the vast audience sat thrilled by the moving play of this new Rachel. Boris Milutin dropped his eyes in the abandonment of his awakened interest, and the sonorous rhythm swept across his soul like the breathings of a wind harp. He did not share in the thunders of applause which greeted the fall of the curtain. He was spellbound. He was lulled into the thoughts of his own adverse fate, for the one face he sought did not kindle at the genius of the beautiful woman whose presence before the curtain was demanded with a general wild acclaim. As he bent forward to gaze again upon the face which was to appear from the shelter of the curtain already drawn backward, at the wing nearest them, pretty Vera de Berg pressed his hand, with a low murmur of sudden delight. Following instinctively the girl's shy glance, he slowly turned, and saw, seated in the next box, the loved object of his silent passion. The young beauty of the Gray House had silently entered, and her wistful dark eyes met his in one look which made his soul ring with the awakened echoes of his silent heart! He had not a single moment to scan the face of the man who, seated in the rear of the woman he had found at last, looked out through the lace veil of the box to the player-queen who was now hailed by a thousand voices, with the wildest bravas. Colonel Milutin's eyes suddenly sought the countenance of Countess Xenia who was gazing spellbound at the great actress, who turned and swept her dark magnetic eyes slowly down the line of boxes to where Boris himself now gazed at her in astonishment.

"By heavens!" he gasped, as he leaned forward to grasp the hand of the still spellbound Countess Xenia. The actress faced them both now, and a sudden look of frozen horror fixed her face in one fleeting expression of indignation and scorn. Before the Russian officer could turn his head to whisper to Countess Xenia, a brief smothered cry in the next box startled him, as the sound of a heavy fall alarmed the three friends! There was no second thought in the impulse which carried Boris to the door of the rear ante-room of the neighboring proscenium box. All he saw, as the attendants hurried to the door, was a lovely girl, bending over the prostrate form of a gray-haired man, who lay across the door between the box and the anteroom, as he had fallen, senseless. It was the recluse of the Gray House !

His quick ear caught the language of the endearing appeals of the distracted girl, and while the earnest officials crowded around the prostrate man, Milutin murmured in all the earnestness of his soul : "Let me aid you, pray, for I, too, am a Russian ! "

At the beck of a grave-faced surgeon, the startled girl was led away by the man who had sprung to her side, at the first cry of her frightened heart. He drew her gently to the spot where Countess Xenia and Vera gazed in affright from their door.

The music of the entracte swelled out high in its majestic sweep, and but few had noticed the accident to the man who had been veiled from general view by his hidden position. While the mother and daughter sought to soothe the girl's alarm, Boris Milutin himself waited at the closed door of the box.

"Does any one know him ? " asked a sub-intendant of the theatre, in a muffled voice, speaking at the door. " The doctor says this is a serious syncope, and he must be removed at once to his home, after a free blood-letting. The slightest panic here might cost us a thousand lives ! "

It was true ! The excitement of the audience had carried them up to that nervous tension in which excited men do the very wildest deeds. In a few words, Boris told of the tenancy of the Gray House.

"You are his neighbor ? " the polite official asked.

"Madame la Comtesse de Berg, my hostess, is here with her daughter. Her villa adjoins this gentleman's home."

"Pray, present me," said the officer, who in a moment had explained to the frightened daughter that her father would be at once removed under the care of the officials. "If Madame would be so kind as to at once retire, with this young lady, it may prevent a scene of excitement, and perhaps a public tumult. I will myself quietly call your carriage, and you can be at home, ready to receive your father on his arrival. Trust me in all! It is imperative!"

The lady who had ruled so long at Warsaw, with stately dignity made herself known to the trembling girl. "It is better so, my child," she kindly said. "Let us escort you home." And, preceded by Colonel Milutin, the three ladies passed out behind the row of boxes into the foyer. Countess Xenia and Vera were already at the door of their carriage, when the agitated girl, suddenly seizing Boris Milutin's arm, cried, "Let me wait and see him, at least, on his way home." And so, while the mother and daughter waited, the officer stood with the unknown beauty gasping at his side, at the foot of the great marble stairway, as eight men carried the still unconscious sufferer down on a hurdle, which had been passed in from the stage door. It needed all the protestations of the chief intendant to persuade the frightened daughter to turn her face homewards. In the gloom of the late night, with no words spoken, Boris Milutin sat in the carriage, with pretty Vera nestling at his side. Across the cramped interior, he could see the eyes of the woman whom he had so long vainly sought. Her breathing sobs told of a loving heart, and the trembling tears on her drooping lashes appealed, in silence, to the young Russian's heart.

Boris Milutin, at thirty-five, had the lesson of love to learn, and here, with her graceful and delicate form near his own, in the sympathy of her sudden sorrow, the young girl's heart seemed to call him to the side of the friendless one so strangely met. Milutin had been busied at the theatre with his strange responsibility, and had not been able to see the face of the man as it lay turned away, and covered by the crowding forms of the attendants, who had run the gauntlet of their dangerous pathway.

All was safe at last, when the door of the intendant's

room closed, but Boris Milutin did not see two eager faces peering down at the prostrate man, as he was lifted from the hurdle into the room where the surgeons waited now. "Yes, the very man!" a man of glittering eyes hoarsely whispered to his friend, as the carriages rolled away.

"What will you do, Stanislas," muttered a dark-faced man, who sought to restrain his too eager companion.

"I shall take the midnight train for Paris!" said the other, who cried "Come on!" and drew the speaker quickly out into the friendly darkness of the night.

Delicacy kept the Russian officer still silent while they approached the hills of Loschwitz, dreaming under the silent stars. "But, I shall know her now," the soldier cried in his rejoicing heart, and his supporting arm thrilled at her touch, when he aided the young stranger up the walk leading to the doors of the mysterious Gray House. The gentle proffers of Countess Xenia, of further assistance, had been declined by the girl, who said, with murmured thanks, "I have begged the intendant to send for our own physician at once, and our household is perfectly familiar with my father's delicate health. This has been his very worst attack."

At the door Boris Milutin only saw again, as the frightened servants stood in wonder, the sweet dark face in all its virginal beauty. She turned, and, pressing both his hands, murmured her thanks, in a voice which left the soldier lingering there in tenderness, as she hastened to direct her household to receive the coming sufferer. Long after the sound of the carriage-wheels had died away, and the sufferer had been aided to his own home, Colonel Milutin walked alone in the night air, under the sweeping branches of the chestnuts in the garden. Few lights gleamed from the fair upper chamber-windows of the old Gray House, and moving athwart the lighted space the Russian noble thought he could descry the graceful form of the sweet girl who had gratefully murmured the "Good-night," still thrilling in his every pulse!

It was only when the morning came, at last, that Boris reflected that he knew little or nothing more of the veiled mystery. In eagerly searching the journals for some mention of the incident, the soldier was again baffled, for beyond the triumphs of the great artist, no mention was made recalling the accident. An unusual wait of the acts was attributed to the effect upon the foreign genius of her triumphant reception in the city on the Elbe.

"It is strange," murmured Boris, as he left the presence of Countess Xenia next morning, for a furtive visit to Dresden. Xenia was almost spell-bound by this woman's appearance, and yet while Vera, too, was full of the artist's triumph, the hostess never spoke. In her own heart she was rejoiced at Boris' departure for a secret quest, for she murmured: "I see the missing clue at last; and if I am not deceived, there is no failure in this. It must be the lost one, and yet they say this genius is an Italian!"

"I regret that I cannot give you any particulars as to the identity of the gentleman who was removed from the theatre last night," said the polite box officer to Colonel Milutin, when that anxious explorer of mysteries stood before the window. "No one seems to know! The box was taken by a servant, and the theatre doctor did not ask the sufferer's name. The coachman of the stranger took him to his residence. I think, however, that he is a Russian," musingly said the official. "Very strangely, another person has also been pressing the same inquiry this morning, and so eagerly that I had actually to be rude to him. But, Dresden is always full of strangers. I would suggest, sir, that you apply to the Russian consul-general, who surely knows all his compatriots, of any note."

Colonel Milutin returned to Loschwitz at nightfall, and had already determined to make a further personal inquiry, when he learned that Countess Xenia had received a note of cordial thanks from the beauty of the Gray House.

"Her father is still ill, but he is now in a fair way of recovery," said Countess Xenia, "and an offering of the most exquisite flowers accompanied her charming note. There it is," said Xenia, with a gentle smile.

And Boris Milutin felt all a lover's fondness, as he gazed at the few simple lines of grateful acknowledgment.

"Marguerite Waldberg," he repeated slowly. "It is strange. She evidently is a Russian. And yet, Waldberg is not a Russian name."

The mystery was still as deep as ever to the anxious soldier. To his chagrin, he had not even the excuse of etiquette to call and ask for the health of the invalid. The prompt acknowledgment of the lonely girl forbade all such intrusions. And so, he bided his time till the future should bring them together again.

A man who gloomily gazed from the car windows eagerly watched for the spires of Cologne on the next morning. It seemed as if some demon drove him on, for even the voyagers in the same compartment gazed in wonder at the dark burden of his face. He stayed not when the train reached the great station, but hurrying to the telegraph window, clutched a sealed paper, and then eagerly read its contents.

"At last," he muttered, "at last!" For the lines traced were: "It is the same man—named Michael Waldberg." Then, for the first time since leaving Dresden, the traveller smiled. But, it was a smile as cold as the last rays of the sun lighting up the Matterhorn, luring on to death and destruction with an unearthly glow.

Gentle Xenia de Berg blushed through her veil, as she drove away the next afternoon from her villa, where Boris sat, and revolved a thousand plans to break down the barriers of the young girl's strange shadowed life.

The lover knew that no dark secret of the past was written on her pure and stainless brow. No! The man who now fought alone his fight against the grim destroyer had the key of the enigma firmly locked in his own heart.

"There is some purpose in this concealment of their real state." An easy luxury was characterizing their secluded life. The father's secret voyages. The daughter's isolation. The death in life of their daily existence. What did it all mean? Boris Milutin knew that the stranger had passed beyond the period of life's gay hopes. "Then, he is either waiting or watching." And for all the young Russian failed to find any clue to the object for which the mysterious man waited under such repression, or to divine what ghastly overhanging doom he feared. A living double mystery!

Countess de Berg had resisted the appeals of ardent Vera to finish the interrupted star-worship of the memorable evening.

"Madame Mazzana is to be here only this one week. It is the third day already." And, alas! the little Countess Vera sadly found that for once her spell was unavailing. Her girlish witchery was for the first time powerless. Even when the Colonel joined the graceful girl in her entreaty, Countess Xenia was firm.

"I have never been very strong since—since the terrible scenes at Warsaw. I could not bear to face that theatre audience again. Our appearance in a party would again draw attention to the strange occurrence of the first night. And, I have also the most important affairs to transact at the Consulate."

"Ah, she is so grand, so noble, so royal in her queenly grief!" murmured Vera, who had drunk in every great flash of the heightened soul expression of the artist's eyes, and had thrilled at each rich modulation of her quavering voice, replete with every appealing accent of the woman's soul, waked by poetry to glowing action. The gentle mother sighed a present refusal.

"You shall see her again, my darling. Such a genius be-

longs to the world, to all time! I am going to take you
later to Italy. And as she plays at Milan, Florence, Rome,
and Venice, as well as Naples, you shall surely see her
again, when my nerves are once more calmed."

Kissing the lips of her child, Countess Xenia went on her
way alone. Her business "at the Consulate," led the widowed patrician to the quiet retreat bowered in the park-gardens
of Dresden, where the great actress sojourned during her
stay. The Russian lady feared to make any personal inquiries
on the subject nearest her heart now. "To what avail," she
murmured, as her carriage drew up at the door of the retired
villa. "I must see her face to face. And, if it is she, the
Lost Lady of Nimovitch, I shall know the truth beyond the
denial of even an actress before whose shrine of genius the
Continenal world bows." The story of Vassili Milutin's silent
sorrows, his clinging to the dear and vanished past, gave
Xenia de Berg a new strength beyond her wont. "I know
this woman's heart must be of a golden fibre. And, even I,
may touch it, and so, work Love's miracle."

The woman who only looked now with appealing eyes
beyond the sealed tomb of her gallant husband, for the
meeting in the dim Beyond, where all wounded hearts will
be bound up by the Healer, felt that the mute pleading of
the General's faithful love, and his loyal vigil of years, would
unlock the banners of even an injured woman's pride.

"She shall raise him, kneeling now before her picture graven
in his heart, to the level of the glowing woman breast which
loves him yet. Proof against luxury and temptation, perhaps, but, what woman is proof against the sufferings of her
loyal lover! I will see her."

In a dim salle d'attente, the Lady of Warsaw counted the
beatings of her heart, as the grave-faced Italian attendant
went noiselessly away, with the card which bore the simple inscription, "The Countess de Berg." Each moment dragged
along, and, with her every faculty sharpened by the intensity

of her emotions, by the gravity of the quest, which might even call back the Eagle of Orenburg to a fond woman's feet, Countess Xenia waited breathlessly.

She could even hear above her the movements of some one pacing the floor in hasty agitation. Her heart sank as she raised her eyes, and the major-domo tendered her a sealed letter. It was with a trembling hand that she took it from the silver salver, and it fell at her feet. When the servant regained it, she noticed, with a lightning intuition, the simple seal—a cluster of forget-me-nots. And, bitter, unavailing tears, filled her eyes as she read the courteous lines in which Madame Mazzana regretted the impossibility of breaking the rule of years. "If I could yield to a desire to bring the world which is veiled from me by the curtain of the theatre, nearer to me, it would afford me gratification to receive the Countess de Berg. It is with regret that I am obliged to say that I lead a life apart, and live only in the shadowy unrealities of the stage. But, let me hope that I shall see you again, in the vast sea of faces which thrills me to the highest exercise of my poor art! I shall know you, and your beautiful daughter, for the world has grown very—very small! And, thus, let me receive your sympathy and know you as a willing friend in the shadows—where I must always linger, and where I regret you must find a barrier —beyond the line of the footlights. And Countess de Berg knew in this guarded defence, that she had found the clue when she read the last words, "Do Swidanya!"

"Do Swidanya!" she murmured. Alas! though she would not lose him, a wall builded by Fate yet divides them! Love's miracle comes not yet! It is in truth, the Lost Lady of Nimovitch! There was no possible appeal, however, from the veiled decision of the letter, and alone and heavy-hearted, the lady drove down through the glories of the beautiful park of Dresden.

It seemed to Countess Xenia as if she alone suffered,—

but, bitterer than the gentle widow's regretful tears, sadder than the longings of the fiery Russian noble, who chafed now wrapped in the mantle of his lonely sorrows at Orenburg, were the sobs which rent the bosom of the woman on whose brows the fadeless laurel now rested. The actress secretly watching saw her visitor disappear!

"Vassili! Vassili!" a suffering woman cried as she watched the carriage sweep away, which bore Xenia de Berg back to her ceaseless imaginings. "It cannot be! For *he* still lives, and a nation's shame walks the earth in the person of the man who once was *my husband!*" And so, in the silence, where her pleading heart called out in vain, the agonized woman bowed her head! "And by his side, by his side, the child whom love brought to me, and whom sorrow has baptized! The child I dare not own!"

That night when the gathered thousands listened to Mazzana's voice swelling in the grand inspiration of Marie Stuart's woes, it was not Scotland's dainty, passionate, graceful queen of arts and hearts, who reigned before them! It was another queen of sorrows! A woman in whose bosom still thrilled the sorrows of a conquered race, of a lost land, a wife betrayed, a mother who wailed for the face of her child, a passionate human being chained to a love which had only brought to her love's last seal of sorrows, a death of absence in her useless life!

The generous Countess de Berg now bore in her bosom the proof which she had sought for years of the existence of Cecile Wizocka. The forget-me-not seal, the tender greeting "Do Swidanya!" and the written letter itself! A sudden impulse seized her as she passed the Gray House and entered her own gardens. "Shall I send this token to Vassili Milutin! Dare I call him on to the quest! What if he were to be led on by me only into deeper sorrows! She pondered during the long evening, while Boris and Vera walked the portico, from whence the enamored Colonel steadily watched the lights in the windows of the Gray House.

And, some whisper of fate murmured to the anxious woman, "Wait—wait, we are the high gods who dispose! and the hour has not yet come!"

"I will follow her to Naples! I will beat at the door of her heart, until—until I see her again walking in the sunshine of love, or I too will share the sorrows of her noble soul!" the Countess murmured, as the angel of sleep folded her in his wings, stealing in upon the sea of her troubled thoughts. For, a sharer of the dark scenes of the intrigues which had swept Cecile Wizocka from the princely home she once ruled, the generous-hearted Russian patrician pledged herself. "She shall be happy yet, happy once again, at Nimovitch!"

There was a new purpose in the visit which Countess de Berg contemplated as she prepared to essay the hitherto hidden mysteries of the Gray House. It was true that a daily message of compliment announced the slow recovery of the patient. Yet, a trace of the social arts learned in the Chateau Royal accentuated a visit which Xenia de Berg now studied with care. Clinging to the involuntary admission of a certain knowledge of Russian, in the greeting of the girl's note, she studied so carefully, and then thinking of the self-chosen token of the "forget-me-not" sapphire ring, Countess Xenia wondered if some scene of this strange past life mystery also involved the recluse of the Gray House. "It is certain that he was stricken at the very moment of her nearest approach to him!"

While the fair widow prepared to gently sound the mind of the young girl who had been her charge for an evening, in his lonely walks, Colonel Boris Milutin wondered at the strange glances of horror and scorn which the tragedienne had cast towards them on the night of the sudden seizure of the stranger. "It is a strange world which we live in! Haunting memories behind us, shadows hovering before us, and, mysteries grouped around us!" He was unable to fathom the reasons for the strange daily life of the Gray House. Judiciously-offered gratuities to the servants whom he could reach, when promptly refused, had shamed him with the answer, "We are not allowed to accept presents!" "They are all too well paid for their silence!" growled Milutin, who felt impelled almost to storm the battlements of this Castle Wonderful. "I will surely know what Countess Xenia discovers!" he mused, as she departed for her visit of strict ceremony.

Face to face with the young girl in the great drawing-room of the old mansion, the Countess de Berg lingered until her own sense of defeat impelled her to return. There was absolutely no sign of any past family history in the modern elegance of the drawing-rooms. Though the signs of wealth, and even a peculiarly refined taste, were everywhere visible, there was not an article going back farther into the past than the reopening of the old mansion.

"You have become fond of this picturesque old home?" hazarded the Russian.

The girl, whose face the visitor was studying, said frankly, "Yes! we have travelled a great deal, for years, in fact, and this is the only home which I have ever known! Our agent purchased it when I left the convent, and I found it already furnished for our reception." There had been the usual conversation as to the invalid's recovery, and, with a sigh, the girl had concluded her guarded remarks. "I had begged my father not to risk the excitement of the theatre! But, he pities my lonely life! He had seen, by chance, the picture of this great actress, and then, decided to break his rule of life and give me a great pleasure!"

The Countess Xenia's eyes were dropped as she carelessly said: "Had your father ever seen her before?"

" I am sure that he had not," the girl earnestly said, " for he has been in the Levant, until he came to take me away from the French convent, where I was educated. Since then, I have been always with him. I have not spoken to him since his illness, as the doctors demand absolute quiet, for his usual malady is insomnia! He only gains rest and tranquillity by going abroad in the silence of the night."

The visitor had finished a fruitless inventory of the objets d' art and crowded memorials of travel. There was no trace of family history or nationality, and she was completely baffled by the frank reception, and yet evident guarded restraint of the charming girl. "Do you like Italy?" queried the Countess, as she prepared for her departure.

"We have never visited it; so it is to me a fairy land of future promise. My father has often spoken of an Italian tour, for he has not yet made his pilgrimage to Rome. The world has been a lonely one for me. I envy your daughter, madame," said Marguerite Waldberg, as she rose, "for I never knew my mother!"

The conversation in French had led Countess Xenia far away from one point of her explanation. "Colonel Milutin tells me that you speak Russian very well," said Countess Xenia, hastily.

The girl laughed softly, as she answered, pleasantly: "My father taught me, and we always use that tongue. It is a refuge of safety in travel, and some day he has promised to take me back to Russia also."

Countess Xenia was fain to depart, and, to her astonishment, the graceful girl went down the long gardens to the shaded linden drive with the departing guest. The widow smiled as she parted from her beautiful escort, for, in that last brief interval, Marguerite Waldberg had learned the outlines of the history of Colonel Boris Milutin. "Pray thank the gentleman for his thoughtful courtesy to me," said Marguerite, with blushes chasing each other on her fair cheek. "I shall certainly ask my father, on his recovery, to personally express his sense of what we owe to him, as well as to your daughter and yourself, madame."

"It is a very thin veil which hides these two ardent young natures from each other," the gentle Countess soliloquized. "And yet, Boris, the star of young Russian chivalry, might choose among our proudest names. This is an unknown stranger. It is the love of mystery—or the mystery of Love —which draws him to her." There were no signs which spoke to her of a previous meeting between the Master of the Gray House and the queen of tragedy. "He is probably some unhappy man who has been chased away from his past surroundings by the memory of the loved and lost. I shall find the key of the mystery yet only in the guarded portals of Madame Mazzana's heart. For, I shall wait, shall watch and wait. All things come at last to the one who waits!"

It was a week later when Marguerite Waldberg for the first time supported her father in a tottering effort to reach the sunny rose bower she loved. His recovery of strength had given way to a strange gloom. He had not spoken of the seizure of the evening, but he was gratefully conscious of his daughter's tenderness. Seated there, gazing on the smiling Elbe valley unrolled at his feet, the invalid turned his feeble eyes to the villa de Berg. Upon the portico, Boris Milutin, pacing to and fro, had already seen the father and daughter on their promenade. There was that in the young girl's heart which waked on this day a vague longing, a moving as of the sweet forces of Spring throwing out each delicate shoot and tendril to bud and blossom. "Father," she said softly, "I am so happy in your strength and recovery. You have been very ill." She laid her hand lightly upon his pale brow. "We owe a debt of gratitude to the Countess de Berg for her aid and escort to me." And then, for the first time, the motherless girl told her father of the prompt aid of their neighbors, the occupants of the next box. "I have already thanked Countess de Berg."

Her father started as he slowly repeated the name. "The Countess de Berg?"

"Yes," said the wondering girl. "And, also to Colonel Milutin, her guest, I owe much. I hope you will personally call and thank him, for I cannot," said the woman whose dreaming eyes rested on the form of the tall officer pacing in sight beyond the garden-wall, on the neighboring knoll.

"Tell me of him! Who is he?" the father said, as a spasm of sudden emotion passed over his face. His daughter dropped her dreaming eyes, as she for the first time, felt the visit of the angel of Love in her awakening heart!

"He is so gallant, so courteous," and the glowing girl told him of the deeds in the far East which had made the name of both sire and son ring throughout all Russia. When she had finished, her father seized her by her slender wrists, and cried, in a sudden rage, "I shall take you away, far from here, as soon as I am well. Never speak that name to me again. It is the very same—Milutin! The very name is accursed. I charge you never to lift your eyes to his face! For, there is blood—blood—between us!" A sharp spasm seized the feeble man, and his eyes closed then, in the fixed stare of a deathly trance. The girl was speechless.

There was the blight of the first great sorrow of her life on Marguerite Waldberg's face as she moved about the darkened rooms of the Gray House, in the long days which followed. Her father's malady had changed. A raging fever burned now in his veins, and the grave physicians nodded ominously to each other, as they listened to his ravings in a tongue unfamiliar to them all. And in his fevered cries, many languages of the East were heard sounding in the brief dream-spasms of his excited mind, slowly revolving backward. There were hours, too, when he was strapped down to save him from the violence of his own wasted clutching hands. A telegram for the man of affairs who handled the sick man's estate at Vienna, brought him to the Gray House. It had been despatched all unknown to the daughter who wondered at the force of the dream-struggles, of the man who had so long veiled her girlhood's history from her.

The representative of a Viennese banker was very grave as he led Marguerite Waldberg aside under the chestnuts in the garden.

" Your father seems to have given some private directions to his regular physician that I should be summoned here, in case of his grave illness. Mademoiselle, it is but just that you should know that all your father's affairs are in the hands of our house. Your own physician here has also sealed letters addressed to you. Should your father not recover his mind, then you will have the gravest responsibility of a young girl cast upon you,—the care of a helpless man. But, you may count upon our house, for the continued devotion of years."

Marguerite trembled as she said, " And when will I know the result ? " Her heart was beating in agony.

" The consultation of physicians to-night will determine, and I am ordered to remain here until your father's health is amended, or,——-" he paused, and softly said, " until you would no longer require my aid."

The hours until the council of physicians had concluded their labors that night were an ordeal of agony to the lonely girl who hardly dared to cast her eyes back to the frightful excitement which Boris Milutin's name had caused. Waiting in an anteroom, she was startled when one of the physicians drew her aside. He was a venerable man, whose flowing beard, bowed shoulders, and full, sparkling eye, proclaimed him an Israelite. He bore a name honored over the whole medical world.

" I am about to ask you a question upon which your father's fate may depend," he said, as he bent his eyes, under bushy brows, upon the anxious girl. " Do you know your father's history ? " he earnestly said.

" He was almost a stranger to me when I left the convent two years ago. I never saw my early home in Russia," she sighed.

" Your mother ? " the old doctor said, his eyes lightening.

" Died when I was two years old, and I have never met any of our family, if such there be."

Fixing his searching eyes upon her, the doctor addressed her in a strange tongue.

She sadly shook her head as the tears trickled through her fingers. " I know not what you mean ! "

The doctor murmured solemnly, " Then, even you cannot aid us, my poor child, for it is the language of my own birth-place—the tongue your father has been speaking in all his fevered dreams. It is Polish—the dying language of a dead people ! I must think—think ! You have never been in Poland ?—never lived there ? "

She firmly answered with wondering eyes, " Never ! "

" And you have not noticed your father's correspondence ? He has had no Polish visitors of late ? No woman ? " The old doctor was now intense in his eagerness.

Marguerite Waldberg was left in a maze of astonishment and doubt, when the old man had listened to all her clear denials.

" I must think—think ! " he said, as he slowly paced the room. " The past of the patient is veiled to us all. The crisis of his disease is on us. And, there is no reaction which we can hope for in the presence of the one he calls on for-ever, always ! "As he rose to join his waiting colleagues, the girl grasped him by the arm.

" Tell me," she implored, " what is my father's disease? What causes these renewed sufferings ? "

The old man laid his hand solemnly on her head. " My poor child ! It is a Polish malady—an old matter of the head and heart ! " For, he alone could read the dark secrets of the sick man's ravings.

CHAPTER IX.

THE REVOLUTIONARY CLUB AT PARIS.

BEAUTIFUL Marguerite Waldberg waited, heavy-hearted, for weary days and many lonely, anxious nights, in the Gray House, a ministering angel of devotion, and eagerly watched the face of the old Jewish doctor as he bent daily over the sufferer. There was a calming influence in the unknown tongue in which the venerable Hebrew physician soothed the ravings of the sick man. Left by his puzzled colleagues to struggle alone against the Destroyer, the bearded patriarch, a Nestor of science, grew to love the gentle, self-sacrificing girl whose eyes rested on him in a last silent appeal.

"God of Jacob!" muttered Abram Cohn, "but this is a fearful punishment. Gazing out on the gleaming stars sweeping westward, the gifted child of a down-trodden race bore with the sealed honor of his profession, the heavy burden of the sick man's disclosures which daily appalled him more. "The Poles were ever the friends of our race," he murmured. "Liberal and kindly when the Russ chased us over the Dnieper, we grew into all the arts of peace under the Polish White Eagle. Only in Poland, has the seed of Abraham ever raised up the roof-tree and tilled the ground in hope, since grim Vespasian and bold Titus bore away the seven-branched golden candlestick to conquering Rome! If he is not worthy of forgiveness, yet this helpless girl's heart beats with the blood of the mighty Paskiewitchs, who always sheltered the defenceless Jews beneath their knightly spears! I will save him! And to what use? To the living hell of his remorse—to the daily chain of newer sorrows eating deeper into the flesh—to the maddening knowledge that his name is accursed of all men!"

Stirred by that warm domestic feeling which is the brightest jewel in the Lost Crown of Judah, the old man cheered the heartbroken girl. "He shall live, my child! Live to watch long over you!"

For, well the aged man of science knew the vain atonement of the troubled and repentant heart of "the man without a country."

Marguerite had poured out her own heart-sorrows to him in the confidences of a soul pent up within itself, and breaking away at last in the silence of her pure heart into a very flowing river of Truth.

One night, two weeks after the seizure, Abram Cohn sat and watched alone by the bedside of the master of the Gray House. The room was silent, and only the graceful form of Marguerite, slumbering in her watching chair in the ante-room, was there to note the glow of silent joy which overspread the face of the aged Jew.

For, the sick man had opened his eyes, and gazed long at the venerable face bending over him. Sorrows and trials, the common lot of humanity, had filled the Hebrew's heart with the "charity which passeth all." He rejoiced in his inmost soul, as he turned to the table, covered with the mysterious aids drawn from Nature's vast treasure-house. As he offered the restored man a subtle cordial, he spoke in words as low and sad as the voice of the wailing prophets by the waters of Babylon.

And, the man in whose eyes the light of reason again shone, turned away his silvered head, and grateful tears trickled down his wasted cheeks. For, it was in the Polish tongue, beloved in the days before the sale of a soul, that the sufferer heard the words of cheer and hope. Michael Waldberg was saved!

When daylight dawned, another physician was at the side of the man who woke to the hopes of another long stretch along the clear highways of Life. " I shall come and visit you, my dear child," said the old Hebrew, as he laid his withered hand in a benediction on Marguerite's brow. " But, let your father not know of me. It will be only a dream of these last days—the mysterious wastage of life. And when he is better, if he demands me of you, I will come to him as a friend, but not for a month. My professional brother, now in charge above, has my daily counsel, and you may tell your waiting messenger from Vienna that he now may go his ways in peace. Your father will live!"

As the old man went forth, his brow glowing with the blessings of the grateful girl, he pondered long upon the unfathomed structure of the human mind. It was in that strange throne of mystery the disease had usurped its brief reign. In "thought's mysterious seat," the fury of discord with snaky hair, had raved as a mastering fiend, sending the burning life-blood throbbing in a poisoned fever through the still strong frame of the man, not yet at his climacteric. Abram Cohn had fought nobly for the life of the unwelcome patient. An heir of the priceless lore of the wise Jews, he was a past-master of all human knowledge. The diamond dust of mortal gropings, swept through Indian, Assyrian, and Chaldean halls down to the labyrinthine temples of Egypt, was the old Jew's noble heritage! Secrets of subtle Persian and lofty-minded Arab, the scattered jewelled thoughts of the races whose bones are blown in the "viewless winds" of Asia Minor; the mighty thoughts of Saracen and Moor, all were garnered, and enriched the casket of his cunning brain. Thoughts too precious for the Talmud and Kabbala—cunning secrets, wrapped in cryptogram and astrologic gibberish, were the weapons with which he had fought the demon of unrest. For the Jews scattered over the world to-day are the heirs to great hidden treasures swept up on the shore of time, whose weighty mass had dropped through the frail web of modern words and types into the darkness of concealment. The Jew has a noble heritage of wisdom!

The gray and scarred world now hides beneath its ever fertile bosom the dust of the forgotten men who have dreamed every dream, who have fallen eagerly on every atom of knowledge which can sweep within the futile grasp of the human mind. There is no song which has not been sung and once echoed down only to be lost on the waves of time, no thought which has not thrilled some vanished, ardent brain. No picture in new tint or shade can ever float before the Raphaels of the ages to come! Its colors have glowed in the past—have "flitted impalpably" before the delighted eyes of artists, forgotten even as the drifted rose leaves lying on Omar Khayvan's tomb. Some later mortal, diving for pearls beneath the sea of life, finds and heralds with glad shouts a single atom of the strewed riches lying deep-hidden there under the throbbing waves which roll around and encompass the world. The New is but a foolish name for the re-discovered Old! The babbling of our later tongues is but a faint echo of the chorus of Babel, and the sounds of its vain discord have never died away. "For thoughts are things!" and are alone, the flashes of the Master Mind, far-darting, blazing with imperishable light, heaven-born and eternal! They are the glances of the great All-seeing Eye; the veiled Jehovah, before whose awful face the devout Hebrew bows, and whose last name may not even be spoken!

"There is nothing new under the sun," murmured old Abram Cohn, as he wandered away from the Gray House of Loschwitz. "For Judas never dies! As all manhood are common heirs to the flickering hopes of the promise of the mild-eyed Christ, so the sons of Adam must ever bear among them, with a tortured heart, that living Judas, who hands down to eternity the one unpardonable crime!" Looking out toward the tranquil western skies, the old Jew, with a brow ploughed deeply by the cares of life, and worn with the burdens of humanity, saw no hope of an immortality in the brightening glow of the western skies. "The Sea of Death is brimming ever with the streams of the Sea of Life," he murmured. "The sum of human joys and woes has been unaltered since the world began, and every cycle only rolls along an unchanging burden of human restlessness !

We are but phases, shadows, a breath upon the glass. Thought, invincible, invisible, unchained and undying, alone is immortal. The baffled tyrant cannot tear even one last word of submission from the racked body within his grasp, in which a victorious chainless thought quivers as true to its heaven-born trust as the magnet to the pole.

"What is man ?" the sage vainly asked himself, and then wandered on his way unanswered. For, his eye rested upon the passing forest bird, winging its swift flight through the silent evening air. "Not all the Cæsars of the sword, not all the immortal Homers, Miltons and Shakespeares—not all the kings of thought, who have ever worn the fool's cap of human eminence,—could give life to one of these little creatures," he mused, as the sparrows, "whose fall is noted," turned their tiny eyes upon the old man, while he wandered away, alone, by the leafy lanes of Loschwitz !

That night, Marguerite Waldberg heard the first tones of her restored father's voice, as it swayed to the rule of reason ; His first conscious speech since the attack which had so suddenly dragged him again near to death's door. "When I am better, I will take you far away from here, Marguerite ; to that distant America, where there is a newer, nobler life, far away under the western sun." The unhappy father even now studied the future of the only living being who cherished him still—his faithful and innocent daughter. Marguerite, kneeling at his side, thought strangely of the hostile aspect of the great actress, as she had peered into their box on that eventful night. "I will know all some day," mused the anxious daughter. A sudden wave of mystic emotion seemed to sweep over her. The reticence of her girlish years had vanished. For, in her anxious mind, the disclosures of Doctor Abram Cohn lingered, to add another enigma to the growing mysteries of the Gray House.

"You have never told me of my mother," she faltered, as an impulse seized her, which was too powerful to resist. The hand of the watching nurse touched her shoulder, in warning, and she was sternly admonished, as the attendant led her from the room. "There is some family sorrow deeply buried here!" the stolid German nurse murmured, though she knew not the Russian tongue, in which, for the first time, Marguerite Waldberg had framed the question asked a thousand times by her own hungry heart.

"Time enough for all this when he is well," the watcher murmured. "There is always time enough for sorrows." It was the watchful Abram Cohn, who had also ordered an immediate sea-voyage, and sternly forbade all the sporadic efforts of the invalid to talk. "He must be subjected to no excitement whatever. To his complete recovery an unbroken silence is necessary, and also a radical change of scene. The one, may save that poor girl, Marguerite's, heart,—for she may not yet have guessed the secret of his nativity,— and, God grant that she may never share the burden of his sorrows! The other, may, perhaps, save him from——" The old man's voice died away in an unfinished whisper, and his teeth chattered in fear.

While Marguerite Waldberg, walking sad and alone under the stars, pondered in an uncontrollable unrest over the now opened mysteries of her early life, she walked in the fragrant rose bowers, from whence she could plainly see the light in Boris Milutin's windows. Though Countess de Berg and pretty Vera had several times joined her in an occasional garden walk, while the sufferer fought his long duel with death, she had not yet crossed the line which now seemed fated to divide her from Boris Milutin forever. A father's curse—an old crime dividing them—some hideous enmity, or a stain upon the noble Russian's honor. Why was that name accursed? Thinking of him, as he had sprang to her aid in the theatre, and listening to loyal Vera's stories of all the wounded hero's deeds of knightly courage,—even under a father's ban,—Marguerite murmured: "It is impossible. He cannot be vile at heart!" And, in the unthinking devotion of her untried girlhood, to the dimly-recognized ideal of manhood which she had waited for,—the child of a vanished mother listened to Countess de Berg speaking with gentle gravity, as she, too, told of the Colonel's past. But, with her new comrade, Vera, she bent her glowing face over the fallen roses, and murmured : "He must be noble, grand, your friend, this Colonel Boris!" and finally, in her gentle heart, born of a sweet jealousy, framed itself: "How can she help loving him herself?" For, the lonely girl was ignorant, as yet, of the fatal skill with which that gay archer, Cupid, had sent his unerring shafts winging over the garden-wall !

There is an obscure little inn in Montmartre, in an old dingy quarter of Paris, where the creaking sign still bears upon its faded blue background a crowned white eagle. It would not need the Polish inscription under the Gallic words, " A l'Aigle Blanche," to tell of the character of the mean little hostelry, known to the French police and the frequenters of the faubourg as the headquarters of the Revolutionary Polish club of Paris. It presented but few signs of interest to the passer-by. Its few squalid tables in the sallé-à-manger, the dismal " beaufet à boire," the one listless, long-haired, greasy waiter, would repel at once the ordinary customer. But, a knot of bright-eyed men of a worn and strange aspect always hovered around its doors ! Their feet resounded on the creaking stair leading up to the one hall, au sécond, above which a few boxed sleeping-dens sheltered these restless children of Sobieski and Kosciusko. Despised by the mouchards of Paris, the poor haunt was left untroubled, for the rickety chairs, greasy tables and worthless furniture alone were visible, when raid after raid had merely resulted in finding a beggarly array of emptiness. A hidden passage to a neighboring "salle au billiards," enabled the sly lodgers to instantly disperse at any quick signal of their own outlying spies. On the night when Marguerite Waldberg had asked her father for tidings of the lost mother she had vainly dreamed of, the volunteer messenger from Dresden was the speaker in a secret meeting in the little hall " au second." To the White Eagle Inn, he had eagerly hastened, on his arrival at Paris, and, gloomy-browed, lonely and sullen, he waited there, until a slowly gathering circle of Polish exiles made the inn a shade more noisy than was its wont. Men in the tattered uniform of the French Foreign Legion, dark-eyed soldiers of the Papal Zouaves, music masters, fencing professors, raffish students, hungry-looking teachers of languages, worn wayfarers, and even returned volunteer soldiers of the great American civil war, walked around the dingy quarters of Paris, in twos and threes, waiting the signal of assembly, or, dispersed in the vilest cabarets of the old faubourg, sought safety in the forbidden company of the scum of Paris. For here, in these dark haunts of misery, the police came not, unless Madame la Guillotine craved a victim for her cold bright kisses ! Sometimes, spurred up by diplomatic uproar, a poor friendless wretch was dragged away from here to be sent to the horrors of Olmutz, the brute slavery of Spandau, or to linger in chains at the flooded mines of Nertschinsk in far Siberia. The cold rain was driving this night in sheets against the window-panes, rattling in their rotten sashes, and a few flaring candles stuck into emptied wine-bottles, lit up the score of hungry, revengeful faces grouped around the messenger of Dresden.

There was not a sound save the occasional entrance of

some qualified member, or the stirring of the keen-eyed watchers in the halls and on stairs, as the speaker, in a suppressed voice, lashed his hearers up to a cold merciless rage.

"Are you sure it is he? Remember how long the time. Fifteen years! We cannot afford to risk the lives of our brothers upon any fatal error," said a gray-bearded listener, as the speaker finally paused. "I was myself in the south of Poland, but I heard all from one who saw the two nobles who escaped. Describe him to me as he is now!"

The speaker rejoined: "It is useless to delay action for any such queries. My companion, now on watch there, saw and marked him in Egypt, when he first arrived from Constantinople, laden with the cursed gold earned by selling his brothers' blood. He will risk his own life as a volunteer. I, too, will give mine, as a sure proof of my faith! Already we have made a plan of the house and grounds, and Pietrow has gained access there once, as a peddler, and penetrated to the main hall. What more would you have? The proof is irresistible. It is the traitor dog himself!

"Did you see him yourself, at the theatre?" growled another voice, whose owner could not be seen.

" Yes, we both had a near view of him as he rested lying at the door of the intendant's room ; only his hair has turned gray, otherwise he is the same. Pietrow knew him well in Egypt, and tried to reach him there, but his Shoubrah villa was too well guarded by the sleepless Nubians. Pietrow was helpless and alone, he was poor, and so lost this wretch, who seems to have fled by Malta, to the south of France, and then worked his way back by Vienna, to hide on the banks of the Elbe, at Dresden. Perhaps he does not yet know that those two Poles escaped. All that I want now here, is three good men, and then some money. This Judas has always rolled in gold. I only demand a vote of death here, and my associates with the poor sum of a thousand francs."

A half-hour was passed in muttered whispers of verification, and the dark projection of a crime still undetermined. A deathly silence reigned in the room, as a hidden voice from behind a screen solemnly said : "The vote."

Upon a table set in front of one wing of the dingy red screen, a human skull lay. It had been fashioned into a grim receptacle. Each man present rose and passing the table in silence, took a pellet from one of two bowls placed in front of the skull. There were pellets of faded white in one, and black balls filled the other. The sign of the doom of Death !

An old blind man, standing in front of the table of judgment, feebly cried : " The vote is made, twenty-three," as he finished a count. And, a hand passed from behind the screen removed in a breathless silence the grim emblem of mortality.

" It is decreed ! " the voice rang out. " Twenty-three black votes, the doom of death, the doom of all here, the doom of man ! " and as the echoes died away a hollow murmur, "Instant death to the Judas of Poland ! " ran through the room. . . . . The conspirators eyed each other in a thrilled silence !

" The lots ! " cried the hidden voice, as the skull was replaced on the table again in full view. " Three crossed lots, twenty blanks. Draw for the executioners. Proceed, brethren, the hour is late ! "

" Stay ! " hoarsely cried a man, leaping to the front of the throng. He was ragged, and a fearful sabre-slash had twisted his wounded face out of the semblance of manhood, but there was the ring of a mortal revenge in his still strong voice ! " I was kept toiling for years in Siberia until an American whaler picked me up floating half dead on an ice floe, in the Ochotsk sea. I gained a safe shelter at San Francisco until I could drag my way back here for my vengeance. I blame not the Russ. I was taken as an open rebel, with arms in my hands. Mouravieff was merciful, or forgetful, when he crossed my name. True, I was too young for a fair butchery. I bore myself, that record tattoed in blood on an old square of linen, to the Golden Gate! I delivered it there to the chief of our order. There were eighty-three names of nobles slain, women scourged, children despoiled, or noble heads which dangled on Mouravieff's oaken forest gallows. My own foster brother died at Nimovitch! It was that which led me into the woods as a human wolf. Tear up one lot. I volunteer. I go willingly!"

"Is it the will of all?" the hidden voice solemnly appealed.

"It is! It is!" the dull murmurs replied. A human sacrifice was accepted. And when the skull was replaced, there was no sound when the words: "Draw for two lots now, brethren!" were heard by all. Silence reigned, as man after man filed past the whitened skull, but a ferocious gleam of joy lit up the face of the scarred volunteer, as he grasped the hands of the two fated ones, who stood now gazing mutely at the crossed slips trembling in their fingers. Again the sound of the hidden commander's voice was heard! "Brothers, let only the four chosen ones remain. Depart ye all until the next call." Before his hollow voice had died away the strange assembly had broken up. But every brother going forth had pressed the hands of the devoted four, and murmured: "Strike, for Poland, to the death!"

That night, by different roads, four murder-planning men departed for Dresden, on the dangerous quest which might not even be named.

For, the table where the skull lay showed them, when they re-entered the lonely room, two rouleaux of shining Napoleons lying there, and there were also four daggers of varying form lying beside the gold. As the avengers gathered around the messenger of Dresden, their self-selected chief, the grave hidden voice broke in again upon their dark imaginings.

"When the moon is full again, we will wait here your

tidings. You know the chief at Berlin. He will also shelter and aid. Go, Brothers!"

A stranger passing by in the stormy night, who might have sheltered himself a moment in the cabaret of the White Eagle, would not have seen the departing forms of those who had voted upon the execution of the master of the Gray House. Lingering in the purlieus of absinthe and King Cognac, they disappeared one by one stealthily, to shelter in the slough of obscurity.

It was in the dim watches of midnight, a few days later, that Marguerite Waldberg was awakened by the sound of a peculiar movement in her father's room. The anxious girl's sleep had been restless, for two weeks had passed in suspense since the question of her life had trembled upon her lips. She had waited until all the preparations for their departure for America were nearly completed. And now, she knew, too, in her own heart, that she would not leave Boris Milutin without a sign of her tender gratitude. Though her father's angry interdict still hung over her, still a veiled communication was not denied to her. Laughing Vera de Berg had brightly evolved a daily rendezvous with the motherless girl at the lowest point of the dividing wall between the two estates. The strange element of mystery and sorrow shading her life seemed ever present and hovering near her. Madame Mazzana had also disappeared from Dresden, and with eager eyes, Marguerite had read of the sudden abandonment of all the great actress' winter engagements, and her hasty retirement to her own villa at Lago Maggiore.

Countess Xenia de Berg had interpreted for herself this sudden change of plan which had so astonished the artistic world, and she waited only until Colonel Milutin should depart for Orenberg, before rejoining his command, till she would herself follow up the clues.

"And this strange man—they must have met—and where? and how?"

The Countess chafed under the delay of a promised future meeting.

"I will throw myself down at her feet. She shall work Love's miracle!" the lady of Warsaw cried.

Marguerite Waldberg never knew what strange warning spirit moved in her bosom on this night, for she had suddenly said, as her father bade her "good-night,"

"I have but one prayer!" and she sobbed as she threw herself in his arms. Father! "For God's sake, tell me of my mother!"

The gray-haired man of mystery folded her lovingly to his breast, and his voice was shaken as he whispered:

"Not now, my darling child! Not yet! But you shall one day know all. In that fair land beyond the sea, I may be brought to tell you. You will know all some day. If I should die suddenly the Prior of the Convent of St. Paul at Jasnagora, in Poland, has a deposit; sealed papers belonging to you; but only at my death!"

The girl started and trembled like a leaf. The words of Doctor Abram Cohn swept suddenly back upon her mind, and the agitated man slowly said, as tears trickled down his cheeks.

"This great genius Mazzana, the woman who is the world's child, she, she too, knew your mother! Go!" he cried, as he kissed her pale forehead. "You may know all too soon!"

And with a faltering step, the astonished girl went slowly to her room. Her mind was still in rebellion. Her heart demanded the flowing waters of truth. Their lonely life, the mad aversion to Milutin's name, the strange event at the theatre, her father's relapse in his awakened rage—all these were unexplained. The obstinate parrying of her tender pleadings to know from his own words, the story of the vanished woman who had once held her at a mother's loving breast in the dim long ago, all this disturbed her very inmost soul.

" Is it a crown of sorrows, or a cross of shame, which marks my poor mother's grave?" the yearning girl cried, as she knelt that night before the little priedieu in her virginal room.

Sheer exhaustion had changed her weeping into a troubled sleep. Her father, who was now able to dispense with nightly attendance, had lingered this night late over his papers, and a last examination of the contents of his open escritoire, for another week would surely see them far on the watery way to the distant New World. Colonel Milutin whose commune at the hand of another, had now grown so dear, would be also a voyager, but, alas, travelling eastward to where the Turcoman's hungry swords were flashing. It was the doom of her love !

" I cannot let him go away without even one parting word !" she murmured, as her eyes closed, and a fond smile still lingered on her face as she slept.

There is a peculiar unmapped mental sense which guards us in the night! Though bright and fearless in the happy innocence of her buoyant nature, Marguerite Waldberg started up in a wild alarm, as from her father's rooms she heard a strange confused noise. It was not the sign of a struggle. There wasno yell to affright the servants, now all sheltered in their distant wing. But, the sudden damp of a nameless terror crept over her brow, as she felt with quick prophetic heart, that a hostile foot was now upon the floor of her parent's lonely room ! She sprang from her rest, and in the excitement of an appeal which was of nature's surest telepathy, she threw herself against her sick father's door, which was, as usual, unlocked ! But a heavy object barred her entrance, and as she heard the slipping of shuffling feet upon the interior carpeting, she threw herself again with all her frenzied force, against the still obstructed door. Her wild cry, " My father !" rending the stillness of the night, was only echoed back by one long hollow groan, as her heart told her of some awful shape of midnight murder !

Before the drowsy servants had roused themselves, to cluster together in fear, she threw open her casement, and then a daughter's voice rang out loudly on the night in the prophetic wail of orphanhood. It was an awful moment!

Colonel Milutin, seated at his window, watching the light in the rooms he had grown to know so well, had seen with surprise several dark shadows move quickly across the shade! "The servants! The last preparations for the voyage!" he gloomily thought, as he watched these unusual movements. And now, filled with his own heart-sorrow, he was helplessly stunned for a moment as that wild cry for help rang out again on the peaceful night of Loschwitz! A single glance told him that the light in the sick man's room was gone. And then, the girl's redoubled call for help from the casement dashed open! His heart told him whose voice it was which called in the despairing agony of lonely danger. Snatching his service revolver, lying there with its sheath and dangling cavalry cord on his table, he sprang lightly down the dark stairway, and threw the sheath away, as he raced madly across the lawn at a headlong speed. He leaped the garden wall at its lowest point with one running spring, and then dashed along under the trees of the old orchard, toward the locked doors of the Gray House! As he raised his eyes toward the darkened angle of the second story, a shapeless evil form sprang out from the vine-shaded porch below, rushing on toward the scarped highway. He saw it but once in the pale-blue starlight, and then, throwing up his hand with the quick snap-shot of a man used to sudden melée and the grapple of the battle-field, he fired quickly twice! The light blinded him, and he saw nothing more, as, led on by Marguerite's wailing voice, he dashed up to the front door. Other voices now joined in the outcry, and in a few moments the sturdy porter and gardener were clamouring with him for admittance! Lights gleamed out now in the Villa de Berg, and slowly the great door of the

Gray House yielded to the trembling fingers within. The quaking domestics led the way to the foot of the stair, and, snatching the nearest candle, Boris Milutin, his smoking pistol ready now in his hand, rushed on up the stairs. His heart cried out "Marguerite!" for his lips did not seem to move. He was at her side, then, and then, with one appealing glance in his face, the gentle girl he had long loved from afar, fell fainting in his arms!

They were not yet near him, the timid followers, when he pressed burning kisses on her pale, cold lips as he bore her to a divan in the great upper hall, now lighted by one feeble lamp. Then, at the head of three excited men, he dashed boldly at the door of the room of death. It was shattered, but yet it did not yield. The butler, his wits slowly returning, suddenly cried: "This way, in through this room!" And, leaping out on the roof of the portico, they reached at last the windows of the master of the Gray House.

They were all open, and a rope-ladder tied to the coping of the portico roof told the story of some skilfully-planned crime.

Boris Milutin was the first in the room. The flickering light which he held showed him a dark form there, lying prone upon the floor, in all the abandonment of the crashing fall of the dead!

The room soon gleamed with lights, and a dozen hands removed the heavy secrétaire from its place, where it had been hastily thrown before the door by stout arms; other articles of furniture had also been piled against it! There were no signs of a long struggle, but, as they turned the body of the murdered man over, a gleaming knife lay at his side! It was a blade of unusual strength and keenness. With a stern cautionary command to all to touch nothing else, the soldier stooped and picked up the bloody knife. It bore, affixed to its blood-stained handle, a parchment label. A name was traced in letters now smeared with the blood of the dead man! Boris Milutin's three years as a staff-officer on the border had taught him Polish, and he was now the only one in the affrighted circle who could read the ominous word, "Judas." He laid the knife down as it had fallen, and, bidding the porter and butler to wait there on a strict guard, he sent two men away to rouse the nearest authorities.

"This is both murder and revenge!" he said, as he went out to tell Marguerite Waldberg, now surrounded by her waiting women, that she was alone in the world. There was no apparent evidence of any robbery, for his money, jewels, and the dead man's watch and trinkets lay upon the secrétaire which had been used to block the door. Milutin had bidden a servant to light up all the lower portions of the house, and he led Marguerite Waldberg, with gentle decision, down to the drawing-room.

"I have already sent to Madame de Berg, and she will be here with your friend Vera, in a few moments. For you must now come to us, at least for to-night," he said, with a tenderness which touched her heart.

She bowed her head in the confidence of her complete trust in his manly protection.

"Tell me," she murmured, "Tell me, is there any hope?"

Milutin's head bowed in a sad silence, which showed her that all was over.

As the first official entered the front hall, the grave-faced gardener touched Boris Milutin's elbow. "Come!" he said, with a signal of his frightened eyes. "They have found one dead man!"

And, led by the flickering candles hastily caught up, the Russian walked down under the roses, where sweet Marguerite Waldberg had whispered her heart's dearest secrets to the listening flowers.

There, his face still strained in the scowl of a violent death, lay a haggard man, clad in the peasant clothes of south Germany. A fearful sabre-slash had some day in the past deeply graven the face now cold in death, and the German Inspector muttered in astonishment: "This is surely no German peasant! Who killed this man?"

And Milutin then handed over to the official the military revolver, of which he had thrown the cord over his neck and shoulders. His face was very sternly sad, as he said:

"I shot him myself, as he was escaping by the rope-ladder still dangling from the house. I give myself up to you. I am Colonel Boris Milutin, of the Russian Army. Please to communicate with the nearest Russian ambassador!"

The official bowed in a grave silence.

There was a hush in the drawing-rooms, as, escorted by her servants, the Countess de Berg soon entered the room, followed by wondering Vera, who had also been roused from her happy girlish sleep.

"My poor child," she murmured, as she clasped the half-unconscious Marguerite in her arms. "Come to us! Let me take you to our home. For you have surely found a mother now."

And, in the house of death soon there was left only that awkward brooding silence which is bred of all catastrophes and crimes. It was only broken by the low voices of the Inspector and Colonel Milutin, sitting there on guard until the daybreak should come, as the official asked a few necessary questions, and made his first notes of the crime.

There, on the bed, now covered with a white cloth, whose angular outlines told the familiar story of the spiritless shell of dead humanity, Count Etienne Wizocki lay—slain at the hands of the man who struck to the death for Poland!

"I surmise this to be the work of some secret society!" said the solemn official, "and I will ask you nothing more to-night. This will be, of course, a very grave official matter. Of yourself, have no fear, for the man who fell under your pistol, earned his death as a murderer!"

Boris Milutin's mind began now to slowly unravel the forgotten past. It was for Marguerite's sake that he determined at once to seal his lips, even from Countess Xenia's queries. "Only to my father! I shall tell him all—for he was in Poland when these things of the past took place. He knows every intrigue of that rebellion."

The first man to come when the sunlight lit up the hills of Loschwitz was the silver-bearded Hebrew doctor. Abram Cohn trembled as he gazed on the still form of the slain man.

"God of Jacob! It is a fearful meting out of man's vengeance! He has gone suddenly—in all his sins—on his long voyage on the dark sea of death. I feared this—I feared this—for his Polish malady has at last been traced to its dark source in the bitter days of the dead past! The avengers of blood have found him out, hidden here in his retreat." And, thinking of the girl whose head bent once more under his benediction, the old man locked the secrets of the dead forever in his aged breast.

The day after the death of " General Michael Waldberg " was one of the wildest excitement at Loschwitz. The darkened chamber where Marguerite Waldberg reposed, under the care of the widowed Countess, was undisturbed. No one dared to break the disclosures of this awful vengeance of the past to the sobbing orphan. Colonel Boris Milutin, with soldier-like promptness, sent a telegraphic message at once to Vienna. Before the dead was laid away in the stranger's burying-ground of Dresden, the Countess de Berg and the Colonel also were aware of the main features of the later mysterious career of the dead man.

"It is strange—very strange!" mused Boris Milutin. "A general officer of our service, and a man of considerable wealth. I have even never heard of him in that capacity. Perhaps he was of the civil rank of Excellence, which has been made to mean 'General' here." And the soldier doubted if he should not at once communicate with his distant father. He would surely know all. Nothing escapes him in Russian society!"

The mystified German anthorities returned in a week, to the orphaned girl, all the sealed papers which they had taken away, and it was true that there was far more light shining upon the death of the disguised Pole at the White Eagle Inn, in Paris, than upon the banks of the Elbe. Already the curtained windows of the upper room of the little tavern told, by their arrangement, to the initiated, who passed by daily, of the fatally successful journey of the avengers. But, one poor window-curtain, tied up with a black ribbon, also indicated that one of the brethren had fallen in the discharge of his grim duty! But there was no one left on earth to weep for the dead volunteer assassin, whose slashed face was now lying cold under the Saxon clay!

Colonel Milutin, with instinctive delicacy, forbore to remain at Villa de Berg, and a strange fate found him for a fortnight acting as the suzerain of the Gray House! His brow was deeply shaded as he walked alone among the rose bowered-arbors, and tried to pierce the shrouding mystery of this dead refugee of wealth. In the brief glimpses at the stilled face of the dead, he had not recognized in the visage, now covered by a sweeping gray beard—in the wasted form of the once stalwart man—the spirited young noble of nearly a score of years before. For, with the instinctive prudence of a Russian, in all things governmental, he had asked no questions. He never doubted that the last Polish Lord of Nimovitch had shared the dark doom of all the unhappy Poles trapped there, to their death! There were but two Russians living who knew the history of that last night of Polish revelry in the old chateau. Dournof was kept mute under the seal of military honor, and his prudent soul guarded, alas! too many other dark secrets. To Vassili Milutin, chafing far away at Orenburg, the gloomy horrors of that night were only goading secret thoughts! "Reaping the whirlwind," he thought bitterly, as the stormy sorrows of his soul tempted him to death, almost to death at his own hands. "It is the work of Nemesis! This revenge of the high gods! She, the lost one, came to me, in sorrow and heart-break, and then left me to the expiation of a wasted life!" The doors of the past were thus sealed to the man who lived in a gloomy silence. He dared not speak of the dead Count.

The curious crowds soon ceased to linger before the Gray House, and when the full moon swept on in radiance, the memory of the dead Judas only lingered in the sorrowing heart of the lonely orphaned girl, who absolutely refused to cross the threshold of the gray mansion again! The Revolutionary Club of Paris, in a grim conclave, listened to the ghastly report of the three who had now returned. "It is well," said the hollow voice, still speaking behind the screen. "So be it ever with traitors!" And the silvery moon shone peacefully down upon the raw red mound in the far-away Loschwitz cemetery, where the dead man of mystery slept, cut off from church, kindred, and country.

Countess Xenia de Berg was pale and anxious as she drew Boris Milutin aside, when, at last, Marguerite Waldberg had given to her a confidence born of the tenderness which lovingly enfolded "the stranger within the gates."

"I shall ask you to escort us now to Vienna. Boris, ask me nothing more at this time! I will tell you all that I can later. Trust to me. It is absolutely vital that Marguerite should confer at once with her bankers at Vienna. It seems that this dead recluse was always prepared for a sudden death, as the great banking house wishes to explain the minute directions of General Waldberg, left to them for his child's guidance. Then, I have also made her a promise that I will go back to Poland with her, on a pilgrimage to recover some family papers of which her father spoke, in view of their contemplated foreign voyage."

"And the house, the Gray House!" said the mystified soldier.

"It will be closed under the direction of the agent here, and a guardian left there. Only his shade will inhabit it."

Colonel Milutin, who was free to depart—for the authorities had vindicated his prompt action in killing the robber—swore a deep oath of silent devotion to Marguerite in his loving heart. "And I, too, will know where that defenceless head is sheltered after her pilgrimage is done!" For he knew now that he fain would have it rest upon his throbbing heart, and never wander more. He loved her with all his heart and soul!

The first duty of Countess Xenia de Berg, on her arrival by the banks of the Danube, in fair Vienna, was to send, with a few words, traced in her own hand, the full published reports of the strange crime and all the legal inquests, to Madame Mazzana, still in her retreat by the waters of Lago Maggiore.

"I feel that this death will unlock for me the seal of the hidden past, the fairy Forget-me-not's trust. Perhaps Love's Miracle may yet be wrought."

CHAPTER X.

GENERAL VASSILI MILUTIN stood at sunset gazing down through the gorge below his castle, as he noted a coming courier, pricking his Tartar pony smartly up the wooded pass. "Letters, perhaps, from Boris," he said, and his face softened as he cast a last look at the grim old fortress of Orenburg, lying there below him. There the Russian flag lazily flapped in the evening air, and a long gray column of troops wound out, seemingly a mere band of ants upon the great parade.

The old soldier straightened himself as the proud martial music floated up to him in the hushed twilight hour. His hill-crowning castle was already gray with moss and creeper, for, long before the White Czar laid out the Orenburg defensive lines, stretching two thousand miles to the Chinese frontier, Milutin's warlike ancestors had here defied the rude Bashkirs and the fierce Khirghiz, in the romantic stronghold which he had now chosen for his last retreat.

"I might ask for one last favor. The Emperor is still grateful, and kind," soliloquized the old commander. "If Boris were to be given the command of these lines, he might be always near me. And yet, it is a ranking General's command. He might be given, however, the trust of the fortress of Orenburg. Ah, why should I so wreck his young life, and cloud his brilliant career? I will drag my own chain on alone—on to the very end of the path!"

The lonely noble cast his eyes away to the north, where

the great Urals broke from their misty heights, into scattered hills, and then, far away over the straggling woods, to the bleak plains of Bashkir-land.

"Still, if Boris were really here, there are the Demidoffs, the Takosleffs. He might find a fitting mate among their princely children. And here, through the wild Ural runs six hundred miles along a chain of armed forts, and two hundred thousand Cossacks are spread out to the far Tobol, Nature was never more lavish. Gold, platinum, silver, gems, all the precious minerals, are found here in our mountains. The chase, too, is royal—royal; and a soldier's sword can surely never rust here. The wild sons of the desert ride up madly in pride to meet us in fight along the lines. Ah, I only dream," said the soldier, as he entered his superb library. Hung with the trophies of twenty campaigns, its windows opened on the "Count's Walk," as the embattled gallery, two hundred feet above the dashing Ural, was known to all the riders-by. General Milutin threw himself moodily on a couch, and then pressed his hands over his aching eyes.

"Boris is of another world than mine. He is of the newer day! His bright young life must not be shadowed with my lonely griefs. He must marry. Yes! Choose one of the fair-faced foes in silken armor, who linger around the throne of Russia's winsome Empress. God! Why did no Turcoman's sword drain these veins of mine? Then my Boris would be even now lord of all my useless wealth. No! I will not call him to the living death here. He shall not burn out his lamp of life in vain! For once—once only —do we live! Marry! He must—he shall marry!"

The General's eyes were resting now on a dear face at which he had fondly gazed in a thousand forgotten nights of vain agony and remorse. His hand trembled as he dropped the miniature case to its place in his bosom, and the sapphire ring called him back again to the Lost Lady of Nimovitch. "Ah, God! If these cruel years would bring me but one token before I die! He buried his head in his hands. "Cecile! It is so long—so drear—so sad! This lonely hell on earth! This agony of a living oblivion! Once again, darling—only to see your face once again! If I went to meet Boris, wandering out into the old paths, would some kind Fate, perhaps, drift us nearer—near to each other's hearts once again—on the trackless sea of life!" For in the darkening hour the spell of the woman who still ruled his stormy soul was on him as he paced his lonely rooms in a vain unrest! Lithe, alert, and with the undying fire of an unsatisfied passion ever burning in his heart, Vassili Milutin was still a man for men to fear and women to doubt. "I will not die till I have seen her! Once again— once again—I swear!" was his bitter cry, and he only ceased abruptly as the knock of his intendant aroused him.

The General's eye was listless, for his mind was far away in the past, as he lifted the two letters from the silver tray held by the servant.

The intendant, bowing low, begged to ask if the courier should wait.

The noble nodded in silence as his trembling hand closed upon the letters.

"Boris!" "Xenia de Berg!" He turned quickly to his table and tore the envelopes open. As he seated himself there, a great white star leaped up over the purpled hill frowning in the East. It was the evening star of hope. The star he had so often watched by the sapphire depths of Sorrento, as Cecile walked with dreaming eyes at his side in the days of that fleeting, mocking happiness! It was midnight before the intendant dared to interrupt the ceaseless, tiger-like tramp of the General's feet as he strode through his lonely rooms.

"Shall the courier wait longer, Your Highness?" questioned the one man who now dared to interrupt his master's "dark hour."

General Milutin looked wonderingly at his servitor. " Is it so late, Ivan ? " he regretfully said. " Stay ! Let this courier rest for the night. Send me one of our own men. Return in half an hour."

Vassili Milutin was hardly left alone before he had finished three laconic epistles. A brief word of fatherly command to Boris bade him await further news at Dresden. " If the ambassador is right, a Turkish bullet may soon finish the work the Turcoman scimitars slighted. The times are truly ripe for war. The great holy war !" And the veteran commander cast his eagle eye southward, toward where the swift Ural ran towards Constantinople. "Will the blue and white cross ever fly on St. Sophia ? God knows !" he murmured. " Boris, my Boris !" his stern face softened, " should be now a major-general and an aide-de-camp to the Czar. As for me, let the old trunk lie where it falls !" The few lines of his veiled references to the death of the mysterious General Waldberg were inscrutable enigmas to the son when he read them three weeks later. " Some of Mouravieff's old mysteries. The fellow himself was of no importance. I believe I do remember a slight skirmish or something else at his old place in Volhynia."

To Countess Xenia, his words were few, but pregnant with his life's purpose : " I have offered my sword again to the Emperor, but only in case of active hostilities. This alone will prevent me joining you now in the search. Should you discover her in the hiding of years, even at the end of the earth, telegraph to me instantly the one word ' Come.' I will then join you, if alive, save only in the one case, that I should be on duty, sword in hand, on the lines. For, my sweet friend, the great war is nearer than even our active generals now believe. Let no false hope lure me away from here ! For God's sake, spare me ! Only for her very self, for the Lost One ! Nothing but her, or the call to my last field, will ever draw me from the Urals. To you alone I have confided the secret key of these dark years. Boris, my beloved son, must never know. If I cannot live to face Cecile in honor, then let him never hear, never dream of the mystery of Sorrento? I trust to you, alone."

The keen veteran's ear soon noted the rushing clatter of hoofs, as his messenger sped away down the glen. He paused, and then looked down in the dashing Ural, where the moon's beautiful broken reflections idly mocked him. He could see the golden cup of the King of Thule lie there hidden in those gleaming northern waters. "In two weeks, I will know if the Czar will send me down to the Danube. There, there, before me, may wait the welcome death. And, so he, the man I wronged, in those years so long ago, has preceded me! Cecile! My God! where, where does she hide?" He clenched his hands. "If she would but speak! If she would only now bend the woman's pride, to the woman's love! "Does she still live?" He gazed up at the stars, and with a face hopeless in its haunting sorrow cried, "Where! O! my God! where! She may not know of this strange death. She may *never* know. And if I could but find her, Love's atonement might at last work Love's miracle! I could now give her my name. I could look into her dear eyes with the honest glances for which she sought so vainly through her tears in those months, those dream days of an earthly Paradise. And, yet, Boris! He must at last know all. His mother's name and memory are dear to me—sacred to him. Would he give the welcome of his noble soul to the widow of a Polish spy. It might even drag him down at court. It might ruin his splendid future. By God! I have it," he suddenly cried, his face kindling. "I will seek the aid of the one man in the old realm who knows the secrets of the old Polish families. The Prior of the Convent of St. Paul at Jasnagora. He guards there, at Piotkrow, all the stories of the great Polish houses. He can touch for me the mystic keys of that vast army of the priests of Rome from whom nothing is hidden. But will he speak ?"

Seated at his table, Vassili Milutin gazed again on the beloved face which had haunted his pillow so long. "I will find her yet, my lost darling, if she is in the world! I will marry her. I will right the wrong I did if I live but one hour and then go forth and ride deep into the heart of battle through the Turkish hosts.

"Then, my Boris will be free! He, the brave boy, will be head of our house. And Cecile, my lost Cecile, can face the very proudest woman of the cold world. The past is hers. It has been mine," the patrician murmured, "and, in these dear unforgotten days, she gave me of her heart's cup to drink —the wine of life! She shall be mine,—if but for one single day. If I live to see the light shine again in her eyes, the light which failed under the false decrees of a world-begotten standard of right and wrong! My God! There are no rights and wrongs in the love of a life!" And the stern soldier's lonely agony of tenderness, remorse and hungering love was as wild as the dark soul-throes of the immortal Dean of St. Patrick's. For, the boldest, coldest, brightest of the men of his day, left behind him, traced in the trembling hand of affection, the epitaph of all his hopes, his very life, his lost reason, his darkened soul, in the simple words of an unavailing sorrow, "Only a woman's hair." But Stella's face was in his heart, and the great Dean died true—if mad. Swift was a self-slain tyrant of Love !

Lord of the Urals, General Vassili Milutin's name was known far beyond the cloud-piercing Hyperborean mountains, to the dim oases of the Khirghiz deserts. Chief of several hereditary tribes, his sword had swept from the Caspian to the Tobolsk. He had often hurled his division into the jaws of death, in red battle's wavering tide—and yet on this lonely night, in his guarded castle, the hundred eager retainers, the hordes of willing clansmen could not banish from his dark soul the wistful pleading of that lost woman's eyes! Powerless in power, the slave of a hopeless passion, only the galley-slave of a vain regret, with his heart riven in a hungry longing for the loved and lost, he seemed to hear in the sweep of the night-winds his own passionate words of old: "I shall meet her at Nimovitch!" And even as Manfred, torn with the superhuman ecstasy of a loving human heart, even stained with guilt, brought back star-eyed Astarte, so did the dear and beloved eyes of Cecile shine down again on the man whose love, whose very madness of devotion, was at once her triumph, and the vengeance of the high gods above us. Vainly opened are the arms, strong in battle, which, in the lonely hour of grief, would draw back from shadowland the loved and lost. And, in the haunting silence of love-haunted lonely chambers, the faithful spirit's cry for the vanished is only echoed back with the raven croak of "Nevermore!" And yet Love rules all! Love wears eternally its own crown of fleeting joys. Its master-song of sorrows is never stilled. When riches flee away, when the sceptre of power trembles in the palsied hand, when the sword has been put away forever, when all life's rosy dreams have faded, the soul of the strong man, stricken by the finger of fate, turns to the undimmed picture of the one darling woman on whose white breast he has tasted earth's highest rapture—the elixir of love! And so, veiled to the vulgar horde, mighty Love walks the earth, a self-crowned god—and whoso is touched with the mystic finger of this great god, becomes, while the beating heart can throb in joy or yield to passion's anguish, a priest of that one undefiled altar on which the sacred fire of humanity flames undying!

For, across the dark ages of the history of mankind, the undimmed light of woman's love shines out, a reflection of the heaven which gave it birth. Tender and gentle, trodden down in the rush of life, the woman-heart rules at last by the eternal power of that love which throbs perennial in the great heart of the world.

While the Prometheus father walked his eyrie, hung high over the Ural River, lit up with the picket-fires of the Cossack sentinels, Boris Milutin, with a troubled face, listened to gentle Countess Xenia de Berg in her boudoir at Vienna. His face was shaded with a living sorrow, as he gazed earnestly in the gentle Russian's eyes.

" Do not ask me, Boris, to lift the veil now from Marguerite Waldberg's past. Her soul is as white as an Alpine eidelweiss. And, dear friend, you must not try your fate now. These are dark days. But be ruled by me. Listen," the fair patrician earnestly said. " I have gained the confidence of this beloved one. Strange as you might deem it, her past life, her very infancy, is guarded by triple keys. I can only tell you that the bankers here have informed her that her continued pension from the Russian government will be that of a major-general's sole heiress. They have even now a large sum of money and valuable properties in their hands. The material future of this dear waif of the world is so far secured. But, the papers, the story of her life, the real key to the enigma of years, rests with the Prior of Jasnagora Convent, in Poland, and in trust to his successors. A sealed letter in her father's hand informs her that the Prior and his council are to be custodians of certain papers until our Marguerite shall reach the age of twenty-five.

" The accounts, money and business matters of the bankers are to be yearly inspected by a representative of the Prior, and in the meantime a further deposit of funds and family jewels awaits Marguerite at the hands of the church dignitary."

" It is a strange, wild story," mused Boris. " The orphaned girl is yet to be shadowed with this darkened past. I see it all ! The true story is guarded by the awful seal of the Roman confessional, for General Michael Waldberg," he said, "was evidently a devout and penitent Roman Catholic."

"You have divined it, Boris," softly replied the lady; "and a father, in his own agony of remorse for some unatoned mortal sin or deadly crime, has thus placed all the past, as well as the direction of the future, in the hands of the passionless priesthood of his faith."

"Yes, and their hierarchy is eternal!" said Boris.

"So, you must wait, my fond lover," sadly smiled Countess Xenia, "until Marguerite has achieved her Polish pilgrimage. True, you may be soon ordered to some new command, but"—she laid her hand gently on his—"even you, chivalric as you are, cannot understand the unsullied virginhood of this sweet girl's mind. Her untroubled affections wait for you, after the flood of sorrow has spent its force. Be patient, Boris, and trust to me." The fair widow smiled at the ardent soldier. "Every day strengthens her growing, shyly-hidden love for you, and when you do put your fate to the touch, her sweet soul will be found waiting at the gates of her heart. But she goes, conducted by my own veteran courier, and my dame d'honneur, first, on a strange secret quest—and she must go alone!"

"Have you, too, abandoned her?" cried the Colonel, his heart sinking.

"Ah, no! She is now a very nestling of my heart," quickly said the Countess; "but, if she would see Madame Mazzana, I may not accompany her."

The lover, with wondering eyes, listened to Countess Xenia, who, opening half the portals of her guarded heart, told him of the positive refusal of the great actress to admit her to an interview in the past.

"Our pilgrim will be armed with her girlish beauty, her gentleness and her lonely sorrow," mused Countess Xenia. "And thus, if victorious, she may be prepared to meet the Prior of Jasnagora, with some knowledge of her cradle days, not gained from the church alone.   God grant she may succeed !"

"Explain !" cried Boris, eagerly.

"Because, my friend, General Waldberg's last important reference to her early life, on the night before his death, was to tell this sweet daughter of mystery, that Madame Mazzana had once known her mother. 'But,' said he, 'you can only appeal to her, should anything suddenly befall me;' and now the assassin's knife has cut the bond of this strange prohibition. It is Marguerite's undoubted right to know the truth, so long withheld now."

"And what must I do ?" earnestly asked the Colonel, with sparkling eyes, as he rose and bent reverently over the graceful hand of his dearest counselor.

"You must allow Marguerite to go out on this Italian journey unquestioned. Wait here a week, be guided by me, and promise me, too, Boris, that you will not speak your love until we have first listened to all the Prior's disclosures."

"I promise!" the knightly Russian said; and yet the lover's heart swelled eagerly within him. "It is so long to wait," he murmured, as he went forth alone and fondly gazed on the light shining from the windows where the "one fayre woman " of the whole world was at that very moment thinking shyly, yet tenderly, of the man whose eyes were turned toward her rooms, as if a holy altar of Love were builded there.

The sun was throwing 'golden gleams into the olive-green foliage of the beautiful promontory of Bellagio, as Marguerite Waldberg, travel-worn and eager, listened, a week later, to the long colloquy between her coachman and the lodge-keeper of Villa Verdi. The old Italian gate-keeper shook his head dubiously as he gazed at the cards thrust upon him, and a letter which he most unwillingly took in charge.

"I tell you that the Eccellenza sees no one—NO ONE !" the stubborn man finally answered.

The orphaned girl was in an agony of tears as she gazed on the gleaming white marble villa, nestling near the shores of the enchanted lake. Her heart sank within her. Prudent Madame Albert had carried in her breast the forebodings of · Countess Xenia, while the train swept past fortressed Innspruck, and clambered over the spider-web way of the Brenner Pass, so the dame de compagnie forgot not to prepare the excited Marguerite for a possible defeat. " Remember, my dear child," she softly said, " every human nature has the royalty of its own retirement. The artistic nature is strange and eccentric. This great lady has abruptly retired from public life, for a season, at least."

So it was most unwillingly that the duenna walked through the exquisite gardens toward the villa, with Marguerite's last words of entreaty ringing in her ears : " For God's sake, beg her for five minutes only. Say to her that Michael Waldberg's orphaned daughter, the child of sorrows, a motherless girl who never knew a mother, bears to her a message from the dead ! "

The lonely girl waited with a soul torn with all youth's awakened ardor, for a final answer through the duenna. A first courteous message requesting the business to be transacted with the major-domo, was all too ominous of failure. The afternoon breeze fanned the cheek of the gentle girl whose deep black robes were sombre settings for the exquisitely tender face, gleaming pale under the dark-brown hair. Her eyes, dark and pleading, were not tempted by the unrivalled loveliness of the three-armed lake. Far above her rose the sculptured pinnacles of the Lepontine and Rhætian Alps, with a mantle of silvery snows wreathing their misty tips. Blue and dreaming in an unbroken silence the forest-fringed shores of the exquisite lake swept away to Bellamo, Como, and Leoco.

The ozone-laden air was fragrant of the forest, and the jewelled lake, the child of the rushing Adda, smiled before her there in its tranquil loveliness. Around its varying shores the patrician homes of the great, towered over little hidden nests, whence the murmur of hidden love-songs never reached the haughty grandees of fashion in their palaces. "It is the world's sweetest hiding-place," said Countess Xenia to Marguerite. "The happiest heart, the darkest soul, the deepest sorrow, the thrilling dream of love's ecstatic possession, all, are buried in the dreaming groves around Bellagio."

"It is an earthly paradise!" murmured fair Marguerite, as the duenna suddenly appeared from a winding walk. There was the sparkle of an unhoped-for success in Madame Albert's shining eyes. "Come!" she said. "Madame Mazzana awaits you there by the cedars." And the bearer of good tidings indicated a little châlet perched upon a rocky crag, below which the sapphire flood of the crystal waters threw back the dainty outlines of the witching bowers of Bellagio. No daintier foot ever trod the springy turf than the young Hebe beauty whose rose-flushed cheeks and parted lips were now lit up with love's eager, memory-treasured, questioning thoughts. She was dreaming of the mother whom she had never known. Her figure, as delicately rounded as a Greek nymph, was as lithe and as stirred with the fire of radiant maidenhood as any Diana of the Olympian groves. In this moment of her supreme womanly anxiety all was forgotten. She would only be worthy of Boris. Her birth, her life story awaited her. The orphaned girl sped along until a quickening thrill awakened to their flood, the mysterious tides of the unanswered love for the lost mother of her childhood, that loving, dream-painted woman who had once bent over a cradle whose only dower was tears. She started as a woman, who had been seated gazing out on the silent, mirrored waters, rose and turned toward her. The moment was supreme! The girl's heart was thrilled with the exquisite music of the voice which softly said, "My child, you would speak to me of yourself. Come!" And before the stranger could note the unrivalled loveliness of the world's mysterious queen of stageland, Marguerite Waldberg was bent by the power of the artist's magnetic master-soul to her slightest bidding. "Tell me what you wish of me," the flute-like voice cadenced, "I know all the sad story of your father's death, and, so, spare me, my dear child, the story of your last sorrows."

The noble face was slightly turned, and Marguerite Waldberg's eyes rested in wonder on the matured loveliness, which only gave a queenly dignity to the Lost Lady of Nimo-vitch. The motherless child knew not that under the rise and fall of the great artist's bosom, was hidden a yearning heart burning to feel her own young life throbbing against it, in the clasping love of the one undefiled and hallowed tie of nature. The pilgrim from Vienna told, in faltering words, the story of her strange childhood, the history of a mother-less child, of the lonely and loveless girlish years, of her embittered father's strange absences, and of the fearful agitations suddenly produced by the unwelcome name of Milutin!

Marguerite, in her own agony of passionate pleading, told, too, of Boris Milutin, of her father's strange and angry prohibition, and of the next quest before her, that visit to where the embattled Convent of Jasnagora hides, on its battle-scarred steeps, the wreck of the wealth of old Poland, the secrets of a thousand nobles, and the broken hearts of the last self-immured aristocrats of the Polish church.

The gentle girl was not skilled in the world's ways. In-tent alone upon touching the heart of the beautiful recluse, she saw not the diamond tear-drops falling, one by one, as her listener, with clasped hands, gazed out on the lake.

"A message from the dead, my child," the lady of Bel-lagio softly murmured, as she turned and laid her slender hand on Marguerite's graceful head. "Were there no papers? Have you no family relics? Nothing to guide you?"

Before the girl, who was now thrilled to her heart with the touch of that loving hand, could reply, her head was resting on the bosom of the queen of the world's artists "It was but a brief sentence, torn unconsciously from his breast by my entreaties," Marguerite sobbed. "He said that you had known my own dear mother. And now, for God's sake, by the mother who bore you, by the woman-heart beating in your own breast, tell me now! Tell me of my mother!"

The daughter of the dead refugee was on her knees, and over her bent the woman without a history, whom the world worshipped as the great Mazzana.

"Your mother loved you—loved you," were the few trembling words which fell from the lips of the Niobe, folding the girl to her breast once more. "Listen, my child! There are chambers of the heart which open slowly, even at the touch of the pure, the good, the innocent. I must think! I have an oath to God to keep! An oath to a dead womanhood. An oath to protect an innocent, a darling child." Her voice broke in sobs. "You have found a mother in this noble Countess Xenia. Stay under her roof. . Listen to her, and then wait and trust to me. I owe nothing to the memory of your father." The splendid woman bent her head in a new storm of sorrow. "But to your dead mother——" There was a pause, while the arms clasping Marguerite to the bosom where her head rested, tightened convulsively. "Go with Countess de Berg to the Prior of Jasnagora. I swear by my life, by my soul, that one year from to-day, you shall know all! The time is not yet come. But, my child, you shall then know of a love which hovered over your childish sleep, and which will bless you from the grave. There is an oath which binds me even now. Here, in this home—which will be open to you—one year from this very day I will wait for you, and you shall then know what the Prior may not tell you. But I ask one return—the obligation of your silence. You will say nothing, even to Colonel Milutin, of my words, and of my promise." The waves lapped the pebbly strand below them in silence, as the girl clasped the noble breast she clung to in an agony of awakened love.

" And my mother did love me?" she faltered.

" More than the happiness of her own heart, the safety of her soul, in this world or the next!" said the actress, as she rose and silently led the way to her villa. " I claim you now as mine—for one day, my Lady Bird, my dear stranger. Then you must let me be to-night your good fairy. I shall ask you to write to me here. Tell me of all your days and weeks. I will watch over you—as if you were mine. To the Countess you must say that a lonely woman's love follows her gracious way in life. And yet I cannot meet her. Not until the seal of the past is broken."

Marguerite Waldberg's kisses clung to the lips speaking in the tenderness of a first loving message from the heart-pictured mother of cloudland, of her childhood's tender imaginings. " You knew my mother. I send to her now a message—a message of my fond love. Bear it in your own tender heart," the girl whispered. " I shall meet her. I shall know her. I shall love her, in this world or the world beyond the strand on which the last waves of sorrow break!"

Hand in hand the two women threaded the bending woods, till at the villa doors the anxious face of Madame Albert greeted them. As the duenna gazed upon the beautiful ones, now knit to each other by a binding secret of love, she started.

" The Countess was right, and yet I dare not speak!" For Xenia de Berg had laid her very strictest commands upon the faithful guardian of the orphan.

Marguerite Waldberg had not noted the fleeting minutes in the sojourn at the châlet, for her strange hostess had led the gentle girl along far over her whole life story. And all things seemed to bend easily to the imperial womanly will of this queen of art and child of genius. The long evening hours passed in a dream, for the strangers heard in rapture Madame Mazzana's word-pictured world wanderings ; and the stars were sparkling far down in the west before the orphaned girl slept in the chamber whose windows opened on the moonlit lake. But the dreams of youth and innocence came quickly to her. Her tired heart beat in deepest slumber under the roof of the mistress of all the human passions—the very magician of womanhood. When the rosy lights of dawn tinted the blue drawn hills, from a happy sleep, Marguerite Waldberg woke and murmured, "Did I dream it, or was it only a vision? Ah, God! that it were not a dream!" For, in the hushed watches of the night, it seemed to her that over the orphan's rest, a beautiful and loving woman leaned, who kissed her dreaming brows and whispered, "God bless you, my own darling!"

There was a tender smile on Madame Mazzana's face, a smile of hope, of bright, brave promise, when she drew the Maid of Dresden aside, and in the dim interior of her own rooms, said at parting, as her arms drew the girl to her breast for the last time, "Trust to me, dear one—wait, and then come to me."

Long after the orphan had seen the Alps fade into the blue mists behind her, veiling the Brenner Pass, that thrilling voice still rang in her ears, freighted with an infinite tenderness. The lovely girl's heart was warmed with the embraces which gave to her lonely life the promise of a happy future. As she recalled all the long conference with the great actress, in her magnificent lonely paradise, Marguerite Waldberg was troubled as she thought of meeting the gallant Russian who had been the first at her side on that awful night. "I am still the child of dark shadows. Some deadly blight of old hangs yet over me," she murmured. For the orphan recalled her dead father's hatred of General Milutin. She now wondered at Madame Mazzana's coldness to her dead parent's memory, and, even in her girlish inexperience, she instinctively felt that the actress knew every detail of General Milutin's life. "Even Boris, has not met this strange beauty. And yet, she is familiar with all his father's history and character. What dark memory of the past comes back with this curse upon the two Milutins?" And yet, when the orphan was once more by the side of Countess Xenia, her first sorrow was to learn that the Colonel was under orders to proceed at once to St. Petersburg "for special service."

"A long, long year!" thought the girl, as she bent her eyes downward to hide her blushing cheeks. "When does the Colonel leave you, Countess?" timidly ventured the dissembling maiden. For she would not lose him now from her brightening life. There was a vindication due to the patrician blood of the Milutins—some explanation of the strange aversion of her dead father.

"Boris will escort us to Jasnagora," said Countess Xenia simply, "and will then, wait at Warsaw to say good-bye."

"He goes back to the East," said the girl, with a sudden fear which she dared not own before her clear-eyed friend.

"Yes, back to the Turcomans! Ah, God! what floods of the best blood of Russia have watered the hills of the Caucasus and the burning plains of Turkestan. Russia's growing empire is cemented with hero blood!" said Countess Xenia.

Marguerite, dreaming of the still hidden past and the mystic veiled future, was strangely silent, but a tender, chastened light crept into her eyes when she welcomed the man who would soon face again the thirsty swords of the bold night-riders of the Jaxartes.

"Boris," said Countess de Berg, in a hushed whisper, as Marguerite and sorrowing Vera communed at the end of the great salon, "you must try to solve the mystery of this

'General Waldberg's' past at St. Petersburg. He must some time have rendered the most signal services to the Emperor. Marguerite has just received an official notification, through her Viennese bankers, that the pension received by her father will be continued for life, to her personally."

Colonel Milutin bent his brows in the deepest thought. " It seems so strange that this dead man's services should have been so conspicuous, and yet, his name has lingered so obscure." The patrician soldier marvelled much over this during the long journey to the Polish frontier, and it haunted him after when he had journeyed on alone to Warsaw. For, guided by Madame de Berg, Marguerite awaited now at Jasnagora the summons of the venerable Prior to receive at his hands the deposits and trusts of the father whose strange connection with a buried past in Poland now filled her with vague fears. For love, stealing into her heart, day by day, was whispering only of the coming parting with Boris Milutin. The child of sorrow knew that a deeper interest than mere sympathy chained the Czar's gallant soldier to her side. With the intuitive defensive feeling of a young girl, Marguerite Waldberg avoided the subject of Colonel Milutin's summons to St. Petersburg. When Countess Xenia told her that the distinguished young field-officer had been given a year's special duty in Asia Minor, the orphan listened with a blanched cheek to the predictions of the Governor-General's widow that the great struggle between Cross and Crescent was now inevitable.

Laughing Vera became suddenly grave as her new friend rose without a word, and walking to the window of the old chateau at Jasnagora, gazed on the great fortress convent where her fate lay hidden. The hour was approaching for the renegade's daughter to know the secret of her parentage. Her eyes filled with tears as a sudden storm of sorrow shook her frame. " He will then go—far away—and, he may never know——"

The girl's plaint died unfinished, as a cowled monk entered the room, and bade the orphan attend the venerable Prior.

Clad in deepest black, escorted only by her faithful maid, the child of mystery went out to climb the threaded paths leading to the venerated shrine of the Polish Virgin Protectress, at once treasure-house and tomb. Far up on the heights, whence Frenchman, Swede, Austrian and Russian had been hurled back headlong by the stout-hearted clerics of the Polish garrison, the last unviolated shrine of Poland drew still the devout Catholic pilgrims by the thousand. There was no word exchanged as the monk, with gleaming eyes, led the fair child of mystery to a great room where an old man awaited her, seated at a table covered with papers. In a corner, the brother on his knees never lifted his eyes in the hour of the solemn interview. His thin lips only trembled with his vehement prayers, and he beat his breast as he vainly tried to shut out the sobs of the pleading girl, who fell, at last, in a swoon at the feet of the aged Prior!

There was the light of martyrdom in Marguerite Waldberg's face as she staggered forth from the room of audience. It was no comfort to her wounded heart that the great prelate had blessed her, as on her knees she implored God's pity and mercy.

" Be ruled, be patient, my daughter ! " came forth the hollow-sounding words of the aged priest. " You are young—innocent. Cherish your faith in God and the Blessed Virgin. The years of waiting will pass, alas! too quickly. Seek not to know all too soon. For the shadow of a great sin—a terrible crime—lies between you and the past you would rashly unfold ! "

The winds were sweeping down over the lonely Polish wastes, and the evening star rose in the far East, when the sobbing girl had told Countess Xenia of the barren harvest of her sadly-ending visit. Property, jewels, money, accounts —all these, were to be explained to her later by a lay brother sent to Warsaw, but, the sealed packets, a dead father's awful legacy—through the confessional—were not to be opened until seven long years more had passed away.

The silent appealing eyes of the girl told the sorrowing Countess of the wounded pride and hopeless self-devotion of the loving orphan.

" It is all over, and, I never can face him with the truth ! For my heart will surely break before then !   He will be lost to me—lost forever ! "

" My dearest !   My God-given child of the heart ! " cried the agitated Countess.   " Look up !   Have courage yet ! For in one year there waits you one at Ballagio who will break the seal in love.   And, Boris will wait ! " said the fair Russian, as the motherless girl threw herself sobbing into the arms of her tender counselor.

It was a gloomy afternoon of storm and sleet, when, summoned by Madame de Berg, Marguerite Waldberg, paler than the unawaked Galatea, timidly faced her departing lover, whose words of burning passion had broke forth only on the night of the yet unsolved enigma of murder.   It was his last day at Warsaw.

" I go, Marguerite," said Boris Milutin, as he took her slender hands in his, " at the summons of the Emperor, to my country's service.   I would have told you sooner of my going, of all I would say here now,"—his voice trembled and he touched the black sleeve of her mourning robe—" if it were not for this.   But, I leave you with the blessed one who replaces to me the mother I lost, the dear one I never knew, as well as to you, the dear, dead woman who gave you birth !   I have never spoken to any woman as I speak to you now, but I ask you, by this sign, to wait for me—to wait but a year."   He placed a slender, worn, golden band upon the girl's finger.   " It was my mother's wedding-ring ! " he said reverently, as he bent his stately head and kissed the trembling little hands he clasped in his bronzed palm.   " I owe a

first duty to the Czar, a duty also to my brave father. I
shall write Countess Xenia of all you would know. She has
told me that you have before you another year of waiting as
well as a year of mourning. Now, my hour is come. Marguerite, will I find you waiting for me when our probation is
over?"

The graceful girl lifted her eyes and searched his very
soul in one last loving glance. "Do you ask it, Boris, to
prove my faith in you? Then, I will wait! And I will wear
your ring—your dead mother's ring." Through her tears,
she smiled as he only kissed her brow, for her icy hands
warmed under the kisses his burning lips pressed on them.
And, when the orphan lifted her eyes, her own soldier was
gone. The path of honour stretched out far before him!
And, on Xenia's breast the child of sorrows sealed her vow
in happy tears. "I will wait, Boris!" rang in his heart for
all the long weary months.

BOOK III.

EXPIATION

CHAPTER XI.

EL ULTIMO SOSPIRO.

COUNTESS XENIA DE BERG marvelled at the stately dignity with which her new daughter of the heart wrapped her hopeless sorrows and her unrest within the shelter of her gentle bosom. Laughing Vera and her mother were drawn to the lonely girl by the sympathy which the first engrossing passion of a woman's life begets, in all who see her wrestling with the angel in her heart.

"The voice that breathed o'er Eden," echoing through the silent halls of the orphan's heart, called forth every energy of her sweet shy nature.

For, while her days were now busied with the grave representative of the Prior of Jasnagora, who was verifying with her all the details of a funded estate of great value, Marguerite Waldberg nestled in the home, set up near the old Chateau Royal by the fair widow who had queened it once over the whole realm of Poland. The days sped away, while the accounts of the Viennese bankers, and the legal formalities of General Waldberg's estate were engrossing cares, driving away other thoughts.

Generous Vera, alone, shared the maiden confidence of the lonely child of a strange destiny. While the two young girls explored all the romantic suburbs of Warsaw, attended by the Countess' faithful duenna, Madame Albert, the widow of the Governor-General took up again the threads of her old social ties. Her secret quest still burned within her bosom ! A diplomate by nature, familiar with the handling of high affairs, Countess Xenia soon traced to its source that mysterious elastic resistance which resolutely covered every unguarded channel of the past history of missing Countess Cecile Wizocka." Marguerite watched in her heart daily the progress of her plighted lover, in his journey to the far East, for the weaving web of diplomacy was now showing out the blood-red threads of a coming war of gigantic proportions. The silence of the higher Polish society of Warsaw, too, was ominous of revolt, and redolent of a bitterness ground in beneath the armed Russian heel. Though Countess Xenia had exhausted all her feminine arts and graces, she never lifted the veil of the past. A month had glided away, and the pale proud children of Sobieski, clinging to the closed circle of their Catholic faith, still jealously guarded every secret which Time had entrusted to the Roman clergy, the only inhabitants of Poland who were free of the ban of the ruling Muscovite. For, with the strange yearning feeling of the Greek orthodox church toward the Roman communion, the Czar's government forbore to crush out the faith which is interwoven in every fibre of the Polish heart. Countess de Berg sighed as she realized at last that it was vain to linger longer on the scene of her happiest days. The quest was a seemingly fruitless one.

"My dear Countess," said the princely Governor-General of Poland, in a final secret interview, "we are all of us baffled by this loyal, able clergy of the Roman Catholic faith in our every political move here. From the cradle to the very grave, they hold the secrets of these born rebels, locked under the seal of the confessional. No order of the Russian government is openly disobeyed, but baptism, marriage, funeral, the

confessional, and all their various religious gatherings we
are forced to allow ! All these convenient occasions serve to
aid the propaganda of revolt in a dead people with only a
living faith left to them, of all their past proud glories. You
will never gain a single secret from these artful Polish beauties.
They dally with our officials, bewitch our officers, and their
smiling eyes hide the very dissimulation of Delilah ! No !
I have never, even with gold, unstinted gold, broken the
inner line of their closed ranks. I remember well, Count
Wizocki, I shall never forget the remarkable beauty of his
wife. Alas ! The flower of Poland's chivalry is scattered to-
day to the four winds of the earth, and, even with our loaded
cannon backing us, we must respect the grave of a people's
past. We have simply annihilated Poland, and in vain
would we now warm the dead ashes to a newer national life !
Should I ever trace out the fate of the Lost Lady of Nimo·
vitch, you shall at once hear, through a staff-officer sent by
me. No, Madame ! Drop the curtain on the sad drama of
Nimovitch ! The play is played out !"

In good time, Countess Xenia herself felt the utter useless-
ness of farther pursuit. A final embassy sent in secret to
the lonely Chateau of Nimovitch, only proved that Boris
Milutin had spent one day, alone, in looking over the strange
gift of his recluse parent. All was sleeping in a haunting
silence there. The peasant drove his teams sullenly afield.
The wild wind wailed as of old in the deep forest, and the
wavelets of the lake rippled on a shore where the returning
foot of Cecile Wizocka left no fairy print as of old. It was
a forgotten Paradise.

Still in the great salon, the empty frame gaped from
whence the Polish beauty's glowing face had been torn by
the midnight prowler. And, greatly Boris Milutin marvelled
thereat.

Day by day Countess Xenia watched the whitening cheeks
of Marguerite Waldberg. There was no longer an excuse

for further delay in Warsaw. The winter was rapidly approaching, and no news came from the east, save a brief greeting from Boris Milutin, forwarded by the military telegraph. The brilliant Colonel was living under that strained repression which makes life in Russia a possible tragedy in its every anxious day. Though love called him back, onward, onward he was driven by the mandates of the White Czar into the dangerous haunts of the desert adherents of the insolent Turk, who relied only now on British guns and British gold, to back up an obstinacy more than fatalistic!

"Marguerite," said Countess Xenia, when the silver snows lay piled high on the frowning bastions of the grim citadel of Warsaw, "let us go southward, my child."

The gentle orphan lifted her head as the bells of the old Warsaw cathedral pealed out in the frosty air. She gazed earnestly at the loving woman by her side. "Any place, any place in the world, save Dresden! I am ready," she murmured. "For, neither in Poland, nor in Russia, will I ever find the secret of the past." And so they journeyed southward to Rome. There were secrets, innocent, yet tenderly knit together by the strange play of the Fates, which divided the two anxious women in heart. Xenia de Berg had exhausted the last resource of a loving heart. For she too, had written a letter to the woman on whose words in the coming year, the very heart-life of the orphan now hung in apprehension and wildest conjecture. Xenia de Berg feared to tell to Madame Mazzana all that she feared, all she divined, and all she hoped. For the stern old noble still lingering at Orenberg was unceasing too in his quest for the loved and lost. In words burning and tender, the proud Russian lady begged for mercy for the girl whose future was still as mist-veiled as her past had been clouded. There was no reading between the lines when the sibyllic answer of the great actress was received by the Countess. In her firmly-traced lines, the words, "Wait and hope, I will keep my word but

only when the appointed time has come ! "   And the positive
tidings that the Lady of Bellagia had gone to the Orient for
the winter closed this one gate of the closed temple of
knowledge.   There had been but one last resort untried.
Alone, and unknown to any of her household, Countess
Xenia sought again the crested heights of Jasnagora.   A
letter from the Czar's great governor, which she gave herself
into the wasted hands of the old Prior, neither added to nor
diminished the grave interest of the silver-haired priest.
To him, all human passion was merely a dream of a dead
and buried past!   Looking backward at the red record of
Poland's fifty years of scourging in chains, he saw in his
scattered flock only poor children of the Almighty, wandering along blindly under His inscrutable will.   " My daughter," he said, as his piercing glance, pointed by the experience of three-score years of clerical life, sought every
hidden thought in the face of the Russian Countess,
" there is a silence which is kinder than speech.   There is
even a love which is veiled behind my denial.   Seek not to
anticipate the time when this beautiful woman shall take up
all the heritage of the past.   Guard and shield her innocence.   Aid us with your woman heart.   For we will watch
over her unceasingly.   On our different ways, we walk as
brethren of one fold, in the great way of life.   There is only
a human pride between your creed and ours.   I may not
break the seal of the past now.   Go, my daughter, go with
my blessing, and may the God of the Fatherless reward you ! "
    As the wayfarers tarried at Vienna on their path to Rome,
Countess de Berg made a last appeal to the head of the
great banking house, whose vaults held the business secrets
of scores of noble families.   The old finance baron, who marvelled at the loving enthusiasm of the Russian lady, was, however, ready with a polite foil to every query which her energy
could suggest.   Though his golden-rimmed lunettes trembled
when he read a brief letter signed " Vassili Milutin," the

parchment-faced old banker's voice was professionally mel-
low, as he measuredly answered his visitor.

"I have been aware for years, Madame la Comtesse, that
the name of the late 'General Michael Waldberg' did not
appear on the official lists of the Russian army! It is very
possible, also, as your friend indicates, that the pension paid
to this charming young lady, is not of a military nature. I
feel that I answer you fully, however, when I state that I
know that the passports of General Michael Waldberg were
veritable, and officially registered. I so ascertained, before
opening his extensive account, by a personal conference
with my friend, the Russian ambassador at this court. The
deceased gentleman was always singularly reticent as to his
private affairs. I have no doubt that all the family archives
are properly under the control of the clergy of the Convent
of Jasnagora. My honor seals my lips!"

"But, as a Russian subject, you are well aware, perhaps,
Baron," persisted the lady, "that Mademoiselle Waldberg
cannot marry without her baptismal and other papers. The
considerable fortune of this dear child, her loveliness, in fact
her whole future, depend upon her further enlightenment.
She must not, she shall not, be legally nameless. Without
the papers we seek, she cannot marry!"

"I believe, Madame la Comtesse, that embarrassment
would only apply to a marriage *with a Russian subject !*" said
the skilful banker. "As a Roman Catholic, under the especial guardianship of the Prior of Jasnagora, who is an ecclesiastical personage, undying and self-succeeding, the young
lady would receive all due consideration from the great
Roman Church in a suitable marriage with any one of
her own faith."

The Countess was foiled. She gazed at him, powerless to
answer.

"I presume, Madame, you may infer that the late General
Waldberg may have skilfully studied this, and so arranged

this property. These restrictions of his last hours prove his wishes to prevent, if possible, his only child *marrying any Russian!* At the age of twenty-five the papers now held by the clergy, may explain all these hidden purposes to this most interesting young lady. I have seen her myself, and, in my similar answers to her, have only respected a trust from the dead. I will say, Madame," concluded the banker, "that the deceased General was a person of no small importance, for the correspondence which he received from Russia, at intervals, bore the seal of the Private Secretary of the Czar."

It was hopeless to continue the duel of useless words.

As Countess Xenia returned alone to her hotel, she saw, at last, shining out, the carefully-veiled resentment of the dead man toward the high source of his considerable income.

" It is strange—it is on the verge of the incredible—that this man, so suddenly swept out of the world, seemed to have had no private life whatever of his own ! "

" My poor Marguerite," mused the Countess, "around you is wrapped the impenetrable mantle of an old sorrow, carried far beyond the grave ; or else, you are walking under the shadow of a crime which would fain hide itself forever under the drifted dust of dead years ! "

So the three wandered far away to where the roofless Coliseum yawns to the blue sky above in the desolate grandeur of ruined Rome. There were no signs of good portent from Boris Milutin as the long winter months wore away. The dark war-cloud was still gathering and rolling up in the East. Its dark shadows were hanging blackly over the Danube, whose historic valley was even now paved with the bones of Russ and Turk. Xenia de Berg watched day by day the silent girl as she wandered over the Campagna at her side, or walked through the galleries where deathless art still mocks at the grave of human empire. In vain the ardent cavaliers who soon thronged the salon of Countess de

Berg's villa on the Pincian, sought the closer acquaintance of the fair girl whose pure face was as set and grave as that of a sibyl. Her hours of self-commune were given up only to Boris, the absent—Boris, the man whose little golden ring spoke to her of the tenderness which wrapped her lonely soul in a mantle of the love of the absent one.

She had found a little retreat of her own, one of those "bits" of Rome which arrest the artist eye and bring the wandering stranger to a sudden halt. A dark-gray wall, crowned by a green climbing ivy, with here and there peeping forth, the socle of some old pillar which had thrown its shadow on Pompey and Cæsar in the dead days; below it there lay a great green pool of plashing water where, from a grotesque mask, a stream still gurgled. Above her hung a patch of the blue Roman sky, the quivering gray silvery-green of a few withered olives, and there was around her a haunting silence, broken only by the distant shouts of the Roman peasant-boys at play in the long drowsy afternoons! Here, proof against all intrusion, possessed by the unrest of her brooding heart, the orphaned girl strove to look out of the folding sorrows of the past into a future lit up with the love of the young hero of the stainless sword. As in the same pathway of life, one side will be in sunshine and the other dreaming in shadow, so side by side, Vera de Berg and Marguerite went along, hand in hand, on the tranquil way of their Roman life. For the play of the rosy hours in the happy heart of the Russian girl was as merry as the murmuring of the leafy brook in June. There was only a glow of gold and crimson before her young eyes! And strangely she loved Marguerite, who seemed to be ever hovering in the opening door of womanhood, her finger pressed upon the delicate lips, still asking the unanswered query of years—the haunting question of old.

It was no unequal division of love which drew the two friends so closely to Countess Xenia. Vera clung to her mother's heart—a laughing nymph—while Marguerite, at the side of her gracious friend, seemed to rest there in peace, shaded by the halo circle of a loving tenderness blended with an infinite pity.

For the affection of mother and daughter for the beautiful waif, was daily moulded into closer ties of love by the heart-born devotion of the orphan to the shadowy mother she worshipped with an ideal fervor.

Countess Xenia marvelled not that Marguerite remained in suspense and without definite tidings. A last faint hope died away which had once flattered her with the idea that some external correspondence might unlock the mystery of years. But, when the fair widow noted that all of her business communications were forwarded through the Prior of the world-famous Polish convent, or by the smooth, astute Vienna banker, she then gave up reluctantly her last lingering belief in the friendly fates. "It seems that his dead hand reaches still out of the tomb yet to grasp the keys of this buried past," thought the patrician Russian, and, day by day, her conviction grew only deeper that it was the shame of a great crime—not merely the shadow of a life's sorrow—which menaced innocent Marguerite. For the grave had closed forever on Michael Waldberg. His bark had "sailed the midnight sea, the sea without a shore!"

"There is no more sorrow there, in that land where his grim shade wanders in a seemingly eternal unrest!" the lady repeated to herself. And, as she watched the noble face of Marguerite bending ever over her beloved books, she trembled to think of the awful sentence of the Almighty, which hovers over us all.

"For I, the Lord thy God, am a jealous God, visiting the iniquity of the fathers upon the children, unto the third and fourth generation of them that hate Me."

In secret, the Countess prayed that this one white lamb might be spared from the unerring law of punishment which strikes from golden throne to peasant hovel with an awful impartiality. So gentle, so true, so tender was the girl, now grown so strangely dear, that the mother of a heart-adoption would have fain taken the burden of that old sorrow upon herself. In the evening hours, at the piano, seated alone, Marguerite's soul seemed to wander out into the infinite upon waves of pleading, passionate melody. It was the voiced prayer of a young and loving heart, the burden of the wordless sorrows which possessed a gentle breast framed by nature for love, for love alone. By a strange hazard, Countess Xenia had failed to note that the beautiful bird of passage never lifted her voice in song although she lingered near Vera in the carols of that vivacious maiden's happy hours.

"Will you not sing for us, Marguerite?" the Countess asked, moved now by a sudden desire, on one of the Roman evenings of the lonely winter. Her listener cast a frightened look at her as she rose hastily, and her eyes filled with tears.

"My father!" she said hastily. "He never would listen to my singing. It seemed to excite him so strangely!"

The silence which followed her departure gave no clue to the strange aversion of dead Michael Waldberg to his own daughter's voice, when in the Gray House, she timidly essayed the songs which, from other lips, seemed to bring delight.

Time had not steeled that man, abandoned of God, and without a human friend, to a self-control in which he could once more hear unmoved the accents of the Lost Lady of Ninovitch, in her daughter's voice. On the waves of her clear, thrilling tones, came back all the haunting memories of a past, dead to him forever. Ever discreet, even with his soul tense in its silent agonies, the shuddering recluse had covered his eyes with his hands in sufferings which were stormy and fanged with a biting remorse. Before his dulled eyes rose again the exquisite form of Cecile Wizocka, her sweet face lit with the light of a delicate inspiration, her fair head bending, as the jewelled, slender hands he had so often kissed, swept over the trembling keys. For, with the touch of a master, the vanished woman he had betrayed also sang with the accent of an angel voice.

Ah, no! The curtain of the past could not hide the sweet despairing eyes which had once watched for him to deny the infamy of the sale of brother blood! In the awful shadow which ever lay "floating on the floor," the doomed man, stumbling blindly along to meet the stroke of fate, clung to the only mercy he could hope for—the mercy of silence, the oblivion of all that had once spoken to him of life and love!

And so, the orphaned girl, waiting in her Roman tarrying place, possessed her soul in a peace only broken by the scattered letters of Boris, which told, in faintly hinted touches, of the great rising tide of war, sweeping down towards the shores of the Black Sea. Moloch was already grinning in the shades of Hell!

"I shall soon meet my father," wrote Boris, when the spring flowers were beginning to dot the Campagna again. "He has been summoned to meet the Czar, at once, at St. Petersburg. If we do fight this year, I shall come to you— if only for one day—before I go to the field. For I must see Marguerite, before Russian and Turkish blood dyes once more the grass of the Danube Valley." And, her heart beating to this promise of hope, Marguerite waited in silent love.

The streets of St. Petersburg were filled with excited crowds eagerly passing the wildest rumours from mouth to mouth, on the evening when Colonel Boris Milutin drove by his father's side down the Nevsky from the Moscow station. It was already the beginning of the four months of the vivid summer of Northern Russia. The Neva had burst its frozen ice-chains of the winter, and the pent-up floods of Lake Ladoga had rushed out to the Gulf of Finland once more. Now that the grass was leaping out of its winter death in life, the armies could move.   And all metropolitan Petersburg waited only the word of that mighty Czar, whose lips could hurl, with one stern command, a half million of fanatic devotees against the unspeakable Turk!   As their open landau dashed down the broad Nevsky Perspective, Boris was strangely, gloomily silent.   His worn and wasted face showed plainly all the fatigues of the eight months of "special service."   While the gray-haired General alternated between returning incessant salutes of passing soldiers, and doffing his cap to the inconveniently numerous shrines and holy images, the son's eyes were lit up by the fire of a strange unrest.   He was himself " in mufti," and his body-servant had remained at the station in charge of the multifarious effects which a Russian is forced to drag along on the distant Asian frontiers.

A single clasping embrace, the simple words, " Boris ! " " Father ! " was all that had signalized their meeting.   Even in the carriage they guarded the repressive, haunting silence of the upper Russian classes.   For there, before them, coachman and footman might be ready to report the faintest word to the Dionysian ear of the " Third Section ! "   A single blunder—one indiscretion, might even cost the head of a man, all of whose personal crimes would go unscathed if they concerned not the political business of the armed Colossus of the North.

An anxious look passed between the two nobles as the War Office was neared.

"I will wait for you.   I will send the carriage back," said the General, in a whisper, as Boris raised a finger to stop the three black Orloffs in their headlong course.

" I will come home in a droschky," answered the Colonel, with a sharp, meaning glance at the backs of the servants. And, to make his instant report, the returning staff-officer leaped lightly from the landau and disappeared into the grim granite corridors of the War Office.

The exile of Orenburg drove slowly down alone to his long-neglected mansion of state, where the timid servants had almost started in affright at his unfamiliar footsteps pacing the salons at night. For, in these two anxious months of "waiting for the word," Vassili Milutin had called up many times the bright witch of the past, and the loving woman whom he had lost haunted his lonely hours. It was gloomy enough in that great, silent house on the Neva, but no dark chamber of its vast interior was as sombre as the locked heart of the stern master, whose eyes rested often with an agonized appeal, upon the glittering token still worn upon his hand! But the long silence of years was unbroken ; the mystery of her disappearance deepened, and even Countess Xenia had deplored the final eclipse of the planet of Hope.

"It is all over," growled Milutin, as, while waiting anxiously for his son, he gazed upon the throng of happy couples whirling by his windows, their faces all beaming in the kindly lights of love.

"The drift of these years of sorrow bears me on, but only to the grave!" he mused. "It is time that Boris should marry now, at once. I wonder——" And the old patrician gazed out for a moment, into the dim future. Should the projected campaign open, then Boris would be in the very blazing focus of battle, the only theatre of Russian advancement, the chosen path to glory.

"He is the last of his line; for I have done with life. He should, he must marry; for the name of Milutin may not lightly die out of Russia. He may mate with the haughtiest, he is worthy of the fairest."

Vassili Milutin, once himself a squire of dames, par excellence, in his now daily palace visits had easily picked up the threads of many old dormant friendships. The distinction of his flattering welcome by the Emperor had been most marked, and many fair heads rested uneasily on satin pillows, awaiting the return of the dauntless young sabreur whose long-deferred Petersburg honors, waited his freshly-laurelled brow.

The great silver mantel clock struck nine before Boris Milutin joined his father, and then, the great doors of the dining-hall were thrown back, as father and son, for the first time in years, faced each other in the hall once ringing with gay life. The elaborate service and lengthened display fatigued the wearied soldier-traveller, who rose at last with a sigh of relief, when the General led the way to the one sanctum cunningly devised for the exclusion of servants, and the baffling of every possible spy. It was a private haven of safety!

"Did you get your orders, Boris?" asked the anxious father, as he offered his own cigarette case to his son, whose face had gained an habitual sternness born of the dangerous trusts confided to him. Boris Milutin's eyes were steady, but his hand trembled as he lifted his coffee-cup.

"Yes. I am to hand in my written report, and then await, daily reporting at the War Office, the decision of peace or war."

"There will be no war, my son; at least, not until next year!" hoarsely whispered the father, now fearful of even the elastic air. And then, bending his head, he whispered a few words, borrowed from a Czar's confidence, to his son. For the exile of Orenburg had long been a master-weaver in that web of Russian policy which was now to be cast out as a net of dissimulation over the lazy Turk, still seated with steadfast eye, imploring Allah for Christian England's help!

"Either of the two, we could fight easily alone; but we are not strong enough for Turkey and England banded as allies—not yet. We must first finally secure the Caucasus, gain a good foothold on the Black Sea in Asia-Minor, reach out with our railroads to Khiva and Pamir, and hang on the flanks of India in a deadly menace, before we can defy hostile England. But then—then—St. Sophia will soon see the blue and white cross waving there!

"No; you will soon be relieved from duty. Come with me, my son. Come back to Orenburg and rest. Take a long leave, and we will see if the breath of the fir forests will not build you up again. You need change and rest."

"You are positive that this great struggle will be delayed for another year?" cried Boris, springing-up and pacing the room. His eye had kindled with a new, strangely-eager light. The young soldier forgot all his prudence, for two dark, wistful eyes seemed to shine upon him now, and a voice, the dearest in the world to him, to whisper once more, "I will wait, Boris. I will wear your ring!"

"I saw myself the orders drafted yesterday which absolutely forbid General Ignatief to bring matters any farther on at present than they are now. Nothing short of a foul, open diplomatic affront, or a serious mêlée will be noticed. Our whole army is first to be carefully rearmed, and every secret preparation fully made for a Danube campaign next year. Beside, the railroad to Vladikaukas is to be doubled in capacity. Without we gain Kars and Batoum, we are powerless to move on later to Merv and Tashkend, which we need in the future. And the inexhaustible petroleum of Baku will then give us the control of the market of Asia, and a fuel for our future desert railways. This supply will ensure the easy navigation of our huge rivers now draining the treeless steppes. No, Boris; we will only fight a part of the great war now; the rest is in the womb of the Future. This is the Czar's own decision. But, hold it locked sacredly in your breast."

"Then, I will take a leave!" gravely said Boris, pausing in his walk.

"And you will come to Orenburg with me?" eagerly cried the General, whose secret mind was now bent upon influencing his son toward a brilliant marriage, worthy of the great name which he bore.

The Colonel fixed his eyes steadily upon his anxious

father's face, and said : "I must go first to Italy—to Rome ! " he answered, speaking slowly, as if under some invisible spell.

Vassili Milutin's hand closed quickly upon the filagree coffee-cup he held, and the porcelain splintered in his sudden grasp. His eyes blazed.

"You *must* go ! you *must leave me ?* And wherefore ? " the great noble cried, a steady light glistening in his eyes. He divined some new force. The two men had never met in any trial of mental strength. Their lives had passed and glided by each other's, and now a sudden light shone upon those lingering months at Dresden. The old General muttered :

"Some woman ! "

"It is a matter of *honor !* " firmly said the young Colonel, as he instinctively assumed a soldier's respectful attitude before the disquieted General.

The fear which suddenly smote proud Vassili Milutin's heart with the flail of a vengeance of the past, too horrible for the noble's haughty nature to brook, quivered in his icy voice. He was white with a silent rage ! "I hope it is not a matter of *dishonor*," the stern General hissed, forgetting that he alone bore the burden of the past shame, that crime against a noble woman nature, which had darkened these long years of lonely agony.

"Explain yourself," said the son, with perfect respect, but in a tone which told General Milutin of a dangerous strain upon the tie which had bound the young man so many years in an implicit obedience.

"Is it to marry that nameless child of the dead Polish traitor, Michael Waldberg, you would leave me ? The man who sold Poland's nobles for Russian gold to the halter and the convict chain ? My curse hangs over such an attempted folly ! You will never enter this house again as my son, while I live ! A nameless adventuress——" When the frantic General, who dreamed not of his sudden self-betrayal, had paused for a moment to note the effect of the interdict, he dropped into a chair with a groan.

For, he was alone in the room! The last glances of Boris Milutin's eyes haunted all the night a haggard and despairing man, who waited in vain for the returning foot of his only son.

The pale yellow sun struggling through the gray mists of the Neva brought no fresh counsel to the lonely father whose outraged pride still tied him within the granite walls of the deserted home, now a very hell to him.

It was three days later when the Minister of War, passing near General Vassili Milutin in the ante-room of the Privy Council, paused to say in a meaning whisper, " It was only the past services and broken health of your brave son which induced the Emperor to ever consider for a moment his unconditional resignation from the army. It is a great loss to the service and his own ruin."

Vassili Milutin gazed mutely at the great minister, and then, bowing deeply, passed out of the Winter Palace portals as if in a dream. His coachman, lashing the frightened steeds along to the Foreign Office, was astounded at the eager manner of the master, whose face wore a look of agony and suspense never seen before, even in the shock of disastrous battle, for his henchman had long shared the soldier's fortunes.

" The Colonel s passport viséed to go abroad was delivered to him, personally, two days ago, General," said an old official, rising with respectful eagerness as the father hid his agitation in an assumed indifference. " And even I, was not aware of his leaving the service until the papers were made out as a simple civilian. It is a great blow to the army, sir. A future general—a coming aide-de-camp of the Czar! He would have reached these honors, and even more. Ah! The folly of these young men !"

But, there was no reply! Soon along the Neva the carriage was bearing away a man whose breaking heart only throbbed: "He has thrown up his rank forever, and left Russia!" Something in his heart seemed to echo, "Forever! Forever!"

Countess Xenia de Berg stood, a week later, at the window of her villa on the Pincian, gazing sadly out on the flaming sun sinking beyond the old Leonine city. In her hand was an opened telegram, and the pale-faced widow saw yet no consolation for her fruitless labors of love in the sunset skies. "Forever and always wrong. Some dark shadow of Nemesis seems to haunt the footsteps of all who have passed under the portal of the Gray House! What is this sudden quarrel? Boris Milutin's hard-won rank and brilliant record are now thrown away. There is some devil of unslaked vengeance hounding down my poor Marguerite!"

There below her in the garden, the dark dress of the orphaned girl was blackened deeper by the shadow of the ruined wall builded over the trodden ashes of forgotten Romans. "I dare not tell her! I fear to warn her! I cannot—I will not—wake her from her dream of love! It is terrible, terrible! Some sudden quarrel of great moment between Vassili and his only son."

Countess Xenia despondently read the fatal words once more.

"Boris has foolishly resigned and gone abroad! Urge him to withdraw his resignation. Act secretly on this. Do not mention my name. Madness and ruin for him—heartbreak for me. You alone can move his heart. Telegraph me to the English quai. Watch for him. He is desperate. I dare not explain. It is the disgrace of our house forever." And it was signed "Vassili."

The patrician lady bowed her head in the deepest dejection. It was a fatal blow to her own bright dreams of a day when the graceful daughter of her heart would walk at last in the sunshine of happiness, when her prisoned voice would break out in the joyous songs of a golden love born out of the sorrows of the past.

"The grim war-cloud has rolled away for another year," mused Countess Xenia, as she watched the form of Marguerite gliding under the ilex trees. She seemed now to be a very Egeria of the fountain whose song rang out ever in mourning over buried Rome. The earnest daily silent appeal of the orphan's eyes had moved her hostess to a new secret alarm. For all knew now that Russia's legions would not be hurled at the foe until the grass had thickened once more the unstained turf destined for their future graves. The critical diplomatic juncture had been passed over in peace, and yet, the Russian lover came not. A noble pride, born of her bright young heart's secret throbbings, scaled the pale lips of Marguerite Waldberg. Day by day passed with no letters—no tidings—and the proud girl had learned to shun the warm sympathy of Vera de Berg, whose flashing eyes were brimming with ready unshed tears. It now lacked but one month of the day when at Bellagio, the child of mystery would face the one human being who had owned to the sacred deposit of the secrets of the sealed past. Walking under the budding branches of the arboured garden trees, Marguerite had seen the blossoms fall under her feet in these long, dragging, weary days of suspense with a rustling sound of "Never! Never again!"

"I dare not answer this appeal of my old friend,—I must wait, wait till Boris himself, comes here," mused the Countess. "There is but one who could aid me now. Ah!" She sprang to her desk, for the Russian journal she had laid aside when the telegram swept all peace from her mind, blazoned the arrival of Major-General Alexis Dournof at Moscow, on a six months' leave of absence. Fate had answered her prayer!

"The Commanding General at Moscow will instantly forward any communication to the returning hero of the Caspian. Yes! yes! I will telegraph at once to Dournof. He, alone, can turn Boris back to the only life which a Milutin can lead. Boris was born under the very shadow of the throne. And Dournof can bring these two warring natures together, in love, again. It is Marguerite's very life which hangs upon this now." And, with her fair head bent over her writing, she tried to hide the meaning of her despatch in words which General Dournof alone would understand. A slight noise at the door caused her to lift her head, as the portière was suddenly swept aside. The astonished face of the Italian major-domo was no check to the onward stride of haggard Boris Milutin, to greet whom Countess Xenia sprang forward, with eager outstretched hands.

"Boris! You here!" she cried with a conscious embarrassment. Her very tone betrayed her eager excitement to learn the sad story which was now written in his face. The lover was gloomily silent.

For, the Master of Ravenswood carried no deeper despair on his pallid countenance than this pale Russian, whose sunken eyes gleamed with a strange fire.

"Marguerite, here? I must see her, at once!" he said, as he wearily sought, with burning eyes, the form of the beloved, in the depths of the great salon. She was not there! His heart stopped its beating.

"Boris, are you ill? Speak to me!" cried the Countess, as she clasped his nerveless hands. But he had followed the direction of her eyes, and then, led on by a hungry love, he sprang through the open door, and, before the girl seated by the plashing fountain could look up, he had clasped her to his breast, in a wild ecstasy of passion! There were no words of welcome to greet him, for Marguerite Waldberg had pressed her hand to her heart, and, in his arms, she sank down upon his breast like a broken lily. Only the murmuring of the falling water kept time to the beating of the lover's heart, as he poured forth those words of tenderness which brought a sudden flood of crimson to the pale face of the woman who had waited so long in vain. It was a strange home-coming of the darling of Russia's young chivalry, for, while Marguerite's lips trembled under his burning kisses, Countess Xenia, in a flood of tears, was praying on her knees before the silver shrine in her own refuge above them.

The eyes of Boris Milutin were fixed upon the slender golden band which he had placed upon the hand he now claimed.

"You said that you would wait for me, my own darling! I have come to make you my own. To take you away to a land where the sorrows of the past shall never cast their shadows upon you again. You must be mine, my Marguerite, mine at once, mine forever!" There was the flush of fever upon his cheek, his hands trembled, and the startled girl quivered under their icy grasp. She gazed timidly at him and her heart sank.

"Is it war? Do you leave us soon? What has happened?" the frightened maiden murmured.

"Ask me nothing!" the Russian answered, his eyes searching her very soul. "I have buried the past! I am a free man now! I have no life but in yours—at your side! I have left the service of the Emperor, and I can marry you —this very day! I am free—free!"

"And your father?" the girl faltered, turning pale and retreating a single step. "Does he know of your presence here—of your purpose?" There was in the quivering young heart now only the memory of the curse which Michael Waldberg had once hurled at the name of Milutin. But out from the grave a dead hand seemed to grasp again at her very heart-strings—a hollow voice to cry "Forbear!"

"I have no father now," gloomily cried the soldier, as he caught the slender waist of the girl trembling beside him.

"I ask of God but one thing now—your life—your love—your hand in marriage! Do you not love me?" The worn traveller gazed in her eyes with a growing despair, for Boris Milutin saw the shadow of parting in the sad glance which pierced his very soul. It was an eternity to him before the girl lifted her eyes to his, and then her new crown of sorrows seemed to be crushing her to the earth. She seated herself by the broken fountain and buried her face in her slender hands. The golden circlet was wet with sudden tears.

"I will never love any one but you, my Boris," she softly said, and each word fell as if ringing out from afar. "Ah! My God! I see all. You have thrown away your splendid life-career for me. I know too well that you cannot marry without the Emperor's permission. Your great house weighs you down with all its past glories. You are the only heir of its vast wealth, the last one to succeed to its hard-won dignities. I have waited for you, Boris,"—her voice trembled— "but the cloud has burst upon us! You cannot marry the nameless girl—the child of mystery—without the ruin of your name and the blighting of your career. No! No! It can never be! Somewhere in the past lies the unatoned burden of a dark crime, which weighs upon our love. It must not be. I will wait until you can take me to your arms in pride and honor. I will wait until my lost mother's history is made known to me. Until the woman you would wed can give to you a hand unstained with that shame which your proud father dreads. I will not drag you down! Never! I will suffer—but alone!"

"For God's sake, Marguerite!" cried the soldier. "You know not what you say. There is but one life—one love before us now. You are mine, by all the promise of your dear eyes, by the words of the lips I love, by the faithful heart you bear in your dear bosom." His arms were stretched out to her, and his voice trembled with the last appeal of his storm-swept soul. "My God! I cannot make known to her the secret of her father's life," he groaned. "My darling! My own innocent darling!" The young noble staggered as if a knife had pierced his heart, as her last words filled him with a fear which froze his heart.

"I have yet a month to wait before my tryst at Bellagio, Boris," she softly said. "It may break my tired heart to hear the story of the veiled past. I may never be your wife. But I am yet a true woman. A woman who has given you her life's love—her whole heart—all that I could give to the one whose soul is dearest to me! And for all this I will not wreck your life. I will not see you, my Boris, an alien from your land, and know of your lost rank, your blighted career. You are free, Boris—free—until your proud father shall open his heart to you again—until the Czar himself shall give you that sanction which preserves to your line your rank and honors."

Boris raised his head to interrupt this sentence of death falling upon his last cherished hopes.

A slender hand stole into his. "I knew this. I feared it. Take back your ring!" she softly said through her broken sobs. "I shall go to Bellagio, and by the memory of my own loved mother, I swear that I will hide my sorrows forever far away from you behind those convent doors, which close for life, unless I can bring to you a stainless name as your wife!"

Her lover's heart thrilled with an infinite sadness as the girl's light foot fled away, and he was left alone by the fountain where she had waited for him so many weary days. His brain whirled. The darkling shadows closed down over the man who stood alone clasping, in his fevered palm, his dead mother's worn wedding-ring. A loneliness as of the grave swept over him, for in his own loyal heart he knew the tender and devoted girl would not easily be moulded to his wild will. And the stars were shining down before the Countess forced him, with a gentle tyranny, to leave the place where still he lingered.

"Where is she?" he hoarsely whispered,

"Vera is watching with her now, Boris," sadly answered the woman, who feared to draw nearer to the barrier of this new sorrow thrilling the sundered hearts of the ruined noble and the motherless girl.

With a trembling heart, Xenia de Berg strove to guard her own double secret. "I will not answer the General. Time and God's providence will alone lift this load of sorrow. And, even General Dournof can now do no more than I, myself. For the curse of the past has wrapped these unhappy lovers in its clinging folds."

"Tell me, Xenia," cried Boris in his anguish, "what is the double secret of the olden days? If you know aught, by the God above us, speak, and save that child's throbbing heart the pain which rends a bosom made to be the throne of purest love."

It was with a fear and sorrow which benumbed her very soul that Countess Xenia saw the disinherited noble go forth in his lonely agony. For Marguerite was too sadly resolute.

"Tell her that I have gone away alone to Nimovitch! I will await there the words which either doom me to hell or lift me to heaven. For, there is nothing before me now but the unbroken level of a death in life."

With a courage born of despair, Marguerite Waldberg hid herself from the man who had waked her young heart to its sudden bloom of an overmastering love. "Tell him that he shall know, through you, the whole sad truth." A proud sadness rang out in her voice as she murmured, "Boris knows that no human love but his can ever touch my heart! If a sacrifice, a life's sacrifice, is demanded by the God who 'visits the sins,' let me walk alone in clouds and sorrow. I will never wreck his life. If I am base-born, if I am the child of shame, as a Russian, I may not drag him down."

The house was strangely lonely when the orphaned girl went forth to Bellagio. For Boris Milutin was already wandering by the lonely lake at Nimovitch. He wandered through the silent halls of the old chateau, and no whisper of the murmuring forest ever broke the clinging silence of the vanished years. " Here I am, indeed alone, with my sorrows," he mused, "for the voiceless past has hallowed this deserted home to the dark angel of oblivion." And it was true that nothing smiled around him, for the rustling leaves, falling softly at his feet, spoke to him only of the distant loved one whose courage and fortitude had been too strong for the pleading of the passion which burned in his heart's core. And, so there, at Nimovitch, he dwelt in darkness !

A lonely old man in St. Petersburg was haggard and wan, as he listened to General Dournof's brave and earnest appeals to the unbroken friendship of a life. "I can do naught, Alexis," the old noble cried, in his despair. " Read this letter from Countess Xenia." And the words of Madame de Berg found an echo in General Dournof's heart.

"I am powerless," she wrote. " Boris absolutely declines to hold any communication with General Milutin," were the words which had shaken the haughty noble's soul to its centre. " There is but one way. The work which was done at St. Petersburg must be undone at Nimovitch ! Some one's pride must give way before madness or suicide leaves the house of Milutin without an heir." And, his eyes drooping in self-confessed shame, the great patrician faltered, " I must, then, trust to God—to the future ; I cannot, I will not, go to Nimovitch." A sudden light showed General Dournof the quaking fear which unnerved the lord of fifty manors.

" He dares not face the ghosts of a haunted past there," mused the baffled friend, as he too departed, leaving the stricken man alone in his sorrow. And Boris, his heart aflame, counted the moments until he might know, under the sighing trees of Nimovitch, the tidings from far-away Bellagio.

CHAPTER XII.

THE BAN OF THE PAST—THE TRUMPET CALLS.

"THERE is some ban of the dark past, of those old bloody days in Poland, which has blighted the affections of both father and son here. What a tumult of warring emotions is hidden in the human heart! Age may take away the glamour of Love, the eye may fade, the step grow feeble, but the door of the heart is ever open to cold hatred, to sudden rage, to the vilest storms of anger, up to the very hour when death's pallid hand seals it forever. Milutin is only a wise fool! He has forgotten the new era which we live in. The days of Ivan the Terrible are past."

General Alexis Dournof threw down his hastily-opened letters at the Yacht Club, to greet dozens of his old comrades-in-arms. All these were eager to know the secrets of the strangely-delayed campaign. General Alexis Dournof, at the Winter Palace, the War Ministry, and at every Club, and even in his gayest reunions, only smiled back his answer: "I came here myself for news. I am only a dweller in the Asian wastes. What have you to tell me?"

"I will be glad to see Tashkend again," the loyal soldier murmured, as the troubles of his former patron often returned to him. "My own hands are tied! Countess Xenia's appeals, too, are vain. General Milutin has uselessly stirred up the War Ministry. When even an Imperial Grand Duke's invitation fails to bring Boris back to the service, we must wait till either one of these two strong natures bends or breaks."

There was also consternation among the blossomed buds of

Petersburg society. There was wailing in hall and at mess. For all the friends of the splendid young soldier now absent mourned the breaking off of a dazzling career.

"Some one of these sleek petted devils who always betray us while we kneel before them. Some flinty-hearted woman devil has driven Boris to these lonely Polish woods," growled Colonel Tchernaieff. "I will give Milutin just one year to either drink himself to death, or blow his brains out," he wrathfully concluded, with a general sweeping anathema upon the marble hearts by the Neva. But still Boris gave no sign!

It was indeed true that the most strenuous appeals of the war minister had failed to reawaken the ambition of the voluntary recluse of Nimovitch. His soldier pride seemed slain forever. The brutal Boyar insolence of his father was unanswered. Had any other man dared to take Marguerite Waldberg's name lightly on his lips, Boris' tiger nature would have drank of his foe's heart's blood. But age, nature's ties, and the patriarchal hierarchy of Russian family life estopped the son's active vengeance. "God help my poor darling!" the moody young noble murmured, as he wandered alone under the leafy walks of the deserted park at Nimovitch. The mood of the disinherited son was a stubborn and dangerous one. He had coldly replied to the official appeals of the war minister.

"My best years have been freely given to the service. My blood has been shed for the Czar. Another can easily replace me," he coldly answered. "And, if the Turkish campaign opens next year, a musket will serve me as well as a sword, or I can die for the Czar just as well in the ranks as a simple horseman. Rank shines out but dimly on the battlefield! I shall not fail to do my duty as a loyal Russian subject. But, I absolutely decline to retain any rank whatever in the army." This decision was furtively conveyed to General Milutin by his old confrère the minister, and it filled the cup of the old noble's sorrows. When a friendly Grand Duke, charged by the Empress, hinted also at a matrimonial alliance, which would raise the house of Milutin even higher, the baffled father was forced to admit to the great noble that his son was now a stranger to him. And so, while the ripple of astonishment subsided, but two fiery hearts were left chafing in the undying quarrel of an unavenged insult to the orphaned girl. In his imperious and lonely sorrow, Vassili Milutin affected to ignore the long silence of Dournof, and also the timid Countess Xenia. But, in his own heart, the man who feared the memories of Nimovitch knew that he was now alone in the world. For the last ties which bound him to the memory of the vanished beauty of Sorrento were loosening, and those whom he had relied on to bring his son back to him, all sided with Boris, in this mysterious quarrel. He was friendless now!

There was the deadly white heat of an old man's rage still burning in the heart of Vassili Milutin when he sadly turned his unwilling feet again toward the prisoned luxury of Orenburg. His last night alone in the mansion on the Neva was an agony of silent remorse.

Before him in the library hung the face of his dauntless son, pictured in the flower of his youth. The boy's face seemed to mutely appeal to him. But he gazed unflinchingly at it, and then turned away to where the white stars twinkled on the rushing Neva. The great house was still. The fearful servants dared not to break in upon his mood. General Milutin walked the halls of the mansion house for the last time, alone. The vacant rooms seemed to him now full of haunting whispers. He thought of the fair dead girl-wife, whose face looked so waxen calm as she lay in state, long, long years gone by, in that silent, vaulted hall. Boris, a motherless lad, in his romping around the great rooms seemed to wake again the brooding silence with his merry cries. Then, the bright-eyed page, the manly young ·cadet, and the handsome, gay fellow, gorgeous in his first uniform of the Chevalier Garde! It seemed as if a thousand pleading memories all called to him on this last night of dismal watching.

When the watchful butler dared to timidly demand if aught else was required, the broken old noble divined the kindly patience. He stood a moment longer, irresolute, before the favorite picture which had thrilled his father's heart so often.

"Boris!" he softly muttered. But only the faint whispered echo returned, and the "shadows on the floor" deepened in his heart. "I dare not go to him—at Nimovitch!" the old soldier owned, as his heart swelled in a last throb of sorrow. "For I could not tell him all. The sins of my life are bearing bitter, bitter fruit!" And so Pharaoh hardened his heart again. The ashy-gray morning was no grayer than the face of the father, out of whose eyes all light had faded in these bitter weeks of quarrel. But, making no sign, General Vassili Milutin sought the grim shades of the Ural mountains again. It was only to an Imperial personage that he bowed in deepest humility as he took his leave, saying, "My life, my sword, my poor experience, will replace in your Majesty's service the son who seems now to have forgotten his father!"

In far-away Rome, Countess Xenia de Berg waited with an anxious heart for the coming tidings of the meeting of Marguerite Waldberg with Madame Mazzana. It was a fearful hazard of Marguerite's happiness to unroll the happenings of the last months before the Lady of Bellagio.

"God help me! I am looking to the light," sighed Countess Xenia, as she closed an ultimate appeal to the woman who seemed to be the only avenue of future help. "A woman's love, a woman's life, a woman's honor, and all her earthly happiness, hangs on your words," she wrote. "And may God deal with you as you deal with this gentle orphan, who asks her soul's life now at your hands."

It was in the room where the girl's head had once rested

on her bosom that the woman who had swayed thousands with her witchery read the lines which pierced her heart like a two-edged sword. She gazed from the window at the lake, dreaming still at her feet. It was mantled in sunshine, but a black storm was driving down from the darkening Alps. "In mingled storm and sunshine, in warring light and darkness, we mortals sit with folded hands," she murmured, and she begged the light of wisdom for the future as she knelt with trembling knees before the Cross of Christ.

It was the eve of the appointed day for which Marguerite Waldberg had so long waited, when the Lady of Bellagio watched the dying sunset with the orphaned girl at her side. The blue lake dreamed below them. A pleasure steamer sweeping past woke the evening stillness with the strains of the "Beautiful Blue Danube." The music swelled out, floating over the glassy waters, whose crystal surface moulded a long triangular wake behind the merrily-beating paddles. The gardens smiled with orange trees fragrant and graceful, and on the hills the ashen-silver green of the olives varied "the fields which promised corn and wine." It was a delightful land of brooding happiness, for the sword flashed no longer on the hills of Lombardy, and time had deadened the echoes of the thundering cannon of Napoleon. Here, in the heart of the old quadrilateral, was naught but the golden glow of God's unbroken peace. The gray walls of Como, overhung with the watch-towers of the days of romance, rose far beyond the silver flood. The cathedral spire, pointing to the zenith, drew the eye, while the vesper-bell sounded sweetly on the evening air. The breeze swept down the valley, where, from the ivy-mantled ruins, the song of the forest bird was borne faintly to their ears. On the two harbor piers of Como those drawn to beauty's chosen shrine lingered, where, in the great pavilion, a thousand loiterers watched the sun go down in glory. From the days of Pliny down to the time of Barbarossa, Como's shores had thrilled to every aspiration of the human heart, and its fringing forests listened to the sighs of the lyre of passion ringing out as wayward as the summer wind.   Not even in the days of the lordly Viscontis, had a more delicately lovely face ever gazed upon its own reflected shadow in the crystal wave than was turned toward Madame Mazzana as the girl, swept away by the entrancing loveliness of the hour, murmured, "This is an earthly Paradise." The hostess had studied the face of the beautiful orphan intently since her arrival, and, as yet, she could not read the secret of the saddened calm which seemed to shadow the youthful face with a chastened self-devotion. All night, with a heart swayed between the future and the past, between the memory-wafted gusts of passion, and the gathering love for the girl whose life-bequest was now nearing its close, the recluse of Bellagio strove to find her way out of the dark tangle of the Fates.   Here a sudden lovely vista opened, showing her the future, lit up by the love of the girl at her side.   If she could only ward off the knowledge of a father's crime—of a mother's sin — what golden fruit might not blossom from the heart of the child whom she now yearned to clasp to a mother's heart!   Some way must be found— some womanly excuse—to throw every safeguard around the orphan.   She wished to lavish on her now the pent-up love of years.   She sighed to linger near her, to watch, as she had once before, that fair and innocent face wrapped in the dreamless mantle of innocence.   She longed to kiss her sleeping brows with a love chastened by years of remorse, of silent sorrow.   " I must—I will find the way !" the queen of art cried in her inmost heart.

" It is a Paradise.   It can yet smile even more brightly for me, Marguerite, if you would make it so.   Here we can find peace and happiness together.   We can love and lead a noble life together.   Be ruled by me.   Look not backward.   Let me offer you a home here, and you shall find all that you would wish in the commune of my heart. You have suffered in the past year, my poor child. Stay with me here. Drink of the nepenthe of Como!"

Marguerite Waldberg bent her head in the darkening shadows, and the last strokes of the Angelus then thrilled solemnly over the brooding waters, as she said,

"My life is not my own. I have but one sacred duty—to find out the mother who bore me. To stand by her grave, if she be dead. If living, to speak to her, wherever she be, and say, 'Mother, your child will bear a part of the burden.' For I know, Madame," the girl earnestly cried, "that the past was stormy, was sad, was clouded. Of what use is all my gold, my carefully-arranged provision of veiled assistance, and continued guidance, when the mother who bore me may look hungrily for a child's love. She shall not look in vain. For, to-morrow, you will tell me all. I shall go on, on to the end. For there is another heart waiting, suffering and watching. It is Boris! Far away, in the lonely chateau of Nimovitch, he waits to claim me as his bride. I care not how poor, how friendless, how worn with the world, the mother I would clasp to my heart may be, I shall only kneel at her feet and say, 'There will be your home in far Volhynia, with Boris, who waits with his noble, manly heart.' If I cannot lift the shame of being a nameless child, a waif, from the woman Boris Milutin would make his wife, then ——" her face grew strangely solemn.

"Ah! No rash oaths, no mad vows," cried Madame Mazzana, as her eyes filled with tears. "Wait, wait God's providence, my dear child."

But Marguerite steadily answered in a low voice, "I shall find behind the veil, a peace, which, in the cloister, will drive away all the dreams of the fatal love which has already wrecked Boris' whole career. He must forget me! He shall!" The excited girl was sobbing now, as she turned to the listener, whose hands were folded on her breast. And, in her tender devotion to her absent lover, the girl saw, behind the sorrow struggling on Madame Mazzana's face, the tell-tale consciousness of a full knowledge of the past life of the haughty General. Kneeling at her feet, Marguerite suddenly clasped the agitated woman's hands. "You, you alone, can clear away the tangle of the past. I care not for myself. I ask only mercy for Boris. Ah! if you knew him, so good, so true, so noble. And for me, for my love, he has braved his own haughty father's anger. Listen! General Milutin is still at St. Petersburg. It is not too late. The Czar will restore to Boris his rank and dignities. Only a few words from you. I will tell you all. I will hide nothing of the love which has grown to be my life. For Vera has told me all that her mother would have concealed in her tenderness. You are a woman whom the world has crowned. You knew this great noble. I feel it. I know that he would yield to you. Write to him," the girl pleaded, her voice quivering in her agony. "Tell him that my Boris lives in a hell made only by a father's pride which looks to the very loftiest marriage for the last of the Milutins. But he loves me so! Ah, if you could see his sufferings! I ask not for wealth. I ask not for rank. I only beg to go, with a father's blessing, to the home where the son I love waits for me. But I will not take up the cup of happiness to ruin the man I love. Tell this cold, stern man, my sad story! Tell him that my love asks nothing of God's bounty in this world but Boris' happiness.'

"You will write?" the girl pleaded. "You knew my mother. My whole heart, my soul, my very life, hangs on your words! The Czar will surely give his permission for this marriage if General Milutin's request is made. All yield to the great Czar. Vera has told me of all the loving hearts which the Emperor and Empress have made happy. They will listen to me, to my plea. But, first, the father must take his son back to his arms. And he will yield if you ask it. You can tell him, too, of my mother. A mother's heart would plead for me—I am motherless. Be my mother on this day of days! It is for Boris' very life perhaps. For, oh God, I fear his lonely life in the silent Volhynian woods! It is my future happiness! Ah, my God, tell me that you will write and beg this cold father to forgive the son whose only crime is loving me. At the father's prayer, the Czar will brush away the iron rules which bar me out, and, by that mother's memory, whom you knew, whom I have never clasped in my loving arms, I beg you to write. You have loved, you have lost, your lonely life tells me so!"

The girl sprang up, forgetting her own agony, as the beautiful actress muttered:

" Forbear, for God's sake! You know not what you ask. I cannot." Sinking in her chair, supported by the frightened girl, the Lady of Bellagio's fainting form drooped lower, till her helpless head rested on the throbbing breast of the orphan.

She had fallen, under the agony of a mighty stroke of Fate. Her marble face was drawn and contorted, her lips feebly moaned, " My God, not to him! Not to him! Never!"

There was a ghastly silence hovering between them as Marguerite hastened to support the trembling steps of Madame Mazzana toward the villa, where Frau Albert had long watched furtively the long commune by the lake-shore.

"It is nothing, my dear child, but the keen sorrow of seeing you suffer unavailingly. I must think, think how I can aid you. But what you ask of me is impossible," said the guardian of the past.

Madame Mazzana drew Marguerite with her into the privacy of the room where for long nights she had sought in vain for any pathway toward the happiness of Michael Waldberg's child.

"Listen, my dear one," the actress said, speaking slowly, " I may find a way, one way to help you. Not your way, but my way. I will think of it to-night. To-morrow, at noon, I will keep my word. You shall know what I have guarded in my heart for you. But, only on one condition will I lift the curtain of the past. You must ask no questions. What I may tell you, you shall know, your heart shall not call out to me in vain. What is hidden, then, leave in God's hands, and to-night, to-night, be my own bright darling to-night, and be happy with me to-night. Let this night be mine alone. To-morrow will be your day, and, now, leave me until I call. I must be alone for an hour !"

Marguerite wondered strangely that, while the hands which clasped her own were cold, the lips which clung to her own, in a fondly passionate kiss of tenderness, were burning.

Slowly the orphan girl walked away through the great halls, until Madame Albert's anxious face met her eyes. Side by side, they wandered in the groves until the lights in the dining-hall recalled them at last. Marguerite was trembling in every nerve, with the eagerness of her tryst of the morrow. Her mother's story awaited her.

There was a wild appeal in the last words of the woman whose roof sheltered her, which haunted the girl's heart, even in her loving anxiety for Boris Milutin, now far away by the deserted Volhynian lake.

"She has loved, she has lost ; she, too, has suffered !" mused the gentle girl, as the far lights flashed out in a diamond circle around the lake, jewelling its sapphire depths. Marguerite knew that these sculptured shores had hidden the sorrows of England's half-crazed queen, Caroline, whose fantastic train of adventurers, led by the upstart Bergami, dragged her down from sorrow's crowned heights, to the gulf of sin and shame.

The cast-off consort of "The first gentleman of Europe," even in her agonized despair, never quivered in as keen an anguish, as the stately woman who now silently watched

Marguerite, wandering with her friend, under the tranquil evening skies.

For Madame Mazzana had unlocked an antique cabinet, and, with a strange eagerness, was searching among its contents. Her eyes kindled with an eager light. She lifted a paper heavy with the seals of the Syndic of Como. Seated where her eye could still follow the graceful form of the lonely girl, Madame Mazzana murmured, "Yes, it is right. She shall have Bellagio, and all else, in time! But I must send these papers to the Prior of Jasnagora for her, the only safe depository I know; but how?" As she mused, her hand trembled as she lifted a little packet in replacing the deeds and the formal will, which she had secretly prepared. A tender smile lit up her pale face as she unrolled a silver paper, and its simple contents lay before her. A child's toy bracelet, a lock of soft, dark-brown hair, and a few faded flowers. With a cry of smothered agony the lonely woman bent her beautiful head in sudden tears. "She shall have these, also, my poor darling! My child! My own child! After I am dead!"

And, springing up, with a fearful glance at the darkened corners of the room, as if one lurked there to catch her awful thought, she cried: "Yes, yes! There is a way—there is a way! I know! That is the way!" And her heart froze in the silence of that lonely room.

Before the great Venetian glass, sweeping to the floor, the mistress of Bellagio stood and calmly eyed for a moment her noble image, in the flashing silvered crystal. She shuddered as she slowly said: "It might be, to-night—yes, to-night. And it would cut the knot of the Fates. For Death— Death," she said, with cold and hollow voice, "pays all old scores. I could carry my burden to the grave alone. This will, a last letter to Vassili Milutin, and a few words to my own innocent darling, who knows me not. Boris would be free. The ban of the past would be lifted! And then, in the unbroken silence of the grave, no one—no one could find again poor Cecile Wizocka! The betrayed wife! The childless mother! The woman without a home! The child of a dead country! The poor mistress of a broken heart!"

She bent her head in sudden thought.

"And what holds me back now? Is it Vassili? Ah! my God! The ashes of years are sifted down on the grave of a life long drenched in tears. He might even then think kindly of me. He might feel, in his heart of hearts, that the woman he loved had died to save his son and her child from the shame of that past, whose sweet passion burns now in bitterest gall and myrrh! Ah! No, Vassili!" She swiftly neared the cabinet, and drew out an object hidden for years.

She stood there with the hunting-knife clasped again in her hand. And once again she saw the imperious lover of these dim dead days, as he hurled himself upon the maddened beast who sought her life. The breezes of the woods of Nimovitch swept again across her troubled soul. "It was fated to be so! Ah! my God! Vassili! The bend sinister of shame! And yet—and yet, I loved you so! I loved you once, more than my life. And I have paid the price. The price of God's vengeance. Now, to freedom! But not this!"

Her lips were dreaming in a smile which brought back all the sweetness of the old passion which had once swept her far over the bounds of self-control. "No! The other! It is better. No one will know. And my child's heart must not be racked in vain. The Arabian cordial of Death! The Heart Compeller! Yes!"

She held a tiny colorless flask of cut-glass in her hand, as she swung the door of the cabinet. It held but a few drops, but it controlled the lives of fifty, if its acrid kiss touched lips warmed with that brief fever we call human existence!

"Do I dare?" she murmured. "Why not? I give to my

poor child the last legacy of an unknown mother's love-happiness for her whole life ! And Vassili; he alone will know. He will know how I have loved her, how I would guard, too, the golden fame and name of Boris ; and, when I am gone, he might think of me once again, as when he met me at Nimovitch, beautiful to him, loving and beloved ! In his memory of Love he may learn to adore the memory of the woman who loved her own fatherless child more than the life whose golden days had been his alone ! "

" But one pang tears my heart. But one sorrow now rends. She might even now learn to love me. She might grow to look with pitying, with loving eyes, on the helpless one who fled, in that wild night, from the horror-haunted halls of Nimovitch. Ah, God ! my own darling ! The cold kiss of death will seal our love forever. For her bright, brave, innocent heart will always cling to me. She cannot know. Vassili will atone. He loved me once. He loved me so ! And thus I go out, in peace, but whither ? " She gazed on the twinkling stars of night, and, when she turned again, a high purpose nerved her soul.

" For one night my child shall know all my love, all my tenderness. With a strange wonder in her eyes, at dawn she will think that I passed out in the silent night, touched by the dark angel's wing. Her love for my memory will be unfading. It is better so—better so ! "

Like a royal queen in state, the Lady of Bellagio entered the hall where the waiting daughter she dared not own was startled at her unearthly beauty. For she was secretly robed for the death of a self-devoted Love, and would fain be remembered in all her womanly splendor. " She will always think of me as she sees me to-night. My dear child ! My last shadow-picture shall be a fond legacy." And Cecile's lip trembled.

There was a restraining influence in the presence of Madame Albert. She had been a woman of the world herself, who had now passed all the storms of passion, and was floating serenely down on the ebb-tide of life! She was, however, unable to trace the reason of the reversed relations of the two women at her side. For Madame Mazzana seemed this night to have regained all the sparkling witchery of young womanhood! Her varying moods swept her listeners over all the scenes of a varied and romantic public life.

In vain did Madame Albert essay to trap her into any un-guarded references as to her youth.

It seemed as if this bright genius had burst, full-starred, upon a world which knew not of her infancy. Scenes of beauty rose in living color under her graphic description, and, when the evening hours lengthened, the great salon rang to the sonorous melody of her voice raised in song, after the voyagers had, hushed in delight, followed her in varied declamation, from the kings of the continental languages.

"Your accent, Madame, is puzzling," remarked Madame Albert, tentatively. "Your German is faultless, yet——"

"It is not my native tongue," remarked the hostess with one wary look, which stilled the duenna. Marguerite, grave and tender, hung now upon every movement of the stately woman whose witching mood seemed to grow upon her. It was with wondering emotion she thrilled to her heart, as the great genius smote upon the harp of Love hidden deeply in the girl's heart.

The fairyland of art, the costly thousand reminders of her days of triumph, of her hours of travel, drew the atten-tion of the baffled duenna, who, in her own wisdom, decided to furtively watch her mysterious hostess, but safely, from afar.

"She is ever on guard in my presence, and, I must wait. There is some special reason in her casting her enchant-ment to-night on this sad-hearted girl. Perhaps she may go on to some careless self-betrayal, I will find her secret out, yet!" and Madame Albert's foot sounded distantly in the far picture-gallery, while the two hearts so strangely knitted together were wrapped up in the passing hours which this night seemed to blend their two hearts in one.

"Sing for me, my dearest child," softly said the Lady of Bellagio, as they neared the grand piano once more, from whose pearl keys the rippling accompaniment to Madame Mazzana's own thrilling voice, still trembled.

"I cannot, I dare not. My father would never listen. He would not have me sing!" The girl's eyes filled with the bitter tears of memory.

A gentle and loving hand drew her to the piano, a voice which touched her very soul whispered, as the noble form of the speaker bent over her, "Sing as if your own mother had asked you. The mother whom you never knew."

In a half trance, moved by a feeling which she could not resist, the girl turned the leaf of the nearest sheet, and with misty eyes, followed the simple score. Her voice quavered in feeling, and her pulses beat strangely as the sweet notes swelled out and filled the vaulted room. Marguerite Waldberg was looking out only into cloudland, as she chanted the tender words of a simple little German song of homely praise. A hush fell on the room, and she felt her own heart swell within her in a tide of feeling bearing her onward and upward. A tear fell on her hand as a soft voice murmured, "Noel is an exquisite bit of heart-throbbing. I hear the angels' carol in your gentle voice! Sing this for me." And, before the wanderer could refuse, her yielding soul led her into the music which her only listener placed before her. The slumbering lyre of her soul was stirred, and all her yearning love was voiced in the song which had once haunted her childhood. The last words faltered from her lips "Gute nacht, du mein hertziges kind," and it seemed, when she rose, as if the lost mother whom she had longed for, folded her in loving arms and pressed her to a breast glowing in fond devotion. The very spirit of Love burned in the kisses pressed on her lips.

" You have a gift of God in your glorious voice, my darling," Madame Mazzana whispered, as the astonished face of the delighted duenna appeared in the salon.

"Countess Xenia will surely never be denied your music again, Marguerite ! " cried the startled woman. " Where have I heard that voice ? " she mused, and it was only when the great house was stilled that the excited dowager felt, with a sudden start of surprise, that the two singers of the night were really one in the accent and timbre of the voice.

It was in the last half hour of the eve of the long-waited day, that Madame Mazzana's sudden fire of splendid genius seemed to suddenly die away again into the grave, watchful womanly dignity which had marked their first interviews. For, Marguerite had buried her face in the bosom which held prisoned the secret of a life, and whispered, " To-morrow, you will tell me all ! " The light of another world seemed to linger on the noble brow of the gracious Lady of Bellagio. " You shall know, you shall know, what I may give to you, and then, dear one, ask, seek, to know no more. My child, my strangely dear one, for your mother, from your mother, I give you these good-night kisses ; " and, drawing down the fair young face to her own, the Lost Lady of Nimovitch gazed long and wistfully into the clear and tender eyes of innocence. Marguerite Waldberg lingered and marvelled that, at the door where they had finally parted, with sudden swift steps, and eyes of strangely kindled light, once more, the woman who seemed to read her very soul, came back to fold the stranger, the orphan of the Gray House, to her breast, in a passionate caress.

Seated alone in her own retreat, gazing on the stars sweeping over the silver lake, and dreaming strange dreams in the hushed stillness of the night, Marguerite could hear, for a time her anxious heart counted not, the steps of the one who alone held the key of the future. The Lady of Bellagio was strangely busied.

In the weariness of her double excitement the orphan slumbered fitfully, until, with a sudden start, she awoke, and then some strange unearthly feeling of dread possessed her. It was late; for the waxen tapers had all burned low in their sockets, and a haunting silence, peopled with unknown horrors, brooded in the hushed room !

There was no sound audible in the chamber where the story of her life was yet locked in a woman's heart. And the blackened waters of the lake lay dark and chill as a pall below the windows of the villa. The fair moon had sunk away in sombre clouds to the west, and every sighing, rustling leaf seemed to thrill, with a nameless terror, the ·girl who rose and closed the half-opened sash. The very air itself seemed charged with an indefinable spirit of evil, and, in sheer fear, the girl turned toward the door which hid her hostess from her !

Madame Albert was far away, in a favored guest-chamber, for the two who waited for the coming day would be alone.

A newer dread, a quaking fear, which hastened her timid steps, drew Marguerite to the door between them, which was hidden by a thick portière.

She swept it aside, and a thin pencil of light streamed through the keyhole. There was, then, another watchful one on this night grown so strangely ominous of evil !

With a sudden impulse, the girl sprang into the room, which was dimly lit by a swinging silver-lamp, twinkling at the farther end. One glance told her that the room was untenanted. Fear lent her wings as she fled to the further recess of the great sleeping-chamber. In her frantic eagerness the startled fugitive brushed aside the frail fastenings of a light door which she knew not of.

With a wild cry of alarm she clasped in her arms a woman who stood before a glimmering taper, and pinioned her shaking hands in her desperate grasp.

" Forbear ! For God's sake ! You know not what you do ! " cried Marguerite, for her hand had closed upon a crystal vial that she had wrested away from the grasp of a woman standing on the verge of that dark chasm we mortals call the grave—the gloomy abyss of infinite nothingness, end or beginning of life past, or life to come, around its portals the dark horrors of the Unknown ward back our mortal gaze.

" It was for you ! " the Lady of Bellagio murmured, as she reeled and fell senseless at the feet of the motherless child.

The gray of morning showed a white, wan face, resting on pillows, wet with Marguerite Waldberg's tears. The Lady of Bellagio was like an humbled child in her docile yielding to the love-strengthened spirit of Marguerite. " I need only you, my darling," she whispered. " Wait, wait, and I will yet bring peace to your heart, abiding peace. For, God alone can send you happiness."

The bright sun lit up once more with golden glory the beauties which smiled around Bellagio, and there was no sound in the darkened room save the beating of two hearts now drawn closely to each other by the mystic chrism of a royal sorrow. Their eyes, meeting in silence, spoke of a love which our poor words cannot render, and the Lost Lady of Nimovitch stirred uneasily in a troubled sleep when Marguerite's hand smoothed her brows. But a smile was now lingering on her pale lips, for she had only whispered " Gute nacht, du mein hestziges kind."

Madame Albert was consciously defeated in her effort to solve the riddle of the past, when two weeks later she returned to Countess Xenia's side. The letters of which she was the bearer bore tidings of which she could not divine the import. " I can see the strange power of genius thrilling even a careless world," the duenna mused. " For, these two seem to have now grown into one being."

It was, indeed, a marvel of the hour. Though Marguerite Waldberg's face bore no sunlight of sudden happiness, a calm seemed to have folded her passionate, longing heart in white wings of peace. "I shall divide my future," wrote Marguerite to Countess de Berg, "between your home, my dear shelter in the dark hours of the past, and this new haven of rest. For the light is dawning now! To you—to Vera, I cannot yet disclose all the hopes which fill a heart happier than I ever dared to dream. For, I shall see my mother yet—face to face! She lives! She lives to bless me yet!"

No one ever knew the import of the letter sent by the Lady of Bellagio to the patrician Russian widow, but words of cheer and hope went out from Countess Xenia to the man who lingered under the shadows which time had cast over the mossy roof-tree of the old chateau at Nimovitch.

There were tranquil, happy days stealing on at Bellagio. Marguerite seemed to insensibly glide into the inmost heart-chambers of the great artist whom all the world knew now had taken a silent farewell of the painted unrealities of the mimic scene. In vain the outer world knocked at the gates of Villa Bellagio. Two beautiful women—goddess and nymph—might be seen from the fair road winding down to the lake, but they lived alone—the world forgetting, by the world forgot.

The autumn was turning the leaves of Nimovitch to gold once more before Boris Milutin knew that the woman he loved with an increasing and despairing love was once more sheltered under the roof of Countess de Berg at Dresden. The Russian widow questioned not her returning bird-of-passage.

But a new, tender light shone in Marguerite's clear eyes as she whispered, "My mother lives. She loves me. This I know. It is enough. And the day will come when I shall know her at last. For the shadow of my great sorrow is slowly lifting." This was the burden of her hard-won victory over the sibylline reticence of the woman who had been saved from death at her own hands.

Countess Xenia never knew that Madame Mazzana had solemnly pledged the departing girl to wait for God's summons and tempt not the waters of the "Plutonian shore." "If you will trust me, if you will love me, Marguerite, I will live! Live for you! And you shall know yet, some day, a mother's love, though the path which leads you to her heart be dark and shaded now."

"I will wait!" the loving orphan cried, as she drew the noble head down on a bosom whose every breath was freighted with the hallowed innocence of an unstained womanhood.

Boris Milutin never dared to hope for a single relenting word from the man the stories of whose fierce reign at Orenburg had even reached the shadowed copses of Nimovitch. General Milutin, hardened in his Pharaoh heart, waited only the moment for the brutal flames of war to light up the darkened valley of the Danube. Yet, the sapphire ring still glittered on his hand! The lost love had made no sign in these lonely years, and the old soldier's brow was fierce and gloomy as he waited like a grim hound in the leash day by day. For the Russian sword still slept on in its scabbard. An awful gloom of growing apprehension settled upon Russia, and it was with bated breath the doomed of the Valkyries wore out the long winter in watching. Pride and passion had not yet lost their dark sway when the four women who watched the deadly feud of father and son shuddered as the Czar of all the Russias hurled his vast army at last on the Turks. On the twenty-fourth of April, in the fatal year of seventy-seven, General Vassili Milutin rode with the glittering staff of the Czar, and Boris, his disinherited son, was only a simple volunteer, with General Alexis Dournof under grim old Gourko!

CHAPTER XIII.

BEFORE PLEVNA.

THE last night of Boris Milutin's stay by the memory-haunted lake of Nimovitch had seen him pacing the deserted salon of the old chateau until the birds began to wake the stillness of the lonely park. The soldier's heart was bounding within him. For the comrades of his happiest years were now sweeping down to the Danube. The White Czar had spoken at Kishineff, and the Bosnian horrors had hurled two hundred thousand Russians, under the Cross of Christ, against the two hundred and fifty thousand Turks banded under the Crescent. The struggle in the young Colonel's heart, as he held back, was a terrible one. For the trumpet call had sounded, and, from the military circumscriptions of Wilna, Warsaw and Kiev, the gray-coated Muscovites thronged bravely to the border. The harvest of Death was ripe !

All day the singing columns had been toiling down the road to Rowno, and hospitable Boris Milutin, mounted on his favorite war-horse, rode along the line, greeting the higher officers who had been his battle comrades ! There was waiting store of good cheer in the two great serf-villages of Nimovitch, and the regimental songs sounded gaily as the flaxen-haired peasant maids, with fluttering kerchiefs, waved their fond adieu to the sturdy soldiers. Blue eyes beamed fondly on Ivan and Serge, as the bright tears told of the warm woman-hearts beating in those Volhynian shades.

It was a day of soul-wrestling and agony for Boris; from

the headquarters of the six corps already on the Roumanian frontier, from the mobilization centre at Odessa and the Crimea, the rallying-points of his two familiar corps, with which he had so long served, and, even from the general of the three last corps, waiting in their own distant circles, a sheaf of imploring letters had sought out the man who lingered with his sword yet in the scabbard. Even an Imperial Grand Duke had telegraphed the offer of a chief-of-staff's appointment from far Tiflis, where the Czar's boldest waited to assault the bristling mountains of Kars.

He had been deaf to even the appeal of the Minister of War to indicate the rank and place which would be acceptable to him. He had even thrown the flattering letter down in disgust. He recognized the hand of his own imperious father in the diplomatic invitation. What to him now were star and order glittering over an unhappy heart? What poor bait of fortune even the golden shoulder-crowns of an imperial aide-de-camp? For the battle of life had been fought. He had surely won in blood and desert toil the right to face his future in peace. And so he lingered on in indifference.

It seemed to Boris Milutin that something had gone out of his life forever. The face of the woman he loved haunted him always. By night her eyes seemed to shine down again on him. Her tender voice whispered once more, "Boris, I will wait!" And then, between them, rose up the stern face of his angered father.

Born a Russian subject—a part of the breathing bulwark of human hearts around the Russian Colossus—he knew too well the barrier which kept him from giving his life, his name, his honour, and his vast heritage to Marguerite Waldberg as his wife. For, he was tied down hand and foot by the fetich of law, custom, family rule and Greek orthodoxy!

"There are a thousand ways to be unhappy in Russia," the patrician hermit groaned, as he rode back into his gates when the last columns of the self-devoted soldiers plodded along toward where the shambles of Lovtscha, and the awful butchery of the Grivitza redoubt awaited them.

Seated alone on the south portico of the chateau, gazing at the thousand tints of green which gave tone and depth to the exquisite valley smiling before him, he started up as a mud-bespattered courier handed to him a sealed packet. The commander at Rowno had bidden the Cossack to ride hard, and the horse, staggering now with quivering flanks, at the great portal of the chateau, showed how well the wild soldier had obeyed the stern mandate. Boris Milutin sprang up as the friendly and brief words of General Alexis Dournof roused his sleeping heart.

"Come to me, Boris. It is not any longer a case of ambition. It is for the honor of your old regiment. Telegraph to Galatz. I will have your whole outfit there. Your father's heart is breaking under the sneers provoked now by your absence. I see love's star shining over you here on the Danube. Shall I call on a Milutin in vain, when the army crosses?"

The two other letters lay long before him unopened. One bore the crest of the De Bergs, and the other was a message from the woman whose love had estranged him from the haughty chief now with the Czar at Kishineff. Colonel Milutin thrust the two letters into his bosom, and then sought his room alone. It seemed as if he would hide her sacred words from the every-day world around him. His soul was at war in the narrow confines of his bosom. The trumpet-call had thrilled his soldier blood in its every fiery drop, and this summons to the front braced him with a new energy. On the wall of the salon, hung the sword he had so long wielded against the Turcoman night-riders. It lay across his table as he opened the letters which he feared to exhaust in their freighted burden of friendship and love.

"Vera and I go at once to St. Petersburg," wrote Countess

Xenia, "to join those who are already organizing the Red Cross societies for the sick and wounded. I have shared the confidence of General Dournof, and I write you now, my brother, to add my own feeble words to his imperative call to arms. We do not make our own lives, Boris, but the path of duty lies always clearly cut out before us. I know that you will join Alexis Dournof, and our hearts and prayers go out with you. You shall have our last tidings always sent to his headquarters. Be steadfast, my brave brother, for I can tell you that the future holds for you a crown of royal happiness. Marguerite loves you—loves you beyond all bounds. Her gentle soul cannot find words, perchance, but I know the richly-dowered woman-heart that beats for you in her loyal bosom. She will not consent yet to seal the ruin of your house by dragging you down. Some day the dark veil of the past will be lifted. Around this innocent girl a mantle of shadows have clung since her lonely child-hood. Helpless, devoted, loving, she has the high pride of an unsullied maidenhood, and to you would give the jewelled crown of a life's devotion. She is yours to the very last! Trust to her fidelity, for the steadfast faith she holds for your sake is of the noblest. You, my brother Boris, may finally conquer your princely father to the speaking of that one word which can lift all these shadows. I dare not speak further, save to tell you that a whiter soul never nestled in a mother's bosom. It is for your sake only that she suffers— for the grand old line which sees in you its noblest and its last! I feel that this war will bring us all nearer together. I have had a strange vision. It may seem a mere fancy of my mind, but we were all together in the far land where the Danube flows to the Euxine!"

Boris' eyes were moistened as he read the spirited woman's last words of good-bye, and the lines in which little Vera's brave soul flashed out in an aspiration for holy Russia.

"Shall I go," the soldier murmured. He paced the very

room where Cecil Wizocka had once knelt over her slumbering child and prayed that its father might be true. It was the long deserted haven where the Lost Lady of Nimovitch had seen the lonely days of her living prison death, in the Volhynian forests, where, from her own windows, she had seen stately Vassili Milutin ride up in answer to that ceasless call of his passion-stirred breast. "I shall see her at Nimovitch!"

Before the soldier there lay the last, his beloved one's letter, and the lonely room seemed filled with the very thrill of her presence—that spirit-essence which blends soul and body, which rises above all of stern fate's decrees and cold fortune's frowns, which laughs at time and space, and sets at naught, the physical gulf between the two sundered hearts beating as one!

He read with a bounding heart.

"My own darling! My dearest," he softly said as he lifted the letter. In his heart of hearts, he felt the communion of the two blended soul bodies, two circles converging into one forever. She seemed to haunt the room, as if her very life was hallowing it. "She has been here, she is here, she will always be near me, here," he murmured, for the gallant lover did not coldly reason that she was prisoned in his heart there, in his lonely and loyal heart, where the viewless spirit of love abode, even as the Great Tenant of the Ark abode, though it was empty to all mortal eyes, in the golden temple in the City of David.

He broke the seal, and, as he read, the lines seemed to glow with the very spirit of her love. In wonder, and with a proudly-beating heart, he repeated her words, penned in loving faith, the words which told him of her undying devotion.

"I may not hold you back, Boris, when your country's flag goes into battle! I send you my picture. Let it speak to you in your lonely days. Perhaps my eyes may tell you what I cannot frame in words. For, trust me, my Boris, a loving woman's heart lies buried deep, deep in her own true breast, where the murmur of the lips cannot reach the one secret locked there in its deepest cell ! I will wait for you, my Boris ! I am your own to the end of my life ! My soul, my heart, goes out to you ! I will be nearer to you than even your longing love can picture ; and I pray God for the day when your father, conquered in love, will join our hands ! New laurels on your brow, new honors to your stainless sword, an eternal joy in your heart, and in our souls, we shall taste that double happiness which we alone can know ! Countess Xenia has promised me that I shall know all at once ; and, when you write to me where your new rank will take you, you shall know, from my poor words, that my heart and soul follow you out to the field of victory ! "

The picture of Marguerite Waldberg, lay before him on the table ! Her eyes thrilled him ! He sprang up and rang for the intendant !—" Fresh horses for the courier, and then send him here at once ! "

When the Cossack stood before him, the growing light of a new life danced in Boris Milutin's eyes. " Can you ride back to Rowno to-night ? " he queried, gazing at the compact little Cossack standing there with merry twinkling eyes, " I have a telegram to send to the Commander ! "

" I will ride it in four hours ! " cheerily answered the trooper. " My own sotnia goes at daybreak to the front, and I must be with them—with my comrades ! "

" Molodetz ! " gaily cried Boris, tossing him a couple of gold imperials. " There is your dispatch ! Stay ! Here is my own card to the General. I, too, go to the front,—to Galatz to-morrow. Wait for me at the headquarters. I need an orderly. Have you served ? "

" Three years in the Caucasus, Barin ! " said the soldier, saluting.

" Then you know blood and fire ! You shall go with me."

It seemed as if a liquid fire danced in Milutin's veins,

as he stood and saw the delighted trooper dash away, under the fringing elms drooping over the lonely chapel of
Nimovitch.

Milutin turned, and then took up the sword which had so
often flashed out by the Caspian for the Czar. He smiled
as he lightly swung the pliant Toledo. " For the Czar, for
Russia," he murmured,—" and for you—dearest ! " he smiled.
" I can leave at daybreak.

In an hour, the hurrying feet of the menials, awakened
from the dreaming trance of the every-day lethargy, were
echoing through the lonely halls. A soldier's kit making
was of old-time routine, to Boris, and a new impulse
thrilled his veins ! He would win her now !

The diamond dews of morning were sprinkled on the forget-
me-nots starring the lawn sweeping down to the old park, as
Boris Milutin closed the letter which told Marguerite that her
lover trusted to his sword to win a father's heart once more.
His voice was tender as he sealed the packet with the arms
of the house of Milutin. A few forget-me-nots were folded
in the lines which told of his joining General Dournof.
" They may speak to her, for me, when I am far away on the
Danube or climbing the Balkans." There was a bright sun
leaping over the dreaming meadows of Nimovitch, as, under
a storm of hourras from a thousand peasants, the young
lord of the manor rode out through his park gates ! The
springy black Orloff tossed his mane, and the white star on
his forehead was borne proudly aloft as Milutin turned to
cast a last glance at the white walls of the old chateau.

" I could have been so happy with her here," he mused.
" I shall come back here some day with her and walk by
that lake. Under the listening trees of the old park, I will
tell her of my love. For I shall meet her here, my dearest,
at Nimovitch ! " The reins lay on the horse's neck as the
soldier lifted his hat in passing the chapel and the graveyards on either side of the road where Russ and Pole lay in

their silent opposition. The cool morning breeze drew over the nodding trees shading the dead of a dozen generations. For, stretching before him, the rolling plains of the Nimovitch highlands offered to his eyes a royal field for a cavalry battle. A slight chill shook his frame, and his brow was grave. "I have nothing else to give her. I will make my will at Galatz, and then give this dear old place to Marguerite! For I have loved her so; in these lonely months her memory clings to every garden walk, to the silent wood-paths where I have called up on her name, to the lonely rooms where, in the vigils of the night, I have heard her voice whisper in my dreams, 'I love you!'" And, as he bounded in a stretching gallop over the elastic turf, he repeated, "Nimovitch shall be hers forever!" and he dreamed of her all the long days as he swept down towards the Turkish border.

Boris Milutin's heart grew light as he neared Galatz, for the Russian army was now, at last, over the frontier, and in every halted train he saw the bronzed faces of men dear to him. The banks of the Pruth echoed to the tramp of armed thousands, and the singing bugles waked the distance. Roumania's hills and slopes sped by, and, with a beating heart, the volunteer without rank sprang out of the train at Galatz. A joyous shout welcomed him from a dozen familiar voices, when Alexis Dournof, forgetting the gravity of a new-made Major-General, grasped him in a soldierly embrace,

"By Jove, Boris, you are in the nick of time. We are to push on at once to the Danube. You may have to wait over a day here to read your letters and telegrams." Dournof smiled as he delivered a formidable bundle. "Now, my dear boy, we can talk in the train. The place is full of spies. Dragmiroff there will provide your whole outfit. I have horses for you. As for rank, you are my chief-of-staff!"

Colonel Milutin's voice trembled slightly as he said, in a low voice, "My father?"

"At Ploieste, now, with the Emperor," murmured Dournof. "Our train goes right on, forward."

"Good," cried Colonel Milutin, who was speedily ensconced in the quiet corner of a car, as the train lumbered down toward the waterless and treeless wastes of the sandy Dobrudja.

While his trusty Volhynian Cossack displayed, with pride, the results of hasty foraging, Boris Milutin read new words of cheer from the girl on whose beating heart his last letters were treasured at Bellagio. It was with a gentle sigh that he laid down Countess Xenia's letters from St. Petersburg. "Anything you will ask will be given to you, Boris," the patrician wrote. "Even the Grand Dukes are astonished now, at your father's cold aversion! He is pitiless!"

Looking out to where the ruins of Trajan's wall were no fence against the Russian legions, Colonel Milutin gazed toward Bucharest's distant hills from whence their path led down to Giurgovo, and onward to fifty thousand Turkish enemies waiting on the Danube. "I will either win her by my sword, or find a death over there," he mused, gazing toward the Danube valley, where the marsh mists hung over the valley soon to be one vast graveyard. For the Balkan ravens were whetting their beaks as the old cause came on for the bloody trial of battle once more. Two months later, Boris Milutin was only the keen-eyed, dashing soldier. For his duties were unending. The great army pouring down from Bucharest and Statina, had forced the Danube, led by Dragmiroff and dashing Skobeloff. The sleepy Turks at Zimnitza roused up, and six hundred of the sturdy Volhynians who had cheered as they passed Nimovitch, lay there stark and dead in the marshes on the first day of sharp fight. On, the whole army pouring in, the great Russian octopus crawled, led by grim old Gourko, until Osman Pasha, hastening up from Widdin, confronted Schilder-Shuldener and Krudener at Plevna. Then came an ominous halt,—before those fresh red mounds!

There were only a few low redoubts to be seen around the town yet without a history, on the day when Boris Milutin himself galloped up with a Grand Duke's order, "to occupy Plevna as soon as possible!" On the twentieth of July, the Grivitza ridge saw the first red harvest field of the horrible struggle to come. Though the Russian standard had floated all day in the very gardens of Plevna, there were three thousand of the best and bravest of the Czar's troops lying on that field of blood where the brave Russians were driven out, fighting inch by inch, that bitter night, to the dismay of their blundering Generals! The Turk was waking up!

Though four thousand Turks also lay dead and wounded on the field, it was a night of fruitless horror which followed the first battle-day of Plevna.

Boris Milutin had charged with the Nineteenth regiment, into the bloody gardens of the dead, and it was only on foot, wounded and bleeding, that he rejoined the stubborn rallying Russians, after the swarming Turkish reinforcements had driven the temporary victors back!

Milutin lay by a watch-fire, on a few trusses of muddy straw, and was drinking the coffee which his nimble Cossack had prepared, while his tired comrades of the staff spoke to him words which brought a flush of blood to his cheeks! This was the real game of war, and, beyond the red hills of Plevna, he saw the way to where Marguerite waited for him at Bellagio! The night was gloomily dark, and down below, in the dismal valleys, between their sheltered ridge and the Turkish position, faint cries and yells were borne back upon the night wind. A patter and trampling as of hundreds of feet sounded heavily on the thickened air!

"What is that, Ivan?" demanded Milutin, his still shaken nerves trembling.

"The Bashi Bazouks are going over the field and killing all our wounded!" simply said the rude Cossack, as he peered out into the night. "But we will get even some day!"

Alas! As Milutin bowed his head on his breast, he could not foresee the time when the Circassians would cut down three thousand of these same marauders, in one wild ride at Phillipopolis. He only knew that the wounded men whose eyes had glanced bravely into his own, that battle morn, lay helpless there under the merciless scimetar! For the pyramid of human heads before Plevna was already begun. It was a horrible night!

Milutin's voice was choking with emotion, when a dozen officers rode up, with a half company of Circassian cavalry as an escort.

"General Dournof!" cried out a stern voice. A soldier wrapped in a huge horseman's cloak, spoke briefly as the dauntless Dournof emerged from his shelter tent.

"The Grand Duke wishes the name of the officer who led the assault on the garden to-day. He wishes that officer, if still living, to report to him at once, at headquarters, for staff duty."

"He is here with me now, General!" said Dournof, his voice ringing out strangely.

"Then, send him here at once! The Grand Duke has sent to him the Cross of St. Vladimir, taken from his own breast!"

"You must go. It is an Imperial order!" whispered General Dournof, as he laid his friendly hand on silent Boris Milutin's shoulder. All the circle around the camp-fire uncovered as Alexis Dournof led forward the wounded hero of the hour. The flickering light of the bivouac fire lit up Boris Milutin's face, as he stood, silent, there before his own father.

"Colonel Boris Milutin! General," said Alexis Dournof, as he stepped back, leaving the son at the side of the stern old General, who sat, speechless, on his horse.

"You!" gasped the veteran; but, he coldly said in an official tone, "I am directed to hand this to you, sir, on behalf of His Highness, the Grand Duke, in admiration of your gallantry in to-day's assault. You will also report at once to His Highness for staff duty."

There was a silence of the grave as the son bowed. His hand dropped to his side from the salute, and his nerveless fingers closed on the glittering cross. No one heard the whisper in which he simply said, "I shall not report! I am sick and wounded, my rank is only provisional!"

"You must, sir!" angrily cried the irate father.

"I shall leave the army first," slowly said Milutin, as he bowed and walked back to the camp-fire.

No one heard the humble supplication of the veteran whose heart was divided between pride and rage. "Boris!" he whispered.

But the face of the insulted Marguerite Waldberg rose up between them; and, while the father rode away along the very picket line, wrapped in his stern sorrow, Boris Milutin fell moodily asleep in his hut with the cross of the Grand Duke clasped in his hand! Though the awful chorus of the battle shambles drifted sadly on the trampled clay, under the shining benison of two dear eyes far away at Bellagio, one step was already gained on the ladder of fame to reach her!

The weary days of fruitless battle and bootless bravery dragged slowly along. Already, the grim Grivitza redoubt was known over a world, shuddering at the carnage which destined seventy thousand men of the warring two hundred thousand now grouped around Plevna, for the battlefield's yawning grave trenches!

There was no further insistence by the gloomy old patrician General Milutin, who watched at headquarters the growing despondency of the aged Emperor of all the Russias. Already over far Russia the sound of bitter mourning was heard.

Though the laurels of Melikoff shone out brightly in Asia Minor, there was on the Danube only a fearful procession of calamities, awaiting the two hundred thousand Russians now crowded into the unhealthy, swampy Dobrudska.

Boris Milutin's eyes grew haggard, his cheeks thin and ghastly as the luckless months dragged along. In vain, long train-loads of sturdy Russians were drawn in daily as reinforcements from the lonely woods of their own distant land, or the vast silent steppes. The maw of the demon Death seemed insatiable.

The fearful record of August, September and October, only further disheartened the vast Russian host. For the hordes of Osman Pasha and Suleiman seemed to have only commenced to fight where all others leave off! Dournof's brow was dark. Even the Russian soldier can waver at last! Around the great table of the ageing Emperor, men spoke only in sadly-dejected whispers.

The spade and the American rifle, in the hands of the desperate Turks, sheltered by the huge reddened mounds of Plevna, defied the desperation of even Russian valor!

The hospitals along the Danube were now all filled with the dead and the dying. The one slender line of railroad open to Russia broke down at last under the increasing demands of the campaign. All was sadness, defeat and woe.

Even Boris Milutin scorned now the hopes of vain promotion; he only clung, with devoted fidelity, to the loved and absent one, whose letters from Bellagio ceased now to bring him life and hope. Even the postal lines were paralyzed!

"I can do nothing for you, my dear friend," said General Dournof, as they rode alone, in rear of the shelter trenches, on an early October evening. "All is incapacity, disorganization and defeat. Our brave troops are thrown in, under poor leaders, and without concert. Only great Todleben's arrival, —a regular siege—and starving these devils out, will ever take us into Plevna!"

As Dournof spoke, a chance ball carried away the very whip he flourished. He calmly continued :

"See our failures! The second and third battles of Plevna. The fruitless heroism of glorious Skobeloff at Loftcha,—the miseries of the Shipka Pass,—and now, this last horrible desperate assault of the Grivitza redoubt! This army is not fitly generalled,—the orders conflict—our sick list is appalling, and the supplies are lamentably insufficient. Nothing but a regular siege will ever take us in!" General Dournof sighed again as he recalled the peerless Skobeloff's manly rage on his return from the fiery graveyard of his devoted troops. Hatless, his white uniform stained and blackened, his scabbardless sword in his hand, the "White General,"—on foot,—came out crowned with glory from that fatal day of Loftcha, an inspired demigod, and yet, even he confessed defeat!

Dournof gazed at the heart-sore Milutin who, for forty long days, had never received tidings of the woman whom he was now determined to marry, even though the Czar himself cried "Forbear!" "My poor Boris! you know not what a romantic girl may do! Why, one of the Emperor's aids told me to-day that. Countess Xenia de Berg and her daughter Vera would soon join the Red Cross Sisters, now vainly toiling with our poor rotting wounded, and nursing our doomed sick! Marguerite might also be mad enough to come!"

Milutin turned and quickly faced his chief. "For God's sake, Dournof, speak no more! Dachkof told me to-day that the Russian volunteer nurses were dying by scores over there, and the best blood of our land is being shovelled into the sand-trenches with our poor butchered soldiers. God bless these darling women! My God! It is a horrible campaign. Could you spare me only a few days to go over to headquarters? I might perhaps find out there some tidings!"

Dournof sighed, as he turned his horse's head back to the camp, for even at a mile and a half, the Peabody-martini was killing its score daily. The high-born Grand Duke of

Leuchtenberg's corpse attested the skill of the Turkish sharp-shooters at a long mile.

"Boris," gently said his friend and General, "I can let no man leave this army now! General Todleben will soon be here! a cordon will be established, by a heavy force, round Plevna; and then a grand assault may follow. But, I will have from you, no more forlorn-hope business! I must save you, my friend! For I will see you yet in your castle at Orenburg, with happy Marguerite at your side! Will you not let me make overtures now to your father? He might yield if you would ask!"

Colonel Milutin gazed fondly at his friend, "Dournof, he said, with his breast heaving, "I cannot! There is some old-time feud which shadowed both my father and this girl's dead father—the dead man who has locked up the childhood of the woman I adore! General Milutin himself has led a life of shaded chapters. I know not what cold bitterness of the dark past pointed their hatred! Some personal quarrel, it may be, perhaps, over a worthless woman, or a game of cards, or a painted actress! I only know that my father, for once in his life—once only—I admit, acted the coward, when he hurled his insults on the dear, defenceless head of the girl I would marry. I will not sue to him! No! Sooner would I climb once more the red embrasures of that mouth of Hell there!" He pointed to where Grivitza lay, a silent, yellowish tiger, with all its black guns waiting to deal out a ready death! Twenty thousand Russians had died around it! And Boris himself had come out, stunned and breath-less, of the awful fifteen minutes in which the Russians had held its gorge, fighting there with shortened bayonets, on the blood-soaked slopes!

"Let me tell you, too, something, Boris!" cried Dournof, his face lighting up with a tender love. "You are a gallant soldier, and a loyal lover! I feel that Countess Xenia holds the real key to the mystery of your father's hate! Did you ever think that another might have pointed the venom which thrills in your father's heart? Waldberg was certainly a Pole! Your father's high command in Poland took him into every circle in those old days! Can it be that Waldberg and your father had a feud to the death over some woman beloved by both?"

Colonel Milutin dropped his head in deep thought. "I will demand of that dearest of women, Xenia, this long-hidden secret, if it be one! But, Dournof, all is veiled to me! Nothing seems real here but death, defeat, misery and the sufferings of my poor soldiers! If I ever had a heart, it is buried here, at Plevna! But, even on my last battle-day, while a heart-throb is left to me, I am the plighted husband of Marguerite Waldberg! Should this ghastly drama leave me still on the scene, I will legally renounce my name, then leave Russia forever, and the house of Milutin will be left without an heir. But, I will not sue to my father!" The sadness of Dournof's eyes spoke of the sorrow of his silent heart.

And thus it was that the daily companion of the Czar, the trusted counselor, the old patrician General, bowed his head in silent tears when General Dournof returned to him his son's final answer. The official offer of a general's commission was also coldly declined by Boris, who said to General Dournof:

"There is but one answer possible to my father in this affair. He knows the reparation which is due to the past. I thank the Emperor most humbly for the proffered distinction. If I live through this terrible campaign, I shall then quit Russia forever, and formally give up my citizenship. I have nothing to take with me but a broken heart! Nimovitch I have already inscribed to Marguerite Waldberg. If I live, we may go back there together some day. If I die, she may think of me there, where my heart has burned with love for her; alone in the lonely and sleepless nights. No, Dournof! The first love of a

pure woman's heart, my only love of a life, cannot be outraged! Trust me, friend. A man who loves as I do, loves
but once. By heaven! this love does not end with life! I
will not let time, tide, a father's hate, or the Czar's unfairly-
drawn rules for noble marriages—aught that binds or ham-
pers—tear that beloved woman from my heart. In all the
world's varying phases, that one darling face is all I see!
And I swear she shall be my wife yet, on a soldier's honor,
so help me God! This is final!"

"Dournof! Dournof!" feebly muttered General Vassili
Milutin, when he had listened to the confidant's relation,
"there is a burden resting on my soul which I pray God to
lift! If a Turkish bullet would end it all it would be a fortunate one for me. May God bless Boris, for the burden
resting on me is a dark legacy of the past. I tell you, friend,
that I dare not face my son and read the riddle which is
even now half veiled from me. After my death Boris
is free, but till then I am a ruined man, whose past holds
him mute before the altar of a broken heart! I cannot atone,
save by my death!"

And General Dournof, on his return, dared not tell the
darling of the young army that his father feared to look into
his eyes. "If Countess Xenia were only here," he cried,
"she might work Love's miracle!"

It was on a stormy night in the dying days of October that
the General and his chief-of-staff sat in their rude log hut
shelter, planning out the details of the movements of the
next two days, when a courier with letters clattered up. The
spade was now triumphant. The great defender of Sebastopol had arrived, and a new energy and a uniformity of
plan gave life at last to the baffled besiegers.

"That, Boris, if the investment is promptly carried out,
will cut off all supplies from Osman, and give us Plevna at
last, in six weeks," cried Dournof, throwing down his pencil.

Colonel Milutin, tracing out the new positions, where the

best and truest would soon die by thousands in the "great movement," hardly lifted his eyes when General Dournof, raising his eyes, murmured, "She is here." For a note from Countess Xenia de Berg, now at the great main hospital at Nikopolis, begged for news of the two soldiers so dear to her.

"We are both here, and I must see you. On this depends Boris' future happiness," she wrote urgently. "Send an orderly down· to me at once with your location, and I will then tell you all. For Boris must be saved for a life of honor and love—for the devoted woman who is now daring all to see his face once more in life."

And Dournof, gazing at Boris, his handsome head bent over the plan of death, with moist eyes, prayed, "God guard and shield them both!"

The hoarse cries of the sentinels and the trampling of a cavalry escort drew General Dournof to the hut door. "Instant delivery! For General Alexis Dournof in person," was the superscription of the packet which the General receipted for, in his own hand. Turning to Colonel Milutin, the General ordered "the usual courtesies" to a representative of headquarters.

"General Gourko's orders were for my instant return, without a moment's waiting, sir!" was the reply of the young adjutant, who was already a hundred yards away before Dournof had unsealed the envelope. His face paled slightly. "Report to me, with your chief-of-staff, forthwith. The Guards are all up. I myself go over the lines to-morrow. Order your next in command to let not one man leave the lines on any pretext—whatever his rank!" The scrawl "Gourko," under the brief lines, made it the Czar's own fiat! Half an hour later, against a flying scud of chilling wet mist, under the dim, straggling starlight, General Dournof breasted the storm with the heart-tortured Milutin at his side. The gruesome night-winds wailed down from the hills where Osman Pasha, Suleiman, Mehemet Ali, and Chefket Pasha, with seventy thousand devoted fatalists had hurled back again the Russian army. Even the bold Roumanian allies who had, two days before, paved the Grivitza redoubt once more, with dead Christian bodies, had failed to break the lines of those desperate Turks! The Cesarevitch,—soon to wear the heavy diadem of Russia,—sheltered behind the genius of old Todleben, the Sebastopol defender, now commanded the Guards and Grenadiers, seventy thousand peerless fresh troops. As Dournof plunged on in the night, a repressed wail broke from his lips. "My God! what folly! what butchery! If the Guards do not go in to win, the Russian cause is lost!"

Boris Milutin spoke out gravely, "General! our Guard was never beaten! It won deathless laurels, even at Austerlitz If the lines are closed up around Plevna, then, Chefket Pasha's twelve thousand men and two thousand wagons will only swell our final triumph. Dellinghausen can easily hold Mehemet Ali on the left. Radetsky, too, can ward off Suleiman at Shipka Pass. If Gourko is given this task by our old Nestor, Todleben, we can firmly girdle Plevna and starve bold Osman out. Then, with a hundred thousand men, we will force the Balkans. After that, ho for Adrianople and the city of Constantine! That's the very move! There has been here so much defeat that the Guard will be surely sent in while it is fresh, and,—the Guards will go in to win!"

Suddenly, Dournof remembered the appeal of Countess Xenia. Dare he tell Boris Milutin that the woman whom he had sworn on his honor to marry, was coming now to join the devoted sisters of the Red Cross? "I must spare him the agony for a time, the useless agony," groaned Dournof. "Not a single man can leave the lines now, and Gourko will take us all with him on this duty of closing up the lines, and posting the corps of the Guard. For we, alas! know these positions but too well!"

Gallant Dournof sighed as he thought of the five thousand of his twelve thousand brave soldiers now lying a prey to the ravens of that fatal field.

The long night was nearly over when General Gourko had gathered together all the principal officers of the superb force which was now secretly destined to spring on the four fortified places, covering the one open Sophia road. It was the very last link to close up in the chain of a mighty investment. The names of Dolni-Dubnik, Gorni-Dubnik, Telis and Radomitza fell upon the ears of men, who heard for the first time the mention of their waiting tombs. When the long council was ended, the flower of Gourko's great command sought in silence the soldiers' bivouac rest.

At dawn, gray Gourko rode, hawk-eyed, over the route whence thirty-five thousand choice infantry, ten thousand peerless horse, and fifty heavy guns, were to be hurled in surprise, against the foe's weak points.

The curled darlings of St. Petersburg were impatiently waiting now before these ranks of flaxen-haired giants all ready to go in, smiling, where every flash of a Turkish rifle might break a gentle heart in the circle of the Winter Palace!

The night of the twenty-third of October, brought to Alexis Dournof the crowning mental struggle of his life. " I can trust no one but you, General Dournof, to lead your Division to-morrow," said Gourko. " If there is any fight in the Guards, then, to-morrow night will see Osman's doom sealed. The road to Constantinople will be open. I will keep your Colonel Milutin with me. He is a man who never loses his head. His iron courage at the Garden assault, too, gives his very name a cheering prestige. I give to you the attack on the main redoubt, at Gorni-Dubnik. All depends on that. The honor of forty thousand men! The success of the whole investment.

" Milutin to-night will, with a company of our choicest riflemen, get as near to that ugly redoubt as he can. To-morrow, he will know all that you can hope to know, until you are inside of that one vitally-demanded redoubt. The enemy will fight like fiends there. It is their last key-point! Once ours, the Czar can sleep in peace, for the closing scenes of the drama will unroll there, like a panorama. To-morrow night will see you the first man of this army, if you give me that redoubt!"

Alexis Dournof grasped his gallant chief's hand in silence! It was only when a mile away on their road, as Boris Milutin turned to ride back, that General Dournof felt his heart-strings suddenly snap! "Alexis!" said the young chief-of-staff, "here are two letters! Leave them at your head-quarters to be sent on by a special messenger, if—if Gorni-Dubnik is won!"

"What do you mean, Boris?" cried Dournof.

"I shall not live to come out! For, I will go in with the Guards! To-morrow will be no time for talk. My father! Marguerite! These letters tell them all! But, Countess Xenia,—say to her that Vera's words of cheer, that her own loving tenderness, must help the woman I may never see through the dark hours—if I fall!" Dournof's bosom heaved!

And, hand in hand, their swords girded on, the soldier-friends gazed in each other's fond eyes!—"Till to-morrow, Boris! And, God be with you!"—cried Dournof, as he dashed the spurs into his steed's sides. "My God! I cannot tell him that Marguerite may perhaps almost hear the thunder of our guns to-morrow—at Nikopolis. It would only drive him mad, and I do not know the truth myself! Who can it be who guides this lonely dear one to Countess Xenia's side, to seek a lover in these gloomy shambles of death. For they cannot have come alone—through the lines! If we come out all right, I will then send Boris down at once with despatches, and Countess Xenia shall tell him all that she knows. It is all my duty will allow me, and it is bitter hard! The gallant veteran's mind lingered upon the disinherited son who was chosen to lead Russia's flower on the morn against that grim sleeping polygon of Gorni-Dubnik! Dournof never wasted a single thought on himself, for, side by side, the friends of years would face the flashing rifles on the morrow! " I have no one to love me! No heart to break over me if—if——" he paused, but, as a bright shooting-star crossed the wintry sky in its fall, he sighed: " Ah, God! It is a pity for Boris!"—and the two letters burned lying there upon his gallant heart.

CHAPTER XIV.

THE GUARDS GO IN TO WIN.

The morning of the twenty-fourth of October, in the battle year of seventy-seven, dawned cold and cheerless on the banks of the Vid River. All night long its sedgy banks, wrapped in a friendly darkness, had been thronged with the hurrying forms of the forty battalions and eighty squadrons, now creeping out into the darkness, followed by their double-charged artillery. In four great groups, the army crawled out toward Gorni-Dubnik, where Colonel Boris Milutin now lay hidden on the picket line, in the cold wet grass, with his eyes strained to the midnight gloom, lest he stumble on a Turkish sentinel! The gloomy silence of the battle-eve was peopled with the ghosts of the gallant slain of Plevna, and, with strained hearts, the anxious soldiers crawled slowly into position! There was not one straggling shot to waken the echoes. For a single chance volley of a few careless Cossacks would have defeated the investment of Plevna. The cordon of stout hearts was to be knotted around the desperate Turks at last!

Silence, a brooding silence, as the stars hid behind the clouds—and the Death-angel's dark wing stretched in shadow from the far Loka to the distant defiles of the Shipka Pass, its rocky sides already red with the best blood of two armies. In the world-famed Grivitza Redoubt, the doubled battalions of Turks lay,—with piles of extra guns at hand,—ready to grasp the seed of death from the open boxes of cartridges now piled along those blood-stained ramparts! Over the whole world, on this stilled night, clicking telegraph and careworn writers were busied with the flashing forth of vague rumors! For, the mysterious thrill "that something was on," spread over a waiting Europe, and the debated fall of Plevna was the theme of a world public greedy for blood, and battle's dread game! Silence, dreaming silence, out on the wastes around the scarred landscape of Plevna! Even the Turkish sentinels droned there on their posts, for sleep came to their jaded eyes, his grim brother Death waiting only for daylight to choose his choicest prey!

Far away, aching woman-hearts from the Volga to the balsam-laden groves of Finland clung tenderly to the men in gray who were now stealing up for the red ecstasy of the coming battle-day! The sleeping hell of human passion burned this awful night with banked fires! And yet, the grim spirits of the night hovered over the opposing lines to haunt the soldier's uneasy rest! The world waited hungrily for tidings from Plevna, while a heart-sore Czar, anxious princess, and the despairing generals of the army, trusted now alone to Todleben's masterly genius! And so the long night crawled on,—until the lifting fogs brought on the mad battle once more!

At daybreak, a pale-faced woman was awakened by a vigorous knocking at the door of her room in the great Red-Cross hospital of Nikopolis. Countess Xenia sprang up and aroused Vera, who had grown to be an earnest-faced woman in these months of sad heart-trial. Under the guns of the great fortress of Nikopolis, in seven outlying villages, a sixth of the vast Russian host lay sick or wounded! "There was lack of woman's nursing, and dearth of woman's tears!"

Xenia de Berg hastily trimmed the little night-lamp and then answered the loud summons. An officer, booted and spurred, bowed low, in the gray of the dawn, as he murmured, "Pardon! Madame la Comtesse. From General Dournof, with all haste."

The Countess eagerly cried, " Can I answer ? "

" Alas ! " the messenger said, " Madame, there is a great movement. I go on at once to Bucharest for reserve ammunition. The special train starts in an hour. For a long week, I fear that nothing but sick, wounded, and dying will come to you from the front. It is impossible. I fear they will attack the Turkish positions again to-day. God help the army ! "

The young soldier, a beardless lad, fresh from the dancing-class of the cadet school, stood there, cap in hand, while Vera clutched her mother's arm, as the Countess read the few lines. " Boris ! " she cried, with a sudden apprehension.

" Mother, mother ! we might go on to Bucharest ! " the quick-witted girl said.

" Alas ! Even if we did, I can get no pass back for Marguerite. Not another volunteer woman nurse will now be permitted to cross the lines."

It was indeed true, for dozens of the devoted ladies lay buried in the huge graveyards spreading around the hills of the Danube at Nikopolis. A useless sacrifice of brave sweet Russian hearts !

" But Marguerite could take my Red Cross uniform, and then return with you. I can stay at Bucharest with Madame Mazzana. My pass will bring her back. And so she can see Boris at last, after the battle ! "

The girl's voice trembled in her eagerness, and the mother bent her stately head and kissed the girl's forehead. " Can you take us to Bucharest with you, Captain ? " softly said the " Angel of Nikopolis." For hundreds of the sick and wounded had so blessed the woman whose eyes shone down in pity on their helpless beds of pain.

" I will return in an hour, Madame ! " the Captain said. " Be ready ! You may have forgotten me. But, I am always Serge Platoff ! "

" You were only a page when I saw you," smiled the

gentle lady, holding out her hand, "and now, a soldier of the Czar!"

"As God wills," the handsome lad said, kissing her hand and then stealing a glance at the blushing girl now sheltered behind her mother.

Serge Platoff had sprung from cadet to captain in five months, and yet, Love's archery was more potent than the rain of the Turkish bullets.

"Then we will gladly go with you!"

Platoff bowed, and before his feet were silent in the hall the simple kits of the two women were hastily thrown together.

The gray chilly dawn came and, far below them, it showed the dark reedy Vid, which sluggishly rolled into the Danube its turbid stream. Light fogs wreathed the sleeping islands of the broad river, and the scream of the toiling locomotive was heard at the head of the one pontoon bridge which swayed every moment of the day and night, now, under the vast traffic of the army of a hundred thousand.

"Have you the telegram, Vera?" cried Countess Xenia, as she threw her mantle over the dark dress with its linen facings where the red Geneva cross glowed, like the stain of hero's blood.

"It is here, mother. They are at the Hotel de Russie, and we will go there at once."

Out of the great hospital, past the long wards where hundreds of the veterans lay waiting the morning visits of the surgeon, the two voyagers hastened in silence. Dozens of the sleepers lay there, stark and cold, only waiting the removal of the ticket, the transfer of another sufferer, and the bearing away of those who had "gone out with the tide," this grim work being the first matin duty of the attendants. Such is the shade behind the glory of war.

Countess Xenia's eyes filled with sudden tears. "Hearts in Russia, homes desolate forever, loved ones waiting some where for these poor fellows who go out in silence forever. All this!" she cried, "for Glory! For the Czar! For the Cause of the peaceful Nazarene!" And the patrician woman wept that Hell's game of war had ever cursed mankind to be the play of pampered princes, and the scourge of helpless womanhood, in every age and clime—the dark legacy of Cain! Down to the river banks, over the broad flowing Danube, on the swaying pontoon bridge of the Roumanians, the ladies journeyed through all the débris of a vast army.

The silent waters of the Vid rippled gently over the sandbar into the Danube, and a dull distant booming broke heavily upon the morning air. Countess Xenia's voice was shaken as frightened Vera clung to her side. They shuddered at each far-rolling deep vibration sweeping down the river.

"What is that, Captain?" the Countess asked, as Serge Platoff threw up his fair head like a racer.

The young soldier's cheek was pale, as he whispered with white lips, "The Guards have attacked Gorni-Dubnik, and that is the cannonade of the assault!"

"God keep our soldiers to-day!" cried Xenia, her voice almost rising to a shriek, as the river breeze bore afar the dull sounds now growing more rapid, which told that the battle was on once more. The whistle shrieked a requiem as they dashed away. In an hour the mother and daughter looked back from the hills toward the mist-veiled Danube. They were speeding on now to meet the distracted Marguerite and Madame Mazzana.

The silence of death hung over the valley of the doomed, and far away, the Vid, running down from the old Turkish hamlet of Gorni-Dubnik, was crimson with blood; for the polygon redoubt was now a flaming hell, and the wild yells of battle broke on the morning air.

While Captain Serge Platoff told wistful Vera the last news

of the great battle-field of forty miles, the Countess mused upon the fight which was now on. She thought of the unhappy Marguerite Waldberg, whose loving, tortured heart had brought her down to these pestilent banks of the Danube, in all the hazards of war, only to see her lover's face once more. Woman's quest!

" If Boris to-day——Oh, my God !" thought Xenia, as the train dashed along to Bucharest, where the two heart-sick women had waited in vain for seven long days for any tidings of the Countess and Vera. And when Marguerite threw herself in the arms of the woman who was now a second mother, the Russian widow's eyes were streaming with fond tears, as she answered, " Safe ! safe ! darling, till yesterday." And yet, she dared not tell that gentle woman, her breast now thrilled with the exquisite tumult of love, that the seething hell of fight raged around her lover in that wild fight to the death at Gorni-Dubnik !

The shaven Turkish soldiers, swarming on the ramparts of the Grivitza redoubt, peered anxiously out at morn over the trampled cornfields, where the Roumanian corses of the last assault still lay uuburied. But, all was silent in their front ! No gleaming lines of the gray-coated Russian foes swept up, as when, to the sound of their regimental hymn, the Muscovites had kneeled and fired back three volleys, blank into the faces of the victorious Moslems, only a month before. Plevna's half-starved defenders then dropped on their knees and invoked the Allah who had so long spared the crescent flag, fluttering proudly on those low clay heaps famed for all the future as the Grivitza redoubt. But, far away on the left flank of the line, the crashing roar of fifty guns swelled and rose and thrilled on the quaking air for hours. Their thunder died away to the ominous silence of death in the afternoon. Who had won ?

At daybreak, the Turkish pickets around Gorni-Dubnik began slowly falling back upon the village. The crimson sun, rising over distant Plevna, lit up a low ravine, where a slender water-course ran gurgling down into the Vid river near by. The Sophia road, the last open causeway into Plevna, wound under a steep, high hill, where a low red polygon, only three hundred yards in diameter, showed four heavy guns grinning from an old Turkish burial-mound. A few shelter trenches below the low parapet, in a dead space near the gully, a clump of rifle-pits two thousand yards away, and well hidden by woods, sheltered the outlying Turkish pickets.

Below the hill, where this ugly redoubt now gleamed raw and red, a triangular lunette, fifty yards on a side, covered the old stone post-road station. It was the very weakest point of the Plevna line of defence.

When the pious Moslem sentinel at dawn laid down his Yankee-made rifle and bowed devoutly to the east, he prayed to Allah, ignorant that General Dournof and Colonel Boris Milutin had secretly placed the very last detachment of Russian troops in position for the assault. Yet, though not a man was in sight, it was true. Three great columns had poured along over the Cirakova ford, from midnight till early dawn.

At six o'clock, Alexis Dournof turned and wrung his friend's hand for the last time!

"We are going out on the line now, Alexis," said Milutin, who had now dismounted and was loosening his oft-tried sword in its scabbard. As he swung around his heavy revolver to the front on its looped cord, he quietly handed to the General, his long-treasured field-glasses. "Take them, Dournof," he said, with a quiet smile. "Where I am going,— I can see the Turks without them."

"What do you mean?" cried Dournof, with a growing fear.

Boris Milutin threw up his handsome head and nervously laughed. "I am going in with the Guards! Ellis has the right, Zeddeler the centre, Rosenbach the left, and the Cir-

cassians will pound away at the Turks, from that hill over
there. Now, Lioubovitsky and I have a bet, that his Grenadier regiment will not be in that redoubt at sunset!" Milutin
drew his sword and then, pointed over the valley a half mile, to
where the rising smoke told of the hasty cooking of the
soldiers' morning coffee.

The General sprang from his horse and caught Boris in
his arms. "This is madness! Your duties are only general.
You are needed all along the whole line. Think of Marguerite Waldberg! You will throw your life away like a common rifleman!"

" I think only of Russia to-day!" gravely said Milutin, and
a smile brighter than the morning flash, lit up his stern
young face. "I shall go in with Lioubovitsky, and you
know him,—the way he fights,—at the head of the column!"

The steady tramp of the devoted stormers then shook the
ground, and the mist of tears over Alexis Dournof's eyes
veiled Boris from sight as he waved his hand, when he gaily
fell in beside the dashing Grenadier Colonel.

The young patrician had stopped one moment, as he
turned toward his friend. No one saw him kiss that picture
of Marguerite, which had lain on his heart in all those nights
of dread before defiant Plevna. Alexis Dournof galloped
away, his heart bounding, with the light of battle flashing in
his eyes, but his heart was sore this battle day.

Dropping shots sounded now all along a line of two miles,
as the columns closed in for the grapple. The firing grew
sharp, for the Turks were stubborn at this first touch of the
steel net of Todleben.

By half-past eight, all the three columns and the deployed
reserve were in position. A fateful word from grim old
Gourko in his lair, a half-mile away, opened the sudden mad
roar of fifty-six guns upon the still silent redoubt—the lunette—and the station at the post-road crossing. All the
parapets were now packed with thousands of grimly-defiant

Turks. Shell after shell bursting in their midst, only made them more fiercely hungry for the coming rush, when the awful unending roar of the Peabody-Martinis would send its sheeted hail of lead tearing through stout Russian hearts. Peering over a hill, looking down to the lunette, which was the Grenadiers' first goal, Boris turned brightly to their bold Colonel, " It is like an old Petersburg field-day, Colonel ! —The Moscow, Paul, Grenadier and Finland regiments, the Rifle Brigade and Ismailoff regiment. By Jove ! There are the Caucasian Cossacks too, now on the hill !" The ground shook as the sharp ring of a horse-battery of six guns on the northeast hill screamed out high over the roar of the heavy artillery. The Grenadier Colonel glanced at his watch, and he firmly gripped Milutin's hand, " Ten o'clock ! old fellow !" and, without another word, dauntless Lioubovitsky sprang forward on a run, the eager fire in his eyes loosening a mad tumult in Milutin's breast. For the Guards were going in to win !

With a wild "hourra," the peerless Grenadiers hurled themselves down the slope, and in ten minutes the sickening clash of the bayonets was the only sound audible in the interior of the lunette, where the desperate Turks died defiantly in silence. The red redoubt was still silent, for three thousand friends and foes were mingled in that sea of life and death. Neither side dared to open fire on the lunette !

" On, on !" yelled the Colonel, as the fleeing survivors of the Moslems streamed out toward the red redoubt. And then from the right and left, the crash and roar of battle at Dolni-Dubnik and Telis, told that the other columns were also now closing in on the penned-up Turks !

Milutin sprang lightly up the slope, sword and revolver in hand, and now the parapet of the red redoubt, was one sheet of living fire ! The very ground trembled, and men went down in rows. In the wild rush of ten minutes, Boris, who was drinking deeply of the mad frenzy of battle, saw nothing as the wave of the Russian assault was rolled back to the lunette—the stone house with its bayoneted Turkish garrison lying dead there! The Grenadiers reformed in the trenches and were covered by the friendly road ditches. Gallant General Zeddeler (the column commander), heroic Lioubovitsky, and bold Colonel Scaton were now lying dead or wounded on the shot-swept field, as Boris Milutin quickly headed and reformed all that was left of his fallen friend's splendid Grenadiers. It was now eleven o'clock, and the Moscow Regiment, with two batteries, closed in like bull-dogs, to aid the Grenadiers, still holding firmly on to the outworks of the red redoubt, where two thousand Turks screamed "Allah-il-Allah!" in wild derision as they rained down bullets on their deadly foes, which were answered with defiant volleys!

Milutin's heart grew sick as the Russian advance was stayed by that flaming red wall. The Rifles poured in now to aid, but the red redoubt quaked again under the discharge of its four heavy guns, and the supporting Russian batteries were forced to pause, for their fire now only swept off their own men. It was a hell on earth!

With wild yells of rage, the Finland and Paul regiments boldly climbed the steep hill on the left of the redoubt, and, after a terrific struggle, were finally driven back to shelter under the very shadow of the still flaming fort. Rosenbach and Rounoff too, lay out on the field of honor between the lines of fire. The day seemed lost! The sun climbed on slowly to high noon, and, for three long hours, the bloody duel to the death was hotly waged. And, still the grim Turks held out!

For, the Guards were now lodged so close to the invincible work that even raging Gourko could not hope to retire them to reform in shelter. They must lie there in the jaws of death! A dreadful suspense clung now to the horrible fight, only blazing up in its highest rage at Telis, where the Jagers had been cut to pieces, and the yelling Turkish reserves were now pouring in to swarm on Gorni-Dubnik hill, over the bodies of the vanquished forlorn hope.

While Boris Milutin cheered on his officers who were moving among the men, then all lying down and firing deliberately now, at every head raised above the great redoubt, a wounded staff-officer staggered up to him.

"General Gourko himself is in the field, sir. He has now ordered three volleys from all the batteries in the order, right, centre and left. When the last volley on the left, mind you, the left, has been fired, the whole three columns will rush on, in one last assault!" and, as the officer spoke, he staggered and fell on his face.

While Milutin quickly explained these grave orders to all the surviving officers of the centre column, a few scouts had safely crawled up to his lines. "General Gourko is crazed with rage. He has rebuked Brock and Ellis, and, is now with Count Shouvaloff, who holds the Reserve Guard. If we are ever to get into Plevna, that work must be won to-night!" So spoke a lieutenant of Rifles. "If we do not, good-bye to Plevna!"

"Poor Lioubovitsky, he has lost his bet!" mused Boris, as he gazed at the corner where, behind a rough shelter, the heroic Grenadier colonel lay gasping in a covered ditch, bleeding from his terrible wounds. They waited now only for the last volley from the left. Two thousand stormers!

"My God!" screamed Boris, as his officers with horror, pointed out to him the gray masses of the right column, rushing on alone into the cross-fire of the Moslem reserve, and the grim blood-red redoubt! For they had not waited, but rushed on, heedlessly, when their *own* batteries had fired their three volleys. And the centre and left were unprepared to aid them, and the supporting guns were silent. It was a fearful mistake!

With a wild yell, a mounted staff-officer swept down the hill under a storm of shot.

" Commanding officer ! " he screamed, as Colonel Milutin sprang out in the open.

" Lead in your men ! Go in with a hourra ! quick ! Support the right. Gourko's orders ! "

A wild cheer from two thousand throats rose up in a grand shout, as the daring officer galloped to the left, and in five minutes, was himself leading the last column in ! Alas ! The flaming ramparts of the Turkish stronghold blazed out again in lines of living red flashes. With tears in his eyes, stern old Gourko saw his devoted columns melt away, and, when General Lavroff fell dead at the head of the Finland Regiment, as it recoiled from the flail of the awful fire, the great General dropped his head with a hollow groan. " The day is lost ! "

" General ! " said Alexis Dournof, whose left arm was now slung in a blood-soaked bandage, " our men have all dropped down there in the dead angles under the walls." The speaker reeled in his saddle. He was faint with wounds and this maddening suspense.

" Well, well ! " roared Gourko, " If they hold on there till night, one rush will carry them in at dark. Let the batteries cease firing. They are only killing our own poor men." So the quick-eyed Dournof suggested !

The staff separated with these orders, at a signal from the stern commander, and soon a terrible silence reigned over the field where the five choicest Guard regiments now lay panting on the bloody slopes of that one rough outwork, on which Plevna's fate now depended. The four Turkish guns were silent at last, for they had been shot from their carriages bodily ! But the fourfold line of shaven heads still lay, with their eyeballs strained, behind that now silent parapet. To lift up a head anywhere was instant death !

General Gourko, with a deadly bitterness in his heart,

never spoke as he rode up to the hill overlooking Gorni-Dubnik. It was a miracle of defiant human opposition. Victor and vanquished were alike powerless. The staff-officers grew pale and sickened one by one, as the dying day flamed down over a field where not a single rifle's ring broke the horrible silence. Behind the bloody parapet, the surrounded Turks glared desperately into each other's eyes, in the last agony of a grim despair. For, with knives, tin cups, bayonets sharpened on stones, and even with the officers' sabres, the Russians were busied throwing up little shelter mounds and, as the twilight deepened, they crept inch by inch, nearer to the parapets of the redoubt of blood. The whole army for forty miles, knew now of the dead-lock, and even Osman Pasha in Plevna, bowed his head in despair. For, nightfall would bring on at least the last struggle of desperation! If the red redoubt fell, then Plevna was locked in the iron grasp of the Russian bear. Grim starvation would soon do that work of Death which failed at the Grivitza re-doubt. The lonely howl of the wolf and the shriek of the night-owl sounded out while this awful unnatural silence still clung to the field of the undecided battle. The last rays of the sun faded slowly in the west, and a deeper gloom stole silently over the rolling ridges where the Turks, now cut off, awaited their death. For hell raged in the hearts of the nine thousand Russians waiting there, bayonet in hand, for the darkness to close down!

Boris Milutin, lying on the very outer slope of the polygon, had passed the word to a hundred brave fellows who had crawled up near to him : "When we hear the first Russian 'hourra,' then, every man over the parapet!" And so the word of doom was passed on to the scattered groups of the six bodies of troops creeping nigher every fifteen minutes.

The heated guns of the Russians were silent on the far ridges where Gourko and Shouvaloff waited, sick at heart, for the one supreme moment! A wild, distant yell was borne on by the night breeze to the distant commander, whose world-wide fame, and even the honor of the Guards under his command, hung on the issue of this last mad rush. It was the time!

"Now!" yelled Boris, as the frantic sounds of the onset of the struggling Ismailoff regiment broke on the night air. General Ellis himself, had leaped, at their head, over the parapet, sword in hand. And, with one mighty shout of vengeance, the Russians poured in a resistless tide, over the parapet, with one supreme effort, and then closed in on the frantic Turks with the cold steel!

A vast flame suddenly leaped up in the centre of the work, as the thousands of infuriated men reeled to and fro in the struggle of death. Even the ready revolver ceased its deadly bark, and, when the sword and bayonet had ceased their hand-to-hand work of slaughter, the blue and white cross floated out on the hard-held Red Redoubt, where never again would the Turkish bayonets gleam. And it was the hand of a gallant lad who threw the Czar's battle-flag out to the kiss of Victory!

The Red Redoubt was won, and Plevna lay at the Czar's mercy! Two thousand stubborn prisoners were disarmed and quickly herded, like dogs, out of the redoubt, where fifteen hundred Moslem corpses lay, now stiffening.

"One Pasha, fifty officers, four dismantled guns and two thousand prisoners!" shouted an aid, as he raced up to General Gourko, surrounded by his rejoicing staff.

"And Plevna!" cried the old hero, as he turned to Alexis Dournof. "General!" he cried, "take every staff-officer that you can find! Gallop over there and help Count Shouvaloff to reform the lines! Post every gun in the work that you can get in there! Take command, and hold that work and road crossing—on the honor of a soldier—to the last man!"

Dournof was bounding madly away before the last word

was spoken! But, his heart was heavy as his horse sprang aside from the heaped-up bodies of the devoted Grenadier regiment. At the lunette, he met the first wounded men crawling out.

"Your colonel?" he cried, as an officer of Grenadiers was carried by.

"Mortally wounded," was the feeble answer.

"And Colonel Milutin?" Dournof's voice was raised almost in a shriek.

"Up there in the work, hard hit!"

Over the débris of exploded caissons, lanes of dead Turks and scattered weapons, General Dournof rode on, in search of the Ismailoff's colonel, who now held the proud honor of having stormed the gate of hell.

"Milutin!" he cried, as he saw the first companies of the Grenadiers slowly crawling together.

"Here!" cried a voice in the dark.

By the side of an overturned gun limber Boris Milutin lay, pale and senseless. His left arm, badly shattered, was hanging, twisted helplessly, at his side, and over him, leaned the adoring men, who had clamped a rough tourniquet, improvised out of sword-belts, on the shattered arm.

"He took us over the parapet!" cried a dozen officers, crowding round.

Dournof was on his knees in an instant, beside his wounded friend, and he heard them not, for he was busied forcing a draught of cognac upon the stunned and helpless man. Boris Milutin feebly opened his staring eyes. His right hand still firmly grasped his sword, whose knot had twisted round his right wrist as he fell.

"Alexis!" he muttered, and then feebly pointed to his left breast. General Dournof tore open the soldier's coat. "The pocket," whispered Milutin, as the torch-bearers gazed to see if his life-blood welled out from another hidden wound. Dournof drew out a picture. It was soaked with the blood of the shattered arm. Boris Milutin gasped. "Marguerite! Tell her "———and his head fell back in the deathly agony of his shattered and twisted arm—for the hero of the Red Redoubt had seen his last battle-day!

The stars glittered calmly down, in the crawling night hours, on this Aceldama of blood, where four thousand of the Czar's peerless guards lay dead on the field of honor. Before Alexis Dournof departed, to reform the troops, and turn the redoubt's guns inward, on Plevna, his trusted aid was personally charged with the removal of Colonel Milutin to the field hospital, beyond the rivulet, now swollen with the human blood, shed in the devil grapple of Gorni-Dubnik.

The awful shades of night deepened over the blood-bought polygon, and even at daybreak, sleepless Alexis Dournof was still busied with the posting of the twenty thousand Russians, who were now a wall of fire and steel, between Osman Pasha and his last avenue of help, the distant Turkish depot at Sophia.

In the little room which she called her own, at Bucharest, Marguerite Waldberg was this night sleeping with the smile upon her face which greeted the last thought of Boris, in her maidenly prayers, as she sobbed herself to sleep. She prayed for mercy for that beloved head bowed in battle's storm.

The morning brought the news, flashed over the Danube, of a great victory. A silence in every heart brooded as of the judgment hour, as Countess Xenia led Marguerite quickly out of the crowded hotel, to seek the first train back to the Danube. A new and rarely beautiful face wore the garb of the Sisters of the Geneva Cross, and yet no one knew, when the Angel of the Hospital reached Nikopolis, at midnight, that the shuddering girl at her side was a novice in those scenes of woe and suffering. Countess Xenia had left the dearest gage of her life with Madame Mazzana, in place of the gentle pilgrim of Love. And the two loving hearts there at Bucharest, listening to the awful tidings of the day of Gorni-Dubnik, mutely gazed into each other's eyes, and dared not whisper "Boris," for he, the beloved, was yet within the sweeping doom of the battle-field ghoul of war.

Before the next dawn, all the world knew that the investment of Plevna was now completed. Osman Pasha's iron heart was shaken at last, as that cold master of the grim game of war, Todleben, drew in with an iron grasp his six great sectors of the embattled Russian forces, they were now gripping the inclosed Moslems with a relentless grasp of steel, and so, thousands of mourning hearts were added to the teeming, sable hosts of sorrow in Russia. The wail for the absent, the loved and lost, went up too in the land of Othman, and the death angel's dark pinions spread yet a little wider over the awful harvest-field of Plevna. But, the long delayed hour of doom had come !

"Trust me !" cried Captain Serge Platoff, as he bent before Countess Xenia, in his last parting greeting. "On finishing my report to General Gourko, I shall go at once, to General Dournof. You will have a courier from me forthwith, and if hurt,"—the boy-captain's voice trembled—"dead or alive, you shall have Boris Milutin ! I will make the quest my own, as if he were my own brother."

The fair Russian widow kissed the bright boy's brow, as he swore the oath of friendship to search out Marguerite's loyal lover in the awful human wreck of dread Gorni-Dubnik ! For the day of days was over at last, and the Guards had gone in—and won !

Four days later, the news of the fall of Gorni-Dubnik, and the final riveting of the iron chain at Plevna, tying Osman— a new Prometheus—to the rock, was flashed around the waiting world.

Sweet-faced Countess Xenia found a willing assistant at Nikopolis in Marguerite Waldberg. For the great hospitals were thronged with the hundreds of wounded arriving daily from the field in the impressed village wagons of the whole Dobrudsha. Alas! many of the sufferers never reached an iron bed alive, even to have their names ticketed. The thirty miles of rough transport was a terrible ordeal, even to the strongest. And in her borrowed uniform of the Geneva Cross, Marguerite waited now in vain, heart-sore, for news of Boris. For Serge Platoff was silent! Vainly had Countess Xenia tried to open communication with General Dournof.

"He is in command now, of the very crater of the fight," said a visiting Grand Duke, who bowed in admiration of the Angel of the Hospitals. "And General Vassili Milutin—he is in the Lom Valley now, in advisory charge of the fight against Mehemet Ali. Even the Czar himself, is yet without news of the fate of his own personal staff, who went in with the Guards!"

In the awful suspense of three more days of waiting, the watchful Countess Xenia hovered near Marguerite, with an anxiety beyond all measure. For the loving girl was in a gloomy trance of deadly agony.

"Xenia," she softly said, "if he were alive, General Dournof would have sent us tidings. Boris! Boris!" The bride of a soldier's soul fell at last senseless in Countess Xenia's arms when they made their evening rounds of the ward assigned to them.

For a grizzled officer of the Grenadiers, whose foot had been roughly amputated in the field, answered to the surgeon who was dressing his wound, "I fell next to Colonel Milutin, in the works. He put his hand on the first gun, and I claimed the second! Poor fellow!"

"Was he wounded?" the surgeon said. "He has not been sent down here."

"Left arm torn all to pieces! Amputated very close. They fear gangrene fever. He'll be brought down as soon as General Dournof can get transportation. He was the hero of Gorni-Dubnik!"

Even the wounded man started, regardless of his excruciating pain, when the younger nurse beside him fell senseless in Countess Xenia's arms. For Boris Milutin had dearly bought the laurel with the sacrifice of her loving heart!

And, thinking then of the proud, bitter old father, now far away on the Lom, Countess Xenia murmured, "My God! This is the one last stroke! It fills up the cup of misery!"

When the morning dawned, only a pale lily face greeted Countess Xenia, who had stolen in to watch poor stricken Marguerite. The noble Russian Countess had toiled all night by the beds of the wounded and dying, for the threshold of the hall of death was crowded with the brave, who gave no sign, but went out alone into the viewless shades of the Hereafter—Russia's vast shadow-army.

In the dim watches of the night, Countess Xenia had hourly assured herself of the well-being of the orphaned girl who was now under the very darkest shadow of the awful ban of the past.

The surgeon-in-chief had also mercifully given a strong sleeping-potion to the girl, mixed in a glass of cordial. She could not physically suffer.

"Countess Xenia," he said, "why do such slips of girls come down here? They cannot stand the realistic results of carnage."

The gentle countess sighed, as she glanced toward the sleeping maiden, whose slender hand was clasped on a bosom tenanted only by the love of the hero of the Red Redoubt.

"Love led her here! She was to have married him."

The gruff old surgeon stalked away, saying, "Wait here for me, I will see what I can do." For, to return a kindness to the Angel of the Hospital, the old medico would even have charged alone the stoutest Turkish bravo, "vi et armis." Even doctors have hearts!

In fifteen minutes, the surgeon returned. "I have talked

with the blunt old captain who fell by his side. Milutin seems to have almost borne a charmed life, for the awful honors of the day are his. General Ellis of the Ismailoff regiment cried like a child when he learned that Milutin was probably mortally wounded. I have sent out my own squad of twenty Cossacks, up the road, with the strictest orders to single out Colonel Boris Milutin's convoy and to bring him at once direct to my own rooms. If I can have quiet for him, I may be able to save him. The captain showed me just the place of the amputation. With the neglect, the loss of blood, the rough jolting of thirty miles, however, the inciting causes of gangrene fever are reinforced. That I fear the most," mused the old veteran. " But I will fight for his life—for you, and for the girl ! "

"God bless you, doctor," murmured Xenia. " Let me be summoned instantly. For, there is the mistake of a whole life to repair. There is an overhanging curse to baffle, the punishment to avoid which falls too often on the in-nocent."

" Trust me," said the surgeon. " I knew his mother. She was one who passed unsoiled through the wild social whirl on the Neva. God bless her sweet memory ! "

Pale and trembling was Marguerite when she opened her eyes, and, in the dim morning light, saw Countess Xenia bending tenderly over the child of her heart.

" Boris ? " she whispered, as she clung to her friend's bosom.

" Darling, you will need all your strength. Can I trust you ? " Countess Xenia's brow was grave.

Marguerite vainly struggled to rise.

" Not yet. He will be brought here in an hour ! A Cossack has galloped back. He is yet alive, but feeble."

The winter sun was lighting up the strange straggling can-tonment by the Danube as a dozen attendants bore a help-less form into the great room which the surgeon-in-chief had hastily vacated. Countess Xenia, with the male dressers, stood in waiting, as the helpless burden was gently borne into the presence of the woman who had loved him against the decrees of fate.

Standing with her friend's hand grasping her arm, Marguerite Waldberg fixed her eyes at last on the pale noble face of the man who had waited for her, there, under the arching trees of Nimovitch,—who had gone out to the field of honor at her own inspiring call!

Like a wraith, she glided to his side, "Boris," she softly whispered, and then, before them all, she leaned down, with glowing cheeks, and pressed her lips to his. It was the marriage of their souls!

But before the surgeon could begin his grim work, Marguerite was busied with Countess Xenia. It seemed as if her yielding nature had changed with the advent of the man whose life might never be linked to hers. In an anteroom the two women waited with beating hearts, till the surgeon should complete the examination, and then give his special orders in the case.

A sergeant of Cossacks standing in the door touched his cap humbly, "I came down here from Nimovitch, with the Baria. I have never left him in the campaign. General Dournof says that I am to watch with him, to obey you, and to give you this."

Before Xenia had finished the rudely-scrawled note, dated from that grim devil's outwork, the Red Redoubt,—she silently handed to Marguerite a little packet, which she had first examined. "Darling," she whispered, "you went into the Red Redoubt with him!" And there, before the child of destiny, lay her own loving pictured face, but reddened with the life-blood of the man she had kissed as he lay there in the pale shadow of death.

Marguerite was left alone with the Cossack sergeant, for the surgeon-in-chief had called Countess Xenia out with a single grave look. On the long porch they stood, the vast straggling camp, the sweeping Danube, and the overhanging fortress spread out before them. Above them on the hill, the great war-flag of victorious Russia flapped lazily in the morning zephyrs. Huge trains were slowly dragging in, with the wounded, and the quickstep of a military band floated gaily down the river, for a gray-coated line of troops was pushing on to fill up the gaps in the iron line of investment now binding Osman Pasha to the rock.

"Ho, for Adrianople!" was on every lip.

"Will he live! Can he live?" entreated Xenia, as her slender hands closed on the surgeon's fingers in a despairing clutch.

The physician's voice was broken. "It is the fifth day! He is very weak. The ninth day will tell the story. I have sent an express rider away to his father. He could be here in three days."

"What do you mean?" almost screamed the Countess. "My God! He must not die! He shall not die!"

"General Milutin may be too late!" the sorrowing surgeon said, "although His Highness the Grand Duke, has telegraphed, at my urging, an order for the father to report instantly here, unless there is a battle actually in progress."

"Will he be conscious?" whispered Xenia, with quivering lips.

"Yes, until the turning point of the fever. It is then always ended in a delirium,—and death!" said the old man who had in the old days worshipped from afar, the wounded hero's mother. His eyes were moist as he said:

"I have placed two of my best medical cadets on duty. One will never leave him an instant. You and she may divide the night-watches, but, no conversation, no excitement. I can rally him a little, and—and—I will give you fair warning." The old man turned away to hide a veteran's weakness.

It was on the second day of the vigil that the wounded man's eyes opened with a slight semblance of his old self, in their clear gaze. He had lain, fluttering in pulse, his bosom slightly heaving, and the tide of life barely moving in his veins. Countess Xenia was seated by the window, and in her hand she held a telegraph message which told of General Vassili Milutin's departure for Nikopolis. Marguerite was seated where she never lost sight of the face of the beloved one. The watchful cadet glided out of the room, and, in a few moments, the chief surgeon gazed down earnestly upon the wounded officer's countenance. There was a solemn silence for a few moments, and then the old man turned to where Marguerite stood in an ecstasy of fear and hope. Her hands were clasped on her bosom. With a warning gesture, the surgeon bade her wait. In a few moments a few drops of a cordial had moistened the lips of pale-faced Boris Milutin. There was a slight flutter of his one hand, that good right hand which had so stoutly clung to his sword, as he lay beside the captured gun of the hard-won Red Redoubt.

The old doctor led the breathless girl gently up to the couch of her wounded lover. There was a sudden dilation of the longing, wistful eyes of the silent sufferer. As Marguerite bent low over him, his glance was fixed upon her beloved face shining down on him there, and a faint color flamed out upon his cheeks. Speechless, yet loving, there was an appeal which needed no words. In her trance of thrilled love, the girl turned to the surgeon who bent low over the man who seemed also to welcome his coming.

The old man raised his head, and, placing the slender hand of Marguerite in the helpless fingers of Boris, he whispered: "Not one word, wait here in silence, just as you are!" and, there were tears in his eye as he drew Countess Xenia gently out of the room.

The sunlight stole in through the opened window, and

threw golden gleams into the far corners of the rude hospital shelter. From the great wards of the huge sick rooms, only a faint distant sound now and then reached the lovers. But, their souls spoke out to each other, for their eyes met in the pledge of a love—deathless, eternal, and thrilled them with the unsatisfied longing of two hearts, proof against even the frown of fortune.

The only heir of twenty fiefs was now but a shattered wreck, and the child, born to all the splendid fortunes of the Wizocki, and the natural mistress of Nimovitch, " had met 'neath the sounding rafter, and, the walls around were bare ! " It seemed an age to Marguerite, as she held her lover's hand, and waited there in suspense. When she raised her eyes a robed priest of the orthodox Greek communion stood beside her, followed by two acolytes.

There was one near who lovingly held her left hand in a gentle and tender grasp, and her right hand was softly clinging to the one chilled hand of her lover, the hero of Gorni-Dubnik ! He was her husband, by the blessing of God, before her beating heart could call back the blood which had flamed to her marble cheeks. She stooped then, and bent her head over him, in all the pride and daring of her virginal heart ; once only, did she whisper, as her lips clung to his for the consecration of a life, " Boris ! My Boris ! Boris my husband ! " And the shadows of pain and parting seemed then to flee away, as the deep voice of the priest intoned the last consecration of the Almighty upon them. For Boris Milutin had made her his wife !

The eyes of her lover-husband called her down near to him, and Countess Xenia leaned beside the wife of a moment, as he softly whispered : " Nimovitch, your own, my darling ! "

His eyes were closed in weakness, as a kindly hand led the Countess and Marguerite aside. In the adjoining room, the surgeon led the two watchers up to the grave-faced priest.

The old surgeon spoke. "The Russian law demands that both the parties shall be of their right mind in a marriage. And, Boris would have it hastened! It is better. The fever may return! Your papers and records will be all counter-signed by me as witness, and may God bless you, my beautiful child! You are now the Countess Milutin!"

The stars were shining that night when Marguerite, who had been excluded from the sick man's room, for her soldier husband was sleeping in the exhaustion of his mental effort, awoke from a troubled rest. Countess Xenia was seated at the table by the one lamp which was their star of hope, in this lonely barrack-room.

"It is impossible to communicate yet with Madame Mazzana and Vera, but the surgeon promises me to send a convalescent patient up to Bucharest to-morrow. General Milutin will be here at noon to-morrow, and it is the eighth day."

"Can I not go to him?" pleaded Marguerite.

"I am to take care of you for to-night, my own darling!" answered Countess Xenia, as she folded the girl-bride to her breast.

When the dawn broke upon them, they were still clasped in each other's arms, but the sunlight showed no fire in the eyes of the pale sufferer, whose wasted body now burned with the insidious sparkle of a new fire in his fevered veins. Countess Xenia led Marguerite to the room of her husband, after a last conference with the sad-eyed surgeon.

"I have directed that the General sees you alone, first. You know the family history, my dear Countess. I also know his stormy nature. Tell him, from me, on the honor of my poor art, that even the Czar can give no earthly honors or rewards now, to this noble young soldier. The pulse is rising, the fatal fire creeping in, and—and—the end is near! One more sacrifice for that!" and he pointed solemnly to the great blue and white cross, waving on the grim fortress.

"Summon me when General Milutin arrives. He must not even see him, without my presence."

It was high noon when a dozen travel-stained horsemen reined up before the great hospital. One sat there, gray, martial, erect, defiant, and covered with the stars and decorations of a general officer. He sprang down and strode toward the surgeon's abandoned quarters. Vassili Milutin's cap dropped from his hand, and sudden tears filled his eyes, as Countess Xenia gravely drew him aside to the nearest angle of the portico.

Standing there, a mighty chieftain of that great army, the old patrician, the last of his line, bowed his head, in the crowning grief of a lifetime. He listened, and the low sweet voice of his faithful friend seemed to pierce his very heart. It was too late !

When he raised his eyes, he murmured : "Take me to him ! I will do your bidding."

There was the sound of an anxious rustling of feet in the sick room, and then, the surgeon-in-chief hastily entered the room alone. In a few moments he returned, and when the General saw his son, the heir to all the vast patrimony of the Milutins, there was no smile of recognition flickering on the face of the dying man. For all the windows were opened now, and, the full light of the growing day streamed in upon them.

"The fresh air may revive him—for a few moments !" softly whispered the surgeon.

Some one had laid a silken camp color on the table, where the Cossack sergeant had placed the sword which he had taken from his master's hand in the Red Redoubt ! There was no sound, but the stifled sobbing of the girl-wife. She was in her bridal-place, kneeling now by the side of the husband of her heart ! The old General with opened arms, would fain have clasped his son to his bosom, but the old surgeon gravely whispered :

"Too late ! He would not know you !"

One cry of repentant anguish welled from the father's heart, and he cried out, in the returning tenderness of the supreme moment, "Boris! Boris, my son!"

But, the pale-browed soldier had only opened his eyes in one last flicker of life's expiring current! His glances rested on his wife—Marguerite. Her dark hair was falling low over her shoulders as she kissed his hand, already cold, with the rosy lips of love! A look of infinite tenderness thrilled her to the very soul, as he whispered:

"Together—always—darling—at Nimovitch!"

And, with a sigh like that of a tired child, the soul of the strong man winged its way beyond the stars!

There was a silence in the room of death, until Countess Xenia pointed to the girl-wife, still on her knees! It seemed as if their kindred souls had gone out together over the bounds of the finite, in a happy union of death.

No one dared to break the grasp of her nerveless hand, closed upon that of her dead husband!

The only words Marguerite heard, as Countess Xenia laid her slender hand upon her, with the surgeon's arms wound around her childish form, were the broken utterances of a stricken man, a man whose pride was dead forever.

"My son's wife shall be the daughter of my heart!" And so, royal Death, cold and imperious, had wrung from the father's heart a boon which his only son had died in vain, to win!

CHAPTER XV.

LOVE'S MIRACLE.

THREE days after Boris Milutin had gone out into the land of shadows, there was a sad procession winding up the scarped road to the casemates of the great fortress of Nikopolis. . . All was quiet on the broad flowing Danube, and not a bellowing gun boomed in the distance! Only a few puffing tugs, and a snaky torpedo boat moving here and there, were visible, watching the Turkish monitors, cooped up, in a cowardly inaction, at Braila.

General Alexis Dournof rode at the head of a regiment, which followed with reversed arms, the ten colonels holding up the black silken pall over the body of the young hero of the Red Redoubt! There was a special distinction given to these obsequies by the presence of a Grand Duke who had also borne a sealed order from the Czar's headquarters, addressed to "General Boris Milutin!"

This order, with its seal intact, was the sorrow's crown of the young widow, whose pale beauty thrilled Captain Serge Platoff, as he rode, in knightly escort, by the carriage where Marguerite and Countess Xenia followed Boris Milutin's riderless horse. The stout sergeant, the Cossack of Nimovitch, groaned as he gazed at the crape-decked saddle, the reversed boots, and the sheathed sword, of his dead master.

Following the bride-widow, General Vassili Milutin rode alone, his soldierly face as stern as carven marble. He had passed a half hour of awful introspection in the room where he took his final leave of Boris, the last of the Milutins, forever and aye.

But, it was loving Marguerite, Countess Xenia, General Dournof and Captain Platoff who sat together, in that long mute vigil, before the dawn of the funeral day.

The old patrician chief of the house of Milutin was closeted alone in those hours with the surgeon-in-chief. Vassili Milutin had not dared to even think of the future of Marguerite, the stranger daughter whom he could not now approach, in her stately dignity of a bridal sorrow, at once the eternal union and last parting, of two lives which had been moulded into one !

The strangest timidity moved the broken father now, when he had requested that his son should be later laid in the great family vault at Orenburg.

Countess Xenia, standing pale but resolute before him, said : "Vassili, the years have drifted us both far down the tide of life, in a close friendship. There are things I would say, but, I dare not at this time, in this place ! But, as you will know later, Boris, our dear one, deeded, before going to the field, the domain of Nimovitch to Marguerite, as a last gift of his loving heart, before he left Galatz. General Dournof is the witness. I know not what Marguerite may wish to do. My home is ever open to her. But, I feel that she will wish that Boris should rest at Nimovitch by the lake, where he waited so long for her coming, as his bride !"

The Countess paused in pity, for Vassili Milutin lifted not his despairing eyes. He spoke not, but bowed humbly, for he was not bold enough to challenge the beautiful girl-widow's claim to her husband's ashes.

"And what do you intend to do with her?" murmured the old man.

"She has asked General Dournof to represent all her interests, with my help, in any necessary conferences with you."

"And then—she does not wish to see me?" the proud old noble groaned in his helpless sorrow.

Countess Xenia laid her hand gently on his arm. "Vassili, it is well that you should part, for a time, at least. Our noble friend, Surgeon Cheskowitch has bidden me to go with her at once to Bucharest—there to rest till she can go on, back to Bellagio. She has a faithful friend waiting now for her at Bucharest. Only this will prevent her going mad," Xenia sobbed, "for the surgeon warns me that her nature may give way finally under this awful blow."

"Who is the friend whom she will remain with?" General Milutin eagerly demanded.

"That I cannot tell you yet, Vassili," replied Countess Xenia, with a sudden alarm. " But, you will soon hear all from General Dournof and myself,—certainly before you go."

The great noble bowed his head in a vain anguish. The thunder of the cannon on the Lom already called him back, and although Gourko had driven the Turks from Telis, and thrown Chesket Pasha, a beaten fugitive, up into the snowy Balkans, the sword of Dournof was still needed in the last grand dash at Plevna.

Down from the old fortress the troops marched at a quick-step, after giving the three last crashing volleys, and the wailing bugles had sounded wildly the stern requiem of the bravest of the brave.

Marguerite Milutin felt that the laurels of honour were blooming still, even in that open grave, as the Grand Duke, who had arrived with his whole staff, himself laid the great white cross "for valor," on the coffin of the man who led the Guards into the Red Redoubt! The mute token of a Czar's gratitude.

"Madame la Comtesse," the august prince. said, as he approached the group where Dournof, Platoff, the surgeon, and Countess Xenia, supported the bride-widow, "a special train is ordered to convey you to Bucharest. From there,

Captain Serge Platoff will escort you to our nearest large city, or to any frontier town, and your passports have been sent to Surgeon Cheskowitch en règle for you. They are viséed for all our frontiers. The personal gratitude of the Emperor will be a gracious reminder to effect his future especial protection to yourself!"

With a bow of grave respect, the great imperial prince departed, acknowledging coldly the salute of General Vassili Milutin, who had never moved until the rocky casemate had been sealed, which hid his only son forever from a father's eyes!

In stately guise, he conducted Marguerite, the daughter of an unknown mother, to her carriage, for she was now the Countess Milutin, and the Czar himself, through the Grand Duke, had confirmed and sanctioned the legal marriage, in sending the imperial passports to the bride-widow!

General Alexis Dournof exchanged a few murmured words with the stricken old patrician, and then, with a last glance at pale Countess Xenia, he rode away at the side of the carriage, as it descended the hill. Captain Platoff and the Cossack sergeant were his funeral staff.

As the carriage swept around the last rocky point, Marguerite turned her eyes to where she had last seen all that remained of the hero of Gorni-Dubnik.

Old General Vassili Milutin, the great corps commander, was now left standing, bareheaded and alone, by the rocky vault, in which were, sorrow-sealed forever, the dead hopes of a princely line.

Something came into the woman's heart, which melted her very soul. A feeling of infinite pity, and a shade of growing tenderness. She gazed upon that stern, martial figure lingering there, friendless and alone, in his great sorrow—and then, her eyes glistened in sudden tears of compassion. She bowed her head, and gently whispered, " For Boris' sake,— he must learn to love me now!"

No one on earth ever knew the words which passed in adieu between Countess Xenia, General Dournof, and the old chieftain, whose armed escort wanted to ride out toward the Lom.

It was Alexis Dournof who, stately and with gentle dignity, declined every offer of the great noble to make a munificent present provision for Countess Marguerite Milutin.

"Believe me, Vassili, it is well to let time bring you both nearer together!" Dournof had said. And, even gentle Countess Xenia, holding out the hand of womanly sympathy, gently urged the head of the house to wait and hope.

"You can surely trust her to me?" the bright-eyed Angel of the Hospitals said. "Wait for the future, Vassili; wait for Love's miracle!"

And so, the old general started, even in his sudden sorrow, for an older grief awoke and gnawed at his heart once more. Somewhere on the weary earth, now grown so hateful to him, there lingered a beloved woman who should long have been a wife, barred from his sight by sorrow's clouds, and the mists of vanished years. That woman was Countess Marguerite's lost mother—the loved and lost beauty of Sorrento!

"Is this all that you have to tell me, Xenia?" brokenly said General Milutin, as the bugles sounded for the rally and mounting of his men. His own charger neighed at the door. He touched the sapphire forget-me-not ring which still shone on his finger. Countess Xenia buried her face in her hands in silence.

"Then I pray to God that the first Turkish bullet I hear whistle, may be my death-knell!" cried the stern noble, as he sprang to the door. For, he had wrung General Dournof's hands, and had tenderly kissed Countess Xenia's forehead, as she sat sobbing in silence. She dared not speak.

The General started back as he reached the door, for a graceful figure, robed in deepest black, gently barred the way. His hand closed upon a little packet which Marguerite held toward him. "From Boris!" she softly whispered.

The lonely father's eyes were dim as he gazed at one lock of curling brown hair which she had cut from the cold temples of the man whose reckless gallantry had thrilled a weary and unnerved army.

Vassili Milutin never knew that he had clasped that gentle girl to his breast, and brokenly murmured, "My child, my poor child!" as he kissed her pale lips. For, springing on his horse, the wild cry "Forward!" was the last good-bye of the proud man who rode madly on to the open court of King Death!

His conquered heart never told him he had already taken her to be his sacred trust, in spirit. It was a miracle of Love!

Two months later, the town of Bucharest echoed the wildest, maddest rejoicings of a population gone mad with joy. The capital of Roumania rang with the hot frenzy of the multitude who thronged the streets. The dissolute metropolis of Wallachia was en fête. The living forgot the dead! It seemed almost incredible. For, when a dispatch was posted on the bulletins, that the heroic Roumanians were at last in the Grivitza Redoubt, and that Plevna had fallen, then the long-echoing cheers of frantic joy rose on the winter air, in wild acclaim! Though Osman Pasha had yielded at last to Ganetsky and his bold Grenadiers, the grim chase over the Balkans still lay before the Russians, now bounding like tigers on the foe. For, grim, revengeful Gourko and the immortal Skobeleff yearned to see the Russian cross floating to the breeze on the Golden Horn. The straggling, unpaved streets of the town were soon filled with crowds of drunken peasants, while café and gilded hell, the hotels, the square of the Prince's Palace, and all the resorts were soon tenanted by the wildest crowd of adventurers who had ever followed a victorious army. In the Corso, a dozen massed bands were playing the "Emperor's Hymn," and bands of invalided soldiers rushed through the streets, chanting their regimental songs, for Plevna had fallen at last!

As the night closed down, the light of bonfires and fire-works, turned the darkness into day, and the sounds of shrill-voiced, wanton women voices swelled out in the bacchanalian chorus. For, of all the devil's auction-marts of the world Bucharest is the wildest, the least restrained!

Three lonely women were seated in the anteroom of a secluded apartment in the Hotel de Russie. They shuddered as the wild yells without rang out around them. For through an open door, the white curtains of a sick couch hid Marguerite Milutin from the distraction of this frantic mirth.

Countess Xenia's face was thinned and pale, and yet, in her eyes, shone out a strange new light. She leaned to where Madame Mazzana was seated, ever watching that room, where a feeble lamp glimmered by the gentle sufferer.

"It is the beginning of the end!" said Xenia, and then, she dropped her eyes before the clear glances of the Lost Lady of Nimovitch! For Alexis Dournof, the dauntless general, who was already leading his battalions up the Balkans, had spoken to her words which told her of all his own heart-longings in the lonely years by the far Caspian.

"You will find me, Alexis, at Nimovitch by the side of Marguerite, when this cruel war is over!"

"And may I come there, come to hear the answer to what I dare not ask now?" The bronzed General's heart leaped up as Countess Xenia softly whispered:

"You may come, your answer will be ready, if God spares you, Alexis."

A certain dashing Captain Serge Platoff, now chief-of-staff to the beloved Dournof, also wondered if he would wear the epaulette of a major, when he claimed Vera de Berg for a long tour abroad, as a soldier's bride.

" Yes, it is the beginning of the end!" calmly replied Madame Mazzana, "and we must now move Marguerite, at once. If the surgeon would only come! For this town will soon be thronged with all the reflux wave of the army of victory, as well as thousands of sightseers. We must leave here at once."

" Still, dearest, we dare not risk the journey to Bellagio,— until dear old Cheskowitch finds her strong enough for this last ordeal."

The mother of the hidden heart bowed in assent.

Vera de Berg had counted every day of the long illness which chained the girl-widow to her darkened room. Heart, mind, body, and soul, all were in the dark eclipse of her sorrow, the relaxation of that hopelessness which possessed her soul. There was a new secret, a sweet mysterious hovering blessing, which blended with the sick girl's dreams! It was the vision of a beautiful, loving woman, whose warm bosom beat often against her own, a gracious and tender guardian-angel who murmured, as kiss followed kiss, " My beloved child ! "

But, Surgeon Cheskowitch, still in charge of the huge hospital at Nikopolis, had bidden the two anxious women who shared this sweet secret, to wait for his final coming.

" In her weak state, any shock, even of joy, might kill our poor nestling!" the old man said. " Let me hold back yet, the only happiness which this sad year has brought. But, I will soon come. Wait for me!" And so their hearts counted the very hours.

While the loving council watched the sufferer, who stirred uneasily at all the clamor of the growing orgie, a fateful despatch was handed to Countess Xenia, by an orderly.

" I come for one day only. Remember my orders. General Milutin is with me. He will say, ' Good-bye,' for he follows the army over the Balkans."

When Countess Xenia raised her eyes, Cecile Wizocka, no longer Madame Mazzana, had vanished.

On her knees, in the solitude of her room, the Lost Lady of Nimovitch cried :

"Give me strength ! Oh, my God, for I must see him to-morrow !"

Nothing could tear her away now from the child whose motherless life was drawing to the close of the long mystery of years, and yet, the sobbing woman clasped her hands in anguish.

" My God ! I cannot tell her all ! I cannot tell her the dark story of a mother's sin, a mother's shame ! " And, her bosom, strangely shaken, thrilled with the lost love of years. " I shall see Vassili to-morrow, face to face ! " And even in her prayer that she might not fear to face her beloved child, heart-hidden in all these weary years, she trembled in every limb ! For she saw again, across the gulf of the vanished years, Vassili Milutin, brave, glowing, manly, his eyes lit up with a life's passion, as on that day, under the rustling forest branches of Nimovitch, when he threw himself upon the giant bear to save her imperilled life ! The light of other years flamed a moment in her splendid eyes. And then in fancy she sat again at his side, and saw that white sail, blown seaward, over the sapphire depths of the Gulf of Sorrento! Then, the sacrifice of a woman's love, to a mother's heart, a contrite offering, was made in this last dark hour. " Marguerite ! My Marguerite ! She shall never know the dark past ! " And she turned away her beautiful face from the haunting vision of the past, those dreams of the hour when the splendid noble had first clasped her to his breast, at still unforgotten Nimovitch.

It was in the dusk of the next day when Cecile Wizocka returned to her watch, near the bedside of the child who had never yet known a mother's love, save in the fond dreams of her fevered brain.

There was an air of positive decision in the commands which Countess Xenia had laid upon Vera to take the Lady of Bellagio on a long drive through the Corso, the only safe outing in this land now overrun with reckless marauders.

Very strangely, Surgeon Cheskowitch beamed into the sick room, shortly after the carriage had driven away. His gray beard bristled with delight, his steady blue eyes gleamed as he finished a long professional scrutiny of the mental and physical condition of the new owner of the great domain of Nimovitch! Then, the old surgeon's eyes twinkled with the sudden impulse of a happy thought. Drawing Countess Xenia aside, he sat down with her at the table, where the three women had so long watched over the gentle girl whom the blood-bought victory of Gorni-Dubnik had made both bride and widow. "Countess Xenia," he said, there is a man here now, waiting, with beating heart, to obey my summons to this sick room. I know not yet what dark shadow of the past has blighted Vassili Milutin's mind. Last of his line, he would fain make a full reparation to the girl, to the wife, whose picture Boris carried on his heart into the Red Redoubt. Milutin leaves us to-morrow. It is now the golden hour! He may yet find a soldier's grave in the Balkans, for his courage at sixty-two is as fiery as when he was the wildest swordsman of his regiment. I will bring him in with me on my return to say 'good-bye,' and his full recognition of his son's widow, will not only ensure her an enormous fortune, but also place this dear one where the court circles and all the old nobility of Russia will surround her with ever honor due to her rank, when he is gone. Her mother——"

"Shall be there! Leave that to me!" said Xenia de Berg, as she flashed her mind back to the past. She was yet ignorant of the lost dead love which had grown up so quickly on that day of the hunt, under the golden forest leaves of Nimovitch'

"They will both be ruled by the gravity of the hour. Perhaps the issue may be fortunate. If Vassili Milutin has thus once met the woman who gave life to Marguerite in the olden days, their common love for the helpless one may bring them nearer to each other."

The carriage was returning. As Vera's light foot bounded up the stairs, Countess Xenia went out quickly to meet them. She instantly decided. " I will give her no time to think, no time to prepare, for a possible meeting with Boris' haughty father ! "

Without a word, Xenia led Cecile Wizocka at once to the side of her child.

There was a new strong light of life and hope shining in the girl's clear eyes, as her slender fingers closed around the firm white hand of the woman now bending over her in an infinite tenderness.

Doctor Cheskowitch had a little theory of his own. It was that good news never kills !

The dark eyes of Marguerite were fixed this moment upon the Lady of Bellagio with a yearning, which melted the longing mother's very soul !

Countess Xenia stood at the head of the couch, and Vera's eyes too were lit up in wonder as a tall form silently followed the bustling surgeon, who came quickly in, hat in hand. In affected cheerfulness, he glanced at the man who was now hidden behind Countess Xenia.

" Now, my child, I promised you that you should soon have your answer when you were able to leave here for your home ! I would ask you with an old man's blessing, before you go to Nimovitch, to ask of this lady where your mother is now ! "

Cecile Wizocka's stately head was bent over the fluttering hand of the girl, who suddenly raised herself and then threw her arms silently around the one whose head was pillowed on her bosom ! The Lost Lady of Nimovitch had not seen the man whose very senses reeled, as Cecile clasped

Marguerite in a mother's embrace, for the first time, before them all !

"My child ! My own darling ! Nothing shall ever part us now !" she cried. And, as her voice thrilled every heart, there was one, on his knees beside her who cried out, in pain, "Cecile ! My God ! Speak to me !"

It was the proud Lord of Orenburg, over whose stormy soul that mother's cry had swept with the accents of an angel's voice !

There was a breathless silence in the room, for the stately head of Madame Mazzana was not lifted from her daughter's bosom ! A thin wasted hand stole out, and then another, its feeble fellow, guided the trembling fingers of the woman who seemed to have lost this world from her ken !

"For Boris' sake !" whispered the now happy girl.

When Cecile Wizocka raised her head, she gazed steadily into the eyes of the man who had sought her for long years. "Is this General Milutin !" she faltered. There was but one in the room, who knew that they had ever met before !— With a last mighty effort, Vassili Milutin controlled the tide of passion sweeping through a wildly throbbing heart."

"I will now tell you, sir," she said, and her eyes rested on his, "that your dead son's wife, my own child, was born his equal in rank ! My friend tells me that you would repair the past !" and, Cecile led up Countess Xenia. "My own fortune, my whole life, shall be given up to this dear one ! Your love—your protection is all that she need ask ! For my probation is over ! She has a mother now !"

But, Vassili Milutin heard not ! He only stood as if some sweet dream of the past had broken through the darkness of all these awful years ! He was standing heart torn, in the corridor, led out in silence by Countess Xenia, for the surgeon's authoritative gesture had cleared the room. Marguerite Milutin had fainted in the thrill of rapture which told her that her haunting dream was a sweet reality. But, now a mother leaned over her in rapture!

Beside the two, in the corridor, the surgeon, with a hopeful face, as he emerged, gave to General Milutin his brief orders.

"You will show yourself the man I have always known you, Vassili, if you go now, without another word! Another scene might kill this mother, on whose life Marguerite's fate hangs now!"

"I must speak to her,—I must!" cried Vassili Milutin, and a look of love flashed over his brow, as he strode toward the door of the room where only Vera de Berg watched with the mother who, folding her child to her breast, was telling in fond whispers all the long pent-up story of a new-found love.

"You must do nothing!" the energetic surgeon cried. "Remember Edmond Dantes! 'Wait and hope!' Go, now! Come back from Constantinople! And you can then easily win back the regard of Marguerite's mother in loving and cherishing her child!"

Vassili Milutin gazed dumbly into Countess Xenia's eyes! Suddenly, he seized the trembling hands which she held out to him and kissed them. "Tell her—tell her! oh! God! I dare not speak!" And he was gone, before Countess Xenia fled away to her own room!

"My God!" she cried, in happy tears, as she sank to her knees "No one knows! And the ban of the Past is lifted now! The olden days are sealed with the seal of a new love, —for Boris' sake!"

The June roses were blushing again at Bellagio, when Madame Mazzana sat in the summer-house by the lake, with her beautiful daughter. It was the eve of another parting—but of a happy parting—a parting in peace and love and hope. The brow of the stately mother was as unruffled as the dreaming lake, murmuring there below the walls of the wooded island with faint musical pulsations, as the wavelets reached the silver strand.

Marguerite Milutin raised her eyes to her mother's in a sudden surprise, which brought the Lady of Bellagio to her daughter's side.

For, a formidable pile of letters and despatches lay upon the table in their favorite arbor. It was a time of dreaming peace, for the battle summer had passed away, and the flags of victory had been borne home to Russia, in triumph, from far San Stefano. The issue of the war had been most glorious. Turkey had disappeared forever as a first-class power from history, when the baffling treaty was signed, on March 3, 1878. It sealed a peace, and yet, it kept bold Skobeleff out of Constantinople, and muzzled the waiting guns of the English fleet. Ivan and Serge, all the other hardy peasants, the wild Cossack, even the fierce Circassians, had streamed back to Holy Russia, leaving only their thousands of dead comrades under the Dobrudsha sands, or whelmed in Plevna's Golgotha. By the Balkan Pass, at Shipka, before Philippopolis, at distant Kars, and before Adrianople, the line of the brave Russian dead but too plainly marked the path of the Czar's juggernaut car of glory! The pyramid of Russian heads had disappeared from Plevna's fatal plains, and the laurels of war blood tinged, rested on the brows of the Grand Duke Nicholas, great Todleben, and that superb trio of heroes, Gourko, Radetsky, and the white-coated Skobeleff, the one darling of the victorious soldiery!

The great Grand Duke had insisted on a winter campaign. The war, begun with half the necessary forces, and under ill-distributed commanders, swept on at last in a splendid frenzy of victory, as the reinforced legions poured on under Gourko, and his two great associates, over the Balkans, in the winter snow, and finally crushed the Turks at Philippopolis. They herded up an army of Moslems, prisoners at Shipka Pass, and rushing through Adrianople's forced gates, dictated a peace in the very sight of St. Sophia !

So the Czar's flags were furled in honor ! It was four long months after Madame Mazzana had recrossed the threshold of her Bellagio home, with her now acknowledged daughter, when Countess Xenia and Vera returned to Dresden. For, Surgeon Cheskowitch would not allow the Angel of the Hospitals to tarry longer at Nikopolis.

The tide of war had rolled far away beyond the Balkans ! There were secrets even between the loving mother and the gentle daughter, on this dreaming June day, when Marguerite called her loving guardian to her side.

Only Marguerite knew that Lieutenant-General Alexis Dournof and Major Serge Platoff fretted uneasily even in the great triumphs of St. Petersburg, until they could seek together a certain villa at Dresden.

The inmost secret of Marguerite Milutin's heart was also a tryst at Nimovitch, for with true womanly art, Countess Xenia waited to send Platoff and his bride away on their foreign tour, before she met General Alexis Dournof again ! The widow of Boris Milutin must not come home to a lonely house, and so there were secrets and secrets, in these happier days !

Both Countess Xenia and Marguerite knew that General Vassili Milutin's attendance on the Czar would soon cease. He had not scrupled to use the gentle intercession of Countess Xenia to effect a surprise of the fair garrison of Bellagio.

Marguerite Milutin, in her solicitude for others, had listened to only a part of the sorrows of her mother's early life. When Madame Mazzana had gently touched upon some of the sorrows of a past which sealed the frontiers of Russia to her, Marguerite's loving eyes kindled.

"I shall always watch over those poor people at Nimovitch ! It seems as if my dead Boris left them to my tenderest care. But, a divided love will always bring me back to you

here at Bellagio! I know he would have wished me to care
for those hundreds of peasants, struggling onward to the
light!"

The young widow knew that a too-suddenly given freedom
had left these enfranchised serfs all at sea—equal in inexperience—and all unfit to rule themselves, although generous
gifts of lands, and even the dangerous freedom of idleness
had been granted them, in the sudden generosity of an
honest and too liberal Czar.

"I will live among them, I will guide them onward, and
upward, as he would have done!" she said.

Neither Dournof, Countess Xenia, Cheskowitch, Vera,
nor the widowed-heiress of two great fortunes had ever been
able to link the name of that vanished shade Cecile Wizocka
to the now happy Madame Mazzana. Countess Xenia
mused and studied the darkened past by the flash-light of
memory. But even she, could not fathom the purposes of
Marguerite's mother! Still, the marvellous stage-play of her
noble countenance in that sick room at Bucharest, on the
day of the surprise, gave to absent Vassili Milutin, hopeless
as he was, the key of a future campaign! The glittering
revels of the Winter Palace could not blind him to the
mother's pleading self abnegation. For Cecile Wizocka would
surely go to the grave locking the past in her breast!

"Boris dead," the still loving woman mused, "Vassili
Milutin has offered his only son up upon the altar of a guilty
past. He would shield and honor the widow of the hero of
the Red Redoubt! Here, afar, I can know her, steadfast,
tranquil, and happy, at Nimovitch. She will live on there,
God bless her, walking in the very way she would have gone
with him."

Her own prayers, then, consecrated a new woman to the
future. It was with fear, a last horrible fear, that Cecile
Wizocka dreamed of the day when the Prior of the Pietrow
convent might open the sealed packets left by the dead

Polish spy, the father whose dark history must still be sealed from Marguerite's wondering soul. And on this very last day of her daughter's sojourn, the mother quaked at heart, for she had seen the packets and letters, before her child began their perusal. There was a danger signal there!

"And so I shall never know? It is well," said Marguerite. Milutin suddenly, as she handed a letter from the Prior to her mother. Cecile's heart beat in the last exquisite agony of a life's sorrows! Her face was very pale as she dropped the letter, but her daughter's loving arms were folded round her. The old Prelate for the first time had recognized her marriage to Boris Milutin. The wheels of slow-revolving ecclesiastical law had ground out a decision in Rome which forever silenced Cecile Wizocka's last apprehensions.

The Viennese banker and the old Prior had jointly destroyed unopened every vestige of the private papers left by General Michael Waldberg!

"Your sudden marriage on the Danube officially terminated our joint trust," wrote the old Prior. "As the late Colonel Boris Milutin was a Russian, we had then but one duty left to perform, under the positive directions of your dead father! That duty was the destruction of all the papers otherwise to be delivered to you at the age of twenty-five. The final duty of the delivery of all your other valuable property will be discharged at once, upon your naming a proper representative to accept it at our hands."

Even in long later years of happiness, Marguerite, Countess Milutin, never knew that General Dournof had effected the decisive action which disarmed the hand of Fate stretching out from a dead father's tomb!

For, a great Russian Metropolitan of the orthodox faith, after weeks of prayer and consideration, had long turned over in his heart a matter learned in the confessional.

It was he who had sent General Alexis Dournof secretly

to the Prior of Jasnagora, on an errand of hidden mercy, charity, and Christian brotherhood!

Cecile Wizocka's arms clasped her daughter's head, in a new rapture, to a happy bosom. When she rose and walked away, there was a newer light on lake and shore which shone in her very soul. Peace for herself at last, safety and silence for the blameless girl who lingered alone by the lake!

"I will atone!" murmured Cecile Wizocka, as she buried forever the mocking past. For now she could look forward to a future of soul repose. "I have only God to make my peace with,—now!" she murmured.

The daughter of her heart knew only that the union of the past must have been a sad, an unhappy one. That separation and aversion had held her father and mother apart for long years.

But, the woods of Nimovitch never whispered the guarded secrets of those olden days, when brothers' blood was sold under the guise of hospitality by the man whose wife had been driven to self-overthrow of a neglected woman's passion!

"Shall I tell her? Dare I betray the confidence of one who trusts me now with his proud heart's choicest hope!" murmured Marguerite, as she walked alone beside the lake. For, she had now read the last letter of the enclosures. On the morrow her own departure for Nimovitch, would lead her back to the little realm where she would reign, a widowed queen, in Boris' name.

"I cannot," she faltered. "I dare not! If Countess Xenia or the General were only here to advise?" But the girl was alone in her uncertainty. Laughing Vera would soon be a happy bride, away on her world-wandering, and only after her own arrival would Countess Xenia, General Dournof, and Surgeon Cheskowitch join her at Nimovitch.

"It seems all so sad, so strange, this gift of the beautiful old domain," Marguerite mused, as she faced the lingering problems of her own strange history. "I must decide everything for myself, for General Milutin's letter gives me no hope that he will ever visit me in Poland."

The widow read again this frank avowal: "The memories of the unhappy years of the Polish insurrection have planted in my heart an aversion to all the scenes of the dark past, where so many cruelties and tragedies darkened my early command there! I shall await you, my child, at Moscow, whenever you will grant me the honor of taking you to see your Orenburg home, and seeing your own dear face in the house where Boris made all the days once light and happy for me—in his page and cadet life!"

Suddenly the star of hope peeped out in the early evening skies. "I will leave him to plead his own cause, for he will surely be gentle and manly. My mother cannot refuse to listen. They will be drawn nearer together now,—for Boris' sake!"

The General's letter was, bit by bit, scattered on the rippling waves of the lake, as Marguerite, rejoiced at heart, knew that her own departure would be the signal for the secret arrival of General Vassili Milutin. "I have not broken in upon your last sojourn with your mother, for I must be alone with her to plead with her for the errors of the past."

And so, the mystery of the old days was dropped forever from the mind of the young mistress of Nimovitch! "I will guard his secret. He would now repair the sorrows caused by his haughty refusal to allow the marriage of his princely son to a poor girl."

In this dreaming self-confidence, the young Countess Milutin passed all her future days, for the veil of the past was never lifted upon the history of Cecile Wizocka. Even the great empty frame had disappeared from the salon of the old chateau, when Marguerite Milutin's light foot, stepping over the threshold, brought back the holy charm of youth and innocent womanhood.

"You shall claim me as yours soon—soon again, madre mia," promised Countess Milutin, as she bore away the smiling benison of a thankful woman's love, "and you will have soon our happy visitors, Vera and Serge Platoff! Before you are lonely here, I, too, will return with Countess Xenia, but I must first take up the sceptre at Nimovitch!"

The loving widowed bride could not bring herself to speak of the last home-coming of Boris Milutin. For, already the stout Cossack sergeant at the old chateau watched over Boris' riderless charger with loving pride. And the imperial courtesy of the great Grand Duke, who had himself not yet forgotten the terrible day of Gorni-Dubnik, was manifest in the stately transfer of the dead soldier's remains to the elm-shaded God's-acre at Nimovitch.

There was one who, from a distant point of view, had secretly marked the parting of mother and daughter! It was a man thrilled now in every fibre by the memories of Nimovitch—the dear dead days of Sorrento, and the heroic self-command of the passion-thrilled tableau of Bucharest!

A faithful servant who had the private orders of Countess Marguerite, led the great noble by a shaded path to the shores of the throbbing lake.

"Every evening Madame Mazzana comes here to see the sunset," the Italian briefly declared, as he grasped the gold pieces held out to him.

There was no sound now upon the brooding waters! The very roses listened in the faint hush of evening to the earliest awakened song of the nightingale. Cecile Wizocka's eyes were fixed upon a little dainty pleasure-boat, floating down towards her from the enchanted regions of the upper lake. "It bears, perhaps, happy hearts on to some joyous meeting. The loving, the parted—all around is a paradise dreaming here, but no white sail drifting down from the dead years can bring back my lost love to my side! For, sin has buried the dear days that were under the cold ashes of sorrow, and I must never see him again!"

The sound of a single word led her back in an instant to the cliffs of Sorrento! For, Vassili Milutin's head was bowed as he knelt before her. "Cecile!" he whispered! Her trembling hands lay in his. He cried, "Deny me not again, my punishment has wrecked my life! There is one, one way alone to atone! For the fair fame of your child! For your own happiness! For my peace! Let us atone. The path of honor lies clear before us now! In the name of the God, whose chastening hand has been laid upon me, I ask for mercy! I am the last of my line! I ask you to let me give you the name of Milutin!"

The stern old soldier's voice was broken, and his loyal love had led him back again to her feet! Something born not of earthly passion thrilled quickly through her wearied heart, as the woman who had held herself true in passion's storms through years, to the broken bond between them, the bond of a love long buried under the roses of that time of brief delight, gazed in his eyes, and he read her answer there! Her heart would not be denied. She turned her eyes in trust to him.

"For Boris' sake!" she whispered, as they went out, together—one in heart—toward the villa, where a daughter's loving arms had once stayed a woman's madly-uplifted hand!

In all the glory of the autumn leaves, the woods of Nimovitch burned again, in their olden glory, as the sun's last rays lit up a little group lingering upon the south portico of the old chateau.

General Alexis Dournof gazed upon his wife with a smile of tenderness, as he watched the bright glowing face of his hostess, Countess Marguerite Milutin. "You have been so happy here with me at Nimovitch," she said softly. "You must come here again, for the leaves will always rustle you their welcome! You will find the dreaming peace still unbroken, and I wili be here to greet you always! My peasants and my pensioners will be your only world, but in the old chateau, you will always think tenderly of these first days of your wedded happiness!"

Countess Xenia Dournof watched Marguerite very keenly as the bronzed General found the moment opportune, for the telling of a secret which he had silently guarded for some days! The Dournofs, going to Italy, would soon be forced to return to the high duties which called the General and the Countess to the great Winter Palace on the Neva!

"There will be a summons for you also very soon! One that even you must obey! For, Serge Platoff and Vera will await you at Warsaw, and perhaps they will even come here, if you will throw open to them the hospitable doors of the dear old chateau! Have you heard from your mother lately?"

The young widowed Countess gazed from one to the other, in a strange growing surprise. "Tell me!" she said, as she stood before Countess Xenia, her eyes searching the very soul of the friend who had gone with her in all the dark days!

Countess Dournof eyed her fondly in silence. "There is a beautiful old villa on the cliffs of Sorrento," said General Dournof, affecting a careless tone, "which once belonged to Vassili Milutin's mother! It has been reopened, and the General intends to make his future home there. It is very dear to him! He has written to me to ask you, nay to implore you, to join your mother there, for the winter!"

Marguerite's heart was throbbing wildly, as she sought for an explanation in vain! But Xenia's eyes were dropt down, and General Dournof's glances rested on a marble shaft rising far away by the lake among the distant trees!

"I cannot bear to go away!" she said.

"Not even, if the Countess Milutin asks her daughter to her new home by the sea?" .

The stern soldier walked away, as the two loving women both faltered the same words. "For Boris' sake!"

And, far away, seated where the blue gulf of Sorrento spread its sapphire breast to the fairest skies on earth, were two happy ones whose hearts lingered with the beloved woman at Nimovitch, whose love, in its innocence and truth, had wrought Love's Miracle, and lifted the ban of the guilty Past!

THE END.

9 783337 298678